THE

CONGRUENT
APPRENTICE

Book One of the Congruent Mage Series

To Kayla —
Enjoy the magic!

My best —
Dave Schroeder

The Congruent Mage Series

www.CongruentMage.com

The Xenotech Support Series

www.XenotechSupport.com

Dedication

To my wonderful mom,
Jeanette Schroeder,
for reading to me as a child
and nurturing my love of fantasy.

Cover and Map designs by Dan Paulson

ISBN-13: 978-0-09978319-2-4

Spiral Arm Press
1725 Carlington Court
Grayson, GA 30017

www.SpiralArmPress.com

Prologue

Two wizards dueled in the dark and roiling clouds, exchanging glowing fireballs, bolts of crackling energy, and blasts of sound so solid they struck like giants' fists. Their combat lit up the night sky brighter and louder than a thousand midsummer fireworks and transformed half the descending rain into sizzling steam before it could reach the ground. Their long, wet robes flapped in the wind, rattling like sails in a hurricane. Cold drops of water pelted their faces, stinging like hail. The battle wasn't going well for either combatant.

"Give up, Fercha!" shouted Verro, the wizard in green, in a moment of calm between sonic attacks. "I don't want to kill you."

The wizard in blue answered with a jagged lightning bolt that disappeared into a circular shield of solidified sound held by her opponent, leaving the air charged with power. Fercha's short auburn hair stood straight out, making her head look like a dandelion in seed.

Verro shot a trio of glowing fireballs in response. They bounced off a magical shield projected by the wizard in blue, exploding in a shower of green sparks.

The pair traded words instead of spells for their next round of exchanges.

"Surrender!" commanded Verro over the roar of the wind.

"Hah!" shouted Fercha. "Will *you* surrender to *me*, Verro? These are the Kingdom of Dâron's lands, not Tamloch's. Why are you here?"

"I came here to find something," Verro replied, "and I did. Now I want to get back to the palace in Riyas without your interference."

Both wizards were standing on thin glowing disks a yard wide. The disks kept them aloft, but slipped left and right, tossed by shifting currents of air.

"Not until you answer my question!" exclaimed Fercha.

The pair exchanged another attack and riposte, with Fercha shooting a beam of cold sapphire light from something in her right hand and Verro countering it with a beam of emerald light from a green magestone set in a wide gold cuff on his wrist.

The beams turned a harsh, pulsing cyan where they intersected and filled the space nearby with magical potential, like marsh vapors ready to ignite.

The twin streams of interlocked energy bound the two of them together and for a moment the winds went calm, causing their flying disks to stop shifting.

"You can't win," said Verro. His wet green robes pressed tight against his tall form and the magical potential surrounding him had frosted the tips of his thick black hair with white.

Fercha finally spoke, biting her words out from the strain of holding her beam.

"The wizard. Makes. The artifact."

She furrowed her brow in concentration. The sapphire-blue segment of the beam lengthened, getting closer to the wizard in green.

"The artifact. Does not. Make. The wizard," she continued.

Fercha reached down along the folds of her blue robes with her left hand and found a small, cocked crossbow. In one smooth motion, she raised it and released a barbed quarrel that crossed the distance between the two opponents in half a second and embedded itself in Verro's right calf, pinning his green robes to his leg.

The injured wizard's attention faltered and his emerald beam cut off as if struck by an axe.

Fercha's azure beam moved lower and intersected with Verro's flying disk, shattering it into dozens of shards and leaving its rider unsupported.

"Blast you!" he said as he fell. "That was my favorite flying disk!"

Before falling more than a dozen feet, Verro raised his golden wrist cuff and sent out a blast of solid sound that caught the bottom front edge of Fercha's flying disk and flipped it almost vertical. Caught by surprise, Fercha threw her arms up and opened her hands, sending the crossbow and what had been in her right hand sailing away overhead. Her body slid off her flying disk and began to fall.

Moments before the wizards struck the ground, black circles opened beneath them. Fercha and Verro passed through their respective circles and disappeared. The pair of round, dark gateways dematerialized with a pair of soft pops.

Above, a bolt of natural lightning jumped from cloud to cloud, triggering the magical potential in the nearby air and generating a shimmering aurora in red, blue, green and gold. Then the rain abruptly stopped and the clouds moved east.

Below, bats and flying frogs continued their nocturnal search for supper, oblivious to what had landed in the mud nearby.

PART ONE

Chapter 1

"Ah, to be young again and wear the holly."
— Ealdamon's *Epigrams*

Eynon leaned down, but his sister still had to stand on her tiptoes to pin the ceremonial holly to his high-peaked cap to mark his wander year. He was tall, thin as a sapling, and awkward, like a pup who hasn't yet grown to match his feet. His sister Braith kissed his cheek. Eynon hugged her awkwardly and teased her by kissing the tip of her nose. They both laughed.

"Stay out of trouble," Braith whispered, hugging him close.

"I'll try," he replied.

He was hoping for adventures, not trouble, but understood the two often came together.

Taking a wander year was a matter of long-established custom in the Kingdom of Dâron, not a practice dictated by royal decree. Eynon remembered what his grandmother had told him when he was small and had asked her why young people went wandering. Her answer was as wise as one of Ealdamon's epigrams. "Customs count more than crowns," she'd said. He'd been looking forward to his own wander year ever since.

Eynon hugged his mother and father, but didn't linger. He'd miss them both. He'd even miss Braith's freckled face and their mutual sibling squabbles. His years of waiting were over—it was time to toss his arrow. He'd been up before dawn, too excited to sleep. Everyone knew he'd set off in the direction his arrow pointed when it landed.

Some young men and women, when they reached their sixteenth year, would toss their arrows so they would point in the direction they wanted to go, like the gentle western slope up to Brynhill, the nearest village to Haywall, or the southern way to the castle town of Caercadel that boasted seven inns, each with its own fine brew.

Eynon wasn't one to cheat, however. He wasn't the best-looking lad in Haywall, but he *was* the best cook and by far the most curious.

All the stories he'd read or heard told him it was best to trust his wander year to chance, so he tossed his arrow high and gave it a twist to set it turning so his future direction would not be predetermined.

When the missile landed, it was pointing east, so that's the direction Eynon would head. It was as good a course as many and better than most. His pack, cloak and bedroll were already on his back. He wore a quilted jacket, perfect for changeable spring weather, comfortable hemp-cloth pants and sturdy hiking boots.

There was only enough food in his pack for three days—dried meat and twice-baked hardtack he'd made himself, bread and cheese prepared by his mother, and well water stored in a goatskin he'd cured by hand. The pack had been his father's, given to him last night with a firm handshake, a short tale of how the pack had served the men in his family well for three generations, and manful attempts to hold back tears. His mother and sister had been the ones to weep after dinner the previous evening. He was glad they hadn't cried again this morning.

"I promise I'll be back in a year and a day," said Eynon.

"See that you are," said Braith, "and bring back a worthy wife."

Eynon turned away so his sister couldn't see his face turn red. He adjusted his pack, waved to his family over his shoulder, and set out.

The Coombe was an upland valley encircled by modest mountains. Long and broad, it ran southwest to northeast, eight leagues by three. Eynon had walked much of its length and breadth and knew a great many of its roads, paths and cattle tracks. He was glad his chance-chosen course would soon lead him somewhere new.

Ten minutes and half a mile of uphill walking later, Eynon turned and looked down into Haywall and the bowl of the Coombe. He was at the top of a familiar rise and could see the twisting blue line of the Wentwash, the small stream that flowed through the center of the Coombe in lazy arcs. Thatch-roofed homes for five dozen families clustered on either side of the water, looking like so many heaped up, out of season haystacks.

Well-tended fields beginning to turn green surrounded his village, except upstream where the blossoming fruit trees of communal orchards marched in neat rows farther back toward Wherrel, the village at the Coombe's northwest gap, near the quarry.

His mother was looking up the hill in his direction, so Eynon waved and watched her wave back—then he turned and continued in the direction his arrow had pointed. He was glad he'd been born in the spring and wasn't starting his wander year by trudging through snow. Once it rained, he'd be coping with mud, but today was sunny and the ground was firm. Above him, a few fluffy clouds were scudding in front of the sun like wandering sheep. Eynon could see a small flock of darker clouds to the northeast, past the mountains, and hoped it wouldn't be raining on the other side.

He'd gone to bed early and had heard what sounded like quite a thunderstorm on the east side of the mountains last night, but those sorts of storms usually swept by quickly.

Two hours later, Eynon had made substantial progress. He'd been a similar distance from his home village before, but never so far in this direction. Eynon had passed familiar farmsteads for the first hour, but after that he was in new territory. Pastures, fields and orchards gave way to scrub grass and thickets, then deeper woods blocked most of the light on either side of the cart track he was following. He kept to the rounded center of the path rather than the ruts because he liked the way it gave him an extra few inches of height, improving his view. It was dim and peaceful underneath the canopy of the arching trees, even at mid-morning.

The woods were alive with the sounds of spring. Squirrels were chittering and jumping from branch to branch. He could hear the grunts of a wild boar or sow rooting for mast deep in the woods and smiled at the melodies of the colorful, newly-returned songbirds. Eynon considered whistling along—he was good at whistling, despite his sister's protests when she was in earshot—but decided it would be wiser to listen quietly and pay attention to his surroundings.

He could see that someone was keeping the cart track clear. Stumps of young trees no more than four fingers thick marked the axe work of some unknown maintainer of the way. Perhaps one of the crofters farther along cut things back as part of their service to

the baron. Eynon put his hand on his own small axe at his belt, its
weight on his left hip balanced by his knife on the opposite side.
He'd done his part to keep the path from Haywall to Brynhill clear
where it passed through a similar stretch of forest.

His parents and the people of Haywall were free tenants of the
baron in Caercadel with its seven inns. Eynon's family owed service
as well as a share of their crops and stock. For the last three years,
Eynon had been old enough to help take their tithe of fruit, grain
and vegetables to the castle town. If not for his wander year, he
would have been one of the young men driving his village's offering
of sheep and lambs there in a few weeks for the celebration of the
spring equinox. Now he'd have to wait until he returned to make
another circuit of the inns and sample all seven brews again.

The sun rose higher as Eynon continued. He was climbing in
earnest now. The modest mountains surrounding the Coombe
didn't have a natural gap to the east, so Eynon had to get over
them the hard way. Thick woods changed to scattered trees, then
patches of mountain laurel bushes starting to show their pink and
white flowers.

Eynon was ascending a rocky talus slope on switchbacks that
resembled the twists and turns of the Wentwash. It was difficult
going because the small stone fragments acted almost like water as
he tried to plow through them. He would push them out of the
way only to have more flow around his feet from uphill, slowing
his progress. He began to wish he'd been sensible, like so many
other young people in the village, and had tried to influence his
arrow's direction.

When he reached the end of the talus section, Eynon found a wide
spot on the trail and stopped to sit on a sunny, flat-topped boulder
and swallow a few sips of water. Another half hour of climbing would
take him to the top of the mountain and it would be all downhill
from there—he'd be outside the Coombe for the first time.

Eynon thought about the words of Ealdamon the Wise in the copy
of the sage's *Epigrams* he'd borrowed from his uncle. *"If you don't
know where you're going, take joy in the journey."*

He'd been waiting for his sixteenth birthday and the start of his wander year with a joyful anticipation that far exceeded his sister's eagerness for the arrival of new kittens. It wasn't a matter of taking joy in his journey, it was a matter of tightly constraining his body's excitement so he wouldn't explode before he reached the summit.

He hoped he'd have adventures like the ones described in Robin Oddfellow's *Peregrinations*. Eynon had a cousin in Liamston who had a copy and allowed Eynon to borrow it for a month in return for building him a new hen house. Eynon lost count of the number of times he'd read Oddfellow's traveler's tale before he'd had to return it.

Circumstances reminded Eynon that adventures weren't always pleasant, however. He heard a hiss and realized the dangerous part of his journey had already commenced. A mottled brown and gray batsnake had been sunning on the flat rock behind him and Eynon had disturbed its slumber. The snake's camouflage blended perfectly into the boulder's surface, so Eynon hadn't even noticed it was there.

The snake closed its wings with a snap, then lifted its head off the rock and reopened them, waving its wings wildly to make itself look larger than it was. It hissed at him again to make its displeasure clear.

Eynon stood quickly. He backed away and moved ten paces up the trail, leaving the boulder and its occupant plenty of room. He knew batsnake venom wouldn't kill him, but it would be difficult to walk far with a swollen leg. Eynon wasn't worried about the batsnake flying after him because the creature's wings were more a matter of helping it stay warm than supporting flight.

According to the stories he'd heard, the same wasn't true for dragons. Eynon smiled. Encountering one of *them* on his wanderings would be quite a tale to tell—if he lived through it.

"Sorry to disturb you," said Eynon.

The batsnake didn't answer—they never did—though there *were* tales of talking dragons. Eynon wondered what he'd ask a dragon if he ever had the chance. He waved goodbye to the batsnake, which ignored Eynon and resumed soaking up sun on top of the boulder.

Half an hour later, Eynon reached the top of the mountain. He could see across the broad valley to the mountains ringing the Coombe to the west and north. Communal fields looked like counting boards, laid out in grids with two out of three fields green and one brown and fallow. The big milking barn near his cottage was the only building still visible in Haywall. He could see the wavy blue line of the Wentwash and the darker green of the woods near Brynhill. Eynon stared for a few moments, taking in the view of his home like a basking batsnake absorbing the sun's rays. Then he turned his back and started down the other side, leaving the Coombe at last.

It was easier walking downhill. There wasn't any talus on this side and the woods were thicker once he moved a few hundred yards down from the summit. The trees' leafy branches kept him cool and shaded. Eynon made good time and even cut across several switchbacks. He was on foot, after all, not guiding a goat cart.

He avoided flat rocks—not wanting to surprise more batsnakes— but did manage to frighten a covey of grouse and annoy assorted squirrels and chipmunks. He thought he might have seen a vicious, big-eyed aloysius the size of an eagle sleeping high in a sugar maple, but couldn't be sure and didn't stop to confirm. It could have been an extraordinarily large hawk.

The slope suddenly grew steeper and Eynon had to run to keep his feet under him. He nearly tumbled down a bank but managed to stay upright until he reached a flat section that was clearly a road, wide enough for two carts to pass abreast. To the east he could hear running water and considered that it must the Rhuthro, the same river that flowed through Caercadel. He'd seen a map in the castle town showing the river flowing out through the south-east gap in the Coombe's ring wall, then turning east and sharply north.

Eynon decided to follow the road north and was pleased to see the dark forest open up, giving way to sunny meadows. The thunderstorm he'd heard last night must have been on this side of the mountain. The ground was damp and a little muddy—not so much that it slowed him down, but enough for him to stick to the crown of the road and avoid the wet ruts.

His step was light even though he'd been walking since dawn.

Mud wouldn't dampen Eynon's spirits. Now the sun was almost directly overhead and he was pleasantly warm. For the thirtieth time, he reached up and touched the sprig of holly pinned to his cap. The spikes on the green leaves pricked his fingers and reminded him he wasn't dreaming.

Ahead, he could see another road intersecting with this one at right angles. It came from the east, maybe from the river, and faded to a small track to the west. The road he was on continued north. To the northeast, a dozen yards into a fenced pasture, stood an ancient oak. It was tall, with bare, gnarled branches, and bore no leaves. Even in death the tree served a purpose— marking the intersection.

Eynon was glad to see the split-log fencing. It meant the land was tended and some farm family must live close by. It would be a pleasure to meet people who didn't live in the Coombe. Meeting new people was supposed to be a big part of a villager's wander year.

For months, his sister had teased him that he'd better return with a wife, since none of the Coombe girls would have him. He'd told her she'd better return with a husband in two years when she went wandering—for the same reason. He knew he'd be too tongue-tied to talk to a girl, inside or outside of the Coombe, and so did his sister. But teasing was what siblings did, and Braith meant well.

When Eynon reached the middle of the crossroads, he looked left and right and saw he cast no shadow. It was high noon. Something felt odd under his left boot. He moved his foot and saw a shimmer of silver in the mud. Reaching down, he worked what he'd spotted out of the wet soil. It was a thin and dirty oval, nearly the size of his palm. He washed it with squirts of water from his goatskin, then marveled at what was revealed.

He'd found a silver amulet, worked with complex, interlaced floral designs. An oval blue gem more than an inch across, with deep facets, was set in its center. Once he cleaned the amulet, the silver danced with reflected sunlight and the gem seemed to be filled with sparks. It was the most beautifully-crafted thing he'd ever seen.

Eynon dried his hands on his tunic and inspected the amulet carefully. There were sixteen small studs around its edge and odd-looking symbols engraved on its back. Some of the symbols looked familiar, but he wasn't sure what they meant. He turned the oval back and forth in his hands, tipping it this way and that to find any identifying details. He needed to find out who owned the lovely thing so he could return it.

He was holding the amulet close to eye level in one hand, trying to discern more about the unknown symbols, when his finger inadvertently pressed one of the small studs. A tremendous blast of blue fire shot out from the gem on the opposite side, striking the ancient oak and turning it into a flaming torch.

Eynon dropped the amulet as if it had burned *him* and stepped back. His eyes were as big as an owl's and his mouth was wide-open in shock. Someone behind him made an impressed whistle and Eynon jumped.

He turned around quickly and saw an older man leaning on a shovel a few feet away. He wore sturdy clothing and a broad-brimmed straw hat.

A farmer, thought Eynon.

"Well, young man," said the farmer, shaking his head slowly from side to side. "It looks like you're going to need a wizard."

Chapter 2

"Never underestimate a man who tills the land."
— Ealdamon's *Epigrams*

"I'm very sorry about your tree, sir," said Eynon.

"It's not your fault," said the farmer. "I'd been meaning to chop the old thing down and turn it into charcoal for years now. You've just saved me a step."

Eynon didn't respond. He was watching the oak burn, still in shock. The farmer handed his shovel to Eynon, who grasped it by reflex.

"I'm going to need your help trenching around the tree so the fire doesn't spread, young man," he said in a kind voice. "Thank goodness it rained last night and the grass is still damp."

Reflected flames danced in Eynon's eyes, then he lowered his head to stare at the amulet where it sat in the mud of the path.

"Go ahead," said the farmer. "Pick that thing up and put it away."

"It can stay where it is," said Eynon. "I don't want anything to do with it."

"Who better than you to take it to a wizard, lad?" said the farmer. "You've just started your wander year if I read things right."

The farmer's observation triggered Eynon's curiosity and caused Eynon to raise his head.

"I did just start. How did you know?"

"Your holly looks fresh-cut this morning," said the farmer, "and several other things besides. Now pick that thing up before one of my fool neighbors comes by and kills himself—or me—with it."

"Yes, sir."

Eynon leaned on the shovel and bent down to recover the amulet. He stuck the shovel's blade in the ground to free his hands. Then he squirted more water from his goatskin to clean it off, handling the silver oval like a wolfhornet's nest. Eynon wiped off the amulet with the hem of his shirt and buried it deep in his pack. He slipped the pack over one shoulder, retrieved the farmer's shovel and followed the older man as he climbed over the pasture's fence and approached the burning oak. Eynon looked to his companion for advice on where to start digging.

"Here is good," said the farmer, indicating a spot about six feet away from the tree.

"I'm sorry again, sir."

"Just dig," said the farmer. "That's the best way you can make it up to me."

Eynon placed his pack on a flat rock, added his jacket beside it, and walked over to where the farmer was standing. He pressed the shovel blade in deep and began to turn ground. It helped to have something to take his mind off the amulet.

"I imagine you're from the Coombe," said the farmer. "I'm Derwen, but you can call me Derry."

He pushed his straw hat a bit farther back on his head and smiled.

Eynon paused from shoveling to answer.

"I'm Eynon," he said. Part of his mind wondered if the farmer kept a herd of milk cows.

"Is your father a smith?" asked Derry while loosening soil ahead of Eynon with the blade of his axe.

"No, sir," said Eynon. "He's a farmer."

"Seems odd for farmer to name his son *Anvil*," said Derry. "At least that's what I was told your name means."

"I think that's right," said Eynon. "It's what my mother told me, anyway. She said she just liked the name."

Eynon paused to lean on the shovel for a moment, then turned another clod of dirt. "My father liked it, too. He said it had a strong, solid sound. My sister used to say my head was as solid as an anvil."

"Being hard-headed can be a virtue," said Derry. "Ask my daughter."

"Your daughter, sir?"

"Call me Derry, lad. I'm not your father."

"Yes, sir. I mean Derry. I was raised to be polite to my elders."

Derry chuckled. "That's one reason why I thought you were from the Coombe. Wait until you get to Tyford."

"Sir?"

Eynon realized what he'd done and he and Derry both shared a laugh.

"You can take the boy off the farm, but he'll still have straw in his hair," said Derry as if he was repeating a proverb. "Tyford is on the Moravon—the great river. It's the biggest city this side of the capital. You and Merry can head there in the morning."

"Merry?" said Eynon.

"Meredith. My daughter," said Derry. "She's taking four barrels of hard cider to Taffaern the Innkeeper, my best customer in Tyford. I'm sure she would be glad to have company on the way. You should be able to find a free wizard or three in the city. One of them will know what to do with it."

"Oh," said Eynon, wondering if the trip would be the kind of adventure he'd hoped for.

An hour of hard work took their firebreak half way around the tree. Derry gave Eynon some dried meat and raisins from his pouch and the two paused to eat. Eynon shared water from his goatskin with Derry.

While the farmer was drinking, Eynon went back to retrieve his pack. He felt uncomfortable when the amulet inside it was too far away. As he returned, he saw something reflecting sunlight in a patch of tall grass.

Eynon moved closer to see what it was—a small crossbow, almost a toy, really, the kind a child would use for hunting squirrels. It was finely crafted, however—the steel of the bow was polished and high quality. It hadn't started to rust, so it must not have been in the pasture very long. There were slots for five quarrels in its stock. One of them was missing.

"Is this yours?" asked Eynon when he returned. "It's well-made."

"It's not mine, lad," said Derry. He looked the weapon over. "And it doesn't belong to any of my neighbors. I suppose it's yours now, unless its owner finds you and claims it."

"I'll take good care of it until they do," said Eynon.

Derry returned the goatskin. Eynon hefted it and reminded himself he'd need to refill it soon. He clipped the one-handed crossbow to his goatskin's shoulder strap with a small strip of metal on the stock that looked like it had been designed for that purpose. He was glad it would be easy to carry.

They continued to loosen the soil and dig. Eynon and Derry found several odd-looking shards of something that wasn't wood and wasn't metal on the ground on the far side of the burning tree as they cut turf and turned dirt. They looked like the sheets of ice that slid off the green slate roofs of the stone houses in Wherrel in winter and shattered on cobblestones. Being from the Coombe-town near the quarry made it easier for the folk in Wherrel to build with stone.

"What are these, sir?" asked Eynon. "I've never seen anything like them. Are they made from some sort of animal horn?"

"Your guess is as good as mine," said Derry, "but I'd say they're wizard-made. They could have been blown here by the storm last night. I went to bed early, but we had quite a thunderstorm. Wizard weather, some call it."

"I heard the thunder from this side of the mountain in the Coombe," said Eynon, "but I went to bed early, too. I wanted to get a good night's sleep before starting my wander year."

Derry laughed. "Most lads wouldn't be able to sleep on the night before their wander year," he said. "Or they'd be drinking ale behind a barn with their friends."

"I'm not most lads, then," said Eynon.

"No," said Derry, stroking his chin. "You're not."

"Would you mind if I took the shards?" asked Eynon. "If you don't have a use for them, that is. Maybe someone in Tyford will know what they are."

"Help yourself," said Derry, "but mind your fingers. They look sharp."

Eynon gathered all the shards he could find with the blade of the shovel, rolled them in his second-best linen shirt, and stowed them in his pack. He hoped they wouldn't cut holes in the soft fabric. Then he got back to the job at hand.

After another hour of shovel and axe work, they finished turning up a one-foot circle of dirt around the tree. The fire had burned down to the point where the blackened trunk was only glowing.

"Thank you, lad," said Derry. "You're a hard worker."

"It's the least I could do after the trouble I caused you," said Eynon.

He stretched to loosen his muscles and looked at the old tree's shadow. It stretched like the gnomon on a sundial and told Eynon that a good portion of the afternoon was gone. Derry followed his eyes.

"I wouldn't be good at respecting your wander year if I didn't invite you home for dinner and offer you a place to spend the night," said Derry. "Grab your pack and do me another favor by carrying my shovel. I've got fish in a cage under my boat, but I promised my wife I'd bring her marshapples, too. If we hurry, there should be enough time to dig some up and bring them home so she can roast them before we eat."

"Thank you, sir," said Eynon. "I loved marshapples the one time I'd tried them. My mother traded for some from a peddler last year and served them for our winter solstice feast."

"You've got a good mother," said Derry.

"You're right about that," said Eynon, smiling and thinking about the food she'd prepared for his journey. He loved working with her in the kitchen.

Eynon put on his jacket and pack. He rested the shovel on his shoulder, and walked alongside Derry as they climbed back over the fence around the pasture and headed east from the crossroads, toward the sound of running water.

"The river's this way," said Derry.

If Derry had been his sister, Eynon would have teased him about stating the obvious.

The mix of trees was changing, confirming Derry's words. The oaks, maples, hemlocks and pines he'd walked through earlier transitioned to moisture-loving hickories, beeches, and birches on the far side of the clearing. Ahead he could see the unmistakable shape of a large willow. As they walked, Eynon saw Derry watching him as Eynon swiveled his head from side to side, taking in his new surroundings.

"There's not much river land in the Coombe," said Derry.

"No, sir," said Eynon. "The Wentwash isn't what I'd call a river, though I did see the Rhuthro upstream from here at Caercadel. There's hardly any marshland in the Coombe, either."

"We don't have that problem around here," said Derry. "Most of the land on the far side of the river is marsh, except where tenants have drained it. We're headed for one of the few spots of marsh on *this* side of the river."

"By that willow?" asked Eynon.

"Exactly," said Derry. He nodded his approval. "You've got a good eye and don't miss much."

"Except the nose on my face, if you listen to my sister," said Eynon.

"I'd bet your sister would get along well with my daughter," said Derry.

Eynon didn't know what to think about that observation.

Soon they reached the willow. They brushed aside some of the hanging branches and paused in the shade beneath the tree's canopy. The rush of running water was much closer.

"The river's less than a stone's throw past this tree," said Derry, "and the ground between here and there is perfect for marshapples. Do you know how to find them?"

"They're underneath tall reeds that look like they have sausages on top," said Eynon.

"And how would a boy from the Coombe know that?" asked Derry.

"I read about them in Robin Oddfellow's *Peregrinations*," said Eynon.

"Hmmm," said Derry, more to himself than to Eynon. "A reader. It's going to be an interesting trip down the river."

Derry led Eynon through the willow branches on the far side. A few feet beyond the circle of the tree was a bog. Eynon noted the marshland's unique unpleasant smell combining decaying vegetation and stagnant water for future reference. He could see hundreds of marshapple reeds waving in front of him and could hear the river was close at hand. Eynon was surprised to note that only the lower third of each marshapple reed was green. The upper portions with the odd sausage-shaped growths were a dried-out light brown.

"The lower stalks are good eating," said Derry, as if reading Eynon's mind, "and the tops are useful, too."

Eynon grinned at the farmer. He seemed wise and competent. If Derry had lived in Haywall, the village would have appointed him to negotiate their annual service to the baron.

"Time to use that shovel again, lad," said Derry. "I'll show you."

Derry took the implement from Eynon and inserted the shovel's blade near the closest reeds so he didn't have to get his boots wet. He stuck it in deep, then levered it back, revealing thick, round root-balls three times the size of an apple-tree apple.

"Pull, lad," said Derry, indicating the reeds attached to the roots he'd revealed.

Eynon pulled on the reeds and they came free, roots and all. A good bit of wet soil came with them. He switched places with Derry and between the two of them they collected more than a dozen plants.

"I'll take the shovel now," said Derry. "You take the marshapples."

Eynon gathered up the reeds, keeping the dirty ends as far away from his jacket as he could manage. He trailed behind Derry as they skirted the marsh and got back on the road. A hundred feet farther along, the road descended abruptly and they were at the bank of the Rhuthro. Rows of stones across the river marked this as a ford. Eynon could see where the road continued on the far bank. Something that looked like a giant round basket was tied to a small wooden dock to the left of the ford.

"Wash those off," said Derry. "I'll get the boat ready."

"Where's your boat?" asked Eynon.

Derry laughed and walked along the dock to the big basket.

Eynon knelt near the dock and rinsed the roots of the marshapple plants in the swift-flowing river water. Clouds of dirt sluiced off and dispersed downstream. Eynon followed the flow and saw Derry sitting in the big basket not far away. *What would the farmer need to store in a basket that large,* Eynon wondered? He finished cleaning the roots, then remembered to fill his goatskin. That accomplished, he stood up, resting the stiff stalks on his shoulder with the damp root-balls away from his back.

His eyes scanned up and down this side of the river, looking for a boat, but couldn't spot one. He'd read about boats and had seen the baron's barge at Caercadel, but he'd never ridden in one before. The Wentwash was narrow enough to jump across with a running start and too shallow for even the smallest craft to navigate, except for the tiny sailboat his uncle had carved for him when Eynon was seven.

"Come along, we need to go," said Derry.

"Where's your boat?" asked Eynon as he walked toward the dock.

"I'm sitting in it," said Derry.

"You're sitting in a basket," said Eynon.

"It's a coracle."

"What's that?"

"It's a boat."

"It *looks* like a basket," said Eynon.

"Get in, boy."

"Yes, sir."

Eynon moved to the end of the dock. Derry was sitting on a board that went from one side of the center of the basket to the other, like a flat handle. The farmer was sitting on the side next to the dock, holding on to a post with one hand.

"Pass those down to me," said Derry, indicating the marshapple plants.

Eynon extended the plants to Derry, who took them one-handed and positioned them in the middle of basket next to his shovel and something else about the same shape Eynon didn't recognize.

"Now climb in. Carefully," said Derry.

Eynon felt awkward wearing his pack and goatskin. The basket didn't look very sturdy.

"How?" Eynon asked. "I don't want to put my foot through the bottom."

"It's stronger than it looks, lad," said Derry. "Step over me and put your foot on the thwart."

"The what?" asked Eynon.

"The board I'm sitting on," said Derry.

Eynon could sense the farmer was starting to lose his patience, so he sat on the edge of the dock and extended one foot over Derry until it reached the board, touching it tentatively, like he was dipping his toe into a farm pond in early spring. Derry surprised him by releasing the dock, grabbing Eynon's hips with both hands, twisting him, and forcing him down on the thwart in the empty spot next to Derry. The basket boat bobbed and spun away from the dock, heading downriver.

"There," said the farmer. "Sit still and don't shift your weight. You don't want to capsize us."

"Yes, sir," said Eynon. He sat very still, clutching the board with white knuckles and feeling like he had the first time he'd mounted his cousin's riding horse bareback when he was eleven.

Derry pulled a long, flat-bladed length of carved wood from underneath the thwart and used it to stabilize the circular craft and steer it to the center of the flowing water. Eynon could see more woodland on his left as the river took them north. There was a wall of waving marshapple reeds with their sausage tops to his right. He'd read that bogs bred midges and was glad it was still too early in the season for them.

Taking time to observe his surroundings gave Eynon a chance to slow his breathing. His panic diminished and he no longer felt one wrong move would flip the basket boat and toss him into the current.

"Are midges a problem in the summer?" he asked.

"Are they?" asked Derry. "On the far side of the river they'll be so thick you could walk on them high enough to touch a cloud in a few months."

"That bad?" responded Eynon, playing along with the farmer's exaggeration. "How do you manage?"

"We ward our homes and nearby fields," said Derry, "but the midges are only a problem for a week or so. Then the swallows and martins arrive to feast during the day and the flying frogs do their part to gobble 'em up after dark."

"We don't get many swallows or martins on our side of the mountain," said Eynon. "Now I know why. We do have a few flying frogs by the Wentwash, though. When my sister was little she caught one and kept it as a pet. They sure can jump and glide."

"You know the story about the flying frog and the pail of milk, don't you?" asked Derry.

Eynon politely said he didn't, even though his father had first told him that tale when Eynon was small. Derry winked, aware of Eynon's dissembling. The farmer shifted his carved length of wood in the current, centered the coracle on the river, and gave his version. He recounted the story well, explaining how the flying frog who'd fallen into the milk pail kept swimming so vigorously that he churned a raft of butter and used that as a platform to jump out of the pail and glide away. He added an extra twist, saying that anyone who drank the milk or ate the butter from the pail would have their dreams come true.

"I like that part," said Eynon. "It makes it more of a fairy tale than a simple teaching story."

"One of my neighbors sells Flying Frog Butter at markets down-river and gets a few pence more per pound for the name," said Derry.

"Sounds like *his* dream is coming true," said Eynon.

"He gets by," said Derry. "Cider is *my* cash crop. You'll have to try some with your dinner tonight."

"I'm looking forward to it," said Eynon.

He loved cider. His father had once given him a sip of the strong version he made by pouring off the liquid that didn't freeze on cold nights. It burned his tongue and tasted strange, but Eynon felt mature for trying it. He wondered if Derry left his cider out on cold winter nights.

Ahead, on the left bank of the river, Eynon could see a gap in the trees. Large flat rocks lined the shore and two long docks on piles extended out into the water. Three boats were tied to them, each a different size. None were round baskets.

"We're almost there," said Derry. "Stay where you are when we get to the dock and don't try to move. Let me do the work until we're moored and I've got all the lines tied. That way, we won't tip over."

"Yes, sir," said Eynon. He didn't have any plans to move until the little basket boat was secured.

Once they arrived at the dock, Derry firmly connected the boat to the upper piles with ropes, lashing it tight in three places. Derry stowed his carved length of wood and climbed out of the coracle with practiced ease. He took the shovel and marshapple plants Eynon passed up to him. Derry put them on the dock, then reached down to help Eynon disembark. Eynon made the transition without mishap. He considered that boats might not be as frightening as he'd first imagined—though he might have felt differently if the coracle had tipped over. He was also surprised to realize that he hadn't thought once about the amulet in his pack while he was on the water. Now that he was on dry land, his worry returned. How would he find a free wizard to help him?

Eynon shrugged to stretch his muscles and adjusted the straps on his pack. Worrying about the amulet could wait until after supper. He put the shovel on one shoulder and the marshapple plants on the other. Both of his hands were full, but it was a convenient way to carry everything. Eynon prepared to follow Derry up a well-worn path and could see a low, wide house with a turf roof behind a screen of oaks and maples up ahead, well back from the river. He smelled smoke from a cooking fire and saw a figure striding down the path to meet them. It was a challenge to make out any details until the figure emerged from the shadow of the trees. It was a young woman with auburn hair and a concerned expression.

"It's about time you got home," said the young woman sharply. "Mother is worried sick. We saw the smoke and didn't know what to think. If you didn't catch anything and don't have the marshapples mother asked for there won't be much on the table for supper."

"Don't worry, there are six trout in the cage under the coracle. I'll clean them before we come up," said Derry.

The young woman pecked Derry on his cheek and finally took notice of Eynon and his burden.

"Who's this hayseed?" asked the redheaded young woman. "Another one of your strays?"

"I'm a Hay*wall*," said Eynon. "My uncle is a Hayseed."

"Eynon, this charming young lady is my daughter, Meredith," said Derry. "Merry, this is Eynon. He's from the other side of the mountain, in the Coombe. If you'd bothered to look on his hat to see his holly you'd know he's on his wander year. I've invited him to dinner and volunteered him to go with you tomorrow to help get those cider barrels to Tyford."

"Pleased to meet you," said Eynon, giving a slight bow.

Meredith looked him over, took the marshapples off his shoulder with a sniff, turned, and strode away from him up the path.

"Welcome to Applegarth," said Derry. "Let's clean some fish."

Chapter 3

"More is shared at meals than food and drink."
— Ealdamon's *Epigrams*

"The fish is delicious, ma'am," said Eynon. "It's the first time I've had any." He wiped his lips, then added, "I love the greens, too."

Eynon and his hosts were seated around a square dark-wood table on chairs made from birch and willow branches. The table was in front of a wide hearth and rested on a floor tiled with smooth flat stones. A pair of windows—with real glass—faced east and west to the right and left of the hearth. The western window showed a warm red and orange sunset. When Eynon saw the window glass, he realized Derry must be quite wealthy, at least by Coombe standards. Few homes in the Coombe had glass windows.

In the center of the table were tallow candles in tall wooden candlesticks, but they weren't yet lit. Still, even without their light, Applegarth's interior had a warm, welcoming glow.

Derry sat at the head of the table with his daughter across from him. His wife, Mabli, sat across from Eynon with her back to the hearth.

Mabli smiled at Eynon. She was a short, round, older woman with cheeks as rosy as apples. Eynon thought she must have dressed up for supper, since she was wearing an embroidered red skirt, a white blouse, and a black vest with more embroidery. His mother had a similar ensemble for festival days and so did his sister.

"The marshapple root is also wonderful," Eynon continued.

"Thank you, Eynon," she said. "You're so polite."

"All the boys from the Coombe are like that," said Derry.

Eynon admired Derry's talent for exaggeration. Some of his friends were a good deal less polite, but he was pleased his parents had raised him to be respectful.

"I made the fish and the roots, but Merry prepared the greens," continued Mabli as if Derry hadn't spoken. "She adds spring onions to the tender part of marshapple reeds to give them more flavor."

"They're very good," said Eynon to Meredith.

The girl ignored him and busied herself putting another serving of boiled marshapple root on her plate. She added butter and drank cider from her mug while waiting for it to melt.

Eynon was used to this sort of behavior when his sister was in a snit and took it in stride. He had another sip from his own mug of cider.

"What kind of apples is your cider pressed from?" Eynon asked the parties at the table who were speaking to him. "It's better than what we make in Haywall."

"It's a special blend," said Derry. "A little sharp, like me. A little sweet, like my charming wife—and a little bit of who knows what, like..." He waved his hand, indicating his daughter, who intentionally ignored him.

"However you make it, I can see why you have regular customers," said Eynon. The cider had a pleasant alcoholic bite, but wasn't nearly as strong as the potent version his father made each winter. That was better when saved for special occasions. For everyday drinking, Applegarth cider was perfect. He liked it a lot better than what he and his family usually drank—his mother's small beer.

Derry beamed and looked proud, acknowledging Eynon's praise. Mabli glanced from Meredith to Eynon and back again, as if willing her daughter to stop being rude and join the conversation.

Meredith was still wearing the simple dress she'd worn when she'd come down the path to meet her father and Eynon. There were wet spots on her sleeves—probably from preparing the greens, Eynon thought. He liked the way she seemed to take pleasure in her eating and didn't pick at her food like some of the Haywall girls did on festival days when they wanted to impress boys with their dainty appetites, pretending to be high ladies from Caercadel. She had managed to finish almost everything on her plate without looking directly at Eynon once.

"Would you like more marshapple root, Eynon?" asked Mabli. "And more greens? Remember to save room for the baked apples with honey. I'm keeping them warm by the side of the hearth. They're Merry's favorite."

Like a quarrel from the small crossbow Eynon had found by the tree, Meredith shot a sharp look at her mother and returned to removing the last bits of her fish from their bones.

"I'd love more marshapple root," said Eynon, "and more greens, too." *I'll never be accused of having a dainty appetite,* he thought. Digging the firebreak had made him quite hungry. So had the flood of fear he'd felt when a fireball had blazed from his hand.

Mabli gently slid two bowls down the table to Eynon.

"Pass the butter to our guest," Mabli instructed her daughter.

"Yes, *Mother,*" said Meredith, shoving the butter crock toward Eynon. She raised her head defiantly and shifted her strategy, deciding to be actively hostile instead of simply ignoring him. Eynon had been waiting for the change—his sister could only stay silent for so long before her temper appeared when she had moods like this. He buttered his roots and greens and savored generous portions of both. After he'd eaten half a plateful, he had an idea.

"Do you think I could make a go of hauling marshapple plants over the mountain to the Coombe when I get back from my wander year?" Eynon asked. "Would you sell me some? I'm sure they'd be popular in Haywall and Brynhill, especially if there was a regular supply."

Derry rubbed his chin, considering. "I've got acres of wet land on the far side of the river that's good for nothing *except* marshapples," he said. "I expect we could work out a trade. What would you carry from the Coombe to this side of the mountain?"

Eynon considered the question. It would have to be something light—and valuable—to make the exchange worthwhile. He didn't want to tell Derry about his father's trick with freezing cider. He suspected Derry knew about that already, since cider was his business. The women of the Coombe did excellent embroidery, but judging from Mabli's vest and skirt, so did the people of the Rhuthro valley. The village hives in Haywall produced fine honey, though, and there were enough wildflowers to support more bees.

"I don't know, sir," said Eynon. "I'm not sure what you need here. Honey, maybe?"

"I like a lad who knows how to say, 'I don't know,'" said Derry. "Most would try to force an answer and prove their ignorance."

"He seems pretty ignorant to me," said Meredith with a frown.

Eynon grinned at Meredith to show that her new strategy wasn't working.

"Merry!" said Mabli.

Meredith pouted at her mother and turned to her father.

"Really, Da, how can he carry enough marshapple plants to make it worth his while? He's only one boy and two dozen would be more than he could manage on any one trip."

"What do you say to that?" Derry asked Eynon. "Could you transport enough plants to make it pay?"

"I don't know, sir," Eynon repeated.

Derry smiled and winked at his wife.

"That's a good answer at this stage," said the farmer. "You'll have to learn a lot more before you'll know if it makes sense. And honey might be something good to trade. Bog flowers don't make the best tasting honey, so a new flavor might find buyers on this side of the mountain."

"Thank you," said Eynon. "I hope I'll have a chance to discuss the idea in more detail when I get back. I'll need to talk to my mother about what she paid the peddler for marshapple roots. I could probably get more if I sold the fresh greens, too."

"That's smart," said Mabli.

She looked at her daughter as if daring her to say it wasn't.

"Did you know the dried upper part of marshapple reeds makes good baskets?" asked Mabli. "You could sell that part, too. We use them to make coracles."

"The round boats?" Eynon asked.

Merry shook her head and stared at Eynon, a silent comment on his lack of knowledge.

"That's right," said Mabli. "And other sturdy baskets, since it's clear you don't have much use for boats in the Coombe."

"True enough," said Eynon. "I'd been meaning to ask," he continued. "I saw how to go downstream in a basket boat, but how to you move one against the current?"

Derry, Merry, and Mabli laughed.

"What?" asked Eynon.

"You don't," said Merry, her voice sounding like her name for the first time. "Coracles are so light you can carry them on your back until you're upstream, then put them in the river and float back."

"In the summer, when the water level is lower and the flow isn't as strong, you can paddle a coracle up the Rhuthro," said Derry, "but it's still faster and easier carrying it up the path on this side of the river even then."

"The load of a man is his coracle," said Mabli.

"What does that mean?" asked Eynon.

"It's just a saying," said Merry before her mother could reply. "It means you never build a coracle you can't carry."

"That sounds wise," said Eynon.

"Most sayings are," said Mabli, getting in the last word. "Let me get the baked apples."

While Mabli turned to the hearth, Merry questioned her father.

"Why were you so late today, Da?" she asked. "I thought you were just going to check for storm damage by the old oak, dig marshapples, and be home early. We have to get the cider barrels ready for loading in the morning."

"You're right," said Derry. "That was what I'd planned. I carried the coracle up the path to the south dock and put it in the water. Then I transferred six trout from my traps to the nice cage you made me."

"I made that fish cage when I was ten, Da," said Meredith. "You don't have to go on about how I wove it."

"Yes, my merry maid," said Derry. "I put the fish in my favorite cage and headed south from the crossroads to fill in that spot in the road that always washes out when we get a heavy rain."

Merry frowned at her father, then her expression softened and she smiled.

"So *that's* why you were carrying a shovel," said Eynon.

"Did you think I was burying a body in the woods?" asked Derry.

Eynon pretended to look shocked. "Perhaps," he said, the corners of his mouth turning up.

"In these parts, we don't bury inconvenient bodies. We weigh their clothes down with rocks and throw them in the river," said Derry.

"Da!" said Merry with mock outrage. "Don't say things like that in front of the hayseed. He'll think you're serious."

"If you need help finding rocks and tossing bodies out into the current, I'm glad to pitch in," said Eynon.

"Why don't you pitch in and carry bowls of baked apples to the table, Eynon?" asked Mabli from her position by the hearth. "I'd have my daughter do it, but I don't know if her response would be sweet or tart."

"I thought we were having baked apples with honey, not sweet tarts," replied Merry.

"I'm glad your mood is changing for the better or I'd have to give your portion of baked apples to our dinner guest," said Mabli. "Thank you, Eynon."

Eynon had taken two full bowls from Mabli and delivered them to Derry and Meredith at the table. When he delivered Merry's bowl, the young woman raised one eyebrow and gave him a tight why-did-you-bother-me look, like a cat interrupted at its grooming. Eynon gave Merry a slight nod to show he'd received her message. Despite Merry's attitude, he was enjoying the conversation around the table. Derry and Mabli were doing their best to make him feel welcome. He started to return to the hearth, but Mabli waved him back to his seat. She put steaming bowls of baked apples with honey in front of Eynon and herself. He tasted his portion and didn't have to work to make his face look pleased.

"Go on," Mabli said to her husband when she'd had her first taste of baked apple. "You never did explain why you were late."

"I was trying," said Derry, "but was rudely interrupted."

Merry stuck her tongue out. Derry saw it, but ignored it.

"I was walking back north to the crossroads when I saw a young man standing there," said Derry. "He'd just found..."

"...out that the old oak had been struck by lightning last night and caught fire," said Eynon. He stared at Derry, willing him not to mention the amulet.

"Da had to walk by the old oak to fill in the spot that washes out," said Merry. "Wouldn't he have seen it burning?"

"Maybe it had been smoldering?" suggested Eynon.

"That must have been it," said Derry, rubbing his chin.

"There would have been smoke if it was smoldering," said Merry. "You're hiding something."

"If he is, he's got a good reason for it," said Mabli. She put her hand on her husband's arm affectionately.

Merry gave her father a stern look, then focused on Eynon.

"He's hiding something," said Merry, sharpening her gaze on their guest.

Eynon's cheeks turned red.

"If Eynon has a secret, it's his to tell if he wishes," said Derry. "We need to respect his privacy."

"I'll be alone with him on a boat for most of a week," said Merry. "I'll talk it out of him on the first day."

She set her jaw in a way that dared any of them to contradict her.

Mabli and Derry nodded. Eynon's cheeks turned even redder. After a deep breath, Eynon grinned and nodded, too. Then he laughed.

"A wise man knows when he's defeated," said Eynon. "I'll get my pack."

Eynon retrieved his pack and goatskin from where they were hanging on pegs by the front door. He moved his empty dessert bowl to the side and placed his pack and skin on the table. Merry moved the unlit wooden candlesticks to make more room. Before Eynon opened his pack, he unclipped the small crossbow from the strap on his goatskin.

"Derry and I found this while we were digging the firebreak," said Eynon.

"You mean *you* found it," said Derry. "You've got a good eye."

"Thank you, sir," said Eynon.

"Do you know how to shoot a crossbow?" asked Merry. Her voice sounded like a captain of soldiers ordering a new recruit to report.

She extended her hand and Eynon passed the small device to her. Merry pulled back the bowstring and engaged it, then released it by hand, not using the trigger. She stared at Eynon, waiting for his answer.

"I can hit what I aim at, with bow and crossbow and sling," said Eynon after a brief hesitation. "I wasn't the best at the weekly shoots, but I wasn't the worst, either."

"Good to know," said Merry. She removed one of the four bolts from the stock. "We may have more quarrels this size in the barn. I'll check in the morning. I think one of them has a line tied to it and would be good for fishing."

Eynon was pleased Merry had had offered to help him—or maybe she just wanted fresh fish on their trip.

"I'd be glad to give fishing with it a try," he said. "It would help me get used to the way it shoots."

Eynon was confident the crossbow would shoot straight and true, but it would still be smart to practice.

"Remind me tomorrow," said Merry.

Eynon was tempted to reply, "Yes, dear," the way his father usually answered his mother, but he nodded instead. He finished opening his pack and lifted out his second-best linen shirt. The rolled-up garment clattered when he placed it on the table. He tugged at the fabric and the odd-looking shards were revealed. Mabli, Derry, and Meredith examined to strange shapes.

"I've never seen anything like *these* before," said Merry.

She rubbed a shard between her fingertips, being careful to stay away from its sharp edges.

"They're smooth, but not cold, like metal," continued Merry. "They don't have a grain, like wood, either."

"They feel like obsidian," said Mabli.

Everyone turned to look at her.

"When did you ever see obsidian?" said Derry, surprised that his wife had managed to surprise him.

"A peddler let me hold his knife," said Mabli. "He said he got it from the Eagle People and they brought it here over the Sea."

Merry grinned. "Did his knife get longer as you held it?"

"Meredith!" said her mother. "Sometimes a knife is just a knife."

Eynon held back a chuckle, entertained by Merry teasing her mother the way she had. Back in the Coombe, young people made such jokes about each other, but not about their parents, and especially not to their faces. *Maybe it's different if you're an only child,* he thought.

Mabli continued, laughing off her daughter's interruption. "This one wasn't metal. It was black and very sharp. It felt like glass. These shards aren't quite the same. They're oily, somehow, like they're glass made from plants, not sand."

"That's a good way of describing them," said Derry. He'd been examining one of the shards himself. "I think they're wizard-made."

"Why would you say that, Da?" asked Merry.

"Show them, Eynon," said Derry.

Eynon unwrapped the amulet while it was still inside his pack and slowly withdrew the silver oval with the blue stone. He held it very carefully, like a butterfly, and didn't point the stone at anyone. He placed the amulet face up in the center of the table.

"That's why," said Derry. "I watched the lad find the thing and send a fireball at the old oak before he knew what he held."

Merry and Mabli leaned in to examine the amulet.

"How beautiful," said Mabli. "It's the largest magestone I've ever seen—and the metalwork is exquisite."

Light from the fading sun reflected off the amulet's surface and sparkled in Mabli's eyes.

Derry took his wife's arm to prevent her from getting too close.

"Watch out," he said. "I don't want to lose you if it shoots out another fireball."

"How many magestones have you seen, *Mother?*" asked Merry.

Mabli frowned at her daughter, more amused than annoyed, but she waggled her finger before switching to a smile.

Merry moved to pick up the amulet, but Eynon blocked her hand and returned it to the bottom of his pack.

"I wanted a closer look," said Merry.

"Sorry," said Eynon, "but I don't want to set fire to your house, even by accident."

Merry glared at him, shooting fireballs of a different sort with her expression.

"Thank you for showing it to us," said Mabli. "I've never seen anything like it before."

"Not even from a peddler?" teased Merry, shifting her gaze to her mother and changing her mood like a spinning weather vane.

Derry touched Eynon's arm. "It's mage-made for sure," he said. "You're wise to keep it hidden until you can find the right wizard in Tyford to advise you."

Merry's mood shifted again, this time to storm clouds. "I still want to see it again. I need a better look at it."

Eynon didn't reply. He finished repacking his pack and returned it and the goatskin to their pegs.

"You need to respect our guest's privacy," said Mabli.

Merry put her hands on her hips. Eynon smiled at her and tried to change the subject.

"I'd really appreciate it if you could look for those extra crossbow quarrels in the morning," he said.

"I said I would," said Merry. "I always do what I say."

"And so does everyone around her," said Derry.

"I wonder where I got that from?" his daughter rejoined.

Derry looked toward the ceiling and pretended to whistle. Eynon and Mabli laughed. After a beat, so did Merry.

"If we've got to find him a free wizard in Tyford," said Merry, "I'll be a few days longer than usual."

"So long as you're home in time to start your wander year," said Mabli. "I want to give you a proper send-off."

"You should be able to find a couple of passengers heading upriver to help you row your way back," said Derry.

Merry shook her head slowly.

"How many times have I made this trip, Da?"

"Once a month for nine months a year for the past two years on your own," said her father. "And three years of trips with me before that."

"Thank you," said Merry. "I'll be back as fast as I can—well before I have to leave on my wander year."

Mabli smiled at Merry.

"Happy birthday," said Eynon, "and happy wandering."

"My birthday's not for a month," said Merry, "and I'm always happy when I'm traveling. That usually means when I'm in a boat—alone—on the river."

"That's not the point of a wander year," said Mabli. "You're supposed to meet new people, visit new places, try new things. You can be a hermit here at home."

"Maybe I'll wander across the Sea to find my own obsidian knife," teased Merry.

"If only," said her mother.

"Come along Merry, Eynon," said Derry. "We need to get the cider barrels staged for loading. It will go faster with three of us."

"Yes, sir," said Eynon, rising. He followed Derry and his daughter toward the door, then turned over his shoulder to speak to Mabli. "Thank you for supper," he said. "The baked apples with honey were a treat."

"It's a pleasure to have you as a guest," said Mabli to Eynon's retreating back. Her voice carried as he closed the door. Eynon was just able to catch her words.

"Such a *nice* young man."

Half an hour later, after the four surprisingly large cider barrels were staged for loading and Merry left to get ready for bed, Derry invited Eynon to have a drink of winter-fortified extra-hard cider.

"Sit," said Derry, indicating a bench inside the shed where the barrels were kept before shipping. "Have some applejack."

Eynon was glad he hadn't told Derry about his father's trick to make cider stronger. Clearly, Derry had already mastered the technique. The farmer took a swig from a thick-sided crockery jug and offered the heavy container to Eynon, who took a small sip.

"That's very good," said Eynon. "And very strong."

"But smooth, don't you think?"

Eynon nodded, but Derry hadn't waited for a reply.

"Magical artifacts are dangerous, lad," he said. "And lost artifacts probably have wizards looking for them."

"Wouldn't it be easier if the wizard who lost it found me?" asked Eynon. "Then I could just give it back."

"Maybe," said Derry, after he'd had another generous drink from the jug. "But how would you know any particular wizard is the one who lost it? Not all wizards are kind and helpful, my lad. Remember—crown wizards serve their noble masters—and free wizards serve only themselves."

Eynon thought about it and had another sip. The liquor really *was* smooth.

"So what should I do?" he asked. The applejack was making him feel warm and more than a bit sleepy.

"You've already learned not to claim you know something when you don't," said the farmer. "Be curious, and keep your wits about you. Don't take what others say at face value."

"That's good advice in almost any situation," said Eynon.

"Yes, but you've lived too long around friendly, honest people," said Derry. "It's different in places like Tyford. You don't have much practice spotting those who'd lie for their own ends."

"You're right about that," said Eynon. "I promise I'll try my best, sir."

"And that will have to do," said Derry. "I've been hearing troubling rumors from the capital and hope they're not true. I don't want you and Merry caught up in the squabbles of kings and nobles."

"Rumors?" asked Eynon.

"Let's hope that's all they are," Derry replied.

The farmer put the stopper back in the heavy jug and stood up. Eynon also got to his feet. To his surprise, Derry gave him a quick, fatherly hug.

"Time to call it a night," said Derry. "You'll need your rest if you're going to keep your temper around my daughter."

Eynon nodded and smiled.

Derry, he thought, *was most assuredly right.*

Fercha

The wizard in blue fell through her escape gate's black circle and pointed her toes. She knew she only had a fraction of a second before she hit deep water—with luck, more like a knife than a rock. Then she entered the frigid lake, her form somewhere between the two extremes. It was dark in the cavern, and darker still below the surface until she struggled her way back up to take a welcome breath.

"*Llachar!*" she commanded while blindly treading water.

Fercha was distracted from the chill by the echoes of her voice reflecting in the underground space. Then balls of bright light appeared near the cavern's ceiling, dancing around the stalactites and casting strange shadows all around her.

Now that Fercha could see, she identified the tall upright stone pillar she'd placed on the shore to mark the easiest place to get out of the water. Behind the stone, in a high niche on the wall where rising water levels wouldn't damage it, was her emergency kit. She swam to the pillar and crawled out of the lake, water dripping from her robes. Fercha pulled herself up the pillar get to her feet. Once standing, she removed her clothing. She was still a blue wizard—at least her lips were blue.

There were towels in her kit, but before she dried her body she retrieved a silver pendant holding a small blue magestone and placed its delicate chain around her neck. When the stone touched her skin, she could feel its energy.

The pendant held her original training stone. It was the first artifact she'd received when she was an apprentice and its familiar resonance reassured her, even as she considered how far her understanding of magic had increased since she'd been given it. Losing her fully-linked true artifact was like losing a limb, but wearing her original training pendant somewhat eased the ache inside her.

With a word, she magically added heat-energy to a towel and wrapped it around her body, savoring its warmth. She preferred that approach to spells that increased her temperature directly. Color returned to her lips and she donned the dry blue robes in her kit. It was cool in the cavern, so she put a dark blue cloak around her shoulders as well.

Fercha turned her shoulders left, then right, feeling the cloak's fabric swirl around her long legs and tall, muscular body. She'd almost defeated Verro with wizardry alone, even though he was taller, with a greater reach. Still, they were equally matched in magical talent. Their duel could have gone either way.

It's a good thing I used my crossbow to end things quickly!

She summoned one of the balls of light to float above her head with a gesture and extinguished the others with a one-syllable command. It was time to find her lost true artifact and confront Verro, the arrogant, green-clad Tamloch crown wizard, once again. This time, she promised herself, the outcome would be different.

Fercha had hidden a spare flying disk just inside the entrance to the cave complex. She set off to retrieve it.

Chapter 4

"Rivers are older than mountains and stubborn
enough to wear right through them."
— Ealdamon's *Epigrams*

Derry and his daughter had gotten everything on board the boat quickly and seemed to know exactly what to put where. After a few minutes of observation, Eynon realized he was seeing a process refined over many repetitions, much like his routine for feeding the stock back home.

Eynon was glad *this* boat was much larger and wasn't round. It looked like a river cargo vessel Robin Oddfellow had described in *Peregrinations*. Eynon guessed it was close to forty feet long with a flat bottom, a pointed front, and a raised back. He knew he had a lot to learn about boats, but didn't know if he could learn much from Merry. Her hostility to his presence was palpable.

At least Eynon had managed to follow Derry's advice and get a good night's sleep. As the current took them downstream, he considered that the trip itself must not be too dangerous or Merry wouldn't have been planning to travel to Tyford on her own before Eynon arrived. The real danger, Eynon realized, was from Merry. Days of forced proximity to her could easily end up with more than lost tempers. Eynon took comfort in knowing he was bigger than Merry—but her tongue was sharper. He took slow, deep breaths.

"Did they teach you anything about boats in the Coombe?" asked Merry. "Or wasn't that part of a farm boy's education?"

Merry was seated at the raised rear of the boat, setting its course with a broad-bladed sweep rudder. The four very large barrels of hard cider were carefully stowed amidships on curved bases designed to hold them securely in place. Derry had called them *tuns* and they were not what Eynon had expected. He'd initially thought they'd be much smaller, the sort of barrel that would serve as a convenient seat if set upright, but had learned differently last night when he'd helped stage them for loading. They were huge—five feet in diameter and closer to six feet tall, from flat bottom to top.

People in Tyford must love their cider, thought Eynon.

The boat wasn't even eight feet wide, so there was barely enough space to squeeze through sideways to get from the front to the back. Eynon sat facing Merry on a board—a thwart, he remembered—that went from side to side near the front. Looking at the narrow space on either side of the barrels, he thought it would be easier to climb over them than to make his way beside them if he ever wanted to reach the rear of the vessel.

In front of Eynon, two dozen crockery jugs with oak-heartwood stoppers rested on the bottom of the boat between him and the tuns. Derry had said the jugs held hard cider when they'd loaded them before the sun was fully up this morning. Eynon had passed the jugs down to Derry from the dock. He felt like the farmer was trying to give him something to do, rather than truly needing his help.

A coil of rope, a tent, food, supplies and sleeping gear were packed in the space under the raised part at the back, below where Merry sat. Eynon tossed his bedroll in with the rest. He looked over the side and smiled when he noticed colorful knotwork patterns intertwined with red apples painted there all the way from the back to the front.

"Is your tongue glued to the roof of your mouth?" asked Merry. "Or is it just a matter of having manure between your ears?"

Eynon didn't rise to her bait and respond in anger. He hoped staying calm would put her off balance.

"We don't have anywhere to put boats in my part of the Coombe," he said. "All we have are small ponds and a narrow stream."

Merry sniffed, loud enough so Eynon could hear it forty feet away at the other end of the boat.

"It can't be much of a place to live if it doesn't have any lakes or rivers."

"We have excellent farm land and fine forage for sheep, goats, and cattle," said Eynon. "There's also a quarry for green slate, marble, limestone and soapstone."

"Manure and *rocks* in your head, then," said Merry. "Turn around."

"What?" asked Eynon.

"Turn around," Merry repeated. "The bow man needs to watch the river and call out rocks."

"I thought you said I was a farm boy," replied Eynon.

He carefully shifted on the board until he was facing downstream.

"Good," said Merry. "Look for rocks sticking out above the surface and ripples from rocks underneath it. The river is high, so we shouldn't have too much trouble, but it's also moving fast, so I'll have less time to steer around them.

Eynon observed the water flowing ahead of him. There were ripples on the left, but if they kept going straight they'd miss them.

"Do you want me to tell you which way to steer or where the rocks are?" asked Eynon.

"Where the rocks are," said Merry. "Other than the ones in your head, of course."

"Are you always this charming?"

"You're seeing me on a good day," said Merry. "I love it when my father and mother stick me with a useless stray and expect me to get him to Tyford."

"Sorry," said Eynon. He rolled his eyes, but then remembered Merry couldn't see his face. "Rock right," he called out.

"I see it," said Merry.

She adjusted their course to miss the rock—it was two feet out of the water and impossible to overlook.

"I like to take these trips on my own," she said. "They give me time to think."

"What do you think about?" asked Eynon. "Rock left."

Merry corrected their path through the water and didn't reply. Eynon didn't say anything. He scanned the river and the river banks. The right bank was a thick marsh, choked with marshapple reeds. The left bank alternated between fields showing green shoots and orchards with apple, pear, plum, and cherry trees in bloom. Tiny white and pink blossoms blown by the wind dotted the surface of the river nearby.

"I like to think about the world outside the Coombe," said Eynon. "I want to travel, like Robin Oddfellow, and maybe become wise someday, like Ealdamon."

"Wisdom is a journey," said Merry. "It's unwise to think you've arrived at your destination."

Eynon recognized the quote. "You've read Ealdamon's *Epigrams?*" he asked.

"Every word," said Merry. "Four or five times. My father has a copy. I think I've memorized most of the aphorisms."

"You're lucky," said Eynon. "I had to read my uncle's copy and he lived a two-hour walk away."

"My father also has a copy of *The Venerable History of Dâron from the First Ships,*" said Merry proudly. "It's so big and heavy I couldn't pick it up when he bought it."

"How old were you then?" asked Eynon.

"Seven," said Merry. "I read it cover to cover before I was ten."

"You're lucky," said Eynon. "I wish I could read it."

"Father likes you," said Merry. "If you stop back at Applegarth after you've dealt with what you found, I'm sure he'd let you."

"That would be wonderful," said Eynon.

He turned back to face Merry and she could see his excitement.

"Watch for rocks," she instructed.

Eynon reluctantly turned around and scanned the river.

"Where did he find such a treasure?" he asked.

"On the street of the booksellers in Tyford," said Merry.

"There's a *street* of booksellers?" said Eynon, his voice rising in pitch.

"A whole block of them, anyway," said Merry. "They're near the street of wizards."

"A street of *wizards*, too?" asked Eynon. "There's only one hedge wizard in the entire Coombe and she's at the baron's castle in Caercadel. She mostly makes charms so men and women can choose when to have children. She also helps with healing, when she can get there in time. My cousin's right foot was crushed by an ox's hoof while bringing Brynhill's tithe to the baron and she saved it for him. He says he can tell the weather with it now."

Merry laughed. "My mother's shoulder can do that," she said. "I think the best wizards prefer cities or remote towers. We're not so different from the Coombe on this side of the mountain. There's only one hedge wizard for all the holdings along this part of the Rhuthro. We'll be passing his cottage in a few hours."

"Do you think he can advise me on what to do with what I found?" asked Eynon. He turned around and looked at his pack leaning against one of the crockery jugs.

"From what you told me, I think you'll need more than a hedge wizard to figure out what to do about *that,*" said Merry. "You'll need someone in the Conclave—a crown wizard or one of the stronger free wizards."

"I know as much about wizards as I do about boats," said Eynon. "Rock right."

Merry laughed. It sounded as melodic as rippling water. Eynon realized she hadn't insulted him for several minutes.

"The front is the bow, the rear is the stern, the center is amidships, and I'm guiding our course with a sweep oar or rudder," she said in a teasing voice as she made a minor adjustment to the boat's direction. "Starboard is right and port is left."

"Large rocks port and starboard," said Eynon, his tone light. *Maybe he* could *learn from Merry,* he thought.

"I see them," said Merry. "Those are old friends. They mean we'll be stopping soon."

"But we just started!"

"We have to pay our first toll," said Merry. "And I have to off-load the ale I had for breakfast."

"I was going to ask you about that," said Eynon.

He could have handled the situation by doing what was necessary over the side, but Merry's presence observing him from the stern made him reluctant to do so.

Merry laughed again.

"Will you tell me about wizards—and history—after we stop?"

"If you ask politely."

"I'm always polite."

"I've noticed," said Merry with another sniff.

Eynon turned around and saw Merry grinning. He grinned back and dipped his head in a quick bow to demonstrate how polite he could be.

When he faced downriver again, he saw a pair of squat buildings made from limestone blocks, one on either side of a narrow point in the river, a few hundred yards ahead. There was a stone dock next to the building on the western bank. Half a dozen links of a heavy chain, each as big as a newly weaned piglet, were wrapped around a foot-thick log standing vertical near the end. The chain trailed off into the water and surfaced at the building on the opposite bank.

"Is that where we're stopping?" he asked.

"Yes," said Merry. "Do they have their chain up?"

"What?" asked Eynon.

"Their chain," said Merry. "To block our path."

"No," said Eynon. "Or not that I can tell. It looks slack. There's a tall, solid-looking man with yellow hair and a sword on the dock. He's waving at us."

Merry sighed.

"He's waving at *me*," she said. "That's Gruffyd. I've known him all my life and he's been trying to woo me since before he left on his wander year. I was afraid he'd be back now. It's too bad he didn't find some nice girl farther downriver and decide to stay with her and her family."

"You're not in favor of his courtship?" asked Eynon.

"He's a nice enough sort, but has even more rocks and manure between his ears than you do."

"Thank you, I think," said Eynon.

"You're welcome," said Merry. "Gruffyd doesn't know how to take no for an answer."

Eynon heard a note of anger in Merry's voice, but before he could comment, she continued.

"He also doesn't know how to read. His mother tried to teach him, but didn't have much luck. I can't talk to him about books."

Merry shifted the boat toward the west bank of the river where the current was slower. She talked as she worked.

"Gruffyd wants to be a soldier and serve in the royal guard. He cares more about his sword than any future wife."

They were getting close to the river toll station. Merry spoke softly, but urgently enough to carry from the stern and get his attention.

"Eynon," she asked. "Can you help me?"

Eynon turned.

"How may I be of service, dear lady?"

"Pretend to be my suitor," she said, reluctantly. "If Gruffyd thinks I've decided to accept you, maybe he'll focus his unwanted attentions elsewhere. Calling me 'dear lady' is perfect."

"Yes, dear lady," said Eynon.

He winked at Merry. She looked exasperated for a moment, then pasted a sweet, but insincere smile on her face.

Eynon faced forward and admired the way she maneuvered the boat up to the dock. Without being told, he tied a rope he found near the bow to a convenient and well-worn cleat close at hand. Gruffyd helped Merry out of the boat after she tied off the stern. She moved to stand a few feet away from him and beckoned to Eynon. He jumped awkwardly from the bow thwart to the dock. Three strides from his long legs later, he was standing next to Merry.

To his surprise, she hugged him, holding him in a pleasingly tight embrace. Her auburn hair smelled like apple blossoms. When they separated a few seconds later, Merry turned Eynon around to face the other youth.

"Eynon, this is Gruffyd," she said. "We've been friends since we were children. We're practically brother and sister."

Smiling at Merry's tactic, Eynon extended his hand to Gruffyd.

"I'm very pleased to meet you," said Eynon. "My dear, sweet Merry has told me so much about you. Best of luck traveling to Brendinas to serve in the royal guard."

"Uh, thanks," said Gruffyd. He was a bit slow to process the unexpected situation.

Merry rested her hand on Eynon's forearm, as if claiming him. Eynon admired the way she was sending an unambiguous message to her childhood friend.

Eynon was a few inches taller than Gruffyd, but the yellow-haired young man outweighed him by seventy or eighty pounds. His upper arms were larger than Eynon's thighs and his wrists were thick from sword practice. Eynon had no trouble carrying large sacks of grain from the mill to his family's kitchen for making porridge and bread, or lifting hay up to the second level of their barn, but his muscles didn't bulge like Gruffyd's. He stood before the larger youth, feigning a confidence he didn't feel.

"You two get acquainted," said Merry. "I'll fetch a jug for your father."

Merry left them and headed farther out the dock. Eynon searched his mind for a safe topic of conversation.

"How was your wander year?" he asked. "Did you travel far?"

"I went to Brendinas," said Gruffyd. "I found a retired royal guardsman there who taught me advanced sword work."

"A valuable skill, I expect," said Eynon. "I'm sure your training will help you in the royal guard. We're headed to Tyford."

Gruffyd nodded.

"Tyford's nice," he said, "but it's not Brendinas."

"I doubt I'll ever get all the way to the capital," said Eynon.

Gruffyd was silent, staring at Eynon. After two heartbeats, Eynon asked a question.

"How did you win a spot in the guard?"

"My teacher got me in," said Gruffyd after his own long pause. "He put in a good word for me with the senior guard captain. They served together when the old King was still on the throne."

"I'm sure you'll be an asset to the realm's defense," said Eynon.

"Thank you," said Gruffyd stiffly, like one dog taking the measure of another.

He looked at Eynon's cap and the wreath of holly around it.

"How long have you been wandering?"

"Only a little while," said Eynon. He didn't want to admit it was only his second day away from home.

"So you'll be gone for a long time after Merry gets back?"

Eynon was saved from having to reply by Merry returning to stand beside him. She carried one of the jugs of hard cider and

passed it to Gruffyd with both hands. After Gruffyd accepted the
jug, Merry took Eynon's near hand and held it. She felt warm and
Eynon decided he liked holding hands with Merry, even if it was
only a subterfuge.

"That's for your father," Merry told Gruffyd, indicating the jug.
"See that he gets it unopened. If not, our mothers will talk and I'll
know and the next cider jug you try to steal a drink from will be
filled with vinegar."

"I'll give it to him," said Gruffyd, shaking his head. "He'll share
it with me, anyway."

"So long as he's the first to taste it," said Merry. "My da says it's
some of his best."

She smiled and leaned into Eynon's shoulder. He was almost a
foot taller than Merry and involuntarily dropped her hand and put
his arm around her. She cuddled into his chest and stared up into
Eynon's eyes before looking at Gruffyd again. The three of them
stood awkwardly and Merry squeezed Eynon's hand.

"We should probably be going," said Eynon. "We have a lot of
miles to travel."

"That's right," said Merry. "Nice to see you again, Gruffyd.
Good luck with joining the royal guard. I'm sure you'll be happy
in Brendinas."

"Wait," said Gruffyd. "I want you to meet someone."

A young woman about Eynon's age was walking onto the dock.
She was of medium height with fine features and had lips so red
she looked like she'd been eating fresh cherries. She was lithe and
her hair was long, blonde, and braided. She wore a fashionable
sky-blue dress, complemented by a belt around her hips made
from shiny brass plates. A thin sword with a polished hilt hung
from the belt.

When the young woman reached Gruffyd, she put her arm
around his waist and he draped his across her shoulders.

"I'd like you to meet my fiancée, Nyssia," said Gruffyd, slowly.
"She's from Brendinas. Her father is my sword master. She's started
learning from him as well."

Gruffyd looked at Merry expectantly, as if worried about her reaction, but his concern quickly disappeared.

"I'm *so* very pleased to meet you," said Merry. "Welcome to the Rhuthro valley!"

Merry stepped close and embraced Nyssia, who seemed pleased, but a bit surprised at Merry's actions.

"But," said Nyssia, "I thought, I mean Gruff said, that is..."

"Did Gruffyd tell you we were once sweethearts?" asked Merry. "Don't worry. That was long ago, when we were children. I couldn't be happier that he found a charming woman like you to be his wife."

The young woman from the capital smiled and looked relieved.

"Thank you," she said. "That makes me feel *so* much better."

Merry stepped back to take Eynon's hand, then cuddle in under his arm again.

"You can see my affections are now bestowed on another," she said.

Eynon smiled and squeezed Merry's shoulder to reinforce her message.

"I'm glad you're not angry with me," said Gruffyd.

"No," said Merry. "I'm very happy for you both. May your years together be filled with joy, health, love and peace."

Gruffyd smiled, looking like a big dog who's been praised by its owner. Nyssia beamed at Merry and Eynon.

"And we wish the two of you the same," she said.

"Now we really must be on our way," said Merry.

"It was a pleasure meeting you both," said Eynon.

"Nyssia and I leave for the capital in the morning," said Gruffyd. "Her father said we should return quickly to be in place for the muster."

"The muster?" asked Eynon.

"Shush, now," said Nyssia to Gruffyd. "Father said not to say..."

"I'm sorry," said Gruffyd. "Safe travels. Perhaps we'll meet downriver."

"Perhaps," said Merry.

With only a few more pleasantries, Eynon and Merry returned to their boat and cast off. They waved at Gruffyd and Nyssia as they pulled away and didn't talk for several minutes, until they were well out of earshot. The sun was higher and the light scattered off the water. It was going to be a warm day. The river carried them at least a quarter mile beyond the squat buildings at the toll station.

"That was interesting," said Eynon from the bow.

"It was," said Merry. "I never suspected Gruffyd would find room inside his thick skull to care as much about a woman as does about his sword."

"I think you're selling him short," said Eynon. "The man is obviously besotted, and Nyssia seems very nice, for a city girl."

"How many city girls do you know?"

"One," said Eynon. "And she seems very nice, so that proves it."

"Your logic is dubious," said Merry, "but in this case I'm so relieved to be free of Gruffyd's attentions, I'll take it."

Eynon turned and nodded his head.

"So glad I have your approval, dear lady. It was a delight to assist you in your unneeded subterfuge."

"Well, we didn't know it was unneeded until we got there, did we?" she asked. "And thank you, you played your part well."

Merry paused as they followed the current downriver. They she abruptly changed the course of the conversation, if not their boat.

"I think Gruffyd is in for a surprise with Nyssia."

"How so?" asked Eynon.

"When we hugged, I could feel her muscles," said Merry. "I don't think Nyssia is new to the art of the sword—I think she's been learning since she could walk."

"Hah!" said Eynon. He looked ahead and rubbed his chin. "Why would she be interested in someone like Gruffyd?"

"He's a baron's eldest son," said Merry, as if that explained everything.

Eynon didn't say anything for a minute.

"It was nice to hold your hand," said Merry to break the silence. "Just don't get any ideas."

"That was the furthest thing from my mind," said Eynon quickly.

He looked over his shoulder and waggled his eyebrows.

"Stop that," she sniffed. Then she giggled.

"Oh no," said Merry, putting one hand to her mouth. "We forgot to use the privy."

Chapter 5

"Wizards are never what you expect.
It's a requirement of the profession."
— Ealdamon's *Epigrams*

Merry eased the boat up to a sturdy wooden dock near a small tower with crenellations at the top, a few miles farther down the river on the east bank. The tower was set back from the water on top of a stone outcropping that increased its elevation and surely gave anyone standing on top of it an excellent view up and down the Rhuthro valley. Eynon wondered if it was the home of the hedge wizard Merry had mentioned.

"That's where our hedge wizard lives," said Merry.

Eynon smiled. He'd been making good guesses lately.

"I like to drop off a jug of cider for him on my trips to Tyford," she continued. "He also has a real privy so I don't have to go in the woods."

"I can appreciate the advantages of that," said Eynon. "In the castle at Caercadel I've heard they have garderobes—privies on the inside that are open to the river at the bottom of their chutes."

"They do," said Merry, "and they're trouble. The settlements downstream would be happier if the chutes on the Caercadel garderobes led to a pit or a moat or something. I'm glad we're far enough downstream for fish to deal with their waste before it gets to us."

Eynon thought for a few seconds.

"Where does Applegarth get its water?"

"From a well," said Merry. "A deep well."

"I'm glad to hear it," said Eynon.

Once the boat was in place, Merry tied off her end and Eynon did likewise. He was pleased when he stepped up to the dock as easily as he would have hopped on top of a stump back home. He couldn't match Merry's effortless motions as she transferred from the boat's raised rear deck to the dock in two quick steps, but he was getting better at it.

Eynon could see why Merry wore a short tunic, trousers and sturdy boots. Her outfit was much more practical than long skirts for a boat master.

He was surprised that no one had come to meet them.

"Is your hedge wizard home?" asked Eynon.

"He doesn't have a flag out to say he's elsewhere," Merry replied. "I think he's in. He's probably preoccupied."

Eynon noticed there was a pole extending from a niche between the battlements on top of the tower, but didn't see anything flying from it.

"A flag?"

"Yes. Holdings along the river have different colors and symbols to represent them," said Merry. "We carry them when we bring our tithes to the earl. When all the holdings' nobles parade into court together it's almost like a rainbow."

"That sounds pretty," said Eynon. "Maybe I'll get to see it someday. We don't do things that way in the Coombe, except for the baron."

He paused and looked up at the tower, wondering if the hedge wizard's privy had one hole or two.

"What does Applegarth's flag look like?"

"It's white with a wide, wavy blue line from top to bottom, between two red apples," said Merry.

"Will you teach me the flags of the holdings along the river?"

"Maybe—after I visit the privy," she said. "Stay with the boat and guard it."

"I can do that," said Eynon. "Now hurry. I need to pay a visit there myself."

Merry walked quickly up the gravel path from the dock and around the granite outcrop below the tower. Eynon watched the river for a few moments, then decided staring at running water made things worse. He shifted his weight from foot to foot and moved a few yards up the path to examine the hedge wizard's tower in more detail.

It was built like the circular stone keep at Caercadel, but on a much smaller scale. The baron's main keep was eighty feet across, while the tower before him was only twenty. From the placement of its narrow windows, the squat tower had only two levels, compared to Caercadel's five.

"Excuse me, young man. Are you traveling with Merry?"

Eynon nearly levitated with surprise. He turned around to see a man in his forties or fifties with a weathered face, wearing a bleached-white linen tunic and a sky-blue cloak. He was bald, with a fringe of long, graying hair. The man wore a wide gold circlet with a blue gem on his brow. The band of the circlet was etched with intricate knotwork patterns. A solid-looking ironwood staff as tall as his shoulders was in his right hand, while a mesh bag holding three large, iridescent, and still squirming fish was in his left. The fish, the mesh bag, and the old man's clothes were dripping wet.

Eynon stared at the older man and consciously closed his mouth.

"I didn't mean to startle you," said the man with wet clothes. "But you *had* been standing on my dock."

Eynon spoke without taking time to think.

"Where did you *come* from?"

"There are many ways to answer that question," said the man. "You could ask my parents for details about of the physical act that led to my birth, but alas, they're no longer living. Or I could respond philosophically and discuss various theories concerning the origin of my mind, my body, and my innermost self."

This was not what Eynon had expected. He had no idea how to reply.

"Instead," continued the old man, "I will follow the example of an ancient teacher and answer a question with another question."

He paused and looked at Eynon thoughtfully, as if determining whether or not he was worth instructing, and decided in the affirmative.

"Where do *you* think I came from?"

Eynon shook his head to clear it, took a deep breath, and puzzled out an answer.

"You're clearly the hedge wizard who lives in this tower," said Eynon. "Merry told me about you. She's..."

"...behind the tower using the *necessarium*, I know," said the man.

"I think she's in the privy," said Eynon.

The man in wet robes smiled at him and waved the hand holding the mesh bag with the fish to urge Eynon to continue.

"Given that your clothes are wet, and you're carrying fish," said Eynon, "I expect I didn't see you because you were under the dock checking some sort of trap."

"Very good," said the older man, smiling more broadly. "You're observant and reached a reasonable conclusion. I was actually walking underwater collecting fish that like to congregate under overhanging rocks on the banks," he said. "Since very few people are familiar with the capabilities of wizards, your response was well-reasoned, if not entirely accurate."

Eynon appreciated what he took to be a compliment, of a sort, and remembered his manners.

"Thank you, good wizard," he said, bowing deeply. "I'm Eynon of Haywall—in the Coombe."

"I should visit the Coombe someday," said the man in wet robes. "I've intended to for many years, but never found the time."

While the hedge wizard spoke, his robes went from wet to dry in front of Eynon's eyes.

Eynon managed to keep his mouth closed, but his eyebrows rose. He went back to shifting from foot to foot.

"I'd be glad to advise you on the highlights of the region," said Eynon, "should you ever have a chance to visit."

The wizard released his staff, which remained perfectly balanced and vertical. He took a step toward Eynon and extended his hand.

"Thank you, Eynon," he said as the two shook hands. "I may take you up on your offer. I'm Doethan. Pleased to meet you, young man. Let's head up the hill so you can eliminate what's distracting you and I can fry up these fish for our lunch."

"Pleased to meet you as well, your wizardness, sir," said Eynon.

"Doethan," said the man in a kindly voice.

"Doethan," said Eynon. "I'd be glad to come up the hill with you, but I promised Merry I'd guard the boat until she got back."

"Don't worry," said Doethan. "I'll ward the boat and its cargo so no one will bother them. Grab a jug of cider for me and I'll see to it."

Eynon walked back on the dock and stepped down into the boat. He remembered Merry had said one of the cider jugs was for the hedge wizard, so he put a jug on the dock and stepped up to stand beside it.

Doethan reclaimed his staff and joined Eynon, handing him the mesh bag of trout and encouraging Eynon to stand behind him. Then the hedge wizard made several passes with his staff pointed toward the boat while reciting words Eynon didn't understand. The blue magestone in his circlet glowed and the knotwork etched in the gold band sparkled.

When Doethan finished speaking, the circlet's glow briefly brightened, then disappeared. Doethan lowered his staff and tilted it up the hill to indicate it was time for Eynon to get moving, but Eynon didn't budge.

"How did you protect the boat, sir?" Eynon asked. "It looks the same."

"Try getting on board," said Doethan.

Eynon did. He stepped forward. The closer he got to the boat, the more he *didn't* want to get in it. He fought that feeling and put his foot on the thwart at the bow, then pulled it back quickly. It felt like he'd hugged a nest of unhappy wolfhornets. His toes buzzed and tingled painfully. The fish in the mesh bag were squirming. The sound of a pack of angry dogs baying came from the tower, while the unmistakable *clank* and *click* of crossbows being cocked echoed from its battlements.

Eynon backed up rapidly. The loop on the bag of fish slid down to his elbow as he clapped his hands.

"That's marvelous!" he said. "The avoidance spell discourages anyone from getting aboard and the hounds and crossbow sounds reinforce your intent, while alerting anyone in the tower that an attempted robbery is in progress."

"Correct," said the hedge wizard. "I especially like the crossbow sounds. They're very good at deterring thieves. How did you know the sounds weren't real?"

"Real dogs would have started barking the minute our boat reached the dock," said Eynon. "And real archers with crossbows wouldn't have waited this long to threaten us."

Doethan looked thoughtful, as if he was calculating sums in his head. He was interrupted a few moments later, when Merry appeared at the top of the hill by the tower.

"Are you showing off again, Doethan?" she shouted down.

"Maybe a little," he replied.

"I'm sure Eynon was impressed, but we have quite a few more miles to cover today."

Eynon waved at her with his hand holding the bag of fish and started walking up the hill. Doethan fell in beside him.

"Oooo," said Merry, "are those for lunch? We *do* have to eat, after all."

"They are," said the wizard. "Once Eynon cleans them."

"I'll take care of that," said Merry, "I think Eynon has other priorities."

* * * * *

"Thank you, sir," said Eynon as he separated the last of the flesh from the bones on his plate. "I'm really learning to like fish. We don't have any at my end of the Coombe, unless you count the tiny armored clawfish in the Wentwash."

"Clawfish aren't fish," said Doethan. "No scales. No gills. No backbones." He nodded at Eynon. "Unlike your companion, here." Doethan's eyes moved to Merry and back. "She has *plenty* of backbone."

"Are you saying I'm stubborn?" asked Merry, the corners of her mouth turning up.

"Maybe a little," said Doethan, echoing his earlier response.

Merry and the hedge wizard laughed. Eynon did too, a beat later, though he suspected the other two were sharing a private joke. He leaned back from the table where they had recently finished their meal of fried fish and marshapple slices.

"Where's Rowsch," Merry asked Doethan. "Asleep in the sun on the roof? I'd like to say hello."

"Rowsch?" asked Eynon.

"My familiar," said Doethan. "A large tan dog."

Merry jumped in.

"He was the model for the baying hounds in the wards, wasn't he?"

"That he was," said Doethan. "Unfortunately, he's off on business of his own at present. Something about discussing fine points of hunting philosophy with the leader of the local wolf pack."

"Please give him my best when he returns," said Merry.

She gave Doethan a slight bow. He nodded his head in return and focused his attention on the two young people.

"I know where *you're* going," said Doethan to Merry, "but why is this young man traveling with you? I'd expect someone from the Coombe to spend his wander year on roads, not rivers."

"Father asked me to take him to Tyford," said Merry. "Eynon needs to find someone there who can help him."

Doethan looked Eynon over, appraising him.

"Help him with what?"

Merry was silent. Eynon lowered his head, then raised it, deciding Doethan was someone he could trust.

"Derry said I needed to find a wizard," Eynon replied.

"And what am I?" protested Doethan with a smile. "A crock of fermented fish guts?"

"I was told you were a *hedge* wizard, sir," said Eynon, "and I think I need a free wizard or a Crown wizard."

"Someone with truly powerful magic, you mean?" asked Doethan. "A full member of the Conclave, not a mere maker of petty charms or a setter of bones."

"Pretty much, sir," said Eynon. "Meaning no offense."

"None taken, young man," said Doethan.

"I didn't just stop here to invite myself for lunch," said Merry. "I wanted your advice—for Eynon."

"Hmmm..." said Doethan, stroking his smooth chin. "Advice about what?"

"That's up to Eynon to tell," said Merry. "But who should he seek to advise him on the street of wizards? Is there someone in particular you'd recommend?"

Doethan's eyebrows moved up a fraction, then his mouth turned up in a knowing smile.

"Do you want to become a wizard's apprentice?" said Doethan, still smiling. "That's quite an ambition for a boy from the Coombe."

"No sir," said Eynon quickly. "I just need help knowing what to do with something I found."

"Something you found?" asked Doethan.

"Something powerful," said Eynon.

"He set fire to an old oak at a crossroads," blurted Merry.

Eynon stared at Merry and she stared back, defiantly.

"It was an accident," said Eynon.

"No doubt," said Doethan. "I know I'm only a *hedge* wizard, but might I see whatever it is you found?"

"I'd rather not, sir," said Eynon. "I don't know how it works and I don't want to hurt anyone, even by accident, by unwrapping it again."

"That's understandable," said Doethan. "Even commendable. Magic needs to be handled with care."

"I just want to get to Tyford and pass on the responsibility for what I found to a powerful wizard who can deal with it safely."

"Also commendable," said Doethan, "and wise, if you select the correct wizard."

"Where should I take him?" asked Merry. "I've only walked along the street of wizards on my way to the booksellers."

"It will depend on which mages are currently residing in Tyford," said Doethan, considering the question.

He looked at his hands, which Eynon noticed were graced with rings of different metals, stones, and colors. Doethan removed a plain black ring from his right hand, held it to his eye, and looked carefully at Eynon. Then he smiled again and nodded. The hedge wizard pushed his wooden chair back from the table and looked through the ring at the pack beneath Eynon's chair. Eynon saw Doethan's unobstructed eye grow large, then the wizard lowered the black ring and returned it to his hand.

Eynon felt uncomfortable after the hedge wizard's scrutiny, so Merry spoke to fill the silence.

"Well?" she said.

"I know where you should take him," said Doethan, "but he's not going to like it."

"Excuse me?" asked Eynon.

"You'll be going on a long journey," said the hedge wizard.

"I thought I was *already* going on a long journey."

"To Tyford?" exclaimed Merry. "Tyford's not far. Brendinas is *far*."

"He doesn't need to go to the capital," said Doethan. "In fact, it's a very good idea if he *doesn't* go to the capital. It's bad enough he has to go to Tyford."

"You can be very mysterious when you want to," said Merry.

"I *am* a wizard, young lady."

"A *hedge* wizard," said Merry, her eyes twinkling.

"As you say," said Doethan.

The older man muttered something under his breath. Eynon could only pick up bits and pieces of what he said.

"The one below Taffy's inn would be best... can't use hers without her permission... wouldn't be wise, not at all... should have built my own..."

Then Doethan realized he was ignoring his guests and removed a plain gold ring from his left hand.

"Here," he said, giving the ring to Eynon.

Eynon immediately tried to return it. He'd heard the old stories about the dangers of accepting rings from wizards, but Doethan wouldn't take it back.

"It's not evil," said Doethan. "It's simply for staying in touch. I'll show you. Pull on the sides of the ring."

Eynon did and was surprised to see the gold circle thin and expand to the width of a dinner plate.

"Hold on to it," said the hedge wizard. He removed an identical ring from his right hand and pulled it to the same size as the one Eynon held.

"Gwaloeaden!" said Doethan in a commanding voice. Three bells from nowhere chimed different notes in succession.

Eynon nearly dropped the golden circle. Doethan's face had appeared in the center of it.

"*Your* face is staring out from Doethan's," said Merry. "Don't look so shocked."

"You'd be shocked too, if it happened to you," said Eynon.

"Use the ring to contact me when you get to Tyford," said Doethan. "Be sure to stay in Taffaern's inn. Once you know which wizards are in residence, I can advise you from here. You can bring the ring back when you return to the Coombe at the end of your wander year."

"Yes, sir," he said.

Merry looked at Eynon. He couldn't tell if she wanted to be the one to hold the ring or if she was glad she hadn't been given it.

"Repeat after me," said Doethan. "*Gwal-o-e-a-den.*"

"*Gwal-o-e-a-den,*" said Merry and Eynon. Each time the two rings linked and unlinked in succession, with three soft chimes for accompaniment.

"I think you've got it," said the hedge wizard. "Collapse your ring and be on your way. I'll clean up."

Eynon pushed on the sides of the large gold circle and it shrank back to the shape of a ring that perfectly fit the middle finger of his left hand. Doethan did the same to his ring. All three stood and pushed their chairs back from the table.

"Thank you, Doethan," said Merry, giving him a hug. "We'll get in touch with you as soon as we reach Tyford and have a chance to scout out the street of wizards."

"Yes, thank you," said Eynon. "You're very kind."

"I wish I was in this case," said the hedge wizard, "but that remains to be seen. Safe travels. I've heard word of trouble on the river, so be careful."

"Did a little bird tell you?" asked Merry.

"No," said Doethan. "A not-so-little hound."

"Remember to tell Rowsch I'm sorry I missed him," said Merry.

"I will," said Doethan. "Time to be on your way. I'll come with you to cancel the wards."

Back at the boat, Doethan touched his circlet and issued a word of command in a language Eynon didn't recocognize.

"That should do it," said Doethan. "Be careful and stay safe."

"Thank you," said Eynon and Merry simultaneously.

They resumed their stations in the bow and stern. Shortly after, Eynon and Merry were back on the river, riding the current downstream. Eynon held up his hand and admired the ring.

"Don't get too attached to that," said Merry. "You have to give it back, in a year."

"I know," said Eynon, "but all this convinces me there's a *lot* more I need to learn about magic."

"Very true," said Merry. Her eyes were reflecting the sun bouncing off the water when Eynon turned around.

"So," said Eynon. *"Now* will you tell me about wizards?"

Chapter 6

"Never pass up an opportunity to sleep or learn something new."
— Ealdamon's *Epigrams*

"I'll tell you about wizards, if you keep your eyes on the river and call out rocks."

"Yes, dear lady."

"Stop that," said Merry, "and turn around."

Eynon saw she was grinning and returned her smile. He shifted to face the bow, looking ahead for rocks as instructed. It was growing warm, so he took off his jacket.

This stretch of the river narrowed and twisted like a batsnake. The current was faster and Eynon had to pay close attention to give Merry enough warning about rocks and other obstacles. He focused on his eyes and ears so he could keep watch and listen simultaneously.

"There are three kinds of wizards," said Merry in a matter of fact tone, as if she was teaching children their letters. "Hedge wizards, free wizards, and crown wizards."

Everybody knows that, thought Eynon.

"Hedge wizards know simple charms and healing magic. Free wizards are stronger. They've crafted powerful artifacts and know potent spells, but serve no master."

"Which is why they're called *free,* I suppose," said Eynon without turning around.

"Precisely," said Merry.

"Rock left," said Eynon.

Merry adjusted their course with her steering oar and continued.

"The most powerful wizards are crown wizards. They serve the king and the great nobles and protect us from foreign magic."

"Are crown wizards always stronger than free wizards?" asked Eynon.

"I don't know," said Merry. "I'm just sharing what I read in *The Venerable History of Dâron.*"

"Right," said Eynon. "Tell me more."

"The first wizards were from a territory across the Ocean called Athica, east of the Eagle People," said Merry. "The Athicans discovered the secret of wizardry and were the first to make artifacts to harness its power systematically."

"Are they the ones who had a blind bard who wrote poems about *The War* and *The Wandering?*" asked Eynon. "My uncle served in the levies and told me stories about them he'd heard around campfires."

"Yes," said Merry. "My father has books recording those tales in his library."

"He does?" said Eynon, the pitch of his voice rising. "Do you think he'd let me read them?"

He turned around to see Merry's reaction and saw she was holding back laughter.

"I expect so," she said. "If you ask politely."

"I'm always polite."

"I know," said Merry. "To a fault."

Eynon knew she was teasing him, but was so excited about the prospect of reading books about the Athicans he held his tongue and didn't tease back. He turned to face downstream and listened.

"Then the Eagle People conquered the city-states of the Athicans and enslaved them."

"How could they conquer the Athicans if the Athicans had wizards and the Eagle People didn't?"

"I don't know for sure," said Merry. "There was only a page or two about the Athicans near the beginning of *The Venerable History,* but from reading between the lines, it sounded like the Athican cities got along with each other about as well as the mountain clans do."

Eynon nodded, then realized Merry probably couldn't see him do so.

"Meaning not at all," he said. "That makes sense. The Eagle People always divide and conquer."

"Some Athican wizards worked for the emperor of the Eagle People and shared their knowledge," said Merry, "but many of them would not. Some self-exiled wizards journeyed far to the west, to Cymryn, our original homeland across the Ocean. *The Venerable History* says they took apprentices, teaching them the secret of wizardry."

"What *is* the secret of wizardry?" asked Eynon.

The prow of the boat suddenly shifted left and right, then back left again. Eynon turned around and saw Merry was holding her side, trying to keep from laughing. He stuck his tongue out at her. She made a face back at him, then took a deep breath.

"If I knew that," she said, "I'd be a wizard."

"Right," said Eynon. He turned back around. "Look out!" Eynon shouted.

The boat had rounded a bend and was accelerating in a fast current. Directly ahead of them was the trunk of a great ancient oak, even larger than the one Eynon had set aflame at the crossroads. High water had undercut its roots and the giant tree had fallen into the river, its massive bulk going almost from shore to shore. There was no clear channel for them to get by and the current was flowing even faster. Eynon could see water roiling like a boiling pot where it was dammed behind the trunk.

"Hang on!" shouted Merry.

Eynon bent his calves under the thwart and gripped the sides of the boat near the prow with both hands. He couldn't see what Merry was doing, but felt the boat rotate until it was parallel to the trunk, turned by the rushing water. He watched as the boat moved toward the east bank, away from the trunk's tangle of roots and toward the end where only a few broken branches remained. The water wasn't as rough here, but Eynon missed calling out a rock hidden under bubbling backwash from the trunk.

The front of the boat suddenly rose with a force strong enough to break Eynon's grip. He felt his body fly up over the prow and into the churning river.

His body was spinning and rolling, like he was tumbling down a hill as a child, but without the luxury of breathing. The water was cold and stung his exposed skin. He waved his arms frantically, trying to stop his twisting motion and find the surface, but he felt one of the few remaining branches on the trunk holding him down. *At least my pack is still in the boat,* Eynon thought as he began to run short of air.

Then he felt a tremendous blow in the center of his back that forced out all the air remaining inside him. Eynon went deeper and the tree released him. He bobbed up, his body rushing downstream beyond the grasping branches. Eynon's face was out of the water for a few seconds. He gasped to fill his lungs—then his head struck a rock and consciousness fled.

* * * * *

Eynon woke suddenly to find Merry kissing him and pinching his nose. His mind was puzzled by the situation, but his body had its own reaction. He rolled on his stomach, got on all fours, and coughed up half the river into the grass. Eynon slowly leaned back until he was kneeling. Merry stood above him and put her arms around his waist, just above his hips. She pulled up—hard—and the other half of the river left his lungs. Then he fell on his back and looked up at Merry and the sky, glad to be alive. His chest hurt. His legs hurt. His arms hurt, his back hurt, and most especially, his *head* hurt. He gave Merry a pained smile.

"Thank you," he croaked.

"You'll live," she said.

"Not so sure of that, but I'll try," said Eynon.

"Try hard," she said. "I'll need your help to free the boat."

"Is my pack safe?" Eynon asked.

"Yes," said Merry, "and I'm fine. Thanks for asking."

"I said thank you."

"You're welcome."

Merry knelt close beside him and stared into Eynon's eyes. He liked that.

"The centers of your eyes are bigger than they should be, but not too big," she said. "Doethan taught me to check for that when someone gets a blow to their head."

"Doethan's smart."

"Yes, he is."

Merry's fingers moved gingerly around Eynon's scalp.

"Ow!" he said.

Her fingers kept pressing.

"Ow! Ow! Ow!"

"Don't be a baby," said Merry. "It's a small lump, no bigger than a couple of cherries. It will be gone in a day or two."

Eynon took Merry's hand. It was damp. He realized both of them were soaked.

"Help me up," he said.

Merry did and Eynon sat up, then got to his knees, then stood. He shook his head and didn't like the way it felt, but his mind was starting to work again. The center of his back was sore. His left side ached, then hurt more as he bent over and coughed up a minor tributary. He kept coughing until there was no more water left in his lungs or his stomach. Merry stood a few feet away and looked at Eynon sympathetically.

"I think that's it," Eynon said when he'd finished.

He looked puzzled and turned around, scanning the ground.

"Have you seen my hat?" he asked.

"No," said Merry. "I had a choice. I could save you, or save your hat. Don't make me regret my decision."

"I'm sorry," said Eynon. "Thank you again for saving me. How are *you* doing?"

"I'm wet and I'm tired and I'm worried about the boat, but it could have been a lot worse."

"Oh?"

"If I hadn't been able to push us to the right, the boat would have flipped when we hit the eddies near the roots."

"That would have been bad."

"You might say that," said Merry. She took Eynon's hand and tugged him along. "Come on, I'll show you."

Eynon squeezed Merry's hand as they walked the two dozen steps to the river.

"Why were you kissing me?" he asked.

"What? I wasn't kissing you."

"Then what *were* you doing? It felt like kissing."

"I was trying to blow air into your lungs."

"Hmmm…" said Eynon. "That explains why you were pinching my nose."

Merry abruptly dropped his hand and pointed down the steep eastern bank. Eynon saw that the boat was wedged into a pair of large branches at the far end of the trunk. Beyond them, there was just enough room to get the boat through and past the waterlogged oak.

"We need to cut those branches and free the boat," said Merry.

Eynon felt for the axe at his belt. It was still there in its protective leather sheath. He'd have to remember to oil and polish it tonight so it wouldn't rust—and do the same for his knife as well.

"Those branches are as thick as my legs," said Eynon. "It's going to take us hours to chop through them."

"Then we'd best get started," said Merry.

"You don't have a saw, do you?"

"No," said Merry. "I only have my axe for cutting firewood. Let's get busy. Chop, chop."

"Chop, chop," repeated Eynon. "How do we get out to the boat to free it?"

"We're wet already," she said, waving her hands to indicate their soaked clothing, "so we swim."

Eynon looked at Merry like she'd grown a second head.

"I *can't* swim."

"Of course you can't," said Merry, shaking her head. "You're from the Coombe, where they don't have boats and they don't eat fish."

She spotted a thick pine branch about four feet long on the bank a few paces away. Half its bark had worn off from its trip downstream.

"This will do," she said. "No time like the present to learn. Pick that up and carry it down to the river."

"Yes, dear lady," said Eynon.

She whacked his upper arm with the back of her hand and Eynon did as he was instructed. The branch was lighter than he'd expected, even though it was as big around as his thigh.

He brought his burden back to Merry at the edge of the water. Eynon was pleased the current wasn't very strong at this end of the great downed tree. Most of the flow was rushing by at the root-end of the trunk.

Merry took the branch and carefully eased it into the river well upstream from the boat. She held on to it with one hand.

"I'm glad the branch floats," said Merry. "We're going to step into the river and hold onto it, so it will help *us* float."

Eynon nodded.

"Push out from the bottom and keep pushing as long as you can stand," Merry continued. "Then kick your feet to move us toward the boat. Do you think you can do that?"

"Step, push, kick," said Eynon.

"Good," said Merry.

The two of them held on to the log and pushed it ahead of them as they entered the river. Eynon moved his legs in a flurry of kicks, sending water flying everywhere, but not helping them move forward.

"Look over your shoulder and watch my legs," said Merry. "Slow and steady is better than fast and choppy."

Eynon turned and observed Merry's technique, then made a reasonable attempt at duplicating it. They soon reached the boat and climbed aboard—or rather, Merry climbed aboard, then helped Eynon. They put the log in the spot where two jugs of cider had been.

"Time to get out your axe," said Merry.

She removed hers while Eynon extracted his from its sheath and began to hone the blade with the whetstone stored in a pouch that rode below the axehead.

"Want me to do yours, too?" he asked.

Merry didn't answer. She located her own whetstone and sharpened her axe silently. Eynon finished first and began to chop at the thicker of the two branches trapping the boat's prow. His initial stroke bounced back from the wood of the old oak and almost hit him in the forehead.

"Be careful," said Merry.

He aimed his next blow at more of an angle. Merry started in on her branch, but both of them found it hard going.

"At this rate, it will be a day or two before we're free," said Merry, "and my delivery will be late."

"It's not like it's your fault," said Eynon.

"I know," said Merry, "but I always do what I say."

And so does everyone around her, thought Eynon, remembering Derry's comment at dinner last night.

"I have an idea," he said.

Eynon put his axe down on the bow thwart and reached beneath to extract his pack, which had somehow managed not to get wet. He noticed that the floor of the boat was covered with widely-spaced wooden slats a few inches above the true bottom, so any water that came on board flowed below instead of on top of them.

I still have a lot to learn about boats, he thought.

Merry kept chopping, glaring at Eynon after each stroke.

After opening his pack, Eynon took out the white linen shirt where he'd wrapped the strange shards. He carefully removed one of them, noting that the shards had cut the fabric in a dozen places. His mother would not be happy—she'd worked hard to weave it.

The shard he selected looked like a picture he'd seen in Robin Goodfellow's *Perigrinations.* The book said it was from a land far to the east across the sea and was called a scimitar. It had a smooth side that described a portion of an arc and a sharp side that seemed very sharp indeed.

Holding it by the smooth side, he put the opposite edge against the branch he'd been chopping and sawed it back and forth. In seconds, he had to step back as the far end of the branch fell into the boat.

"How did you do that so quickly?" asked Merry. "Was the rest of the branch rotten?"

"I'll show you," said Eynon.

He repeated what he'd done on his branch and Merry's branch fell into the boat after only a few sawing motions.

"I'm impressed," said Merry.

"So am I," said Eynon. "I had no idea they were *that* sharp."

Eynon used the shard to smooth off the longer of the two branches, turning it into a thick, sturdy pole. They threw the other branch off the stern and watched as it was swept into the maelstrom near the roots.

"You push and I'll steer," said Merry.

Eynon used his new pole to lever the prow away from the end of the tree and force the boat along to the open channel beyond.

When the nose of the boat was well past the upper trunk, the current caught it and spun the boat around, sending it downstream at an increasingly rapid pace. Both of them cheered.

"Thank you for saving my boat," said Merry.

"Thank you for saving my life," Eynon replied over his shoulder.

"It was nothing," said Merry.

Eynon wasn't sure if Merry was teasing him again, but he didn't have the energy to come up with a witty reply. The afternoon sun was bright and beginning to dry them both out. He struggled to stay awake as the heat of the warm spring day baked him and the sound of flowing water lulled him until his chin was on his chest.

"Wake up!" shouted Merry from the stern.

"Yes, dear lady," he said after a yawn.

Eynon reached down and splashed a handful of cold river water in his face. That should keep him awake for a while.

He'd had more than enough excitement for one day.

Fercha

Where was her flying disk? She remembered hiding it behind a rock the size of a millstone, five paces in from the narrow opening to the cave complex. Now she couldn't see *any* stones large enough to camouflage a flying disk, let alone one the size of a millstone.

Something crunched under her boot. Fercha looked down and saw pieces of a broken fired-clay jug on the stony floor of the cave's entrance. Her avoidance spells must have failed—they were less effective against anyone who was drunk. She picked up a piece of the jug and sniffed, smelling yeast and malt.

Beer, she confirmed.

Fercha stepped outside, angry at herself for not storing the flying disk near her emergency kit by the underground lake. On a level spot halfway up a steep slope, she paused to get her bearings.

The night sky was clear. Stormclouds had left the area some time ago, though the grass was still damp. Fercha dimmed the glow ball above her head to check the stars and confirmed she had four more hours until dawn.

Applegarth was southeast, on the other side of a mountain, she remembered. Below her was a small stream flowing south. She'd follow its course until it was time to head east and start climbing.

It would take at least three days to reach her destination and recover her artifact. Fercha pulled her cloak tighter and set out downhill.

Chapter 7

*"Not every animal that talks and walks
on two legs is truly human."*
— Ealdamon's *Epigrams*

"Merry," said Eynon, "why didn't your father have me talk to *Doethan* about what I found? He seemed like he knew a lot more magic than the hedge wizard in Caercadel."

"I have a theory about that," said Merry. "I'll share it with you later. Why do you think Doethan isn't a simple hedge wizard?"

"When I first met him, he said he'd been walking underwater catching fish," said Eynon. "Then I saw his clothes go from wet to dry in an eye blink."

"Interesting," said Merry.

Eynon twisted the sleeve of his linen shirt and watched drops fall into the river.

"I've been thinking a lot about dry clothes lately."

"Ours will be dry in another hour or so—without any help from wizardry."

"Yes, but the wards he put on the boat were more powerful than anything I'd expect a hedge wizard to cast."

"A physical aversion spell, plus sounds like barking dogs and cocking crossbows?" said Merry. "Do you have so much experience with wizardry you can judge what it takes to work it?"

"I only know what I've read," said Eynon. "What about his magic rings? Rock left."

"Got it," said Merry. She adjusted their course. "I won't second guess Doethan's skill level. He *says* he's a hedge wizard."

Something in Merry's voice made Eynon think she knew more than she was telling.

"Has Doethan been teaching you wizardry?"

"Why would you say a thing like that?"

He *had*. Eynon recognized Doethan's favorite misdirection tactic of answering a question with another question. He smiled, glad Merry couldn't see his face. That explained quite a bit. Eynon wondered if Derry and Mabli knew—and how they'd feel about their only child learning to be a wizard. He realized his own curiosity was growing. He wanted to know the secret of wizardry, too.

"What's your theory?" asked Eynon.

"You're not very patient, are you?"

"Cauldron, meet kettle."

"Fair enough," said Merry. "I think my father—and mother—want us to stay together all the way to Tyford to see what develops."

"Develops?" asked Eynon.

"You *do* have straw behind your ears, don't you?"

"Hey," said Eynon, not turning around.

"My parents have had every eligible boy in the Rhuthro valley at our dinner table," said Merry. "I'm their heir and I'm sure Da wants to start training a prospective son-in-law in how to manage his lands as soon as possible, not that I couldn't do a perfectly fine job of that myself. My mother wants grandchildren, but at least she's willing to wait until I get back from my wander year to start *that* project."

"Now I understand why you were so horrid to me at dinner," said Eynon.

"It was nothing personal," said Merry. "Sorry."

"Uh huh," said Eynon. "I suppose your parents want you to marry Gruffyd and pop out a squad of little royal guardsmen?"

"Now *you're* being horrid," said Merry. "I said *eligible* boys. Gruffyd is only a good match for me in his own head. My parents never invited *him* to dinner."

"Nice to know," said Eynon. "But isn't his family wealthy, like yours?"

"It is," said Merry, "But I'm not a princess and don't have to be pushed into a marriage of state. My parents are just trying to hurry things along, that's all. Most girls in the valley are married by seventeen, and my mother doesn't want me to miss out on the right young man."

"What about your father?"

"He wants me to be happy—but he also wants me to find a suitable husband."

"He knows my family isn't rich, right?"

"Suitable to *me*," said Merry. "He'd be happy with anyone I choose. My future mate could be landless, so long as I select one."

"Even another woman?"

"Yes," said Merry, laughing. "That way there'd be twice as many grandchildren."

"There would, wouldn't there," said Eynon. "Rock left."

"On it."

"In the Coombe, villages farm their lands in common," said Eynon. "There's usually a head man or woman, but all they do is settle disputes and take the lead negotiating with the baron. I think that's easier than how you do things along the river."

"You're probably right," said Merry. "I think my parents like you."

"Where did *that* come from?"

"I wanted you to know. They're polite enough to most of the boys they invite, but they were particularly nice to you."

"Do you think showing up with a magical artifact in my pack might have had anything to do with it?"

"Maybe," said Merry, "but you had good manners."

"I am nothing, if not polite."

"You said it, I didn't."

Both chuckled. Eynon was glad they were beginning to be at ease with each other.

"When will we stop today?" he asked.

"Not for a few hours," answered Merry. "There are two more toll stations coming up and I want to get well past them before finding a spot to stay for the night."

"Do you expect problems?"

"No," said Merry. "Certainly not at the second one. The first toll station is a different matter. Mastlands raises pigs. I usually give them a jug for their toll and two more to trade for a couple of their smoked hams. The family has four sons—the youngest is my age—and their father is often away in Tyford."

"What about their mother?"

"She died last fall, of the old maiden's disease, which is strange because she'd had all those children. She wasn't even as old as my mother."

"I'm sorry she died so young," said Eynon.

"So am I," said Merry, "but that's why I'm worried. I know that the sons can be wild, especially if their father is away. Their mother used to keep them in line, but without her around, I don't know what to expect."

"Could it be worse than Gruffyd?"

"Yes—*far* worse. When they're unsupervised, I've heard tales of the Mastlands sons acting worse than a band of blue-painted mountain-clan raiders after three days of drinking."

"I don't like the sound of *that*."

"Neither do I," said Merry. "Rumor has it they have no respect for person or property."

"We'll have to be prepared, then," said Eynon.

"What do you have in mind?"

* * * * *

"Here comes the toll station," said Eynon from the prow. He was wearing Merry's long blue cloak to give his appearance a sense of mystery, though the effect was somewhat spoiled, because it didn't even reach his knees. His own cloak was far too plain to impress.

"I see it," said Merry. "Is the chain up?"

"It wasn't, but it is now," said Eynon. "Two men are turning the windlass."

"Do you think we can run down the center of the channel and have you cut the chain with the shard as we go?" asked Merry.

"I wouldn't risk it," said Eynon. "One of the brothers has a crossbow."

"We could hide behind the sides of the boat and you could cut the chain on the far side," said Merry.

"I see grapnels on the dock by the windlass," said Eynon.

"Blast," said Merry. "We'll have to hope they'll behave."

"And if not," said Eynon, "we'll bluff."

"I'll take the lead and pretend everything is normal," said Merry.

She steered the boat within a few feet of the Mastlands toll station dock and held up a jug of cider.

"I've got your toll," she said, "and two more of these beside, to trade for a couple of hams."

The four brothers stood close together on the side of the dock near Merry and Eynon. It was clear they'd been drinking for at least a few hours. The men seemed to be well on their way to the belligerent drunk stage.

Eynon didn't know their names, so he mentally dubbed them Oaf, Dolt, Fox and Fool. Oaf and Dolt were tall and muscle-bound, with stubbly beards and stringy blond hair past their shoulders. They appeared to be in their early twenties and showed the exaggerated bravado of large men after several mugs of strong beer. Fox had short dark hair, a sly look, and a pointed beard. He was clearly a few years older and still had his wits about him. Fool was Merry's age and was midway between Fox and Oaf in size. He looked wiry. His hair was shaved to the scalp so there was no way to tell its color.

Lice, thought Eynon.

"We'll help you with mooring," said Fox.

He nodded to Oaf and Dolt and the pair tossed grapnels over the gunwales of the boat and pulled it close against the dock, tying off the lines securely. Fool kept a loaded crossbow aimed at Eynon. Regrettably, Fool's eyes were clear. He must not have matched Oaf and Dolt drink for drink.

"It's not your cider jugs we want for passage past our lands," said Fox. "We'll be taking two of your *barrels* for our toll."

"The barrels already belong to my father's customer in Tyford," protested Merry.

Eynon could hear the worry in her voice.

"It's not our fault you're not prepared for an increased toll," said Fox, "though I will toss in a couple of hams if you stay to enjoy our company while we tap the first barrel."

"No thank you," said Merry, struggling to retain any sense of civility. "You can keep your hams, just allow us to be on our way."

"I think not," said Fox. "Grab the girl and tie her to a post. Do the same with the beanpole."

"This is outrageous," Merry protested. "When my father finds out, you'll have Applegarth's levies and the earl's knights to deal with."

She looked at Eynon and he could see from her expression that the situation was deteriorating far beyond anything Merry had anticipated. He was glad they'd planned ahead.

"What do you think?" said Fox to Fool.

"I think we'd best make sure her father doesn't find out," Fool replied. He nodded at Eynon and Merry. "The river can be quite dangerous at this time of year, after all."

Eynon revised his assessment—the youngest brother was no fool.

"I want the girl first," said Oaf. He began to climb onto the stern deck of the boat, but Merry held him off with her steering oar.

"I'll get the boy," said Dolt. "He'll be an interesting diversion while I wait."

"Keep your crossbow on him so he doesn't cause trouble," said Fox to Fool.

"Don't be an idiot," said Fool. He momentarily aimed the tip of the loaded quarrel at Fox to make his point. "I know my job."

Eynon chose that moment to stand up. He'd discovered a small loop on the back of the silver amulet, so he could hang it and its central blue stone from a thin cord around his neck. The metal glinted in the late afternoon sun and the stone glowed with an inner warmth. A tall staff Eynon had whittled from the thick branch was in his right hand and Merry's cloak swirled. The shard he'd used to shape his staff was on the bow thwart behind him.

"I am the free wizard Eynon," he said, using the same voice Eynon's father employed to get the attention of quarreling village elders. "This woman and her cargo are under my protection. Keep your distance, or I will blast you where you stand."

Oaf paused his attempt to drag Merry off the boat and Dolt didn't come any closer to Eynon.

"Aren't you a little young to be a free wizard?" asked Fox.

Eynon watched Fool shift his crossbow so it pointed at his chest.

He belatedly realized that Dolt hadn't moved to attack him so that he didn't block his brother's shot. As the speeding quarrel rushed toward him, Eynon's staff moved of its own volition and intercepted the bolt in mid-flight. It quivered in the wood a few inches above Eynon's hand. He was as surprised as Fool, but tried his best not to show it. Fool bent to reload.

"Grab them, you idiots," said Fox. "The boy was lucky, that's all."

Oaf pulled Merry's steering oar out of her hands and threw it on the boat's deck near the cider barrels. He leered at her and opened and closed his hands menacingly, as if to illustrate what he soon planned to do.

"Come on, pretty girl," he said. "You know you'll like it."

Merry closed her eyes and muttered a few words under her breath.

"Archers, release the hounds!" shouted Eynon.

Dolt stopped advancing on Eynon. From the woods near the dock came excited bays of hunting dogs. The distinctive *clank-click* of a dozen crossbows being cocked echoed in the trees.

"Begone!" Eynon commanded.

The four Mastlands brothers exchanged glances. They were fine with odds of four to two, but less so when they were the ones outnumbered.

"Back to the keep, boys," said Fox. "Maybe he *is* a wizard."

"I'm still takin' the girl," said Oaf.

"An' I want the wizard's silver," said Dolt.

Then the dogs stopped barking and archers failed to appear from the woods. The two big men exchanged unpleasant smiles. They stood with the toes of their boots sticking over the edge of the dock, about to step down into the boat. Eynon turned and picked up the shard on the bow thwart in his left hand. He twisted his arm back and brought the sharp side of the shard down across Dolt's left boot, a few inches from the tip. Merry did the same to Oaf, using a second shard she'd hidden beneath her steersman's seat. The boot tips fell into the boat as Oaf and Dolt screamed and hopped back, clutching their injured extremities.

Eynon kept swinging his shard to sever the grapnel ropes near the prow, while Merry cut the grapnel ropes at the stern, then jumped down into the cargo area to retrieve her steering oar. When Eynon looked up, he saw that Fool had finished reloading and was trying to decide whether to target Merry or him. Eynon lifted the small crossbow from his belt and loosed the bolt he'd already loaded in Fool's general direction. Even if it didn't hit him, he hoped it would at least distract Fool's aim.

Eynon was astonished to see the small quarrel had done more than distract. The bolt had pierced Fool's left hand and nailed it to the stock of his crossbow. Fool's arms went up, along with his weapon, and his quarrel released, flying harmlessly into the air.

"Push off," said Merry. "It's time to go."

"You won't get far," said Fox. "The chain is still up."

The oldest brother moved to the far end of the dock, behind the windlass. He bent down and was out of sight for a few seconds as Merry and Eynon used the steering oar and Eynon's staff to guide the boat down the length of the dock. Once clear, the current turned them to face downstream, but their progress stopped when the boat bumped into the toll station's massive iron chain.

"Cut it!" shouted Merry.

"Yes, dear lady," said Eynon as he leaned over the starboard bow and began to saw at the chain with his shard. Unfortunately, metal proved much slower to cut through than wood. He finished one side of the nearest link, but needed to cut the other side as well for the barrier to separate. He could feel Merry fighting the current with her steering oar to keep the boat stable and not have it turn broadside to the flowing water. Then the link was completely severed and the chain fell. The boat leapt forward.

"Eynon!" shouted Merry.

He rose and turned to see Fox standing by the now-useless windlass. The oldest brother had a malevolent look on his face. The dark-haired man held a long wooden spear with a tapering steel blade in his right hand, ready to throw.

Must be for stabbing fish, thought part of Eynon's brain.

The boat's stern—and Merry—were almost even with where Fox waited. At that distance, Eynon knew it would be hard for the man to miss. Eynon's hand went to the amulet as Fox hurled the spear toward Merry. An intense beam of blue light shot from the amulet's gem and disintegrated the spear as it flew. The shaft turned into ashes that wafted away on the wind and the spearhead fell into the river with a loud *plop*.

Eynon wasn't sure why or what he did next. He squeezed the amulet and saw a fireball emerge from the blue magestone like a shooting star. It struck the end of the dock and spread out, setting even the damp wood of the pilings ablaze. He watched as Fox and Fool helped Oaf and Dolt off the dock and smiled at the reflection of the blue-white flames on the water until the boat passed around a bend. Only a glow in the sky upriver remained to remind them what had happened.

Eynon was trying to figure out how he felt about the first time he'd ever intentionally harmed other human beings. The fire of the moment had been as hot as the fireball that had set the dock ablaze. He would have done anything to save himself and Merry, but once the heat of trying to survive passed, he was less sure of himself. He would have killed the men, if he needed to, and that didn't fit with the boy he'd been two days before.

Merry was the first to break the silence.

"You saved my life."

"The *amulet* saved your life," said Eynon, "and I'm very glad it did."

"Uh huh," said Merry.

Eynon thought she must feel like he had felt after he'd found the amulet and set fire to the old oak. He waited a few beats, then spoke loud enough to be heard over the rushing river.

"Your sound-magic with the dogs and the crossbowmen was very well-executed."

"I made Doethan teach me that spell so I could protect my boat," said Merry.

"Did he teach you the physical aversion spell, too?"

"No, that's more advanced."

"What a pity," said Eynon. "Maybe it would have kept the Mastlands sons away."

"Even if I knew it, I couldn't very well cast that spell with us still aboard!"

Eynon was pleased to hear her response. It was more like the old Merry—the one that *wasn't* in shock.

"Not interested in tingling like a nest full of wolfhornets?" he asked.

"Not today, thank you."

"Me neither."

The two of them sat watching the river, but not speaking. Eynon silently signaled for rocks by raising his left hand or his right. The sun crept closer to the western horizon before either of them spoke.

"We have to stop at the next toll station," said Merry.

Eynon put his hands over his ears.

"I can't hear you," he said.

"No, really," said Merry. "The next toll station is Flying Frog Farms. It's nothing like those despicable Mastlands barbarians."

"La, la, la," said Eynon.

"Stop that," said Merry.

Eynon put his hands down.

"Rock right."

"Where?" asked Merry.

"We already passed it."

"Be serious. We need to tell them about the Mastlands sons' attack. Llyffan needs to get the earl and the local levies mustered to punish them."

"Llyffan?"

"The owner and squire-reeve at Flying Frog Farms," said Merry.

"Oh," said Eynon. He wondered if that's what Derry was, too?

"Didn't we punish them enough?" asked Eynon. "We shot them, set fire to their dock, and cut off their toes."

"You don't understand," said Merry. "The prosperity of the valley depends on the river trade. If landowners and merchants can't feel safe taking their cargoes up and down the river, it's bad for everyone."

"That makes sense," said Eynon. "Will the earl hang them?"

"He might, if they don't head southwest to join the mountain clans first."

Eynon thought about the choice between exile or death and hoped he'd never have to face it. Then he smiled when he realized at least two of the brothers wouldn't be walking very fast if they *did* head for the mountain clans' lands.

"Will we be staying the night at Flying Frog Farms?" Eynon asked. "Your father told me about their butter."

"Llyffan does know how to charm out extra pennies," said Merry, "but we *won't* be staying the night."

"Does Llyffan keep an inn? Does he charge too much?"

"No, and no," said Merry. "Llyffan is very generous to his friends. Our families have been close since before I was born. It's not Llyffan I'm worried about, it's his wife, Madollyn."

"She doesn't like you?"

"The opposite," said Merry. "Maddy mothers me—smothers me is more like it. She'll want to know everything about the goings on in Applegarth, whether or not my mother has a new dress, who you are, what happened on our trip downriver, and more. She'll keep me up late talking and will stuff us until we can't walk—for dinner *and* for breakfast."

"Sounds like pure torture," said Eynon, "and my aunt from Brynhill. A brief conversation with her takes half a day and I'm always sent home with a full stomach and a bag of honey cakes."

"Good," said Merry. "You understand. I'm hoping they'll have some junior cousins collecting tolls so I can pass the word about the Mastlands problem, tell them about the downed tree across the river, and make a quick escape."

"I'll follow your lead," said Eynon. "I'll even claim urgent business downriver if Madollyn is waiting for you at the dock."

"You're the best," said Merry.

"Thank you, dear lady."

Eynon was pleased she didn't say, "Stop that!" this time. He looked down into the boat for a few seconds to give his eyes a rest from the glare of the sun off the water.

"Hey," said Eynon, pointing down. "What do you want to do about these boot tips?"

He held up the section of scuffed leather he'd cut from the end of Dolt's right boot.

"Hang on to them," said Merry. "We can use their toes for bait."

"I don't think I want to eat any fish that would find their toes appealing," said Eynon.

He rotated Dolt's boot tip, examining it closely.

"Don't worry," said Merry. "I was joking."

"You can tell the Mastlands brothers' mother wasn't around," said Eynon.

"How?"

"This one wasn't wearing socks."

Chapter 8

"No youth is fully responsible in the spring."
— Ealdamon's *Epigrams*

"Go right!" shouted Eynon.

"But there's a rock in that direction," said Merry.

"With my hat behind it. Get me close and I'll try to snag it."

Merry steered the boat as requested and Eynon dipped his new staff in the water. He was glad he hadn't removed the crossbow bolt, because it helped him rescue his waterlogged cap from the back of a moderate-sized chunk of limestone worn smooth by the current. The holly his sister had pinned to the cap was still in place and looked even greener after its immersion. Eynon held the cap up and to one side so it could drip into the river.

"Did you learn Doethan's clothes-drying spell too?"

"If I had, don't you think I would have used it earlier, when both of us were soaked?"

More answering questions with questions, thought Eynon.

He put his wet cap on a thwart in front of the closest cider barrel, where it wouldn't blow away. When he returned to the bow, Eynon stretched his shoulders and felt a sore spot in his upper back. He turned around to catch Merry's eye.

"You might have been hiding the true extent of your powers."

"I wish," said Merry. "I did learn how to make fertility choice charms, though. They're easy."

"Good to know," said Eynon. "Did Doethan have a chance to teach you any healing spells? My back feels like I was punched by a giant."

"Sorry, no," said Merry. "That's one of the reasons I didn't want you to come on this trip. When I'm on my own I get wizardry lessons."

"I didn't mean to interfere with your education," said Eynon.

"Don't worry," said Merry. "I'm sure I'll learn a lot this trip—just in different subjects."

"I've learned more in a day on the river than I would have in a year in the Coombe."

Eynon tried to move an arm around to rub the painful part of his upper back, but couldn't reach.

"I'll get some liniment at Flying Frog Farms and rub it on your back tonight," said Merry. "I'm glad to do it, since I'm the one who gave you the bruise."

"What?" asked Eynon. "When?"

"When you were underwater, held down by tree branches," replied Merry. "I had to hit you in the back with my steering oar to push you free."

"In that case, a bruised back is a small price to pay for my life."

"I'll still rub in liniment."

"That would be nice," said Eynon. "When do we get to Flying Frog Farms?"

Ahead, the Rhuthro was making a sharp bend to the left. Merry waited until they'd rounded it before replying.

"How about now?"

Eynon could see a much larger dock than the previous toll stations ahead on the left. It was twice as wide as the Mastlands dock and the back third of it included rows of stalls covered by a shake-shingled roof. A long yellow banner with a green flying frog in mid-leap hung from a tall pole at the front upstream end of the dock. A smaller dock was on the other side of the river, but there was no sign of a chain.

People must stop here because they want to, thought Eynon.

A tall woman in a yellow dress with a green apron was standing near the banner, waving enthusiastically. A taller man in a green tunic and enormous boots had his arm around her.

"Oh drat," said Merry.

"That must be Madollyn," said Eynon. He covered his mouth with a palm to hold in a laugh and looked forward to a good dinner.

"And Llyffan," said Merry. "I don't see how they knew we were coming. Sometimes I think the real wizardry in the valley is how fast news travels."

"The same thing's true in the Coombe and we don't even have a river to speed word along," said Eynon. "What's your plan? Do we stay the night here or try to make a quick escape?"

"A quick escape," said Merry. "Talk less. Smile more."

"Good advice under the circumstances," said Eynon. "I'll follow your lead."

"Thank you," said Merry.

"One question," said Eynon.

"Ask."

"Do you think we could talk Madollyn into giving us some honey cakes?"

* * * * *

Eynon was impressed that Merry had kept their stop at Flying Frog Farms to a few minutes over an hour. She told Llyffan and Madollyn what had happened at the Mastlands toll station and they agreed to send word to the earl and call out their own levies to take action.

That agreement didn't happen, however, until Madollyn was assured Eynon and Merry were unharmed. The mistress of Flying Frog Farms had hugged them both a dozen times with arms that were extra-strong from years at the churn.

Maddy even pinched Merry's cheeks, making them turn red.

"You're as beautiful as the old king and queen's daughter, Princess Seren, when she was a girl, before we lost her," Madollyn fussed.

"Ummm... Thank you," said Merry, her face blushing an even brighter shade of red.

Eynon turned away so Merry wouldn't see his grin. He wasn't able to escape Madollyn's attentions himself. The older woman pinched *his* cheek and pulled him down to plant a motherly kiss in the middle of his forehead.

"You two look out for each other the rest of the way downriver," she said. "Promise me you'll be extra cautious. The young king doesn't have a tenth the sense of his great-grandfather and I don't like it. We're in for bad times, I can feel it in my bones."

"I'll send a crew upriver to see what can be done about that tree trunk blocking the main channel," said Llyffan, heading off more of his wife's uncomplimentary comments on Dâron's current ruler.

Eynon almost offered to give them one of the larger shards, to help make cutting up the fallen trunk easier, but Merry's eyes warned him not to say anything. Madollyn still kept mothering them, but Merry's insistence that they needed to get to Tyford in three days, not four, kept delays to a minimum.

Merry gave Llyffan and Madollyn four jugs of cider—one as a traditional toll and the three that weren't used for toll or trade at Mastlands. Eynon wasn't quite sure how it happened, but he also ended up with a thick bundle of clothes, including a new-to-him white linen shirt, since Merry let it slip that Eynon's had been slashed and rendered unwearable.

As they pulled away from the dock, Eynon thought it a good omen that a flying frog chasing a dragonfly soared across the boat's prow. He was also pleased to have two new baskets of food resting next to his hat on the midship thwart.

"Nicely done," said Eynon when they'd turned a bend and were out of sight of the Flying Frog Farm's dock.

"Thank you," she said. "You, too."

She held up a pottery bottle about a quarter the size of a cider jug.

"Llyffan found me some liniment."

"I thank you, and my back thanks you—in advance," said Eynon. He removed a canvas sack big enough to hold a copy of Ealdamon's *Epigrams* from under his seat and waved it back and forth to ensure Merry saw it. "Madollyn gave me a bag of freshly baked honey cakes and they smell wonderful. I hope they're as good as my aunt's."

"If they're not, your idea to carry Coombe honey to the Rhuthro valley might be a good one."

"We'll find out after dinner tonight, I expect," said Eynon.

"Go ahead, try one," said Merry.

"I can wait."

Merry smiled and Eynon turned back to watch the river. The barrels stowed amidships made it very difficult for anyone in the bow to get to the stern or vice versa, so it wasn't a simple matter for Eynon to share the honey cakes while they were aboard.

"It's only a couple of hours before sunset," said Eynon. "Where do you plan to stop for the night?"

"We'll lose our light sooner than that," said Merry. "We're in the shadow of the mountains."

Eynon shook his head slowly from side to side, displeased with the gap in his understanding.

"I should have figured that out on my own."

"Don't worry about it," said Merry. "I'm glad to be part of your education." She made a slight course correction with her steering oar, avoiding a snag Eynon hadn't noticed. "There's a stony beach on the east bank a few miles downriver," Merry continued. "It's one of the few places on that side with woodlands, not marsh. I've camped there before."

"Sounds good," said Eynon.

He rubbed the sore spot on the back of his head where he'd hit the rock and was pleased it hadn't turned into a goose egg. Eynon hoped tomorrow wouldn't be more exciting than today. He'd wanted adventures, but not so many so close together. He took several deep breaths and closed his eyes for a moment to block out the late afternoon glare.

"Wake up!" shouted Merry from the stern. "We're almost there!"

Eynon opened his eyes and lifted his chin from his chest. Ahead on the right was a beach of sorts, made of thousands of pebbles. A huge rock the size of Doethan's tower was upstream and the obvious source of the small stones. Two white birch trees incongruously grew amid the pebbles—they'd make good posts for tying off. Behind the beach was a broad clearing, sloping up to a wood of mixed pines and trees with new green leaves.

"Sorry for nodding off," he said.

"Don't worry about it," said Merry. "I knew this stretch of river didn't have many rocks and I'm glad you got some rest. I'm going to bring the boat in by the downstream tree, so tie off the prow there and get ashore. I'll toss you the stern line to tie to the upstream tree."

"Yes, dear lady," said Eynon. He turned back in time to see Merry stick her tongue out at him. Eynon was laughing when he tied up the prow, but stopped by the time he caught the stern line and made it fast. The boat secured, Merry began to pull items from the protected storage area under the raised stern deck. She threw a canvas-wrapped bundle almost as big as a man down to Eynon.

"Oof," he said when he caught it. "What's in here? A dead body?"

"Of course not," teased Merry. "I told you we throw those in the river. It's our tent."

Eynon thought about the words *our tent* for a moment, then put the rolled canvas on the ground and caught two packs, two bed-rolls, and one of the food baskets Madollyn had given them. Merry extended her hand to Eynon and he helped her down to shore. He noticed she'd tied the bottle of liniment to her belt.

"Please get whatever you need for the night," she said, indicating the boat's bow with her hand. "When you're done, I'll set the wards."

Eynon nodded and promptly retrieved his pack, his staff, and the bag of honey cakes. He put them on the ground near the rolled-up tent and the other essentials.

"Can you teach *me* how to set wards?" he asked.

"I can try," said Merry. "I only know the one for baying dogs and cocking crossbows. and that's just a *minor* warding spell. I'm still trying to convince Doethan to teach me one of the *major* wards, like the physical aversion spell that makes your body buzz like a nest of wolfhornets. Like I said, I'd hoped he might show me how to work it on this trip, but..."

"Sorry to get in the way of your lessons," said Eynon. "I'll do my best to learn. Even minor wards would be helpful. Barking dogs frighten off animals, and clanking crossbows make would-be robbers think twice."

"And both wake us up," said Merry.

"And that," said Eynon.

Then Merry surprised him. She pulled a small silver pendant on a fine chain from inside her shirt. In its center was a rounded, highly polished blue gem the size of Eynon's thumbnail.

"Well," said Eynon. "That's something new."

"It's my training artifact," said Merry. "Doethan gave it to me to use while I'm learning the basics. He said I'll get to make my true artifact soon. The wizard makes the artifact, the artifact doesn't make the wizard."

"That's one of Ealdamon's epigrams."

"I know," said Merry. "Watch and listen."

Eynon focused his eyes and ears on Merry. He recognized her hand motions and intonation—they were what she'd used on the Mastlands dock, only now her actions were more obvious. Standing closer this time, he could make out a *woof* from the back of her throat and a *click* with her tongue. The bright blue magestone in her pendant flashed and the fine silver-work around it shimmered. When she lowered her hand and stopped talking, Eynon nodded appreciatively.

"Is that it? They're set?"

"They are," said Merry. "Want to test them?"

Eynon knew *this* was a test—for him.

"No," he said. "I'm sure they'll work. And I've heard enough baying hounds today. Shall we see what Madollyn and her cooks made us for dinner?"

"We have to raise the tent first," she said, smiling. Merry tucked the pendant back into her shirt.

They unrolled the canvas bundle and set the thick rectangular canvas ground cloth on a flat patch of thick grass. Then they spread out the fabric of the tent. Merry positioned stakes and guy ropes around the perimeter, then instructed Eynon to hold the tall pole at the front entrance so she could anchor it properly with ropes and stakes from inside the bundle. She drove in stakes with a heavy ironwood mallet that had also been rolled up in the canvas.

"How did you ever set this up on your own?" asked Eynon.

"Don't be silly," said Merry. "I didn't. I used a one-person tent then, with one center pole and ten stakes around the edges. It went up easily."

"Why not give us two tents like that?" said Eynon.

"I told you why earlier," said Merry. "My parents wanted to see what developed on this trip."

"Oh," said Eynon. He was very thoughtful as they set the rear pole and the four corner poles.

"That's done," said Merry.

"Now can we see what's for dinner?"

"After we lay out the bedrolls."

"I hear and obey," said Eynon.

Eynon and Merry sat close together on a blanket a few minutes later, looking out at the river. Madollyn's dinner basket turned out to contain a pair of thick round, whole-wheat trenchers, a baked chicken stuffed with spring onions, pickled root vegetables, a loaf of freshly-baked dark bread with seeds on top, a jug of water, and a small crock of bright-yellow butter. Eynon laughed when he opened the crock to confirm its contents. The image of a flying frog in mid-leap, like the one on the Flying Frog Farm's banner, was pressed into the butter's golden surface. Merry dug deeper into the basket, then she laughed too. She held up two perfectly round red apples.

"These are ours," she said. "From Applegarth. They're the best eating apples in the Kingdom of Dâron—in all of Orluin, for that matter."

"How many apples from other kingdoms have you tasted?" asked Eynon.

He was grinning and Merry stuck her tongue out.

"Don't try to minimize my bragging with facts," she said. "Wait until you try one before causing trouble."

"Yes, dear lady," he said, cutting her a chicken leg and putting it on her trencher. "Have some fowl first."

"Thank you," she said. "I will."

The rest of the dinner passed pleasantly. Eynon told Merry about hurrying through his rounds of the seven inns in Caercadel last year so he'd have time to visit the castle's library. Merry told Eynon about wandering off on a family trip to Tyford when she was nine. She'd been found hours later on the floor in the back of one of the shops on the street of booksellers with dozens of open volumes around her. Eynon noted it was hard to get lost in the Coombe. Everyone knew everybody and parents kept a watchful eye on each other's children.

"Does that explain why you're so polite?" asked Merry. "Word will always get back to your mother and father?"

"Perhaps," said Eynon, "though they're not likely to hear about today's adventures."

"Until you get home and tell them," said Merry. The corners of her mouth went up, then her expression turned mock-serious. "Take off your jacket and shirt," she said.

"What?" asked Eynon. "Why?"

Merry untied the bottle of liniment from her belt and held it aloft.

"Oh," said Eynon.

He stood, took off his quilted jacket, folded it, and positioned it neatly on the blanket next to the basket. He did the same with his linen shirt. Then he shifted to his knees beside Merry and removed the amulet by its cord. Without touching the silver oval or its blue stone, he placed the magical artifact on his shirt as carefully as he'd return a baby bird's egg to its nest.

"Thank you for being considerate," said Merry. "I didn't want my boat to burn to the waterline if it shot out another fireball."

"I am nothing if not considerate, dear lady."

Merry's mock-serious expression returned.

"Turn around so I can rub this in."

Eynon adjusted his position and moved from kneeling to sitting, giving Merry good access to his back. The liniment—and Merry's strong hands—soothed the large bruise between his shoulder blades. Eynon could smell wintergreen and sensed something in the liniment warming his skin and muscles.

"You may not know any healing spells—yet," he said, "but this is the next best thing."

"I'm glad it's helping."

Merry continued to rub Eynon's back for several minutes before she squeezed his shoulders and stopped.

"That's all for now," she said.

Eynon turned to watch Merry moisten a corner of the cloth covering the basket with water from the jug and use it to clean her hands. He smiled at Merry and she smiled back.

"I'll do it again tomorrow if you're still sore."

"Thank you," said Eynon. "I'd like that."

"I've got something else you'll like," said Merry. "Put your shirt on and sit next to me. I'll feed you an Applegarth eating apple."

Eynon lowered the blue and silver amulet around his neck and pulled his shirt over his head. Merry patted a spot on the blanket and Eynon sat, their knees almost touching.

"We'll only eat one now," Merry decided. "We can save the other for a mid-morning snack tomorrow."

"I defer to your expertise in all things related to apples," said Eynon.

"As well you should," said Merry.

She expertly cut one of the apples with her belt knife and fed slices directly into Eynon's open mouth. After the first few slices, Eynon smiled and sighed.

"I'm sorry I teased you about apples from other kingdoms earlier. These must be the best apples on either side of the Ocean."

"So good of you to acknowledge the truth," she said. Then she kissed him.

Her kiss was every bit as sweet as the apple. Eynon kissed her back. It wasn't his first kiss, but it was the best he'd had in his limited experience.

They kept kissing until the orange glow above the mountains to the west began to fade.

"Time to go in the tent?" asked Merry.

"It *is* getting late," said Eynon.

The two of them stood reluctantly. They held hands to continue their new connection.

"I'll hoist the food out of harm's way if you've got a rope," said Eynon. He didn't know if there were any bears on this side of the river, but he expected there were plenty of raccoons and other clever nocturnal hunters.

"There's a rope and canvas sling over a branch on a tree near the big boulder," said Merry. "If you take care of the food, I'll clean up here."

Now that Eynon was standing and not distracted, he realized he was shifting from foot to foot again.

"Ummm..." he said, uncomfortably.

"Follow the path up to the right behind the boulder. There's a pit, a log across it, a pile of smooth stones, and a wooden shovel. I've got soap for when you come back. You can wash in the river."

Eynon nodded his thanks. He gathered up the leftover food in the basket, then stopped to hand two honey cakes to Merry.

"In case we get hungry later," said Eynon.

"You're so sweet," said Merry. "Now get moving—and be quick about it."

* * * * *

"Eynon?"

"Mmm-hmm?"

"Thank you for being gentle."

"Uh... thank you for being patient. I hope I didn't hurt you."

"No more than I expected."

"I didn't intend to hurt you at all."

"I know," said Merry. "You're nothing, if not considerate."

"And polite. Don't forget polite."

"I won't," said Merry. She kissed him softly.

It wasn't completely dark inside the spacious tent. The moon was approaching half full and the clear night sky was ablaze with stars. The blue magestones in Eynon's amulet and Merry's pendant combined to cast a dim sapphire glow where they rested on the far end of the ground cloth.

"You're not going to start acting strange in the morning, are you?" asked Merry.

"What do you mean?" asked Eynon, shifting up on one elbow.

"Some of the boys in the Rhuthro valley follow around the first girl they've slept with like puppies," said Merry. "Others brag about being a girl's lover."

"Woof!" said Eynon.

"Stop that!" said Merry. "I'm serious."

Eynon took Merry's hand and put it over his heart.

"I promise you that I will not be a puppy or a boor."

"Good," said Merry. "I wouldn't be here with you if I thought you would be."

Eynon shifted Merry's hand from his heart to his lips, where he could kiss her fingertips.

"I do have one condition," he said.

"You're adding conditions?"

"Just one," said Eynon. "I want you to teach me how to do the warding spell with the baying hounds and crossbows."

Merry laughed, and Eynon laughed with her.

"I promise," she said. "But learning a spell takes hours of study and repetition."

"You'll find me a diligent pupil," said Eynon.

Merry snuggled her body against him.

"I know something else that's best learned through hours of study and repetition."

"And what might that be, dear lady?"

"I think you know."

Fercha

Fercha was making good time heading toward Applegarth, drawing on her magic instead of stopping to eat or drink or rest. Every hour, she would pause and use the power of the training magestone in her pendant to scan ahead and attempt to locate her lost, fully-tuned true artifact. Until now, it had been beyond that small stone's limited reach. This time, however, she felt it.

Her artifact wasn't in Applegarth. It was moving north. She didn't want to consider the possibility that Verro may have found it ahead of her, though she was comforted by the thought that if he had, her amulet would be in Tamloch now instead of still in the Rhuthro valley.

She changed course to head east and spent even more of her reserves of magic to increase her pace, pulled toward her artifact across the miles.

It must be on a boat on the Rhuthro—and only a mountain stood between her and the river.

Chapter 9

"Nobles serve themselves and their subjects, in that order."
— Ealdamon's *Epigrams*

Eynon and Merry didn't get an early start the next morning. They hadn't been in a hurry to take down the tent, but when they did, Merry made Eynon laugh and blush with a joke about tent poles. Eynon left to retrieve their food from its high perch and give his face time to return to normal. Merry sped him on his way by repeating her instruction from the previous night—*and be quick about it.*

He was pleased that breakfast wasn't awkward. They sat together on a blanket and shared the chicken they hadn't eaten for dinner and slices of dark, seeded bread slathered with butter. Merry made Eynon blush again by sensuously licking chicken grease from her fingers. Eynon made Merry giggle by running his tongue around his lips to remove a dot of butter. Merry couldn't complain about Eynon acting like a puppy when she was doing the same.

As a treat, they each had a honey cake, or rather they playfully fed each other pieces of honey cake until only crumbs remained around their mouths. It seemed only right for those to be removed with lips and tongues.

Between kisses, Eynon considered that the honey cakes had been good, though not nearly as tasty as his aunt's. That meant his idea for a two-way trade of marshapples and honey could still be viable. Then thoughts of anything except Merry left his brain.

"If we keep this going," said Eynon when he paused for breath, "we'll have to set the tent back up."

"Why?" asked Merry.

Why indeed? considered Eynon.

Sometime later, Merry returned to other aspects of Eynon's education. Step by step, she taught Eynon how to remove the minor wards on the boat. He watched her do it, then practiced resetting and removing them himself.

"You're good," she said. "You have a natural aptitude."

"For wizardry?" asked Eynon.

"And other things," Merry replied with a twinkle in her eye. They both laughed.

"Come on," said Merry. "Let's get everything stowed and go."

The dew had burned off by the time their gear was in place and they were heading back downriver. Merry had turned her seat around and was leaning against it instead of sitting down. Eynon was pleased that his back wasn't nearly as sore as it had been. That was a welcome change.

He noticed that the river was changing, too. Several tributaries had joined the main flow of the Rhuthro and now it was wider, deeper, and slower. There was time for Eynon to look over his shoulder and smile at Merry frequently, without any worry about rocks. Merry smiled back whenever he did, and she didn't give any indication that she objected to his attention.

"Is there anything else you can teach me?" Eynon asked the next time he turned around.

"What do you mean?" teased Merry. "I'm as new at this as you are."

"No," said Eynon, "is there anything else you can teach me about wizardry?"

"Oh," said Merry. She paused for a moment, then spoke. "I know how to move boats upstream against the current."

"You do?" asked Eynon eagerly. "How?"

"Oars," said Merry.

Eynon's face fell.

"I couldn't resist," said Merry.

She blew him a kiss. He frowned back, then smiled and turned around to watch the river.

"Eynon," said Merry. "I do know one more spell. Doethan said it was very similar to the warding spell."

"What does it do?" asked Eynon, looking over his shoulder.

"It's a listening spell," said Merry. "The warding spell creates sounds that aren't there and the listening spell calls in sounds that *are* there."

"How does it work?"

"Give me a second or two to cast it and I'll show you," said Merry. "You're far enough away for a demonstration."

Eynon watched Merry move her lips and gesture with one hand. The motion completed with her index finger touching her ear.

"The spell is working," said Merry. "Turn around and whisper something. There's enough noise from the river to disguise what you say."

"I can do that," said Eynon. He faced downriver and did as instructed.

"Thank you," said Merry. "You're beautiful, I mean *handsome,* too. Now say something I couldn't guess."

Eynon whispered again.

"Your mother's name is Glenys. Your father is Daffyd, and your sister is Braith," said Merry. "Was that right?"

"Three for three," said Eynon, loud enough for his voice to carry. Then he went back to whispering.

"Yes," said Merry. "I'd be glad to teach you how to cast the listening spell. It's very useful."

"For listening to your parents trying to plan out your life?" asked Eynon in his normal voice.

"And for finding out what friends and suitors really think of you," said Merry.

"I think you know in my case," said Eynon.

"I might," said Merry. "Are you a friend, or a suitor?"

"A friend for now," said Eynon, "but I might consider the other when I return from my wander year. I have to stop at Applegarth to see if your father will let me read *The Venerable History of Dâron,* after all."

"But when you return, *I'll* still be on my wander year," said Merry.

"It might take me a while to read through your father's library," teased Eynon. "And I've still got to return a certain something to the wizard it belongs to."

"Who knows where your path will take you," said Merry. "Let's enjoy the present. I'm glad to be your guide until we find a wizard to advise you in Tyford. That's at least three more days—two more on the river, plus one in the city."

"Uh huh," said Eynon. He was already thinking about the pain of saying goodbye.

They were both silent for what must have been a mile. Eynon noticed there were more settlements along the banks of the Rhuthro now. The east bank was still marshy, but beyond the waving reeds and willows he spotted tilled fields and sturdy farm houses. There were plenty of farms on the west bank as well. Stone manors, wooden barns and scattered outbuildings were set back from the river. Each settlement had its own dock or docks with boats from coracles to canoes and cargo vessels moored beside them.

"When's our next stop?" asked Eynon. "Are there any more tolls today?" He was thinking that chains long enough to block traffic on the river when it was this wide would be *very* expensive.

"Our next stop is at Rhuthro Keep," said Merry. "That's the castle for the earl of the Rhuthro valley, my family's liege lord."

"Is an earl more important than a baron?"

"Not as most barons see it," said Merry, "but yes. Earls usually control more territory and sit higher in the Great Hall. They have more knights and soldiers, too."

"The baron in Caercadel only has a dozen knights," said Eynon. "They work with the men at arms that train the levies, drink, and hunt deer."

"Our earl has more than a hundred knights. They do what yours do and serve as cavalry when the king summons the army."

"I can't remember Caercadel's baron and knights ever serving."

"That's because the last time Dâron was at war was before we were born," said Merry.

"Oh," said Eynon. "Who were we fighting?"

"We were fighting who we always fight," said Merry, "at least according to my father and *The Venerable History*. The Kingdom of Tamloch."

Eynon was amused by the way she pronounced the last sound in Tamloch, like she was clearing her throat.

"Do you mean the evil green folk all the stories warn us about?" he asked.

"They're not green—they *wear* green," said Merry. "And they're probably not evil, either. They're a lot like us, I expect. *The Venerable History* says three tribes set sail for the west when the Eagle People took their lands on the White Isle and the Green. Our Cymri ancestors settled here, in the south of Orluin, and founded the Kingdom of Dâron. The Ériu folk from the Green Isle went north and established the Kingdom of Tamloch. And the blue-painted clan folk from the uplands of the White Isle sought out lands like the ones they'd left. They settled in the mountainous Clan Lands to the northeast and southwest of Dâron. For tens of centuries, the Abbenoth, a great river running north to south, was the border between Tamloch and Dâron, while the clan folk mostly kept to themselves. Then the Eagle People landed in Orluin and took both sides of the Abbenoth as a province in their empire."

Eynon clapped in admiration. "Did you memorize that?" he asked.

"Not word for word, but it's pretty close," Merry answered.

"I can't wait to read the book," said Eynon. "Once I return the amulet I'm coming right back to Applegarth and reading every book in your father's library."

"Some of the books belong to my mother, too," teased Merry.

"Every book in your *parents'* library, then."

"If you find the right wizard quickly, maybe you can ride back with me and help me with the oars."

"I'd like that," said Eynon.

"So would I," said Merry. "And maybe you could visit me at Doethan's tower—that's where I'm headed on my wander year."

"Does Doethan have a library?"

"That's right," said Merry. "You didn't see it. Doethan must have a hundred books one floor up from where we had lunch."

"All of a sudden, I'm less interested in going back to Applegarth."

"You don't want more adventures?"

"Learning wizardry—and *other* subjects—will be enough of an adventure for me."

"Good to know," said Merry. "Oh, I just remembered. Doethan said that the Eagle People arriving was probably one of the best things that happened to Dâron and Tamloch."

"An invasion from across the Ocean was good?"

"Doethan says the Eagle People provided a common enemy. Now that they provide a buffer, Dâron and Tamloch go to war every twenty or twenty-five years, not every five," said Merry.

"They're too afraid the Eagle People will attack them both, after they're worn down?" asked Eynon.

"That's what Doethan said."

"Why didn't Dâron and Tamloch attack the Eagle People at the same time and push them back into the sea?"

"I asked the same question," said Merry.

Eynon could hear the smile in her voice.

"What did he say?"

"That getting Dâron and Tamloch to work together was a lot like getting a wolf to make friends with a mountain lion," said Merry.

"Maybe if you raised them together from the time they were pup and kit," mused Eynon.

"Listen," said Merry. "There's more. Doethan also said the Eagle People defeated us every time we tried."

Eynon laughed. "That's a different story," he said. "Wouldn't the armies of the combined kingdoms outnumber the Eagle People's forces?"

"You'd think so," said Merry, "but Doethan said the Eagle People's soldiers had far superior discipline and their martial wizards were better than ours. Doethan thought it was more the former than the latter, but they still beat us and our allies from Tamloch."

"I wonder if Doethan was ever a martial wizard?"

"I thought the same thing," said Merry. "You were right. He *is* more powerful than a hedge wizard."

Eynon was quiet for a few minutes. He looked at the settlements on either side of the Rhuthro as they grew larger and closer together. The listening spell was still in place, so Merry could make out a word or two as Eynon muttered to himself, but nothing he said formed coherent sentences. Finally, he looked over his shoulder and asked a question.

"When was the last war between the kingdoms?"

"I'm not sure," said Merry, "but at least twenty years ago. My father and Doethan fought in it. That's how my da got his lands."

Eynon nodded, encouraging Merry to continue if she had more to say.

"My da was really old—almost twenty-eight—when I was born. He served in Brendinas for several years after the last war ended. I'm almost sixteen and…"

"I've added up the sums," Eynon interrupted. "We don't think much about war in the Coombe, but it looks like we're due for one soon, if Derry was at court for three or four years—not that wars come on precise time tables."

"You may be right," said Merry. "Now I'm even *more* interested in spending my wander year in Doethan's tower."

"Agreed," said Eynon. "We're both prime candidates to be drafted into the levies."

"If we learn something from Doethan," said Merry, "we can aim higher and become crown wizards."

"I think I'm less interested in glory or dying for my kingdom than you are."

"If we're going to be called one way or the other, our odds of dying are a lot higher holding a spear or a crossbow than a wizard's staff," said Merry.

"You've got a point," said Eynon. "Is that Rhuthro Keep?"

Eynon could see a tall, square castle ahead on the left bank. One of its walls was next to the river and it stretched back at least twice as far as the castle at Caercadel.

The structure had massive square towers on each of its four corners while a fifth round tower in the middle formed a large central keep. As they approached, Eynon noticed several stone docks, each as big as the one at Flying Frog Farms, but without the covered merchants' booths at the back.

Soldiers, wearing white and purple surcoats over mail, clinked about checking boats and deliveries. Most of the dock space was in use and hundreds of barrels, crates and casks were stacked several rows high, ready to be moved inside. Dozens of new conscripts were milling around like so many sheep in a pen, waiting to be ordered somewhere by liveried soldiers.

"What's on those surcoats?" asked Eynon. "I can't make out the design, except to tell it's mostly white with some purple."

"You've got a good eye to make out that much at this distance," said Merry. "They *are* white, with a purple V-shape, pointing down, and a black portcullis above that."

"A portcullis?"

"An iron gate. The river narrows up ahead. Rhuthro Keep guards the Rhuthro valley from anyone attacking from downriver."

"Did Tamloch ever drive an army this far into Dâron?" asked Eynon. "We're a long way from their territory."

"Rhuthro Keep more likely guarded the valley from other nobles in Dâron, not foreign armies," said Merry. "Some nobles act like *what's mine is mine and what's yours is mine, too.*"

"The people in the Coombe went west to escape quarreling nobles," said Eynon. "Our baron wishes only to stay in Caercadel and avoid the kingdom's squabbles—at least that's what my father says."

"You've got a wise baron," said Merry.

"We think so," said Eynon. "Long life to him and the heirs of his body who follow."

"Long life," echoed Merry. "If war comes, though, even your baron must answer the king's call."

They were quiet for a span, considering their own thoughts, as their boat neared the bustle of Rhuthro Keep.

"Where do we put in?" asked Eynon.

"The closest dock," said Merry. "The one with a single man-at-arms on duty. I think I recognize him."

"I'll tie up the prow," said Eynon, as Merry carefully brought the boat against the sturdy stone dock. Thick bundles of twigs served as bumpers to prevent the dock from damaging visiting vessels.

"I've got the stern," said Merry, expertly looping a rope around a cleat. "Tally!" she shouted at the young guardsman approaching. "Why is it so busy? Is the king coming to visit?"

"I hope not," said the young man.

Eynon pegged him at no more than eighteen. He was quite a bit shorter than Eynon but sturdy and muscular, probably from months of work with sword and shield, wearing heavy mail. Tally wore a conical steel cap and a worried look.

"The crown has summoned the army," the young soldier continued.

Eynon and Merry exchanged a wary glance.

"I was afraid that might be why," said Merry. "How's your sister?"

"Expecting her first child this summer," said Tally, "but her husband's been drafted and will likely be on campaign along with me when the child arrives."

"I'm glad and sorry to hear that," said Merry. "This is my friend Eynon, from the Coombe," she continued, waving a hand at Eynon. "We've got a jug of cider for the earl."

Eynon reached back and found a jug. He changed his grip to grasp it more securely, then lifted it up to Tally.

"Careful with that," said Eynon. "It's so delicious you won't want to lose a drop."

"I know," said Tally. "I've had a mug or two of Applegarth cider before, when I rowed my sister up to see Merry."

"See that it gets to the earl," said Merry. She followed her words with an obvious wink. Tally laughed, then his face grew serious.

"You'd better leave now," he said, "before some of the more senior people decide to commandeer all four of your barrels to support the war effort. They'd be very popular in the officers' feast hall."

"Good advice," said Merry as she scanned the docks for anyone Tally's superior.

"It's also smart for the two of you to get on your way," said Tally. "The freelance recruiters have slots to fill."

"But I'm only fifteen," Merry protested.

"You look older," said Tally. "Be on your way then. I'll see that this jug is well cared for."

"I'm sure you will," said Merry. This time, Tally winked.

Merry untied the rope at the stern while Eynon did the same at his end. He used his staff to push the prow away from the dock and felt their craft shoot forward as Merry steered them out into the current.

"Congratulations to your sister," shouted Eynon before the boat was out of earshot. Tally waved to confirm he'd heard Eynon's good wishes. Merry directed their boat to the far side of the river until they were well past the castle.

"Doethan was right, it seems," said Merry. "Dâron and Tamloch go to war every twenty years."

"But why did the war have to start three days into my wander year?"

"You can feel sorry for yourself later," said Merry. "Now, I recommend you tie your wrist to the prow line. There's rough water ahead and I don't want to lose you over the side—again."

"Your concern for my welfare is appreciated."

"Pipe down and watch for rocks."

"Yes, dear lady."

The boat shook as they entered a stretch of turbulence. Ahead, the river narrowed sharply, its channel cutting a steep-sided passage through a ridge almost as tall as the nearby mountains. The current moved faster, forcing its volume through the constriction.

"Hang on," said Merry. "It's going to be quite a ride."

Chapter 10

"The swiftest path sometimes meanders."
— Ealdamon's *Epigrams*

Eynon *did* hang on. It wasn't much of a choice. If he didn't, he'd fall overboard and would likely be killed, his body bashed against the boulders flanking the entrance to the channel. Despite its heavy cargo, the boat began to buck like a stallion after knocking over a beehive. The prow tossed up and crashed down as it plowed through the roiling waters. Curtains of water splashed high on either side. Eynon tried to suppress his fear, but failed. He clutched the bow thwart with white-knuckled hands as he sat, soaked and shivering.

Turbulence was replaced by even more speed when they passed the entrance. Eynon felt swept along by a giant's hand shoving them ever faster. He went to his knees and leaned forward to reduce his resistance to the wind. The walls of the gap were a blur. Eynon didn't try to call out rocks—there'd be no time to change course if he did.

He heard a cry from Merry and looked over his shoulder to see what was wrong. To his surprise, he saw she was excited, not troubled. Her eyes were wide, her mouth was open, and her hair streamed out behind her. Merry's face was wet from spray, and her cheeks were bright. She was *enjoying* shooting the gap.

Eynon watched as Merry gripped the steering oar with both hands, using her body to help hold it tight and maintain their course. He saw she had the boat under control and was thrilled to test her skill. Eynon told himself he shouldn't be afraid and took deep breaths to calm his racing heart, but was only partly successful.

Looking back was making him dizzy, so he turned downriver again and tried to take in his surroundings. The walls of the gap were steep and sheer. Curving diagonal layers of rock were exposed on both sides of the channel where the river had cut through the ridge. They went by too fast for Eynon to take in many details.

Ahead, Eynon could see a wide patch of sky. Their boat was caught up by a wave and swept onward. Seconds later they were through, popping from the gap like a stopper from a cider jug. Eynon's heart rate abruptly slowed and he released a breath he hadn't known he was holding.

"Whee!" shouted Merry as they were carried along on a wave.

Eynon turned in his seat.

"Whee," he said, without a trace of Merry's celebratory glee.

They were gliding through a wide section of the river past the gap. It was almost a lake, with a strong current. He saw a queue of boats near the west bank.

"Wasn't that fun?" asked Merry.

"Uh huh," said Eynon. "Fun. Right. Let's row back upstream and do it again."

He shook his head to show that what he said and what he meant were not the same.

Merry laughed.

"You didn't like it?"

"Speed, terror, and the threat of drowning," said Eynon in a flat voice. "Of *course* I liked it."

"I shot the gap just for you," said Merry.

"We had a choice?" asked Eynon. "Come to think of it, how do boats ever get upstream against that current?"

"Easy," said Merry. "There are locks beyond the castle. You couldn't see them because the walls were in the way. Those boats to the west are waiting to use them."

"Aren't locks for keeping people out of places?"

"Not these locks. Boats are *locked* into watertight stone pens, then water is pumped in or out to raise them up or lower them down. There are three side-by-side pairs of locks at the Keep. Think stairways—one for going up, one for going down."

"You mean we didn't *have* to shoot the gap?"

"No, but the locks are a lot slower. And we'd have to pay a toll to use them."

"Did your father know you were going to shoot the gap?"

"No," said Merry, "and don't tell him. He took me through years ago to give me a thrill, but cautioned me never to try it on my own. I've done it every solo trip I've taken since, and sold the toll jugs to buy books in Tyford."

"In that case," said Eynon, "I forgive you for scaring me, even though that was quite a trick to play on someone who's only spending his second day on the river."

"If you forgive me, I'll make it up to you," teased Merry.

"Consider yourself forgiven," said Eynon. "If you teach me that listening spell when we stop to share the last Applegarth eating apple."

"I'm glad to teach you the spell," said Merry. "I said I would—but what makes you think there's only one apple left?"

"I thought Madollyn's cooks only gave us two."

"Yes, but there are more than a dozen of them in a basket stowed below," said Merry. "My mother made sure we were well-supplied."

"I think I'm quite fond of your mother," said Eynon.

"So am I," said Merry, "when we're not under the same roof."

Eynon sat back on the thwart and let the morning sun dry his face and hair.

"There were times when my mother and father joked that wander years became a tradition because it got young people away from home so their parents didn't kill them," he said, "though I get along with my parents well enough."

"You don't know?" asked Merry.

"Know what?"

"Why we have wander years."

"There really is a reason?" asked Eynon. "I thought it was just a tradition. Traditions don't need reasons."

"Of course there's a reason," said Merry. "You're a farmer. You should know what happens when you have a small herd of sheep or cattle and don't bring in a new ram or bull every few years."

"Too many aren't born right," said Eynon. "One of my cousin's cows gave birth to a two-headed calf a few years ago."

"That's the idea," said Merry. "Now think it through."

Eynon thought, then spoke.

"I get it," he said. "If small settlements don't bring in new blood, babies won't be healthy."

"And..." encouraged Merry.

"And sending us out on wander years to meet new people..."

"When you bring them home and marry them, or join their families elsewhere, it..."

"Keeps our lines strong," completed Eynon.

"Precisely," said Merry.

"I'd always thought wander years were there so that we could have adventures before settling down," said Eynon.

"Why can't they be both?" asked Merry. "For adventures, and for healthy babies when their parents are ready?"

"Both it is," said Eynon. "When's our next stop?"

"Not far," said Merry. "There's a wood on the east bank up ahead. It's between two farms and they keep it wild so there are plenty of deer to hunt. I know a private, sheltered spot there where we can anchor and share that apple."

"And teach me the listening spell," said Eynon.

"And find a way to make up for the fright I caused you."

"Will you rub my back?" asked Eynon.

"Something like that," said Merry.

* * * * *

After they shared the apple, Eynon was quite pleased by Merry's means of making up. The two found a euphemism for lovemaking when their cries of passion scared a mother doe and her fawn into running deeper into the forest. *Frightening the deer* became a way for them to secretly joke about spending private time together.

Later, they discovered that not all the animals at their stop were afraid of them. Eynon fed a bold chipmunk a bit of honey cake while Merry enticed the creature with a small piece of apple. It chittered at them happily, then ran back into the forest.

Behind a young maple, Eynon thought he spotted a *raconette,* a small masked beast the size of a kitten with an oversized ringed tail and oversized curiosity to match. He tossed a piece of honey cake and half of his last slice of apple toward where the animal's large copper eyes were visible, then turned his attention back to Merry—and magic.

The listening spell proved easy to learn. It was similar to the hounds-and-crossbows spell and Eynon was a quick study. After the lesson, Merry and Eynon cast it on themselves for practice. They reluctantly left their sheltered clearing, but shared intimate whispers as they continued downstream.

Since their break, Eynon noticed there was more traffic on the river north of the gap. When he thought about it, it seemed only common sense. Wheat and oats and apples were fall crops and wouldn't be transported from the upper reaches of the Rhuthro at this time of year, while men and military supplies would be heading to the earl's castle from Tyford and smaller cities downriver. They passed several cargo vessels making their way upstream and waved to their navigators, since the arms of the crew members pulling oars were otherwise occupied fighting the current.

Eynon tugged his damp, holly-wreathed hat forward. The sun was getting higher in the sky and the day was warming up. He wished he'd brought a broad-brimmed straw hat instead of his high-peaked felt hat that offered little protection for his face.

Ahead, on the right, he saw two long, sleek boats pulled up on the muddy bank. They were black, narrow, and as vicious-looking as a pair of eels. Each eel-boat was barely wider than a man's hips, but as long as their own cider-transport vessel. Six men stood beside them, scanning the river.

As Eynon and Merry neared, the five men—*and one woman,* Eynon realized—slid their boats out into the main channel. The twin eel-boats cut through the water like knives and their crews sculled briskly to flank the Applegarth vessel.

Now that they were closer, on his left and right, Eynon could see the men wore an odd collection of military cast-offs. Most had padded-canvas gambesons with heavy, stiff, boiled-leather paldrons and vambraces, but none of the pieces seemed to match.

The woman, navigating the right-hand boat, wore armor crafted from small, shield-shaped bits of leather that made her look like a pine cone. A dark-leather hat with a broad brim shielded her eyes from the sun, so it was impossible to read her expression.

Too bad they weren't stupid enough to wear plate on the river, thought Eynon.

He didn't like the look of these new arrivals and liked their intent even less when he heard them whisper. His ears sharpened by the listening spell, Eynon caught every word the steersman on the left told his crew.

"Board and subdue, my lads," said the steersman. "We'll claim boat, crew and cargo." He paused and spat into the river, then continued. "The lad and girl should earn us a recruiting bounty, so try to leave them in one piece. Those barrels should fetch us a good price at the Rhuthro Keep's kitchens, too, if they hold what I think they do."

His crew muttered their agreement, excited by the prospect of a prosperous bit of piracy.

"Careful," whispered Merry. "They've got to be some of those freelance recruiters for the earl's army Taffy warned us about."

"They're thieves, plain and simple," said Eynon. "I'll load my crossbow"

"Don't forget kidnappers," said Merry. "It's the only honest way to refer to them."

"What do we do?" asked Eynon.

"We fight," said Merry. "We have the advantage—they'd prefer not to kill us, and we'll kill them if we must."

"I hope it doesn't come to that," said Eynon. "And I don't like the odds."

"We'll deal with them one at a time," said Merry. "If they let you. You take the boat on the left."

"Right," said Eynon.

Merry rolled her eyes and began her own preparations. She didn't say, "No, I said *left*," but he could tell that was what she was thinking.

Eynon wished he could joke in dangerous situations, but he was too worried. He removed a quarrel from the stock of his small crossbow and armed the weapon. Then he put the sharp shard next to him on the thwart. The attackers would probably attempt to board at the bow instead of scaling the raised stern or trying to climb over the cider barrels. He hoped Merry had a plan for dealing with the boat on the right, because Eynon expected to be fully occupied with its opposite number.

He stood with his crossbow at the ready as the prow of the left-hand boat came even with his position. The man in the prow had a week's ragged beard and a jagged scar from his ear to his chin. He held a halberd with a spear point and a wicked hook, ready to give Eynon scars of his own. Scar-man stabbed at Eynon to keep him back, then started to board. Trembling, Eynon shot him in the belly, but the quarrel only went in a few inches.

Blast, thought Eynon.

His attacker's gambeson must include a layer of hardened leather squares. Still, the man's eyes went wide. He screamed in pain and dropped his halberd to clutch his stomach. Eynon smiled—at least some of the quarrel must have entered flesh.

The scarred man bent over and Eynon assumed he was no longer a threat, but he came up from the bottom of his boat with a short sword in one hand and a grapnel in the other. Eynon tried to load another quarrel, but he fumbled the weapon. Crossbow and quarrel fell by his feet. Taking advantage of Eynon's confusion, his attacker set the grapnel into the side of Eynon's boat and lunged with his sword point. Eynon fell back and landed in the center of the bow thwart. As the attacker swung the flat of his blade toward Eynon's head, Eynon instinctively picked up the shard and used it to block the blow.

Both of them were shocked when the far end of the short sword clattered down to join Eynon's crossbow. Pressing his advantage, Eynon swung the shard back and forth in front of him. The man with the scar retreated and tripped over the linked gunwales of the two boats, falling back into his own.

Eynon stepped forward and brought the shard down on the eel boat with as much force as he could manage. It felt like splitting a particularly challenging piece of cord wood back in the Coombe. The shard struck a few inches behind the narrow attacking vessel's pointed prow, cutting all the way through the thin wood. The small section remained attached to Eynon and Merry's boat by the grapnel.

Scar-man scrambled to his knees and quickly moved amidships, away from Eynon, but the damage was done. The left-hand attacking boat started taking on water and began to sink.

"Eynon!" shouted Merry. "Duck!"

He bent to pick up his crossbow and lost quarrel when he felt a rush of air above his back. It registered in his peripheral vision that a second man, from the boat on the right, was swinging a halberd at where Eynon's heart would have been. Driven by instinct, Eynon stretched out his left arm and tried to hold off his new attacker with the point and edge of the curved shard. The shard intersected with the ashwood shaft of the halberd, cutting off its head. The axe-shaped halberd blade joined the front end of scar-man's sword at Eynon's feet.

"Get back!" Eynon shouted.

His opponent closed instead. He shoved the lower half of the halberd's staff into Eynon's solar plexus, knocking him back onto the bow thwart where Eynon bounced and sat, momentarily stunned. The shard fell from his grasp. Then the second man pressed his advantage, taking up a short sword and raising it to deliver a stunning blow. Eynon felt a surge of energy flow through him. He reached over his head and blocked the sword with the small triangle of prow from the left-hand vessel.

The thin wood shattered, but Eynon held on to two longer pieces of the prow and threw them at the second man's head. His attacker stepped back, giving Eynon time to pick up his staff. He got to his knees and rotated his staff through ninety degrees of arc, striking the swordsman on the side of his head with a crisp *thwack*. The man collapsed forward and didn't look like he'd be getting up soon.

"Eynon!" shouted Merry again.

Eynon turned and saw Merry holding off two swordsmen with her steering oar. One attacker was short and wide, the other tall with long hair. Eynon retrieved his crossbow and quarrel and carefully cocked and loaded the weapon. Then he took a deep breath, aimed, and let fly. The bolt hit the short, wide swordsman on the left an inch above the knee. Merry used her steering oar to slap the injured and off-balance man over the side and into the stern of the right-hand attacking boat. The remaining swordsman redoubled his attack.

I've got to load another quarrel, thought Eynon—but the crossbow's stock was empty and he didn't know where Merry had stored the extra ammunition. He grabbed his staff and clambered up and over the four cider barrels until he was close to Merry and the long-haired swordsman. She was losing her end of the fight. Her steering oar had a dozen chips cut from it where it had interposed between her body and the swordsman's blade.

Eynon stood balanced on top of the last barrel and extended his staff to try to tangle the remaining swordsman's legs, but he was a yard too far away to accomplish his goal. The swordsman feinted low, then came in high and smacked Merry's left temple with the flat of his blade. She fell like a stone. Eynon leapt off the top of the barrel, aiming his staff at the man's back, but he misjudged the distance and landed on his face in the narrow space between the last barrel and the raised stern.

The swordsman jumped down beside Eynon—his boots inches from Eynon's eyes. In the next moments, Eynon expected to feel a sword blow that would either end his life or his consciousness. He raised his head an inch or two and tried to clear his brain. A few feet away, in the darkness under the raised deck, he saw a pair of reflective copper eyes. A small, wiry gray shape with a black mask shot out from its hiding place and dug its claws and teeth into the exposed flesh of the swordsman's leg above his boot.

The long-haired swordsman screamed and hopped on one foot, trying to break the creature's hold.

Eynon reclaimed his wits, rolled over, and found his staff by feel. He gripped it from the bottom and thrust the top of his staff up beneath his opponent's gambeson, connecting with the soft spot under the swordsman's breastbone. Blood trickled out. The point of the quarrel embedded in Eynon's staff must have ripped flesh.

The man fell back and landed on the deck like a sack of grain. Eynon's opponent was paralyzed. He wheezed like a covered pot full of water too long on the hearth.

The little beast disengaged his claws and shifted to sit on Eynon's stomach. Eynon stood and carefully cradled his rescuer in his arms before placing it on the boat's raised stern. The animal was a young raconette—probably the one he'd seen in the woods an hour earlier.

He took stock of himself and realized he was whole, except for a collection of bruises that would probably grow over the next few hours. Eynon climbed up on the raised stern deck and felt the pulse at Merry's neck. It was strong. A knot the size of a duck's egg was rising on her temple, but her breathing was steady. He straightened her limbs, put the cushion from her steersman's seat under her head and smiled as the resourceful raconette settled on her chest, tucking its fluffy ringed tail around its body.

Below, he saw the second swordsman stirring. The long-haired man had regained his breath and was kneeling in a small pool of water. Eynon looked at the man, then Merry, then back at the man. He reached down with his staff and whacked the long-haired man on his left temple, none to gently, thinking Merry would be sure to approve. The man fell forward, still kneeling.

Eynon climbed down to stand beside his dazed opponent and dragged him to the side. Then he levered the man over the edge and tipped him into the attackers' remaining boat. The woman in pinecone armor at the stern pushed her hat back and stared at him.

"Who *are* you?" she asked. "We were going about the crown's business and you..."

"Be quiet," snapped Eynon. He clambered up on the stern deck and looked down at her, his staff in his hand. A blue glow pulsed under the neck of his tunic.

"Don't hurt me, good wizard," said the woman. Her steering oar shook in her hands.

"Begone!" shouted Eynon. "Or I'll burn your boat to the waterline."

"Yes, good wizard."

The short, wide swordsman had removed the crossbow quarrel from his leg and wrapped his wound with a sleeve ripped from his undertunic. He took the oars and slowly rowed the thieves and kidnappers' narrow boat upstream while the woman at the steering oar exhorted him to stroke faster. Eynon watched them pick up their comrades, who were clinging to the overturned hull of the other boat. Once they were pulled from the water, he turned around to focus on more important matters.

Eynon confirmed that Merry's pulse and breathing were still good, then took the notched steering oar and slowly guided their boat to a quiet, sheltered spot masked by a short, rocky peninsula. It had been a miracle the river was straight and largely rock free for their most-recent travels, though perhaps that had been one of the reasons their attackers had selected this stretch for their ambush.

With trembling hands, Eynon tied up the boat, then went below. He found a yellow and green towel in one of Madollyn's baskets and dipped it in the river, rolling the fabric into a wide, flat tube. That task completed, he returned to the stern and placed his make-shift cold compress on Merry's bruised head. Her eyes fluttered open when the cool towel touched her skin.

"Did we win?" she asked. Her voice sounded like peach skin.

"Yes, dear lady," said Eynon. "They're gone." He rested his palm on her cheek. "You're safe."

"I'm glad," said Merry. Her eyes closed.

Eynon found Merry's blankets and bedroll under the stern deck and made sure she was comfortable as she slept on the deck before him. The little raconette—a male, he confirmed—shifted from Merry's chest to Eynon's shoulder. The brave beast weighed no more than a six-month-old kitten, but his claws and teeth were sharp and his front paws looked like hands. Eynon decided to feed him more apple, then discovered the small scamp had already discovered their store of them and was halfway through his second.

With his new helper chittering away, Eynon inspected the steering oar and decided it needed reinforcement. He moved over the cider barrels to the bow and returned with his pack, the shard, and one and a half halberds. He used the shard to cut the head off the undamaged halberd and found a coil of rope underneath the stern deck. He used the rope to lash the pieces of halberd to the steering oar and was proud of his work, glad that his grandfather had taught him his knots.

Eynon found the extra quarrels in the storage area while he'd been looking for the rope. Merry had packed them in a wooden box next to a small crockery urn full of dried cherries. He brought the box and the urn on deck and replenished the supply of bolts in his small crossbow's stock. He left the box by the steersman's seat in case he ran into more trouble and had to reload quickly. He ate a few dried cherries, for energy. Their tart sweetness bit his tongue.

The raconette begged and Eynon gave him a few cherries, which he ate greedily on Eynon's shoulder. Then Eynon returned to the storage area and brought a jug of everyday drinking cider and the rest of the honey cakes on deck, too.

It was time to get back on their way, though the day's tone had shifted from innocent joy to near tragedy in the space of a few hours. Eynon's head was whirling as he untied the boat and used the mended steering oar to guide them back out into the center of the current. He would stay the course to Tyford.

Merry was sleeping peacefully. Eynon hoped she would wake before nightfall.

Fercha

Only a mountain stood between Fercha and the river, but that mountain proved to be more of a challenge than she had expected. It was particularly steep and half its slope was covered in slippery talus. She had to use magic to bind the chips of rock together in places to find a firm footing and had to ascend in zigzagging switchbacks instead of moving directly upward.

Her spirits were not diminished by the physical challenge, however. She was confident she knew her exact location. The cluster of dark firs at the top of the mountain were the same stand of trees she knew well from her own trips on the Rhuthro. They weren't far from her tower.

At this rate, it would take Fercha several hours to reach the top—and still more time to make her way down to the river and commandeer a boat. But she was getting closer. She could feel it.

Fercha frightened a batsnake as she made her way to the summit. As it slithered away, she wished it—and herself—good hunting.

Chapter 11

"Healing potions are no substitute for caution."
— Ealdamon's *Epigrams*

Changing course is hard, but going with the current is easy, thought Eynon from the steersman's seat. He smiled when he realized that sounded like one of Ealdamon's epigrams. The few times he had to shift direction to avoid obstacles made him glad his arms and shoulders were muscular from farm work. He smiled again when he realized the strength of Merry's embraces yesterday and this morning likely owed a lot to the physical challenges of navigation.

Eynon kept to the center of the channel and scanned the water and shore for any potential signs of trouble. So far, all he'd seen were small holdings and at one point, a water-powered sawmill on the west bank. The east bank was no longer marsh. Instead, unbroken stands of hardwoods marched in random ranks from the shore of the river, covering the hills and mountains beyond with dense greenery.

The small holdings grew farther and farther apart until there was no sign of human habitation. Four boats hauling cargo upstream had passed them, hugging the west bank. Two were rowing, one was poling its way up a section of shallows, and one seemed to be moving upstream of its own accord, with what looked like a fisherman dangling bait in front of it. Eynon resolved to ask Merry for an explanation of the strange sight when she awoke.

Animals were unafraid of humans along this part of the river. Eynon saw four does and six fawns drinking on the shore upstream from a brown bear sow and her two cubs. A mother possum with more babies than Eynon could count clinging to her back was walking up a log leading from a stony beach to the wooded bank above. A raconette—probably a female from her larger size—was hanging upside down by her tail from a branch that extended over the river, a child's short throw away from Eynon. The raconette on his shoulder waved to the inverted female with one of his human hand-like paws and she waved back solemnly.

There were no signs of more thieves or kidnappers or narrow black eel-boat raiders. Eynon maintained his watch with his crossbow and extra quarrels in easy reach. He realized that Merry must have had a very good view of the water ahead from her raised vantage point. She could see rocks and obstructions sooner from here than he could from the bow, but she hadn't said a word. He was glad she'd given him a chance to feel useful on their journey.

"Hey," said Merry.

"Hello," said Eynon softly, pleased to hear her voice. "How's your head?"

"Still attached, I think."

She tentatively put two fingertips on her duck-egg bruise and winced.

"Stay quiet," said Eynon. "We're making good time downstream."

Merry sat up slowly, but remained seated on the deck. She moved her gaze from side to side like every degree of motion hurt.

"We're in the crown forest lands," she said. "They run for ten miles or so. There ought to be a royal hunting lodge coming up soon on the left."

"Should we stop there?" asked Eynon. "Would they have a hedge wizard who knows how to heal?"

"No, and no," said Merry, slowly. "Unless you want us to be forcibly enlisted in the king's army."

"I'd rather volunteer," said Eynon. "At some point in the future."

"I agree," said Merry. "The lodge should be busy processing venison. It takes a lot of supplies to feed a force in the field."

"So hug the east bank?" asked Eynon.

"Yes," said Merry. "Just don't run us aground."

Still seated, she touched the bruise on her skull again and checked her body for additional injuries.

"There's plain cider in the jug and dried cherries in the urn," said Eynon. "There are honey cakes, too, if you want them. See if you can drink or eat something."

"Cider sounds nice," said Merry. "My mouth is dry."

She had several swallows from the jug and licked her lips.

"Thank you," said Merry, lifting the jug toward Eynon. "That was exactly what I needed. You're a very considerate person."

"You'd do the same for me," said Eynon.

"I stand by what I said. Would you like some?"

"Just a taste."

Eynon took the jug from Merry and drank, then returned it to her. She had a few more sips, then stoppered it and put the jug on the deck. When she opened the urn with the dried cherries, the raconette jumped from Eynon's shoulder to Merry's lap and begged.

"*Chee chee chee chee!*" said the little beast.

Merry put a dried cherry into each of its tiny palms.

"*Cheeeee!*" said the raconette appreciatively.

"I think he has a name now," said Eynon.

"Chee-Chee?" asked Merry.

"That's too long for such a small creature," said Eynon. "I think we should call him *Chee.*"

"Chee," said the raconette definitively, and that was that.

After half a dozen more dried cherries had gone into Chee's mouth and Merry had her fill, she resealed the urn and broke a honey cake into three pieces. Chee stole two of them from her hand and surprised the humans by delivering one of the pieces to Eynon and keeping the other himself. Eynon nodded to Chee and said, "Thank you."

The raconette bobbed its head and said, "Chi-chee!" Then it returned to Merry's lap and curled up to nap. Merry shifted slightly and leaned her upper body against Eynon's legs, so she had a good view downriver. He liked having her close. Eynon spotted smoke ahead on the west bank and guided their boat to the east. Soon, they passed the lodge, pleased not to see anyone on its dock.

Probably all busy butchering deer, thought Eynon. They sat quietly together while the current swept them farther north. Without being told, Eynon recentered the boat in the middle of the river.

"I thought most of Dâron was safe for travelers," said Eynon. "Now it seems anything *but* safe."

"It *is* safe, mostly, or it has been," said Merry. "The king's muster must be seen as a license for lawlessness." She paused, then added, "At least by the men and women whose temperaments tend in that direction already."

"Why couldn't wars come every century, not every twenty years?" asked Eynon.

"So our grandchildren would have to fight them?"

Eynon had no response about either war or grandchildren. Eventually, he spoke.

"Where do we stop tonight?" he asked.

"There's a freeholder on the east bank who lets Applegarth crews stay in a small cabin on his land," said Merry. "He's put in a small dock next to it so we won't need to get our feet wet."

"That sounds good," said Eynon, "and better than staying in a tent."

"Didn't you *like* sleeping in a tent with me?" asked Merry.

"I don't really know," Eynon replied. "I don't recall that we did much sleeping—and you must be feeling better to tease me."

"I am," said Merry, "though my head still feels like it's caught between hammer and anvil."

"I'm sorry," said Eynon. "Is there anything I can do to help?"

"There's some willow bark in a red box down below," she replied. "And a small potion bottle from Doethan."

"You have a healing potion and you didn't tell me?"

"I'm sorry," said Merry, gently rubbing her bruise. "Something must have knocked it out of my head."

* * * * *

Merry held the steering oar while Eynon found the red box with the willow bark and potion in the storage area. He was assisted in that project by an inquisitive raconette. Eynon distracted Chee with half an apple and brought the box to Merry. When he took back the steering oar, she drank the potion in one gulp and washed it down with three generous swallows of cider.

"That's truly vile," she said, wiping her mouth.

"The strongest medicine tastes the worst going down," said Eynon as if he was reciting a lesson.

"That's a good one," said Merry. "You should write it down and compete with Ealdamon."

"It's not original," said Eynon. "I heard it from my grandmother. I think she was talking about fish liver oil."

"Your grandmother makes you drink that foul stuff, too?" asked Merry.

"Everyone's grandmother does," said Eynon. "Hmmm..."

"What?"

"If one of the estates on the Rhuthro presses fish liver oil, I could add that to the marshapples I'll be carrying to the Coombe, instead of our people having to buy their oil from peddlers."

"Wouldn't that make *you* a peddler?" asked Merry.

"True," said Eynon, "but I'd be a *local* peddler, not one of those untrustworthy fast-talking peddlers from Tyford or Brendinas."

"I can see your point," she said. "I'm sure my father can help you find a source for fish livers."

"So long as I don't have to press them myself."

"I agree," said Merry. "I'd rather wrestle a skunk."

They both smiled and sat in companionable silence as they floated north. Merry chewed a piece of willow bark from the red box, making faces from its astringent taste. The sun was going down, but a few hours of daylight and dusk still remained. Eynon noticed a tall, narrow tower ahead on the east bank at the end of a long spit extending out into the river.

"That's the Blue Spiral Tower," said Merry. "It marks the northern border of this section of crown forest lands." She leaned her head back against Eynon's knees and looked up at him. "It belongs to a powerful wizard, but she's not in residence very often from what I've heard."

"It looks well-constructed," said Eynon. "Have you ever been inside?"

He admired the way the tower's spiral of blue accent stones contrasted with the gray stone used for most of the structure. The blue stones circled up from the tower's broad base to its conical tip and the stones in the spiral stuck a few feet out from the tower's walls, like winding stairs.

Something about the structure made him feel warm all over—or maybe it was just Merry leaning against him.

"No," said Merry. "No one has. Wardens sometimes climb the spiral steps on the outside to scan for fires and poachers."

Eynon felt a curious desire to stop and ascend the tower all the way to the crenellated battlements at the top. *The view from up there must be spectacular,* he thought.

"The magestone in your amulet is blinking," said Merry. "I can see it through your shirt."

"It is?" asked Eynon. "What should I do about it?"

"There's not much you *can* do about it except be aware of it," said Merry. "I just hope it's not trying to warn us about danger ahead."

"I don't recall it blinking before we were attacked by the black boats," said Eynon.

"There is that," said Merry.

Chee stirred on Merry's lap and leapt up to Eynon's shoulder in two quick hops. The raconette scanned the horizon, ready to send up a warning cry if necessary.

"Do you think he understands what we're saying?" asked Eynon.

"I don't see how," said Merry. "He's probably reacting to our own anxiety."

"That must be it," said Eynon. He shifted his head to stare at Chee. "Look there—can you see his tail from where you're sitting?"

"Better than you can, I suppose," said Merry. "What about it?"

"It's not fluffy all the way around like a raccoon, or long and sinuous, like a wildcat. Chee's tail is bushy on top, but flat underneath."

"I see it," said Merry. "The bottom has ridges along it, and no hair."

"That must be why the female raconette I saw had such an easy time hanging from a branch," said Eynon.

"When was this?"

"On the east bank. When you were asleep."

"Oh, sorry," said Merry. "Maybe that's what they use when they want to steal *ripe* cherries."

"Could be," said Eynon.

His amulet stopped blinking when the tower disappeared from view behind them. They returned to watching the river, enjoying each other's presence without speaking. Chee made odd noises as he slept on Merry's lap that Eynon interpreted as the raconette's version of snoring.

"The freeholder's cabin is a mile or so north of here," said Merry. "I'm feeling a lot better after that potion. Trade places, please, and let me take the steering oar."

She started to get to her feet.

Eynon inspected the side of her head where the raised bruise had been. Now it was a smooth mark on the skin under her hair, only faintly purple.

"If you're feeling better," said Eynon.

"I am," said Merry. She got up from the deck and spit bits of willow bark over the side. Then she took another drink from the cider jug and ate a few dried cherries. She shared with Chee, who didn't seem unhappy about losing his comfortable napping spot.

"Want some?" she asked.

Eynon answered by opening his mouth, hoping Merry would feed him. Instead, Chee took four cherries from the open urn, climbed to Eynon's shoulder, and fed them to him one by one.

"He's a considerate little fellow," said Merry. She was close to laughing and so was Eynon.

"That he is," said Eynon. "Though I'd prefer it if *you* were the one feeding me."

"Maybe later," said Merry with a twinkle in her eye that signaled she really was feeling better.

He stood up from the navigator's bench and traded places with Merry. Instead of sitting down, he moved behind her and rested one hand on her upper arm. He liked feeling connected. Chee stayed on Eynon's shoulder. Then the raconette began to jump and point.

"That's it," said Merry, following Chee's finger. "There's our cabin."

Eynon saw a simple, one-story log structure with a shake roof set back under the trees. A patch of grass kept short, he assumed, by grazing deer, sloped down to a sturdy wooden dock. A dozen boulders as tall as Eynon blocked a portion of the current upstream from the dock, leaving a quiet pool behind them.

Those boulders looked like they've been dropped in place by erratic ice giants, thought Eynon. Similar stones sat in the middle of fields in the northern part of the Coombe and farmers had no choice but to plow around them. Eynon admired Merry's skill as she brought the boat up to the dock. He tied off the stern, then jumped down and walked along the dock to secure the bowline. That maneuver was much easier than trying to climb over four large barrels of hard cider. Chee found a perch on top of one of the piles supporting the dock and supervised.

Eynon and Merry removed packs, food, bedrolls and other essential supplies from the storage area under the stern deck and put them on the dock. After retrieving his pack, Eynon set the minor wards while Merry observed his technique. Chee seemed to sense their magic and didn't try to hop back on the ship, triggering the wards. Eynon considered that a good thing, since he didn't know how the raconette would react to baying hounds.

Before they left the dock to begin their walk to the cabin, Chee returned to Eynon's shoulder. A few moments later, a gray squirrel ran across their path and paused to chitter an angry protest at the newcomers invading its territory. The raconette wasn't intimidated, even though the squirrel was nearly the same size he was. Chee looked down from his raised vantage point next to Eynon's head and answered back forcefully with *"Ch-ch-ch-chee. Cha-chee!"*

The squirrel reversed course and ran back into the forest.

"That's telling him, my friend," said Eynon.

"Chee," agreed the raconette.

When they reached the cabin, Merry retrieved a cast iron key from a chink between two logs and opened the door. Then they entered and put down what they were carrying. It looked like a pleasant-enough place to spend the night.

Most of the right wall was a broad fireplace made from rounded river rocks. Half a cord of wood was neatly stacked close at hand, while a medium-sized cooking pot hung from a swinging arm, near where the fire would be when they lit one. A simple trestle table and a pair of benches sat half a dozen feet away from the fireplace and four straw-filled canvas mattresses were stacked on the floor by the cabin's left wall. A small oiled-cloth window was in the wall facing west, near the door.

Chee launched himself into the rafters and began exploring that part of the cabin while making soft clicking sounds.

"All the comforts of home," said Eynon.

"Your home, maybe," said Merry.

"What's missing?" asked Eynon. "I'm just a simple farm boy and don't know what a sophisticated Rhuthro-valley squire-reeve's daughter expects."

"We have a pump in our kitchen," said Merry. "It's the height of luxury—even though I have to pump it myself."

"So that's where you get your muscles," teased Eynon. "I thought it was from steering the boat."

"That, too," said Merry. She posed for him and flexed her right bicep. "Plus archery practice."

"Archery practice? Where's your bow, then?"

"I didn't bring my longbow," said Merry. "I only use it for hunting deer and didn't think I'd have the time for that this trip."

"I didn't bring my longbow, either," said Eynon. "I wanted to travel light on my wander year."

"And depend on the kindness of farmers' daughters?"

"Farmers' wives, anyway."

They laughed and exchanged a hug and a quick kiss.

"Fetch some water in the pot and I'll get a fire started," Merry instructed as she moved to the fireplace.

"Yes, dear lady," said Eynon. He didn't move.

"Alright, I deserved that," said Merry. "*Please* fetch some water. I think tonight will be cool, and I want to make soup."

"Glad to," said Eynon. "Where's the well?"

"The *water* is in the river," said Merry with a smile. "Mind you don't fall in."

"Yes, *dear*," said Eynon.

"And bring me some spring onions if you spot any."

* * * * *

The soup was hearty and filling. Venison jerky and dried peas soaked up the water nicely. Fresh marshapple root provided richness and bits of stale bread made it thick. Eynon had found spring onions, and their flavor gave the soup a tasty bite. Even Chee enjoyed the small cup they offered him, though he was more interested in dried cherries and another piece of honey cake.

Merry was looking tired after dinner, so Eynon encouraged her to sit at the table and enjoy the warmth of the fire. He cleaned the pot and their bowls in the river and split more firewood to replace what they'd use, to be fair to the next travelers to stay at the cabin. Merry had assured Eynon he didn't need to split wood, since her father paid for the use of the cabin and any wood they used with jugs of cider, but Eynon insisted.

When he returned, they each stood guard for the other for visits to the privy, then walked down to the riverbank to wash their hands. Once they returned to the cabin, Eynon moved two of the straw mattresses close—but not too close—to the fireplace and arranged their bedrolls. The oiled-cloth window near the door changed from reddish orange to black and the only light inside was the fire's warm glow. Merry cuddled next to Eynon and nestled in his arms. Chee curled up on top of Eynon's pack a foot closer to the fire.

"Thank you," said Merry.

"You're welcome, I think," said Eynon. "But for what?"

"For saving my life."

"They weren't going to kill us," said Eynon. "They wanted to collect bounties on us as conscripts."

"They wanted to steal four barrels of hard cider," said Merry, her eyes slowly closing involuntarily. "The bounties were an extra bonus."

Eynon gave her a gentle squeeze. "You were wonderful, holding off two of them at once," he said. "I got to fight my opponents one at a time."

"You did pretty well for a farm boy," said Merry.

"Farm boys are often underestimated."

"I'll have to remember that."

Eynon felt something odd, like someone was squeezing a finger on his left hand where it was pressing against Merry's back. He checked, and Chee was still sleeping.

"Hold on a minute," said Eynon.

He disengaged himself from their embrace and sat up. Merry did the same beside him. They could both see the plain gold ring on the middle finger of Eynon's left hand slowly pulsing. He took the ring off and held it up. It continued to pulse and vibrate.

"Open it up," said Merry. "It must be Doethan."

Eynon carefully tugged on two sides of the ring and marveled again as it expanded into a wide circle. Three chimes sounded and Doethan's face appeared inside the circumference.

"Are you safe?" the hedge wizard asked.

"Yes," said Merry, "but there's been more trouble on the river over the past two days than in the last five years combined."

"That's what I wanted to warn you about," said Doethan. "The king has summoned the levies. Gangs are kidnapping anyone that has a pulse or can fog a mirror, just to earn the king's bounty. Word is out every wizard of power must come to Brendinas to support the royal army. We're on the brink of war with Tamloch."

"That's old news to us," said Merry. She quickly filled her mentor in on what had happened since they'd left Doethan's tower.

"You were knocked unconscious?" exclaimed the wizard. They could see the concern on his face even as ripples flowed across his image.

"I'm fine," said Merry.

"She really is," confirmed Eynon, "thanks to your healing potion."

"That's a relief," said Doethan. "I was afraid she'd be too stubborn to use it."

Merry stuck her tongue out at Doethan and he raised one eyebrow in reply, then his concerned look returned.

"I'll have to talk fast—these connections are temperamental and only last for a limited time."

"We're listening," said Merry.

Eynon nodded his agreement.

"Where are you now?" asked Doethan.

"In Farnam's cabin," answered Merry.

Farnam must be the freeholder Merry had mentioned, thought Eynon.

"Good," said Doethan. "You haven't gone too far. You're not going to Tyford. There won't be a wizard left there by tomorrow afternoon. They'll all have left for Brendinas."

"Where do you want us to go?" asked Eynon.

"To the Blue Spiral Tower upstream," said Doethan. "I'm sure you saw it on the east bank."

"But what about my cargo?" asked Merry. "I've got to get it to my father's customer in Tyford. Taffaern won't be pleased if his cider doesn't arrive."

"Don't worry about that," said Doethan. "I'll send Old Taffy a letter and tell the old reprobate he'll have to keep selling that weak barley water he calls beer to his patrons instead. He'll understand."

"But I always do what I say..." Merry began.

"Please," said Doethan, his image wavering even more. "Go to the tower, not to Tyford. It's important—and it's not safe for you on the river."

"But..." said Merry.

Eynon squeezed Merry's hand. They exchanged a glance and Merry came around.

"What should we do when we get to the tower, sir?" he asked.

"Find the dock..." said Doethan. Words were lost as his image became less distinct. "...in the rock..."

Chee woke up and joined them, staring into the gold circle as it made rapid clicking noises much like the raconette's own vocalizations.

"...take the west gate..." said a voice that sounded less and less like Doethan's. "...hidden well..."

With three soft chimes, the image vanished. Chee began to mimic the circle's clicking noises until Merry stroked his fur and gently returned him to his spot on Eynon's pack.

Eynon pushed on the sides of the gold circle and it transformed itself back into a ring. Merry slid the ring back on the middle finger of Eynon's left hand. For a moment, they simply sat, overwhelmed. Then Merry spoke.

"Could you understand what Doethan was saying at the end? I know we have to go back to the wizard's tower."

"Right," said Eynon. "Find the dock in the rock."

"That sounds like a child's rhyme," said Merry.

"Yes, but not the second part," said Eynon. "I think I heard that we were supposed to take the well-hidden west gate."

"Maybe," said Merry. "We can try to remember more and figure it out while we sleep." She yawned.

"It's been quite a day," said Eynon. "I didn't think today would be *more* exciting than yesterday."

"Let's hope that trend doesn't continue tomorrow."

"Absolutely," said Eynon.

His brain was racing as he contemplated the challenges of breaking into a wizard's tower—even an unoccupied one. He was restless as he leaned back and tried to find a comfortable spot on his bedroll. Eynon didn't achieve that state until Merry was back in his arms and the two of them were cuddled together again. With Merry beside him, all was right with the world.

"Your heart's beating fast," said Merry. Her ear wasn't far from that organ.

"Yours isn't?" he asked.

"Listen," she said, pulling his head to her chest.

Eynon could hear her heartbeat, too. It was as fast as his. Merry moved his hand.

"You can feel it, too," she said. It felt very nice to feel Merry's heartbeat.

"I know something that could help us get to sleep," said Merry. She moved one of her hands down Eynon's body.

"Stop that," said Eynon without much conviction. "You were hit by the flat of a sword and knocked unconscious only a few hours ago."

"Doethan's healing potions are very powerful. I feel better than ever. Take it slow and we'll be fine."

"What about Chee?" asked Eynon.

"What about him?" replied Merry. "If he wants to watch, maybe he'll learn something."

* * * * *

They were both more relaxed and ready to sleep afterward. Merry was tucked in close, her lips by Eynon's ear. She whispered to him in a sleepy voice.

"Eynon?"

"What, dear lady?"

"Why did you say my father was a squire-reeve?"

"Huh," said Eynon softly. "You mean he's not?"

Maybe Merry's not that far above me after all, he thought.

"No," she said, snuggling closer. "He's a baron."

Chapter 12

"Plans change like the weather—and about as frequently."
— Ealdamon's *Epigrams*

Eynon woke before Merry and rekindled the fire. Chee opened an eye to watch him, then went back to sleep. *Sensible beast,* thought Eynon. Once a log began to burn and the cabin started to warm, Eynon visited the privy, then returned for the pot to fetch water. It would be a pleasure to have warm water to wash with, and it was past time for him to shave as well. Eynon was glad Merry hadn't protested that his beard stubble was scratchy.

It was cool as Eynon walked down the path. The surface of the river was covered in fog where warmer air met water chilled by melting snow. The sun was barely up and only animals—and Eynon—were stirring. He had a lot to think about—like Merry being a baron's daughter.

Why did they live in a house, not a castle, then? Eynon wondered. *And if Merry was the heir to a barony, how could she also be a wizard? That went against all custom.*

He filled the pot and put it on a large flat rock as tall as a table near the river. Eynon was surprised when he looked into the clear water and saw his reflection. In three days' time, his face had matured. It might have been his beard growing in, or it might have been that life beyond the Coombe aged him faster, he wasn't sure. Eynon promised himself he'd check again after he'd shaved, to see if his new, more mature look persisted.

Merry was still asleep when Eynon returned and hung the pot over the fire to heat. Chee had traded in his spot on top of Eynon's pack to curl beside Merry and didn't acknowledge Eynon's arrival.

Their food supplies were on the table—no need to hoist them overhead in the cabin—and Eynon reviewed what was available to see what he might turn into breakfast. There was a small sack of flour, leftover butter in the Flying Frog Farms crock, apples, dried cherries, a round of cheese and a small smoked ham.

He was confident he could turn those ingredients into a breakfast that would please Merry.

Eynon went out again and returned a few minutes later with a dozen green sticks as big around as his little finger and as long as his arm. He leaned them against the fireplace and stripped the bark from the last foot of their length. Eynon left the bark he removed by the fire to dry—it would make good kindling for the next visitors to use the cabin. He carried the trimmed sticks to the table, then dipped a mug in the warming water and placed it beside the sticks.

He opened the drawstring on the bag of flour and poured a generous portion into the clean bowl he'd used for his soup last night. A finger's width of butter, a pinch of salt, and a few dribbles of water joined the flour. Eynon stirred the mixture with a spoon to make a thick dough. When he was happy with its consistency, he turned the dough out onto the tabletop. He worked it with the palms of his hands, kneading it a few dozen times until it became elastic. Then he pressed it out until it was a mostly flat sheet.

He'd tried to keep his preparations quiet, but found a small observer was awake and interested in what he was doing. Chee squatted at the far end of the table and watched as Eynon used his knife to cut long strips an inch wide from the flattened dough. The raconette chittered softly as Eynon wound the strips in tight spirals along the bark-free ends of the sticks. When all the sticks were wrapped, Eynon coated the dough with more butter and carried them to the fire. He used three blocks of split wood to wedge them at an angle so the buttered dough was above glowing coals, not flames.

Chee was fascinated and jumped down to stare at the skewers as they cooked. Eynon remembered that raconettes, like raccoons, washed their food, but he didn't think they cooked it.

Keeping an eye on the dough—and Chee—Eynon returned to the table and put a handful of dried cherries into the remaining warm water in his mug, where he hoped they'd plump up nicely. He carefully peeled and cored one of the Applegarth apples and offered the leavings to Chee, who was glad to return to the table for the treat.

Eynon chopped the apple into the soup bowl, filling it with small, sweet chunks. He added a little cider to keep them moist.

While his knife was out, Eynon cut four generous slices from of the ham and did his best to do the same with the cheese, though it was less cooperative. He rolled the ham slices around the cheese and left them on the table while he checked on the dough.

He was in luck. Thanks to the butter, all the spirals were golden brown. Eynon removed them from their spot over the coals and encouraged each of them off their sticks and onto a wooden plate. He slid the rolled-up ham and cheese slices into four of the dough spirals and carefully spooned apples and dried cherries into the rest. The warm dough melted the cheese and filled the cabin with the homey scents of cooking meat and fruit tarts, of a sort. The enticing aromas woke Merry.

"Mmmm…" she said, as she stretched under her blanket, opened her eyes, and smiled at Eynon. "What's for breakfast?"

"Follow your nose and find out."

"Yes, dear," said Merry, as she stood. "I'll be back in a few minutes."

Merry was as good as her word. When she returned, she looked not only hungry, but much more awake. Her cheeks glowed and drops of water were in her hair.

"The morning is too foggy for you to look so bright," said Eynon.

"I stuck my face in the river," said Merry.

She tossed her hair, sending a fine mist in Eynon's direction.

"I'd prefer cider, not water with breakfast," he said, waving a ham and cheese spiral under Merry's nose.

"I'd prefer *that*," she said, snatching the spiral from his hand.

She took a bite, closed her eyes, and smiled.

"It's delicious," said Merry between mouthfuls.

Eynon teased a thread of cheese off her chin with a finger and Merry licked it off with her tongue.

"Try the fruit ones," he said, handing her another spiral.

Merry tasted one of the apple and cherry versions. Her eyes closed and the corners of her mouth turned up in pleasure.

"Mmmm…" she said. "Will you marry me?"

"I'll consider the idea," he said, smiling.

"If you won't necessarily marry me, will you keep cooking for me?"

"That's easier to answer," said Eynon. "I'd be glad to, when I have the opportunity."

"Good," said Merry.

She was about to say more but Eynon handed her another ham and cheese spiral and she decided eating was better than talking. Eynon picked up one of each type of spiral and nibbled on one, then the other.

"Where did you learn to cook?" asked Merry before she reached for another.

"From my mother and father," Eynon answered. "Isn't that how everyone learns to cook?"

"Men in the Rhuthro valley don't do a lot of cooking," said Merry. "They'll grill a venison steak when they're out hunting, but they tend to leave any more complicated cooking to women."

"Maybe the Coombe isn't as backward as people here seem to think, then," said Eynon. "Cooking skills are highly valued in prospective husbands in the Coombe."

"Sounds like I should plan to head west for my wander year if all the men in the Coombe are good cooks," said Merry. She grinned at Eynon.

"I thought you were going to spend your wander year learning magic from Doethan in his tower," said Eynon.

"After I pick out a husband," said Merry.

She gave Eynon a playful shove.

"A baron's daughter will have a lot of suitors to choose from," said Eynon more seriously.

"Stop that," said Merry. "A baron from the western marches isn't the same as a duke from a huge estate near Brendinas. There's no requirement for me to marry another noble. My father was a yeoman before the king made him a baron, for that matter. And my mother didn't have a title."

"Yes, dear *lady*," said Eynon. He put extra stress on the last word and bowed slightly.

"If you don't want me to throw one of these spirals at your head, you'll lose that attitude."

"That would mean more for me," said Eynon. He mimed catching a thrown spiral. "Forgive me. I'm trying to get used to Derry being a baron—and Mabli a baroness. Why don't you live in a castle instead of a farmhouse?"

"We *do* have a castle," answered Merry. "It's farther upriver."

"Oh," said Eynon softly.

"Da likes to spend time at Applegarth when he can," continued Merry. "He says it's more like where he grew up before he was made Baron of the Upper Rhuthro. He tells me doing his own chores helps him keep his head on straight."

"Your father seems like one of the wisest men I've ever met," said Eynon. "Maybe that's why?"

"It's a bit different when he's *your* father," said Merry, "but he's wise enough. He knows more than he says, which is one of the marks of wisdom."

"That sounds like another epigram, but I don't recognize it," said Eynon.

"I made it up," said Merry.

"Now who's trying to compete with Ealdamon?"

"If I was really as wise as Ealdamon, I'd tell you to hurry up. We need to get upriver to the Blue Spiral Tower."

"Right," said Eynon. "I guess I have a lot of rowing to do in the immediate future."

"Not necessarily," said Merry.

* * * * *

Eynon was surprised when Merry traded places with him and sat in the bow, while he guided the boat from the stern. The surface of the river was still covered with clumps of fog, like clouds descending to rest on the flowing water. Chee had found a warm spot on Eynon's lap and gone back to sleep. Eynon felt like a new man after a chance to clean up and wash with warm water. A shave had not removed his look of new-found maturity.

Merry was looping an arm's length cord around the crossbow bolt still embedded in one end of Eynon's staff. She tied a large teardrop-shaped blue crystal to the cord through a hole drilled in the tapered end and held it out in front of the boat.

Eynon was reminded of the vessel he'd seen heading upriver yesterday, where a person he thought might have been fishing was in a similar position.

"Shouldn't I be at the oars?" he asked.

"Shush," said Merry. "I need to concentrate."

She leaned toward the bow, reciting a spell and gesturing with one hand, while holding Eynon's staff tightly in the other. Soon, the blue crystal hanging in front of the prow began to glow.

It must be some kind of magestone, Eynon realized.

The boat moved toward the crystal and Merry guided their vessel in a full turn until the bow was pointed upstream. They were making good progress against the current, as if a dozen strong backs were pulling oars.

"You're *full* of surprises, aren't you?" said Eynon.

"Shush," Merry repeated. "Just steer. This isn't easy."

"Right," said Eynon.

He stayed quiet and watched for rocks as the boat was pulled briskly along by the magestone's magic. Merry continued to lean forward. She focused on the crystal for a few more minutes, then sat up and stretched.

"It's set now," said Merry. "We can talk."

"When were you going to tell me about *this* bit of magic?" asked Eynon.

"Probably never," said Merry. "I'm only supposed to use it in an emergency, since Da doesn't want to risk someone stealing it from me."

"I'm beginning to see that your father isn't the only one who knows more than he says," teased Eynon. "I saw another boat using something similar to head upstream yesterday while you were sleeping, and had meant to ask you about it."

"Several of the old families and merchant households have pull-stones," said Merry. "So do royal courier boats. They're not *too* uncommon, but they are valuable. I figured that our current circumstances counted as an emergency."

"I think you're right," said Eynon. "At this pace, we'll be at the Blue Spiral Tower in half an hour."

"Less time than that, I think," said Merry. "What should we do when we get there?"

Eynon thought for a few seconds then replied.

"Doethan said, 'Find the dock in the rock.'"

"Uh huh," said Merry.

"I think that means we need to search for some sort of opening in the rocks at the base of the tower," said Eynon. "Maybe there's an opening to some sort of chamber there with a place to tie up?"

"Perhaps," said Merry, "but I've never heard of anything like that at the Blue Spiral Tower."

"Do you have a better idea?"

"No," said Merry. "Should we start the search on the upstream rocks or the downstream ones, do you think?"

"Upstream," said Eynon. "It would be more convenient if boats could enter without fancy maneuvers."

"That makes sense," said Merry. "Let's hope there aren't any gamekeepers or fire wardens at the tower."

"It's been too wet for fire wardens to keep watch," said Eynon, "and from what you said about the king's army needing venison, I'd expect all the royal gamekeepers to be at that hunting lodge."

"I hope you're right," said Merry.

The boat sped south and soon Eynon saw the top of the Blue Spiral Tower through a gap in the fog.

"We're almost there," he shouted.

"Shhh!" said Merry. "Sound carries. Use the listening spell."

A few seconds later, after they'd both cast the spell, they could talk softly and still be heard along the length of the boat.

"I'll stay in the fog as much as I can," said Merry. "Once we get past the tower, swing us around and I'll bring us close to the rocks at its base."

"Understood," said Eynon.

The warm feeling he'd felt the last time they'd been near the tower had returned. A few minutes later, they were staring at the pile of mostly gray rocks at the tower's base. Most of them were huge—twice as tall as a man. Seeing them, Eynon could understand why the river hadn't undermined the foundations. The gigantic rocks were a few feet from Merry's face, though Eynon was farther back.

"I don't see any entrance," said Merry.

She turned back to look at Eynon.

"Your amulet is glowing."

Eynon glanced down. Blue light was radiating from the amulet, giving his face an unhealthy pallor in the fog. He looked up to inspect the rocks again and saw one of the largest boulders, to the right of the tower's base, had a thin blue line bisecting it.

"So it is," he said. Somehow, Eynon was sure he knew what to do next. "Tap my staff against that one," he said.

He pointed at the rock with the thin blue line. Merry gently tapped it with the end of Eynon's staff where the pull-stone was tied. They were both surprised when the massive stone divided on the blue line and the two halves slid aside, revealing a watery passage into the tower's foundations.

"Shall we?" said Eynon.

"What choice do we have?" asked Merry.

She used the pull-stone to direct their craft inside. As soon as the stern was past the entrance, the rock halves closed behind them. In the dim illumination filtering down from glowing balls of light on the high ceiling of the chamber, Merry could see stone docks on the right and left.

"Which side?" she asked, sounding less like her usual confident self.

"I don't know if it matters," said Eynon, "but if we have to choose one, let's go left."

"Right," said Merry.

They both smiled, breaking some of the tension.

Between Eynon's steering oar and Merry's pull-stone, the boat was soon tied to stanchions at the dock on the left. Beyond the dock on the right, Eynon could see broad niches with access to the water. *Storage for boats?* he wondered. His amulet was glowing even brighter, giving them more light to take in their surroundings. Chee had returned to his usual perch on Eynon's shoulder, but the little creature was uncharacteristically subdued.

"Well," said Merry. "We're in the *dock in the rock*. What else did Doethan tell us?"

"Take the west gate..." recited Eynon from memory. "It's hidden well..."

"We're on the west dock, anyway," said Merry. "Good choice, earlier."

"Thanks."

A passage with a tall, wide, rounded arch entryway led farther west, away from the dock. It was big enough for three canvas-topped traders' wagons side by side.

Eynon retrieved his hat, pack, water skin, crossbow, and some food from the boat. He hung the long, curved piece of shard across his back, blade down, attaching it to a leather cord using a pair of holes near the edge that might have once held rivets.

Merry put on her own pack and fashioned a similar sling for a smaller piece of shard, adding a bag with more food as well. She removed the pull-stone from Eynon's staff and put it away carefully. Then she returned his staff and collected a jug of hard cider from near the bow.

"Can you help me secure this on top of my pack?" asked Merry. "You never know when we might need a gift."

"Or a drink," said Eynon. "I'd be glad to." He lashed the heavy jug in place and admired his handiwork. "I hope you don't fall over backwards."

"So do I," said Merry. She leaned forward to restore her balance.

"I'd be glad to..." began Eynon, but he stopped when Merry stared at him with a look that said it would be unwise to complete his statement.

Chee chittered softly, but the sound echoed in the empty space. The raconette pressed against the side of Eynon's head and held on to his hair nervously.

"Easy there, fella," said Eynon. "We'll be careful."

"To the west gate?" asked Merry.

"West it is," said Eynon.

The three of them entered the arched passage. Glowing balls of light on the ceiling every twenty feet or so illuminated their path as they walked. The floors were surprisingly clean and there weren't any cobwebs in odd corners. It wasn't long before they reached a t-intersection. Huge, iron-banded oak double doors were directly ahead, while passages led off to the left and right.

"Where now?" asked Merry.

Eynon was surprised to see Merry deferring to him—he wasn't any more sure of what he was doing than she was, he imagined—but he tried to do his best to lead them.

"We're supposed to take the west gate," he said, "and through these doors is west. See if they're unlocked."

Merry pulled on the right-hand door. It didn't open, though it could have simply been too heavy to move.

"Let me try," said Eynon.

He tugged at the door on the right, then the door on the left, but they didn't budge. There didn't seem to be a lock and even if there was, they didn't have a key. Eynon stepped back.

"I don't see how we're going to go west if these doors won't open."

He tapped the center of the doors with the end of his staff and a blue glow flared from the amulet around his neck. Eynon and Merry had to step back quickly as the doors opened of their own accord, fitting themselves flat against the walls on either side.

"Well," said Merry. "I guess we're on the right track."

"I guess we are," said Eynon.

They continued into a circular room on the same giant scale. It was lit by a much larger glowing ball in the center of its domed ceiling that stretched up three times as high as Eynon was tall. An animated broom danced past them as they entered, followed by a black circle on the floor the size of a dinner plate that trailed behind like a well-trained pet. The pair turned left and were soon out of sight.

Chee set off a series of high-pitched noises that were almost as disconcerting as the broom and its companion. Eynon stroked the little raconette with his free hand until the beast calmed down.

"At least now we know why the place is so clean," said Merry. "I wouldn't mind having a magical broom like that back at Upper Rhuthro Keep."

Eynon filed Derry's castle's name away in his memory for later.

"I understand the broom," said Eynon, "but what was the black circle, I wonder?"

Merry gave him a look that was easy to interpret as *you're an idiot.*

"Don't you see?" she asked. "It's a dustpan."

Eynon shook his head, accepting that he'd missed the obvious, and turned his attention to the room. It was about fifty feet across, and most of that was filled with a low circular stone wall enclosing a broad opening in the floor. With Merry by his side, he crossed to the wall and looked down to see a deep pit. Blue stone steps went around the opening in a spiral, like the stones that wound around the outside of the tower above them. There was a gap in the wall where the steps began.

"Want to bet we're directly below the center of the tower?" asked Merry.

"I don't know much about magic," said Eynon, "but I'd agree. There's a certain symmetry to repeating what's above down below."

"So where's the west gate?" asked Merry.

"It's hidden well," said Eynon.

"Or maybe, it's a hidden well," said Merry.

"That seems like something a wizard would do," said Eynon. "Down we go?"

"After you," said Merry.

She extended her hand to indicate Eynon should go first down the stone steps. He didn't want to disappoint Merry, so he began his descent. At least it wasn't dark—the glowing ball on the ceiling gave off plenty of light and Eynon's amulet was nearly as bright.

"Lean into the wall," said Eynon. "There aren't any railings."

"Yes, *mother,*" said Merry.

Chee was back to clutching Eynon's hair, but Eynon didn't mind—he was focused on not falling.

After seven full turns of the spiral, they were at the bottom. A soft blue light from the lowest row of stones supplemented the light from above and Eynon's amulet.

Merry had been right. There was a well—or at least a wide pool of water—at the bottom, enclosed by another low wall. There wasn't any bucket or windlass, though. It would be a long walk back up seven turns of steps to haul water, assuming the tower's kitchens were at the level of the docks.

"Now what?" asked Merry.

"I don't know," said Eynon.

He fingered the plain gold band on the middle finger of his left hand. "Should we try to ask Doethan?"

"I don't know if even magic can reach through all this stone," said Merry. "Let's rest and have a snack and think first."

"That's a very good idea," said Eynon. "Exploring a wizard's tower is hard work."

"We haven't even gotten into the tower itself, I expect," said Merry. "We're still underneath it."

"Close enough," said Eynon.

They took off their packs and Eynon helped Merry set out strips of venison jerky, two leftover fruit spirals from breakfast, and one of the Applegarth apples on the low wall around the well.

Chee finally relaxed enough to release his grip on Eynon's hair and climb down to sit on his haunches next to the apple. Eynon was impressed that the raconette was patient enough to wait for them to share their food.

He pulled his knife from his belt and cut the apple in wedges, leaving a neat cylindrical core. Eynon put the core on the wall to deal with later. Chee got three apple wedges, but still looked hungry.

Eynon and Merry felt revitalized after having something to eat and taking sips of water from Eynon's goatskin.

Merry was repacking her gear by the outer wall of the chamber, while Eynon, who had already shouldered his pack, was standing next to the well. He picked up his staff to see if the combination of his staff and the blue amulet would help him come up with a solution like they had at the oak doors above.

Chee eyed the apple core, and Eynon smiled. The raconette was welcome to it.

A loud bang from above startled them.

Someone must have opened the doors, thought Eynon.

A strong wind swirled down around them, tipping the apple core into the well. Chee followed, trying to intercept it. The little beast vanished into the water.

Without thinking, Eynon jumped in after him.

Then he was suddenly elsewhere.

PART TWO

Chapter 13

"The journey of a thousand miles begins with a single step."
— Lao Tzu

To his surprise, Eynon wasn't wet—but he *was* cold. There was thick snow on the ground where he had landed. White-topped blue mountains higher than he'd ever known rose on the near horizon. Four tall alabaster pillars striped with blue spirals stuck out from the snow, defining a large square around him.

Wizards must mean something different by the word "gate" than most people, thought Eynon as he stood and brushed snow from his legs.

He felt disoriented and a bit light-headed, like it was hard to catch his breath. Chee jumped up from a mound of snow and burrowed inside Eynon's jacket, for warmth or protection or both, he wasn't sure. The apple core sat abandoned on the cold ground. Merry was nowhere to be seen. Eynon called her name, but heard no reply.

One thing at a time, thought Eynon. *It's freezing here. I should probably get my cloak from my pack—and I have to find shelter before I can do anything to find Merry.*

He surveyed his surroundings. Plumes of smoke rose in the distance from many points of the compass and there was a strange, unpleasant smell in the air. He considered what it might be—then it came to him.

"Rotten eggs," he said aloud.

His breath condensed in puffs of cold when he spoke.

In the distant background was a sound Eynon couldn't identify. It was something like wind through leaves, but the only trees nearby were pines and firs. The sound didn't rise and fall like wind, though. It was steady. Chee stuck his head out of Eynon's jacket. The little raconette wrinkled his nose and immediately retreated back inside.

Eynon stroked Chee through the quilted fabric of his jacket. He spotted something blue in the distance.

"There's a lake to the east, beyond those trees," he told his small companion. "Maybe we should try heading that way to find shelter?"

"Or you could follow me to get warm," said a new voice.

Eynon looked behind him and saw an old man with a kindly face wearing a heavy coat of some sort of brown fur, thick gloves, and a hat that looked like it was made from a beaver pelt. He carried a gnarled walking stick and was much shorter than Eynon, with some odd constructions made from sinew and bent wood attached to his feet.

"Yes, thank you," said Eynon. He rubbed his hands together to keep his fingers from freezing. "Warm would be good."

"Excellent," said the man. "You certainly don't appear to be dressed for the weather."

When Eynon looked at the older man's eyes more closely, he could see well-hidden sadness. He wasn't sure if he should be worried or reassured.

The man turned and set off to the north. Eynon moved slowly, noticing the attachments on the other man's feet helped him walk on top of the snow instead of breaking through with every step. The man looked back.

"Come along, then," he said. "I'm Damon. Follow me."

Without any better options, Eynon stayed close behind, trudging his way through the snow for at least half a mile. Chee stayed safely snuggled inside Eynon's coat, far warmer than he was.

"Where are we going?" asked Eynon. He kept his eyes on his path to find the best places to put his feet.

Damon looked up and pointed ahead. Eynon lifted his gaze and saw the upper portion of a castle larger than the earl's fortress at Rhuthro Keep rising above the trees to the north. It had two tall towers—one broad and solid, the other thin and delicate—showing themselves above the castle's imposing outer walls.

"Oh," said Eynon.

One of the towers looked familiar. It was slender and gray, with a spiral of blue stones winding to its top.

"I've seen a tower like the slender one before," said Eynon. "It looks like the Blue Spiral Tower on the Rhuthro."

The man he was following sighed loud enough for Eynon to hear.

Eynon pressed on. "Is it the same wizard's *summer* residence? I can't see why anyone would *want* to live here in the winter, it's so cold."

"Perhaps you should wait to form conclusions until you have more information," said Damon over his shoulder. He now sounded more amused than displeased. "I'm sure the Master will allow me to tell you *something.*"

"The Master?" asked Eynon.

"The Master Mage," said Damon. "That is why you're here, isn't it? To learn wizardry?"

"Yes, sir. Thank you, sir. I expect I *am* here to learn to be a wizard." Eynon hadn't realized just how *much* he wanted to to learn wizardry until that second.

"The Master knows what it takes to train strong wizards," said Damon, pausing to allow Eynon time to catch up. "There's not a better place to learn wizardry in all the world than here."

They continued on together. Damon took small steps and led them to a narrow path where the snow wasn't very deep, as if most of it had melted away.

"That sounds wonderful, sir," said Eynon, glad to be out of the knee-deep snow. "I want to learn."

"Good," said Damon. "Like you, I am also a student of wizardry."

"But you're so..." began Eynon.

"*Old?*" asked Damon. Then he laughed, sending clouds of crystals into the air around his head. "Not everyone comes to wizardry when they're young. I started late. I've been studying for many years and still have much to learn. Part of my training is teaching new apprentices."

Eynon wondered how long Damon had been studying. He didn't want to be an apprentice for twenty years. And he needed to find Merry.

"Excuse me, sir," said Eynon, trying to think about something less troubling than spending more years than he'd already been alive learning wizardry. "Where *are* we?"

"You're in Melyncárreg," said Damon. "That's the name for the land hereabouts, not the Master's castle. We call that the Academy, and the trees around it are the groves of Academe."

"But the groves are across the Ocean in Athica, where wizardry started," blurted Eynon. "I read about them in Robin Oddfellow's *Peregrinations.*"

"You're already a student, I see," said Damon, nodding. "That's very good. The Master named his school in honor of the one founded by the Most Ancient Masters."

"Oh," said Eynon.

He swiveled his head as they walked.

"Everywhere I look I see smoke rising," said Eynon. "Are there lots of settlements in the area?"

Damon smiled.

"No," he said. "Those aren't hearth fires, they're *cuddio tân,* the hidden fires from deep in the earth, escaping to the surface wherever they can. There's a great fiery cauldron below the ground we stand on."

"Is that why the snow isn't as thick along this path?" asked Eynon.

"Excellent," said Damon. "You've got the beginning of wisdom already and know the importance of studying books *and* your surroundings. I think the Master will find you an acceptable candidate."

Damon's words were disconcerting. Eynon didn't know what was involved in being chosen as a wizard's apprentice. Merry had already been selected as one by Doethan, but things could be a lot different here in Melyncárreg. Then he realized Damon hadn't answered his question.

"Are the *cuddio tân* the reason why the snow isn't as thick along this path?"

Their guide laughed again, loud enough for his voice to echo back to them.

"The Master likes his apprentices to be stubborn," he said. "It's a prerequisite for learning wizardry."

"Sir," said Eynon, trying once again to get an answer. "Are the *cuddio tân* the reason why the snow isn't as thick along this path *and* why it smells like rotten eggs here?"

"Yes, and yes," said Damon with a grin.

"I thought so," said Eynon. "There's a vent in the ground near Wherrel, a village near a quarry back where I'm from, and it smells like that sometimes."

"Is there now?" asked Damon, rubbing his chin. "It smells of sulphur all the time here, except when the wind is strong. You'll get used to it."

Eynon thought it would take him a long time to ignore the smell, but he didn't comment. Damon looked like he'd been in Melyncárreg for decades.

"Are there many students here?" he asked. He was taking in the size of the Academy—it seemed large enough to house an army.

"No," said Damon. "They've all gone east to Brendinas to answer the king's summons, except for Nûd, of course."

"Nûd?" asked Eynon.

"The Master's assistant," said Damon. "He sees to the Master's wishes and keeps things running smoothly."

"I'm sure it will be a pleasure to meet him," said Eynon.

"Once you have, you may be less sure," said Damon.

Eynon shook his head from side to side. Everything was strange in Melyncárreg. As they continued to walk toward the castle the sound of wind through leaves grew louder. Eynon finally identified it.

Idiot, thought Eynon. *It's not rustling leaves—it's running water.*

"Is there a river nearby?" he asked.

"There is," said Damon. "You'll spot it soon enough."

The rushing water sound intensified until it was even louder than the Rhuthro speeding through the Gap. Before them, the ground became more open and sloped up toward the castle. Eynon focused his attention on where he placed his feet and increased his pace.

"Not so fast," said Damon.

He held Eynon back with his walking stick—then he used the stick to point ahead. Eynon gasped when he saw why. A deep valley, a chasm, really, was directly ahead. Its walls were bright yellow in the sunlight, daubed with shades of red and pink and blue and orange.

Guided by the sound of rushing water, Eynon turned to the left. A broad waterfall, taller than the baron's keep in Caercadel, splashed down with a roar into a fast-flowing white river. Collections of polychromatic water droplets danced like steam above it.

Eynon's eyes went wide as they tried to take in everything at once, moving from the waterfall to the river to the spectacular colors of the cliffs across from him.

"It's magnificent," he said, finally finding his voice.

Damon was chuckling.

"It is at that, isn't it, lad," said the older man with a hint of a grin. "I always like to bring newcomers this way. Be thankful it's still winter. In the summer, you'd have flies buzzing around in your open mouth."

"Thank you," said Eynon.

"You're welcome," said Damon. "I had the same reaction the first time *I* stood on this spot." He started to walk northeast, toward the castle. "Come along now—there are more impressive things to see ahead. Melyncárreg is *full* of wonders and I don't want you to freeze to death."

"Yes, sir," said Eynon.

He reluctantly left the lovely scene and followed Damon along a snow-free path that led along the high cliffs on this side of the river. Soon, they were directly opposite the castle. Its gray stone walls were a marked contrast to the yellow cliffs of the river valley marked with splashes of bright colors. Ahead of them was a rope bridge wide enough for a wagon to cross. It was firmly anchored to both cliffs and had a gentle curve in the center as it dipped into the valley.

To the right, Eynon could hear more rushing water. Clouds sparkled on the river's surface, with the sunlight creating dozens of small, shifting rainbows around them.

"Is there another waterfall in that direction?" Eynon asked.

"There is," said Damon. "It's even taller."

"Can we see it?" he asked.

"All in good time," said Damon. "Now we need to get you warm."

Chee stuck his head out of Eynon's jacket and chirped at Damon.

"Both of you," said Damon in a teasing voice.

The shock of everything that had happened was beginning to wear off and Eynon was feeling the cold. A warm fire and a hot drink—or a meal—would be welcome. From the angle of the sun, it seemed earlier here than when he and Merry had entered the Blue Spiral Tower on the Rhuthro. He was hungry again, even though he could tell it was still just an hour or so past sunrise here.

"Are we near the Rhuthro valley?" asked Eynon as they crossed the rope bridge. Walking across it felt a little like riding in a coracle.

"There's near and there's *near*," said Damon. "We're closer to the Rhuthro valley than we are to the stars, but farther than Tyford to Brendinas."

"You could just say, 'I don't want to tell you,'" said Eynon.

"There's nothing enigmatic about *that*," said Damon. "Pay attention and we'll have *you* talking like a wizard in short order."

"Perhaps," said Eynon.

"See?" said Damon. "You've already started."

Two hundred yards ahead and up a gentle slope, a three-story portcullis guarded the main entrance to the castle. It was shut and packed snow reached up to the lower crossbars. It didn't look like the gate had been used recently.

The older man put his arm around Eynon's shoulder and walked him around to a stout wooden door in the castle's wall sixty paces to the left, well back from the portcullis. Damon banged a series of sharp knocks on the door with his walking stick.

"Open up, Nûd, you slug-a-bed," he shouted. "We have a new one for the Master to train."

Damon rapped again and soon the heavy thick door began to open.

"It's too cold to move fast this morning," said a voice like rusty iron hinges from the other side of the door. "I was drinking mulled wine by the side of the fire and I had to put my boots on."

"The Master doesn't pay you to sit and drink," said Damon. "He pays you to work."

"He pays me, but there isn't a tavern or market within two thousand miles to spend my wages in," grumbled the voice, which must belong to Nûd, Eynon supposed.

The door continued to open with the speed of pouring honey in midwinter.

From the sound of Nûd's voice, Eynon expected him to be a short, wizened old man with a face like a gnarled tree root.

Instead, Nûd was young, not more than five years older than Eynon. He was a giant, a head taller than Eynon with shoulders broad enough to nearly fill the doorway. Nûd was wearing a white canvas apron over a saffron-colored linen shirt and blue-plaid braies. His dark hair and most of the front of his body were dusted with flour.

"Come in, come in," said Nûd once he'd spotted Eynon. "Don't let the heat escape. I've made ale-cakes and they should be coming out of the oven in a few minutes. You have time to wash up before breakfast."

Eynon was taken aback by Nûd's size and manner. His friendly words contrasted with his raspy voice, but Eynon finally remembered his manners.

"I'm Eynon of Haywall, from the Coombe," he said with a small bow. "Thank you for your hospitality."

"As Damon must have told you, I'm Nûd," said the giant.

"Don't thank him for his hospitality until you've tasted his ale-cakes," said Damon.

"I'm sure the fire will be warm, no matter how Nûd cooks," said Eynon.

"An astute observation," said Nûd. "And a diplomatic one. Pay no attention to Damon. He's been here for years and still has a lot to learn."

"The Master will deal with you later," said Damon, smiling. "Come along," he said to Eynon. "I'll show you where to wash."

"Thank you, sir," said Eynon as he followed the older man inside the castle. Damon took off his oversized shoes for walking on snow and leaned them against a wall. Then he took off his fur coat, revealing a stained and worn dark blue tunic underneath. He hung his coat on a nearby peg and led Eynon down a flight of stone stairs into what was obviously a well-outfitted kitchen.

"He's polite," said Nûd, mostly to himself as he rubbed flour off his chin, then shoved the oak door closed. "I wonder how long that will last?"

Eynon was wondering why it was time for breakfast in Melyncárreg, when it was almost time for lunch back in the Rhuthro valley. He didn't really know where he was or how he could get back to Merry. Then he realized it might make more sense to figure out how to help Merry come here, since that had seemed to be the intent of Doethan's instructions.

He inhaled. A somewhat-off smell of baking ale-cakes struck his nostrils despite the omnipresent odor of rotten eggs in the air. He was warming up in the hot kitchen, thanks to the fire cheerfully burning in the room's large hearth. Breakfast would do as well as lunch to fill his stomach.

Chee made his way to his usual perch on Eynon's shoulder. The little raconette seemed entranced by the smell of ale-cakes and the prospect of hot food. Chee emitted soft *chi-chi-chi-chee* noises while he sat on the edge of a soapstone sink and washed his hands alongside Eynon and Damon.

Warm and clean, Eynon sat on one side of a long trestle table across from Damon. His pack was on the stone floor between his feet and his staff was leaning against a nearby wall. Nûd sat on an extra-sturdy bench at the end. He'd delivered a pan of hot ale-cakes that joined a small crock of butter and a tub of some kind of blue fruit preserves in front of Eynon and Damon. Links of odd-looking sausage sizzled on a metal platter and polished hardwood plates were in front of each man. Pewter mugs held what smelled like cider. A small saucer was placed next to Eynon's plate for Chee.

"Let's eat," said Nûd.

He offered a two-tined fork to Eynon. Then he held a similar fork in one hand and his eating knife in the other.

Eynon removed his own eating knife and picked up the offered fork to emulate Nûd.

"I'm sure it will all be delicious," said Eynon.

"Don't get your hopes up," said Damon.

Chapter 14

"Surely, I said, knowledge is the food of the soul."
— Plato

Eynon loved to make ale-cakes. They were simple to prepare, with only four ingredients: flour, some sort of fat—like lard, tallow, bacon grease, or butter—salt, and ale-barm to make them rise.

Good ale-cakes were round, the diameter of a beer mug, and as thick as two fingers, with golden brown tops. These were ragged rectangles the size of Eynon's palm and over five fingers thick. Their burnt tops made them look more like bricks of charcoal than ale-cakes.

Eynon scraped most of the char off an ale-cake, then split it and buttered the remains of the upper half. He put some of the blue preserves on the lower half and speared a sausage with his knife. With feigned enthusiasm, he tasted the buttered portion. It was terrible—like rotten-egg-flavored sawdust. Damon had been right. Eynon shouldn't have gotten his hopes up. He tried his best to chew and swallow without revealing his distaste, but wasn't successful.

"I told you," said Damon.

The older man stuffed a large piece of ale-cake in his mouth and swallowed without chewing.

"It's easier to eat if you don't leave it in your mouth very long," he said.

Eynon grimaced and Nûd shook his head sadly.

"I try to make everything at least palatable," said the huge young man, "but never seem to manage."

Chee hopped down from Eynon's shoulder, sat in front of the small plate, and waited while Eynon broke off bits of ale-cake and an inch-long slice of sausage. Nûd produced a child-sized clay cup and filled it with cider for the raconette. As it turned out, Nûd needn't have bothered. The animal sniffed at the food and the cider and turned up his nose. Chee jumped from the table, exploring the kitchen in search of something more edible.

"There's a bowl of apples in the pantry," said Nûd, pointing toward an open door. "You can have *one.*"

The raconette eagerly ran to the place Nûd had indicated.

It was time for Eynon to try another taste. With a resolute expression, Eynon bit off a piece of ale-cake coated in blue preserves. He nearly spit it out, it was so bad. The blue preserves had an astringent taste combining sour cherries, hot peppers, and alum. He closed his eyes and swallowed, following Damon's example. It helped, a little. Eynon took a gulp of cider to wash it down. Unfortunately, the liquid was just this side of vinegar. It didn't help counteract the taste of the ale-cake or the preserves. His face showed his reaction.

Nûd and Damon nodded sympathetically.

"Sorry," said Nûd. "The sulphur in the air and water affects how everything tastes."

"Isn't there anything you can do to make it better?" asked Eynon. "Couldn't you use magic or something?"

"A trained wizard could bring in dishes from the finest inns in Brendinas," said Nûd, "but the Master seems to think eating my food teaches apprentices self-control."

"The Master can think again as far as I'm concerned," said Eynon.

Damon snorted and went back to eating mechanically. Nûd shrugged his massive shoulders and turned up his open palms in a *what can I do about it* expression.

"I'm going to cook my own meals, if you don't mind," Eynon continued.

"Please do," said Nûd. "You can cook for all of us."

"It can't be much worse than this," observed Damon. He drained his mug and wiped his mouth off with the back of his hand to hide his grimace.

"Fine," said Eynon. "Could you show me around the kitchen and the larder when we're finished?"

"Certainly," said Nûd. "Then I can take you to your cell."

"Excuse me?" Eynon asked. "Is this a school, or a prison?"

"Calm down," said Damon. "Students' rooms are known as *cells* and have been for decades. It's a custom."

"Oh," said Eynon. He resolved to keep a closer watch on his tongue until he gained a better understanding of how things were done in the Academy and continued his questions.

"Where are the other students?" he asked. "And when will I meet the Master?"

"You'll meet the Master when the Master wants to meet you, and not before," said Damon. "I've already told you that every half-way trained wizard or hedge wizard left for Brendinas in response to the King's summons."

"My apologies," said Eynon. "You did."

He pushed a link of sausage around on his plate, trying to muster the courage to taste it. To postpone the ordeal, he asked another question.

"How many people are left in the castle, then?" He was curious to learn how large a group he'd be cooking for and assumed that Nûd had fixed a special late breakfast for the three of them.

"Just us," said Nûd.

"The three of us?" asked Eynon. "And the Master?"

"Don't worry about the Master," said Damon. "He has his own ways of getting fed."

"Does he travel to inns in Brendinas to get decent meals?" Eynon joked.

"Sometimes," said Damon.

"But he never takes me with him," said Nûd in a tone that Eynon wasn't sure was teasing or serious. Eynon assumed the former and smiled at Nûd, receiving a smile in return.

Damon leaned back on his bench then reversed course and put his elbows on the table, cupping his chin in his joined hands. He stared at Eynon. Eynon returned his gaze.

"Do you think he'll do?" Damon asked Nûd without turning his head.

"Does it matter as long as he's willing to cook?" Nûd replied.

"True enough," said Damon. "I can already sense magic about him."

Across from Damon, Eynon sat up straight and held his head high. For some reason he didn't pull out the amulet with the blue stone, even though his original mission had been to take the artifact to a wizard to get his assistance. He was afraid Damon or Nûd or the Master would take the amulet away from him, and he didn't know if he'd need it to try to reach Merry. Besides, Damon was still an apprentice—if a rather old one.

After a few seconds more, while it felt like Damon was looking into him, not just at him, Eynon decided it was time to move on.

"What's next?" he said.

Nûd and Damon exchanged a glance and smiled.

"Next, you help me clean up, then I'll show you how to find your cell," said Nûd.

Chee reappeared on top of the trestle table with apple cores in each front paw.

"I said *one,*" said Nûd.

"Chi-cheee," said the raconette, apparently defending itself.

"I know they're small," said Nûd, "but please don't abuse our hospitality."

"Chee," said Chee contritely.

The raconette ran up Nûd's right arm, crossed behind his head, and jumped from Nûd's broad left shoulder to his usual perch on Eynon's narrower one.

"When you've seen your cell, you can meet me in the library and start your training," said Damon.

"Won't the Master be training me?" asked Eynon.

"No," said Damon. "I'm responsible for the first stages of training for all new apprentices. It's supposed to teach me patience."

"Patience is a virtue the Master says Damon really needs to work on," said Nûd.

"Quiet, you," said Damon.

"See what I mean?" teased Nûd.

"Before we get up," said Eynon, "I've got another question."

"Ask," said Damon. "I doubt I could stop you."

"If there aren't many students—or teachers, for that matter— why is the Academy so big?" Eynon asked. "It's as large as the fortifications for the Earl of the Rhuthro valley, but I don't see very many people inside or outside."

Nûd answered, not Damon.

"First," said the big man, "the Master is the most powerful wizard in all of Orluin. Important wizards need impressive strongholds."

"Wizards need towers, not castles," said Damon. "We've been over this before."

"Yes," said Nûd, "but here in the wilderness, a castle provides much-needed defense."

"Defense from what, if there aren't any people nearby?" asked Eynon.

"Wolves, bears, coyotes, mountain lions..." began Damon in a bored tone, like he'd had this conversation many times before.

"...and the odd gryffon or wyvern or dragon," added Nûd with more animation.

"Not to forget annoying herds of wisents, moose, elk, and pronghorn," added Damon.

Something connected in Eynon's brain.

"Was your coat made from a wisent skin?" he asked Damon. "I saw one that wandered into the Coombe through the gap at Wherrel and it had the same dark fur around its head."

"It was," answered Damon. "You've asked enough questions for now. It's past time for you to clean up, find your cell, and start your lessons."

"Was there a two?" asked Eynon as he stood.

"A two?" asked Nûd.

"You said *First*—was there a *Second?*"

"Defense from wildlife *was* second," said Nûd.

"Then was there a third or fourth?" asked Eynon.

"At one time there were more students and apprentices than there are now," said Nûd. "When Dâron and Tamloch and the Eagle People were at war, the Academy was bustling. That's third."

"Now that we're at war again, maybe things will be busier here," said Eynon.

"Maybe," said Nûd. "If the war drags on."

"Don't they always," muttered Damon.

"And fourth?" prompted Eynon.

"Fourth," said Nûd, "is that sometimes the Academy is used for meetings of the Conclave of Wizards, with every practicing mage in the kingdom attending."

Eynon was glad he'd started this line of questions.

"Is there a fifth, like where Melyncárreg *is* and how far away it is from the Rhuthro valley?" Eynon asked, pressing his luck.

"It's time to clean up," said Damon. "Get moving so you can clean up, find your cell, and start your lessons."

"And start cooking lunch," said Nûd.

"Yes, sirs," said Eynon.

"Cleanup first," said Nûd. "You wash, I'll dry."

* * * * *

Eynon didn't start his lessons until *after* lunch. By the time he and Nûd had dealt with the breakfast dishes and the big man had shown Eynon the available cooking utensils and the contents of the larder, it had been past mid-morning. It took still more time for Nûd to escort Eynon to his room. Eynon was reluctant to call it a cell, despite Nûd's insistence.

Unpacking took very little time. Eynon determined he didn't need to carry the shard across his back. He expected the threats inside the Academy would be to his preconceptions, not his body. If he ventured outside again, with the wolves and the wisents, he'd retrieve the weapon. Reluctantly, he left his staff in a corner of the room. Like the shard, it didn't seem appropriate to keep it with him indoors. It was cool inside the castle, so he kept his jacket on.

Nûd showed Eynon how to find his way around the castle, only part of which was technically the Academy. The school itself was an L-shaped collection of buildings to the left of the main entrance, tucked up tight against the castle's outer wall. The kitchens were below ground, which curiously helped them stay cooler in summer and warmer in winter, according to Nûd.

Understanding the layout of the castle and the Academy was made easier by a scale model in a room near the library. It didn't include labels, but it showed top-down views of each level for all the fortifications and buildings except the gray and blue spiral towers. Eynon promised himself he'd come back soon and commit the model to memory.

"We've taken too much time touring," said Nûd. "Let's head back so you can fix us lunch, then you'll have the whole afternoon for your first lessons in wizardry."

Eynon didn't mention that Merry had already started his education in the magical arts.

"Great," he replied.

When they returned to the kitchen, Eynon got a fire going so it would burn down to cooking coals by the time he was ready. He found a deep glazed-ceramic vessel that looked like an upside down bell. With Nûd's help, Eynon filled it with water from the pump near the sink. The water smelled strongly of rotten eggs. Chee left Eynon's shoulder and found a perch in the rafters where he could see what was going on without having to smell it too closely.

"Do you have a wooden whisk?" asked Eynon.

Nûd produced an implement that looked like a big shaving brush. Eynon began whipping the water vigorously, beating it into a froth. The rotten egg smell increased.

"Could you help with this?" Eynon asked Nûd.

"I have no idea what you're doing, but I'd be glad to," said Nûd.

The big man applied the whisk with a will and the sulphur smell grew even stronger. After a few minutes, Nûd's arm grew tired. Chee descended from the rafters and did his part wielding the whisk and creating lots of bubbles. When the raconette grew tired, Eynon took the bowl and held it up to Nûd's nose.

"Sniff," he said.

Nûd inhaled.

"It doesn't smell nearly as much like rotten eggs anymore," said the big man.

"I used a trick I learned from my cousin in Wherrel, back in the Coombe," said Eynon. "It was his job to beat their cooking water before meals."

"I never would have thought of that," said Nûd.

"I wouldn't have either, if my cousin's family hadn't figured it out for themselves," said Eynon. He found a large onion and a bunch of white carrots and began to chop them into small pieces. "What else do you have we could use to make soup?" Eynon asked.

"I have dried beans and dried peas," said Nûd. He fetched small canvas bags for Eynon.

"Thanks," said Eynon. "Do you have any smoked meat?"

"There's half a smoked wisent haunch in the cold pantry," said Nûd.

"Please bring me about a pound of it," said Eynon.

"Glad to."

The big man walked away to fetch the meat. Eynon found a dozen andirons and thick cast iron skewers by the fire. He cleaned them as best he could with sand and a mail scrubber, then put them in the coals to heat. While they were warming, he chopped the onion and the carrots into small pieces and tossed them into the ceramic pot. Then he added generous portions of dried peas and beans.

"Spices," said Eynon to himself. "Where would Nûd keep spices?"

Chee helped Eynon locate the big man's supply. They were on a high shelf, but luckily, Eynon was tall himself, if not as filled out as Nûd. He put salt and pepper and dried parsley into the pot and transferred several of the andirons and skewers to the liquid inside. They sizzled as their heat transferred. The water warmed and soon the kitchen smelled of something a lot more appetizing than rotten eggs.

When Nûd returned with the smoked wisent meat, Eynon cut it into pieces the size of the tips of his fingers and added them to the pot as well. The aroma grew even richer as Eynon switched out cool skewers for hot ones to set the water in the ceramic pot boiling. The rich smell of cooking meat drew Chee's attention and Damon's, too.

"What are you cooking?" asked the older man when he entered the kitchen. "I can smell it all the way up in the library."

"Soup," said Eynon.

"When will it be ready to eat?" asked Damon.

"In a few minutes," Eynon replied.

"Will you have any bread to go with it?"

"Nûd, do you have any flour?" Eynon asked. "Not the kind you used for the ale-cakes this morning."

"That was some old rye flour," said Nûd. "I've got a sack of oat flour in the pantry I haven't opened."

"Please bring it to me, and three or four apples, and some butter."

"Glad to," said Nûd.

Eynon scoured out a small glazed crockery bowl with the piece of mail, then peeled and cored the apples with his belt knife while the soup bubbled.

"Trade out the skewers, please, Nûd," said Eynon.

While the big man did the switch, Eynon chopped the apples into bits so small they were almost a paste. Then he added in oat flour, butter, and a pinch of salt to make a stiff dough. He cut off a strip of dough and showed the other two men how to wind it around a skewer and cook it over the coals, like he had for his first breakfast several hours ago. Thinking about that meal reminded him of Merry. He hoped she was safe and promised himself he'd try to figure out how to contact her as soon as he could.

Chee ate the apple cores—except for the seeds—and ten minutes later there were spirals of oat bread to go with generous portions of soup. There was still a bit of an odd taste, but it wasn't overwhelmingly bad like the meal they'd had earlier. Nûd and Damon were *very* pleased.

"I don't see why you should teach him wizardry when he's already a wizard in the kitchen," said Nûd.

Damon was too busy dipping one of the oat bread spirals in broth to reply.

"If you won't teach me how to be a wizard, you'll find dinner much less to your liking," Eynon noted.

Damon winked at Nûd.

"The lad has many talents," he said.

"True enough," said Nûd. "Why did you cook in a ceramic pot, not a metal one directly over the coals, by the way?"

"Whatever it is in the water that smells bad doesn't like metal," said Eynon. "The people I know in Wherrel mostly cook with green-colored soapstone griddles and vessels. My cousin told me their foul-smelling water can eat right through iron or copper, given enough time."

"I'm glad to see you're an observant young man," said Damon. He'd finished his bowl and wiped his mouth with the back of his sleeve.

"Thank you," said Eynon.

"That was the best meal I've had in months," Damon declared. "Nûd, *you* clean up—it's time for Eynon's first lesson in wizardry."

"Don't get your hopes up," said Nûd, winking at Eynon. Then the big man turned to Damon. "Be sure to finish in time for him to make dinner!"

Merry

Eynon was gone, and so was Chee, the little raconette who'd adopted him. The foolish farm boy had jumped into the well after the even more foolish creature and disappeared.

Merry stared down into the crystal-clear waters in the well. Eynon wasn't there. She'd rushed to the stone wall and had reached into the water to help pull Eynon out, but all she'd gotten for her effort was wet. Merry got on her knees and leaned over the low wall. She smacked her hand against the surface of the well water in slow, methodical pulses of frustration. Slapping sounds echoed in the deep cylindrical chamber and circular ripples radiated out from where she struck.

"Don't waste your time," said a mellow contralto voice above her. "You wouldn't want to go where *that* gate leads."

Merry looked up and saw a tall woman with short auburn hair wearing blue wizard's robes descending the winding stairs. A few moments later, the woman was standing next to Merry. She extended her hands and helped Merry stand. The two women regarded each other at arms'-length. Merry looked at the short-haired woman with imploring eyes.

"Where did he *go?*" asked Merry. "And how can I get there?"

The wizard in blue turned her head from side to side, taking in the young woman before her.

"First," she said, "who are you and what are you doing in my tower?"

Merry pushed back her feelings of shock and tried to deliver an intelligent answer.

"I'm Merry of Applegarth and Doethan sent me here to find a gateway," she asserted. Her brain caught up with her ears. "This is *your* tower?"

"It is," said the short-haired woman. "I built it, or rather, I had it built. My name is Fercha." She extended her hand and Merry shook it, still a bit dazed from what had happened.

Fercha examined Merry more closely. "You're one of Doethan's apprentices?"

"His only current apprentice, as far as I know," said Merry. "Do you know Doethan?"

"We're acquainted," said Fercha with an enigmatic smile. "It sounds like someone with you found my gate."

"Yes," said Merry. "Eynon did. He and Chee fell in the well and disappeared."

"That is how gates work," said Fercha. "Different places are on each side, so it seems like anyone walking—or falling—through them has vanished. Who is *Chee*, by the way?"

"A raconette," said Merry. "Eynon made friends with the little beast when we stopped for lunch two days ago."

"Hmmm," said Fercha. "Raconettes are uncommon familiars, but there are old stories about wizards adopted by them."

"That fits Eynon," said Merry. "He's simultaneously common and uncommon himself, if you know what I mean."

"Is Eynon your lover?" Fercha asked.

"Y-yes," said Merry hesitantly. "And my friend."

Fercha smiled at Merry and seemed to be remembering her own youth and romantic challenges.

"Where is this Eynon person from?"

"From Haywall, in the Coombe, good wizard."

"I told you, call me Fercha," said the imposing woman. "You're a wizard in training, so let's keep things less formal."

Fercha rubbed her chin with her fingers. Merry could barely hear what she was saying.

"From the Coombe to Applegarth... could it be?" Fercha whispered to herself. Then she spoke louder.

"Did Eynon find something on the road?" she asked Merry. "He must have—it's the only answer."

Merry debated not replying, but decided to share what she knew without thinking too hard about it. Fercha was impressive and powerful, but she didn't seem malicious.

"He found an artifact at a crossroads just east of the mountains around the Coombe, *Fercha*," she said.

"Describe it, please," Fercha commanded.

"It was fine silver work, with a large oval blue stone," said Merry. "It glowed when it came near your tower."

"That was *mine!*" said Fercha. Her shoulders slumped. "I was so close..."

"Can't you go through the gate to retrieve it?" asked Merry.

"I could, but I'm not going back through that gate if the legions of the Eagle People *and* the royal army of Tamloch are on my doorstep," said Fercha with a quiet intensity.

"What's on the..." began Merry. Then she stopped. She'd seen the anger and pain in the short-haired wizard's eyes. Merry changed course. "Right," she said. "What do we do now?"

Fercha stood immobile, but seemed to gain strength and stature from her own focused will. She looked up the winding stairway, then at Merry.

"First, I have to rest," said the short-haired wizard. "I need a hot meal and a good night's sleep, in that order. Then I need to craft a new artifact."

She stepped close to Merry and lifted the girl's small silver and blue pendant up by its chain until it was visible outside Merry's shirt.

"While we're at it, it's high time you replaced this trinket with something more powerful."

"Yes, good wizard," said Merry.

"I told you to call me Fercha," said the wizard. She began to climb the spiral stairs and glanced over her shoulder.

Merry's body felt charged with potential. With the right teacher, she was sure she could do *anything*.

"Gather your things and come along," said Fercha. "Until Doethan comes to reclaim you, you're *my* apprentice now. If I read things right, he will be far too busy to instruct you."

Doethan was clearly caught up in the affairs of the kingdom when he'd told them to go to the Blue Spiral Tower, thought Merry. *She knew he was more than a hedge wizard!*

"When he reaches out to apologize for having you and your friend trespass in my tower, you can confirm his agreement with the arrangement."

Merry pressed her lips together tightly. If Doethan couldn't train her, having Fercha as a mentor would be wonderful.

"Dark times are upon us and the kingdom needs more wizards," said Fercha. "I hope you're willing to work harder and learn faster than you ever have in your life."

"Yes, Fercha," said Merry, her voice reflecting her inner joy.

Eynon was on the other side of the gate, but at least he was where Doethan had wanted him to go. She hoped it wouldn't be *too* dangerous there. As soon as she mastered more magic, she'd find a way to contact him.

Merry was more than ready to master the art of wizardry as fast as Fercha could teach her. She slipped on her pack and began to climb, following her new mentor with her feet barely touching the stairs.

Chapter 15

"The wizard makes the artifact,
but the magestone makes the mage."
— Ealdamon's *Epigrams*

The library had high ceilings. Overstuffed bookshelves half-again as tall as Eynon lined nearly every wall. Narrow windows between the shelves let in plenty of light to read by during the day. The ceiling was dark with soot from thousands of hours of oil lamps to prove it saw plenty of use at night as well. There was a fireplace on the inner wall and wood was carefully set, ready to light, inside it. The room smelled of leather and old paper. Eynon was entranced and extremely distracted. He struggled to focus, like a small child who had to attend to lessons on a festival day.

The books will still be here tomorrow, thought Eynon. He took a chair next to Damon at a table made of thick polished wood. Chee climbed down from his shoulder and curled up in a tight ring near Eynon's left hand.

The older man noticed Eynon scanning the shelves and smiled.

"The books will still be here tomorrow, lad," said Damon.

Eynon knew Damon didn't have to read his mind to repeat his thoughts. They were written on his face in large letters.

"You're welcome to read anything in the library," said Damon, *"after* you've worked on your lessons—and cooked our meals."

"Thank you, sir."

"I'm glad you want to learn from books, but the first lessons of wizardry are best learned through practice, not reading."

Eynon couldn't hide his disappointment. For him, books were magical.

"That's not to say you can't find helpful spells and techniques in books," the older man added, "but most elementary wizardry is decidedly hands-on."

"Yes, sir."

"Please," said Damon. "Stop calling me *sir*. It makes me feel old."

"But you *are* old, *sir*," said Eynon with a grin.

"I can see this will be entertaining for both of us," said Damon, returning Eynon's expression. "May you have apprentices just like you someday." The older man shook his head slowly from side to side, regarding Eynon. "That could be good or bad, depending on your attitude."

"I'll try to make you proud—*Damon*."

"Excellent. First, tell me what you know about wizardry."

"That won't take long," said Eynon. "I don't know very much."

He took a slow deep breath, then spoke rapidly.

"Free wizards and crown wizards are very powerful. They command fireballs and lightning and shields—and weapons—made of sound. They can fly and travel from one place to another in the blink of an eye. They can levitate objects and cast wards to protect places or things. They can augment their senses to hear, see, and smell far better than ordinary people. They can also generate illusions—and I'm sure they can do a lot more, as well."

Damon nodded.

"Concise, and accurate, as far as it goes," said the older man. "What about hedge wizards?"

"Hedge wizards work small magics compared to free and crown wizards' big magics," said Eynon. "They make fertility charms, heal injuries, help women with childbirth, and do what they can to make the lives of people and animals in their care easier."

Damon nodded again. "Well said. Those are excellent summaries—but do you have any idea *how* wizards work magic?"

"No, sir," said Eynon. "I mean, no, *Damon*. Does it involve artifacts?"

"It does, but artifacts only serve to channel magic. True magical power comes from the magestones at the heart of every artifact."

"Magestones?"

"Gems formed deep under the earth through heat and pressure that work their way to the surface in various spots," said Damon. "There are many places in Melyncárreg where magestones created by the *cuddio tân* have been washed from rock faces into streams and rivers, or lie about like pebbles on the ground, ready to be selected by a worthy wizard or apprentice."

"When do I start looking for one?" asked Eynon.

"Don't get ahead of yourself, lad," said Damon. "That depends on how well you do with your first lessons. You have to master the basics before you'll be ready to find your magestone and craft your artifact. The ground is covered with snow and the smaller streams are iced over anyway, so you'd be severely limited in where you can look until it warms up around here."

"Oh," said Eynon. He could wait, but he didn't want to.

"Have you ever seen a magestone?" asked Damon.

"Uh huh," said Eynon. "I saw a blue one, once."

He tried not to think of the back of the large blue oval gem in a silver setting pressing against the skin of his chest under his shirt.

Damon looked at Eynon and tilted his head for a moment, staring intently.

"My friend Merry had a small one in her pendant," Eynon explained. "She's learning wizardry from Doethan, a hedge wizard in the Rhuthro valley. Do you know him?"

"I'm acquainted with a wizard by that name," said Damon. He furrowed his brow, then went on. "You should know that most wizards in Dâron have an affinity for blue stones, while those in Tamloch prefer green magestones and the Eagle People's wizards opt for imperial purple."

"Do the stones' colors affect their powers?"

"No," said Damon. "You'll understand why in a few minutes."

"Great," Eynon responded. He thought for a moment, remembering illustrations in *Peregrinations* and Doethan's sky blue cloak.

"Do the colors of wizards' robes tend to match the color of their magestones?" asked Eynon. He included Damon's dark blue tunic in his mental catalog of examples.

"Most do, but not all," said Damon. "It's a custom, not a law."

"I understand," said Eynon. That's how most things worked in the Coombe, after all.

"From the time of the first wars between Dâron and Tamloch, most people wore the colors of their respective kingdoms," explained Damon. "Crown wizards, in particular, wore their kings' livery, and free wizards did the same to show they were as powerful as wizards working for nobles."

"That makes sense," said Eynon. "I expect that blue cloth was less expensive, too, because there was so much of it made for uniforms."

"An insightful observation, and one borne out by the facts, at least here in Dâron," said Damon. "When the Eagle People arrived, they had their own customary colors for uniforms. We're just lucky they favored shades of purple, rather than blue or green. Imagine how confusing it would have been otherwise."

Eynon nodded. "I've never seen one of the Eagle People," he said. "Grandmothers make them out to be monsters eager to steal cattle and children."

"You're more likely to have *that* sort of trouble from Clan Lands raiders than the Eagle People, Eynon," said Damon. "The Eagle legions are disciplined, and their leaders are wise and subtle. They played Tamloch and Dâron against each other like a harp and took the lands of the Abbenoth valley from us after we'd exhausted our armies fighting each other."

"Divide and conquer?" asked Eynon.

"That's their motto," Damon confirmed. "And they do it well."

The older man stood up.

Chee lifted his head when he heard Damon's chair scrape back. The raconette decided nothing important was happening and returned to his nap.

"Nûd!" Damon shouted.

The large young man appeared in the door to the library closest to the kitchen and waited for Damon to say more.

"Has the Master left us any wine in the cellars worth drinking?"

"If he had," said Nûd, "don't you think we'd be drinking it? There are a couple of jugs of Applegarth hard cider I've been saving for special occasions, though."

"Fetch one," said Damon. "I've been doing more talking than I'm used to and the lad looks like he'd appreciate something with a kick to it."

"Yes, Damon. Of course, Damon. Nûd is but a servant and you've been a student here as long as I've been alive."

"Some of us need a lot of time to get it right," said Damon.

"Words more true were never spoken," teased Nûd.

Eynon didn't feel particularly in need of a drink, but he wouldn't turn one down.

Nûd disappeared and returned in short order with a familiar-shaped jug, three pewter goblets, and a small clay cup. He removed a wax seal with his belt knife, pulled the cork, and poured generous portions of cider into the metal vessels and a smaller amount into the cup for Chee.

The popping cork and the smell of hard cider were enough to convince the raconette that it was worth sitting up. The little beast took the clay cup in both hands and tilted it toward his mouth.

Damon imitated Chee, using both hands on his goblet.

"Ah," said the older man. "*This* is worth drinking—it's far better than that bitter stuff you press from local apples."

"Whenever you want to build a gate to Brendinas to get supplies, I'll be glad to serve something better," said Nûd.

"Never mind, then," said Damon. "Unfortunately, gates work in both directions."

"So you've said," Nûd noted.

Eynon had a sip of cider, then put his hand over his mouth to hide a smile. Nûd gave the two of them a comic bow and retreated out of sight toward the kitchen.

Chee tried to insert his head into the clay cup to lick the bottom. Damon and Eynon were amused and left the raconette to his efforts.

The older man returned to his seat and put his goblet on the table with a solid *thunk*. Some of the liquid within sloshed out and down the vessel's pewter sides.

It's a shame to waste even a drop of Applegarth's amazing hard cider, thought Eynon.

"Time for serious talk, lad," said Damon. "Where were we?"

"The Eagle People?" suggested Eynon.

"Before that."

"Why wizards wear colored robes?"

"Before that, too."

"Magestones?" suggested Eynon, tentatively.

"That's it," said Damon. "Magestones. People think they're the source of wizards' power..."

"But they're wrong?" asked Eynon.

"They are. It's not the magestones—it's what's inside them that's at the heart of wizardry."

Eynon forgot about his goblet and the cider it held. He leaned forward, intent on Damon's words. Could he really be learning the secret at the heart of wizardry in the first hour of his first day of magic lessons?

Damon paused. Eynon looked at him expectantly and the older man laughed.

"I can't fault your eagerness to learn, lad," he said. "The secret at the heart of wizardry is congruency."

Eynon's face fell.

"I don't understand," he said.

"Few do," said Damon. "And that's the beginning of wisdom. Do you at least know the word?"

Eynon thought for a few seconds and retrieved a memory of three-sided figures on a slate.

"It's from Euclid's *Elements*," said Eynon. "I remember my geometry teacher making me repeat *side-angle-side, side-side-side, and side-angle-angle* until the words invaded my dreams."

"You're full of surprises," said Damon. "I wouldn't have expected a farm boy from the Coombe to have studied geometry."

"One of the men in Haywall served in the king's army and was promoted to engineer," explained Eynon. "He had a copy of Euclid's book and taught most of us. You'd be amazed how useful geometry is in dealing with farmers' disputes over field shapes and boundaries."

Damon smiled. "Perhaps I would. But no matter—you understand the concept and that's a head start. Do you remember the gate that got you here?"

"How could I forget?" asked Eynon. "One second I was beneath the Blue Spiral Tower and the next I was landing in the snow not far from here."

"Exactly," said Damon. "Congruencies take two places that are separate and bring them together—like that gate."

Eynon considered the concept for a few seconds.

"I can see how that would help you get from one place to another quickly," he said. "But how do you use a gate to make a fireball?"

Damon waved his hand at one of the tall windows facing west.

"Look out there," he said. "What do you see?"

"Mountains," Eynon replied.

"Above the mountains."

"Sky," said Eynon. "And clouds?"

"What *else* is in the sky?"

"The sun."

"Correct," said Damon. "And what is the sun?"

"A big ball of fire."

"What would you get if you opened a congruency to the sun?"

"A big fireball!" Eynon exclaimed. "And opening a gate to a thunderstorm would get you lightning *and* thunder for weapons and defenses made of sound."

"Very good," said Damon, beaming. "You can see the possibilities."

Eynon's brain was spinning. "How do you use congruencies to fly?" he asked.

Damon laughed.

"You'll have plenty of time to learn the nuances of wizardry, now that you've grasped what's at the core of the art," said Damon. "I'll answer that question and the five hundred more I know you'll have—later. Now it's time to practice."

"What do I need to practice?" asked Eynon.

Damon looked him up and down. He removed a tiny silver token the size of a royal mark coin from his belt pouch. A small blue gem not even as large as the nail on his little finger was in its center.

"Use this," said Damon. "Apprentices practice with tokens until they find their true magestone. It will be hard, since you're not as attuned to the token as you would be to an artifact you made yourself, but give it a try. Walk over to the fireplace and see if you can strike a spark."

"I'm reluctant to practice fire magic in a library," said Eynon. "I don't think the Master would be happy with either of us if the contents of this room burned to ash."

Eynon scanned the bookshelves and smiled nervously. He still planned to read every volume and didn't want an accident on his part to interfere.

"Don't worry," said Damon. "I'll deal with the Master if it comes to that—and I can snuff out a fire in an instant if you lose control."

"Very well," said Eynon.

He took the small circular token and carried it to the fireplace. Then he looked through the tiny gem in the center of its disk and focused his thoughts and will. The tiny magestone in the token twinkled.

The gem against his skin did more of the work, however. It seemed that it knew what to do with very little guidance from Eynon. He was glad he'd kept his jacket on to hide any telltale glow.

A beam of sparkling energy shot from the tiny gem and seconds later there was a fire roaring in the fireplace.

"Well done, my lad, well done," said Damon, clapping. "You're a natural at wizardry."

"Thank you," said Eynon. He knew it was the large magestone under his shirt that had provided most of the power for the demonstration.

"You seem to have a knack for fire," said Damon. "Let's see how you manage with lightning."

"Inside?" asked Eynon. "In the *library?*"

"I'm not insisting you call down a thunderbolt," answered Damon. "I want to see if you can summon a spark to your fingertips."

"Like when I rub my feet on my grandmother's braided rug in the winter and shock my sister?"

"Exactly like that," said Damon. "It requires control over the lightning's flow. You want high pressure, but low power to get a good spark without damaging the area around you."

"Couldn't we do this *outside?*" asked Eynon. "I wouldn't want to damage any books."

"Preserving your future reading material should provide plenty of incentive to get it right," said Damon. "Let me show you what I want you to do."

The older man rubbed his palms together, then extended the finger of his right hand. He nodded to Eynon to touch the offered digit.

With a *snap* and a bright pulse, a miniature bolt of lightning crossed the short distance from Damon's finger to Eynon's. Eynon jumped, then rubbed the place where the lightning had landed.

"That was a lot stronger than the sparks I got scuffing about at my grandmother's."

"I'm sure it was," said Damon. "It's very easy to use too much power the first time you try to direct lightning, so why don't you aim for my goblet instead of my finger. Remember—you want pressure, not power."

"If you say so," said Eynon.

He rubbed his palms together the same way Damon had illustrated, then picked up the token in one hand. He extended his other hand and visualized pushing sparks from his fingertips. Once again the gem against his skin seemed to know what was needed.

Clang! Five arcs of lightning jumped from the ends of his fingers to Damon's goblet with enough power to make the metal ring. The damp circle of cider at the goblet's base sizzled. Moments later, the library smelled like apple pie and the sky after a summer thunderstorm.

Damon popped up like a startled flying frog, knocking his chair over in the process. Chee had effectively levitated to the top of a nearby bookcase. The raconette stared down at the pair of humans warily. All his fur was standing on end, puffing him up to twice his normal size.

Eynon was stunned. He sat, frozen, staring at his outstretched hand.

"Too much power?" he asked uncertainly.

"A bit," said Damon as he set his chair upright and remained standing. "Maybe we should save future work with lightning until we're outside."

"That's a good idea," said Eynon.

He stood up as well. It wouldn't be polite to remain seated. Eynon put the token on the table and clasped his hands in front of him, wondering if Damon's lack of judgment as a teacher had anything to do with his long apprenticeship.

"One last lesson before I send you off to cook our dinner," said Damon. The older man looked ready to stop and rest soon, but he pushed on.

Eynon's nerves were jangling. He would have been glad to stop as well, even though he was eager to learn more. Then he realized what was likely coming next and felt re-energized.

"Will you be providing me with *sound* instruction?" Eynon asked.

Damon raised one eye, then a corner of his mouth turned up.

"That's correct," said the older man. "I see you're a step ahead of me. At least you're not likely to damage anything more than your ears—and mine—with sound."

"Let's hope," said Eynon. "Do you want me to shape something offensive or defensive?"

"Defensive might be best for our hearing, lad," said Damon. "I want you to build a simple sonic shield."

Eynon was intrigued.

"Where do I start?" he asked.

"Hold your token between your thumb and index finger and sweep your arm around in a big arc," said Damon. He made a motion for Eynon to copy. "Then imagine a thick circle in that space and pour sound that means something to you into the circle. I use geese honking."

"I'll try," said Eynon.

He centered his mind and thought about his sister, Braith, singing while she practiced archery. There were times when Eynon thought she charmed her arrows into the targets with her voice.

He picked up the token with its tiny magestone, but could feel a resonant link from the large blue magestone against his skin connecting to the small one between his fingers. When he moved his arm, it inscribed a great round shield-shape in the air. With help from both magestones, he poured his memories of his sister's songs into the shield and felt it solidify, invisible, in front of him. Eynon was thrilled to be working a new sort of magic.

He was about to ask Damon to throw something at him, to see if the shield held, when the magestone against his skin twitched. The hot oval felt much warmer and suddenly the invisible shield launched itself toward Damon, knocking the older man over before returning to place in front of Eynon.

Chee chittered a loud *chi-chi-chi-CHEE* from his safe vantage point on top of a bookcase.

Eynon dropped the token onto the tabletop, which dispelled the shield. He hurried over to check on Damon.

"I'm so sorry," he said. "I didn't mean to do that. The shield seemed to have a mind of its own."

He helped the older man up, brushed him off, and guided him to a chair.

"Pay it no mind, lad," said Damon. "I'm no worse for wear, though if I had smacked my head on the floor it might have knocked some sense into me. I let my guard down."

"You shouldn't have had to be on guard against *me*," said Eynon.

"When a new apprentice is first learning magic, his teacher should always be on guard."

"If you say so," said Eynon.

Damon looked at him closely, like a farmer deciding which horse to buy.

"Tell me," said Damon. "How long were you in the Blue Spiral Tower? Days? Weeks?"

"More like minutes, or maybe an hour. It wasn't long."

"That means it couldn't be any sort of residual influence from *her* magics," Damon mused.

"Sir?" said Eynon. He could barely hear what the older man had said, let alone make sense of it.

"Never mind," said Damon. "It's not important. I think we've both had enough lessons for one day."

"Yes, Damon," said Eynon. "I'm *so* sorry if I hurt you."

"I'm fine," said the older man, smiling. "My pride and my backside will both recover quickly."

"That's good," said Eynon, smiling back. "I'll make something especially good for supper—if I can find the necessary ingredients."

"I'd like that," said Damon, "and so would Nûd, I expect, though I doubt he'd say so. Tell him to let you borrow from the Master's private larder if need be."

"I will, Damon, thank you. I hope that won't get you into trouble."

"No, the Master will be so entertained by your skill and my folly that I'm sure he'll be in a good mood."

"May it be so," said Eynon.

"Time for you to go down to the kitchen, lad," Damon directed. "And after that, you'll can head to bed. You'll need a good night's sleep."

Eynon nodded.

"Good advice," he said.

"It's better than you think," said Damon. "You're much farther along than I anticipated. You'll want to be well-rested before setting out to find your own magestone in the morning."

Chapter 16

"Communications spells don't ensure comprehension."
— Ealdamon's *Epigrams*

"That was tasty, lad," said Damon. The older man sighed with contentment.

"Thank you," Eynon replied as he stood up from the table.

"Where did you learn to cook so well?"

Eynon looked over his shoulder as he carried an empty platter to the sink.

"My parents knew their way around a kitchen—I must have picked it up from them."

Damon nodded and smiled.

"And from my grandparents—and my aunts and uncles—and several cousins."

Now Nûd was smiling.

"And Glynneth—she's our neighbor one cottage down. Her sweet cakes are amazing."

"Before you extend credit to every man and woman in the Coombe," said Damon, "know that Nûd and I appreciate their instruction and your aptitude. From what I've seen, you're as quick to learn wizardry as cooking."

The corners of the older man's mouth continued to turn up and laugh lines creased his forehead.

"I hope that proves to be the case," said Eynon, nearly laughing himself once he realized how he'd been going on.

Eynon had worked hard making dinner. He'd fried thin slices of elk steaks with onions and made flatbread with more of the oat flour from breakfast. A crock of pickled cabbage with spicy red peppers Nûd had unearthed from the recesses of the Master's larder had complemented the meal. Its strong flavor counteracted any sulphur smell in the air. To Eynon's surprise, his nose wasn't noticing the odor of rotten eggs nearly as much as it had when he'd first arrived.

"Don't worry about the rest of the dishes," said Nûd after Eynon had returned to the table. "I'll clean up. You need to get your rest."

The young giant glanced at Damon.

"Very true," said the older man. "It's quite a hike to the best places to hunt for magestones. It makes me tired just thinking about it, so I'm heading to my rooms."

Damon stood, wrapped his robes around his torso and leaned on his walking stick.

"Meet me here at dawn," he said. "Nûd can show you where we keep the traveling rations and outfit you for the trip. I'll draw a map for you before I go to bed."

"Can you tell me what I'm looking for?" asked Eynon.

"I thought I was clear about that," said Damon. "You're looking for magestones. Wait, no. You're looking for *your* magestone."

"Yes, sir," said Eynon. He was feeling both puzzled and resigned. *Must all wizards—in training or otherwise—be so intentionally obtuse?*

"Don't stay up late," said Damon as he left the kitchen.

Chee sent him on his way with an energetic, if repetitive chorus of *chee-chee-chee-CHEE*. Eynon stroked the raconette's fur.

"Thanks for collecting the dishes," he said to Nûd. "Please wait a few minutes before you wash them. I want to try something."

"Should I be worried?" asked Nûd cheerfully.

"I hope not," said Eynon. "I want to see if I can improve the quality of the water in the kitchen. The sulphur smell isn't bothering my nose so much now, but the sulphur taste still is. I think I can taste iron in the water, too."

"Iron and who knows what else," Nûd agreed. "I'll put a pot of water over the fire to heat and you can try whatever you've got planned."

"Good idea," said Eynon, "but if what I have in mind works, we won't need it."

Nûd built up a fire and filled his largest pot with water, watching Eynon as he did.

Eynon staked out an empty table against the wall on the far side of the kitchen, near a small sink used for prepping vegetables.

Next to the sink, on top of four sturdy hardwood legs, was a polished granite-slab counter about three feet square. A hand water pump was embedded in the slab with its spigot hanging over the sink's rectangular soapstone basin. Nûd stopped pretending to organize pots and dishes. He stared as Eynon experimented with a combination of sonic shield and fire magic.

First, Eynon pumped a gallon or so of sulphur-tainted water from the hand pump into a basin he constructed from a lens of solidified sound. It floated in the air above the sink. Then he added heat until the liquid boiled. Once steam began to form, Eynon shaped the upper part of the lens to direct the hot water to a second, slightly lower floating lens he contrived to *remove* heat from, so the steam would condense and eventually drip out into the soapstone sink.

Oops, he thought. *I've got to put a stopper in the drain.* He steadied his mind to keep his wizardry working and found a disk of wood on the back edge of the polished granite slab. It was whittled to fit the hole in the bottom of the sink and Eynon wedged it in place. A thin sturdy chain with a hook on one end was connected to the disk to make it easy to remove. Eynon placed the hook over the edge of the sink.

"That's fascinating," Nûd noted.

Eynon had to think about it to realize Nûd meant his magical constructs, not the stopper and chain.

"How does it taste?" Nûd asked.

"I have no idea," said Eynon. "I simply had an idea and wanted to see if it would work."

Nûd stepped away and came back with a pewter mug. He used it to capture some of the clean water dripping down into the sink.

"It's good," Nûd said, after he'd swallowed a third of the mug's contents. "Have some."

Eynon took the mug and drank, though he reserved most of his concentration to hold his spells in place.

"Can you pump more water into the first lens?" asked Eynon.

"Certainly."

Nûd raised and lowered the handle half a dozen times until the first lens was full again. Chee hopped down from Eynon's shoulder and took over pumping, keeping the water level even. He seemed to think pumping was as much fun as eating Applegarth apples.

"Clever beast," said Nûd. "And you're pretty clever, too. Is this something Damon taught you today? It seems quite advanced."

"Damon taught me how to work with heat and sound. The rest was my idea," Eynon answered.

"You have good ideas," said Nûd. "You'll have to ask Damon if there's any way to keep your system going so we'll always have clean water."

"That's an excellent thought. Maybe tomorrow," Eynon equivocated.

He didn't want to tell Damon what he was doing in case the older man would forbid it.

Chee kept pumping and Eynon's spells kept boiling and cooling water until the soapstone sink was full.

"I think I'll bring all the dirty dishes over to this sink, instead of the main one," said Nûd.

"Let's keep the clean water for cooking," Eynon suggested. "I'll replicate my spells where the dishes are."

"I'll cover this sink so it doesn't get dirty," said Nûd.

He located a huge wooden cutting board and placed it over the sink. Chee looked disappointed to stop pumping.

"You can pump over there," said Eynon, pointing to the main sink.

The little raconette scampered across the tops of preparation tables and found the indicated pump.

"Do you think you could handle four lenses?" asked Nûd.

"I think so. Why?" asked Eynon.

"The water from the pump comes out a foot or more above the edge of the main sink," said Nûd. "You capture and heat it in one lens and cool it in a second one."

"Right," said Eynon.

"Can you let the clean water flow out into two more lenses?"

"I think I can," said Eynon. "How will that help?"

"Just do it," said Nûd. "I'll show you."

Eynon concentrated and formed the requested pattern of solidified sound. Chee filled the first lens with water, keeping up a happy *chee chee chee* in the background. Once the two lower lenses began to fill with water, Nûd made another request.

"Can you heat up the lower lenses now? Make them hot, but not boiling."

"I'll try," said Eynon. He concentrated and succeeded.

Nûd pushed a dark brown bar of lye soap into the left-hand lens against the pressure of its solidified sound walls until it popped inside. Eynon smiled when he realized Nûd's plan.

"How clever. Hot soapy water to wash. Clean hot water to rinse."

"Exactly," said Nûd. The big man was pleased his suggestion had worked and started in on washing and rinsing dishes.

"I hope it doesn't take you too long to find your magestone," Nûd remarked as he worked. "I expect this will be a much better way to wash dishes than heating up our foul-tasting water in a pot over the fire."

"Since I don't know what I'm looking for, I have no idea how long it will take," said Eynon.

"I'm sure it won't take you long," said Nûd. "I was told that *She* found her magestone and returned in time for lunch on her first day of searching."

"She?"

"One of the Master's many former apprentices," said Nûd. "Forget I mentioned her."

"Of course," said Eynon. He filed Nûd's comment away as a topic to research when he was finally able to read through the Master's library.

"How long did it take Damon to find *his* magestone?"

"He never told me," replied Nûd. "That was before I came to work here. I'd ask the Master, but he'd never tell me either, I'm sure."

"Do you ever see the Master?"

"Every day," Nûd replied. "Somebody has to make his bed and do his laundry. Come to think of it…"

The big man shook water off a pewter plate and stood it in a rack to dry. Eynon knew what he was about to suggest.

"We can experiment with using solidified sound and heat magic to clean clothes some other day," said Eynon. "Do you have anything to give to Chee as a reward for pumping water?"

"How about a dried cherry dipped in a boiled honey syrup and rolled in crushed walnuts?" asked Nûd.

"I think that would be more than satisfactory," said Eynon. "And I wouldn't turn one of them down, either."

Nûd went a pantry, out of sight of Eynon and Chee, and returned with two small candies wrapped in birch leaves. Chee jumped on a table and begged Nûd for one of the treats. To Eynon's surprise— and frustration—Nûd gave both to the raconette.

Chee took one in each hand, then returned to Eynon and offered him a confection.

"Thank you, Chee," said Eynon, accepting with a small bow. "I'm sorry I doubted you."

The raconette bowed in return and popped the treat he'd kept into one side of his mouth, making him look like a squirrel with a full cheek pouch.

"Delicious," said Eynon after he licked traces of honey from his lips.

"Don't tell Damon, but my mother made them," said Nûd.

"Your mother has talent."

Eynon took a deep breath, then yawned.

"Among other qualities," said Nûd. "You should probably get to bed. Damon wasn't joking about the distance to the best places to find magestones. Tomorrow will likely be a very long day for you. Meet me here an hour before sunrise and I'll find you a heavy coat and a pair of snowshoes."

"Thank you," said Eynon.

He motioned to Chee and the raconette climbed up his arm and perched on his shoulder.

"I'll make breakfast, too," Nûd added.

"No, don't worry about it. I'm glad to cook," said Eynon. He was remembering the inedible breakfast Nûd had made and was far from interested in repeating that dubious pleasure.

"I'll just start the fire in the morning then," said Nûd. "I found a big sack of not-very-old wheat flour hidden behind a barrel in the dry pantry, by the way."

"Wonderful," said Eynon. If Eynon was reading the huge young man's expression correctly, Nûd was happy with the prospect of eating Eynon's cooking rather than his own.

"Bring me some of the wheat flour, plus honey, salt, butter, eggs and water right now," said Eynon. "I'll make up some sweet dough to proof overnight. Then I'll go to bed. I'll sleep better with the prospect of fresh hot rolls in the morning."

* * * * *

Eynon's small cell was cold when he stepped inside. It was a stone rectangle, not much wider than his outstretched arms, with a narrow window at one end and a door at the other. Enough late-afternoon sunlight was coming in the window to see everything clearly. There was a bed on the left and a study table on the right—the room was cramped, but cozy. The remaining furnishings included a chest for his clothes at the foot of the bed and a chair with a padded cushion tucked under the table. His pack was next to the chest and his staff was leaning against the study table.

Nûd had piled two quilts, three goosedown pillows and a thick wisent robe on his bed and stacked plenty of wood by the fireplace. Eynon inspected the split logs and selected enough pieces to last through the night. Even with the waning light coming through his window he felt tired enough to go to bed.

Feeling in his pouch for his flint and steel, Eynon stopped and remembered he was now an apprentice learning wizardry. He focused his will—with help from the blue magestone—and had a fire burning in seconds.

Nûd had laid out a nightshirt and cap for him, so Eynon changed and draped his clothing on top of the chest and over the back of the chair to air out. He positioned his boots close enough to the fireplace to dry, without risk of them catching fire. Eynon's feet were freezing where they touched the cold slate floor, so he climbed into bed.

It was a pleasure to position his body under the quilts and wisent robe. He thought about Merry while his toes warmed.

Where was she? Was she safe? What caused the loud bang and the gust of wind back in the Blue Spiral Tower?

He fingered the plain gold ring Doethan had given him. What was that word of invocation? *Gallo-thee-en?* No.

"Gwal-o-e-a-den," Eynon said in a clear voice. He hadn't realized he'd said the word out loud and resolved to ask Damon, or Doethan, why some spells needed words and some just used thoughts.

So non-wizards can trigger them, Eynon deduced, answering his own question.

The ring slid off his finger and expanded in pulses to form a circle as wide as the distance from his shoulder to his fingertips. Three bells chimed different notes. Doethan's head and shoulders appeared inside the circle. He was wearing a white and blue brocaded dressing gown and a dark-blue knitted nightcap. The hedge-wizard stifled a yawn.

"Eynon! You made it," said Doethan. "I hoped you would—and I'd recognize those cell walls anywhere."

"I'm learning wizardry," said Eynon. "But Merry..."

"Merry must be turning the Academy upside down and making the Master wish he had eight ears to hear all her questions and four mouths to answer them faster than she can come up with new ones."

"Not exactly," said Eynon.

"No matter," said Doethan. "I'm glad you reached out. I have a message you *must* give to the Master. Can you do that?"

"I'll try," said Eynon.

"See that you're successful," said Doethan. "Tell him that he is *urgently* needed in Brendinas. The king is about to do something foolish with the army and the wizards of Tamloch are planning a flying raid somewhere along our western border. We need his wise counsel *and* his magic."

The hedge wizard took a breath.

"Can you do that, Eynon?" asked Doethan. "You must convince him. If you can't, tell Merry. She'll make him listen."

"But she's..."

"A handful?" rejoined Doethan. "Of course she is. Pass the message along as soon as you can, please. I can't stay to talk. I'm expecting company."

The conversation, if you could call it that, abruptly ended. The ring shrank down to its original size with a pop and fell into Eynon's lap. He returned it to his finger, wishing it was equally simple to contact Merry. He felt remarkably comfortable in bed and had very little interest in putting his feet on the cold floor and dressing before he could find Nûd or Damon.

Eynon was spared the need to get out of bed by a knock on the door. It was high enough up that Eynon was sure it was Nûd.

"How are you doing?" came the big man's voice through the door. "I heard someone talking."

"That was me," said Eynon. "Come in."

Nûd did, leaving the door open.

"I heard from Doethan," said Eynon. "The hedge wizard I'd mentioned at breakfast. He's in Brendinas and has an important message for the Master."

"What is it?" said Nûd, looking closely at Eynon's left hand where it rested on top of a quilt.

Eynon passed along Doethan's words.

"Foolish child!" said Nûd when Eynon had finished.

"What did I do?" asked Eynon.

"Not you, Eynon, the king," said Nûd. "Can't they leave him alone?"

Eynon recognized a rhetorical question and didn't answer. He was glad Nûd wasn't calling *him* a foolish child. All in all, he was feeling rather clever after what he'd accomplished. He yawned.

"I heard that," said Nûd. "I'll pass the message on to the Master, but I make no guarantees about his answer."

"Thank you," said Eynon. The first yawn was followed by another.

"Get some sleep," said Nûd in a kindly voice. "I'll wake you in time to make breakfast."

Nûd started to say more, but Eynon's eyes were already closed.

Chapter 17

"There's no disputing about taste."
— Eagle People's maxim

The next day got off to a good start. Eynon woke up two hours before sunrise, feeling refreshed, not tired. Something about Melyncárreg was affecting his sleeping patterns, and not in a bad way.

When he left his cell to go to the kitchen, he adjusted the spell he'd devised for generating heat to create light instead. A soft glowing ball above and behind his head helped him find his way downstairs to the kitchen. From his vantage point on Eynon's shoulder, Chee blinked as his eyes adjusted to the light.

Being up early has its advantages, thought Eynon. *There's more time to practice wizardry.*

Eynon stood by the main sink and recreated his clean-water generating system. He could tell that the large blue gem in the amulet under his shirt was doing a large part of the work, but Eynon didn't mind. He thought of what he needed and the magestone formed the required magical constructs. Once he set up the series of basins, with the last one emptying into the main sink, the blue magestone kept the water flowing without Eynon's ongoing attention.

A spell that alternately heated and cooled water inside a cylinder functioned to operate the pump handle. He'd negate that construct if Chee ever wanted to do more pumping. For now, the raconette curled up to nap in a bowl on a table near the sink.

Eynon carried several seasoned pine logs to the fireplace and used fire magic to set them burning. Then, out of habit, he put clean water in a kettle hanging above the fire to boil for tea in a more conventional fashion. Half an hour later, when the coals were ready, Eynon put a pot with clean water, cut oats and salt in a deep pan on a short iron rack to simmer. He found the remains of a rasher of bacon to fry, and located nuts and honey in one of the pantries to add to the oats.

Nûd entered the kitchen and smiled when he saw Eynon hard at work instead of sleeping in his cell. Eynon was pleased the big man had found him shaping dough for rolls, not in his bed. The rolls were an extra bonus and would be something easy for Eynon to carry with him on his journey after they came out of the cast iron oven positioned above the coals.

Nûd and Damon were quite pleased with their breakfast. The bacon disappeared without the aid of wizardry and Nûd enthusiastically scraped the last bits of sweetened oatmeal out of the pot.

The rolls were cooling on the table near Chee, who was very polite about not stealing any. The raconette was enjoying his own breakfast of apples and one of yesterday's oat-bread spirals topped with honey. Eynon wrapped six of the rolls in a linen napkin and put them in his pack. There were six left.

"Those look good and smell better," said Nûd, admiring the rolls. "May I have two to offer to the Master?"

"Of course," said Eynon.

He reached for his pack, but Nûd stopped Eynon with a hand on his arm.

"Keep yours," said Nûd. "I'll take them from the half dozen you left for us. You did leave them for *us,* didn't you?"

"I did," said Eynon.

"I'll take two of Damon's three for the Master," said Nûd. "I'd give up one of mine, but I'm a growing boy."

"If you keep growing, you'll have trouble fitting through doorways without ducking your head," grumbled Damon.

Eynon hid a smile.

If the Master likes my rolls, maybe he'll come down and share a meal with us, he thought.

When they'd finished eating, Nûd and Damon examined Eynon's magical constructs for making clean water. Nûd was impressed and clapped Eynon on the back. Eynon wasn't used to contact like that from anyone taller than he was. He grinned at Nûd. It felt good to be appreciated.

Damon didn't say anything. He examined the constructs carefully, then stared at Eynon for a few seconds before narrowing his eyes and smiling.

"You're much farther along than you have any right to be, lad."

Nûd smiled and nodded his agreement.

Through a flourish of his hand that resembled wizardry, Damon produced a roll of parchment from the dangling sleeve of his dressing robe and placed it on the table.

"Here's the map I drew last night. Help me unroll it."

Eynon held one end while Damon unrolled the parchment and anchored the other with his forearm. The old man used his free index finger to trace Eynon's route.

"The hot springs are twelve miles due west of here," said Damon. "Keep the sun at your back on the way there and in your eyes when you return."

Eynon knew quite well how to tell east from west, but didn't say anything. Damon continued.

"You'll see towers of white steam from the hot springs when you're halfway there, which should make them easy to find."

"Very good," said Eynon.

"This route should take you on paths where the snow isn't too deep—only a couple of feet," said Damon.

"How deep is the *deep* snow?"

"Taller than I am," said Nûd. "In some places, a lot taller."

"I'll stay on the path," said Eynon.

"That would be wise," said the old man. "You want to be at the hot springs before noon. That way, you'll be able to search and will still have time to make it back before nightfall."

"I'll do my best to get there quickly," said Eynon. "Once I reach the hot springs, how do I find my magestone?"

"The *cuddio tân* melt the snow, so it's easier to find magestones where the ground is warm. Search near the hot springs but not *too* near," said Damon. "If you get too close to them you might fall in and be boiled like beef in a stew pot."

"I'll be careful," said Eynon.

"Don't trust the ground around the hot springs, either," added Nûd. "Sometimes it's very thin and covers sinkholes."

"I see," said Eynon, feeling decidedly less confident than he had a few minutes before.

"Treat them like a dragon with a toothache, lad, and you can't go wrong," said Damon.

Eynon had never encountered a dragon in any context and resolved to be *very* careful around the hot springs, even though he wasn't sure what a hot spring was. He'd been to Wherrel to see the largest spring in the Coombe several times. It was the size of a mill pond, but was cool, not hot. The spring's water was refreshing and Eynon loved the way it bubbled on his tongue.

"If I find magestones, how will I know which one is mine?" Eynon asked.

"You'll know yours when you see it," said Damon.

"That's helpful," said Eynon, thinking it was anything but. "Any other advice?"

"Keep your wits about you, and your crossbow ready."

"Yes, sir."

"Nûd, get him a pair of snowshoes and something warm to wear."

"Get them yourself, old man," said Nûd cheerfully.

Nûd grinned at Eynon while Damon glared at him.

"No, wait. I'll get what he needs," Nûd continued. "You tell Eynon what to do if he runs into any of the larger local fauna."

* * * * *

Eynon snapped a sprig of holly off a tree he passed and tucked it into his warm fur hat to remind himself he was still on his wander year. He was cold, despite the hat, the thick wisent-skin coat Nûd had found for him, the fur-lined gloves on his hands, and the long wool scarf he'd wrapped three times around his neck.

He was beginning to learn how to walk effectively in snowshoes and was pleased they kept his feet on top of the foot or more of snow covering the ground. His staff helped him maintain his balance as he shifted weight from shoe to shoe. It was straightforward to stay on the path because someone had marked the trail with splashes of red paint on tree trunks at regular intervals.

Winters must be harder and longer in Melyncárreg than the Coombe, mused Eynon as he increased his pace and pushed on toward the west. The extra exertion helped him stay warm. Frigid air bit into the exposed parts of his face. He resolved to figure out how to use heat and fire magic to help him cope with the colder climate as soon as he had a chance.

Chee insisted on staying with Eynon on his quest. The raconette wore a discarded woolen mitten Nûd had adapted to fit his small body. He was nestled inside Eynon's coat with only his head poking out above the top fastener. From time to time, a soft *chee-chee-chee* would float up from below Eynon's chin.

The small crossbow Eynon had found near the oak tree back in Applegarth swung at his belt and the long, sharp shard of mysterious magical material he'd been using as a sword was attached to his pack where he could easily reach up and grab it. Old Damon's descriptions of the dangerous animals in the area had been sobering, so Eynon paid close attention to his surroundings.

He'd been climbing for three hours, making his way through stands of tall, straight pine trees with most of their needles clustered on branches far above him. The high boughs had captured some of the snow, which made the forest floor much easier going. He saw a gap in the trees ahead and the ground began to flatten out. When he got closer, he saw the gap opened into a broad meadow where a few sparse stalks of amber grass poked above a blanket of crusted snow.

Eynon froze when he heard bellows of anger and screams like an eagle on the hunt. He could feel Chee's head popping down into his coat in response to the sounds and wished he had a refuge of his own. Slowly, Eynon eased back to the edge of the trees and peered around the trunk of a large pine.

A tawny gryffon with a white-feathered head was facing off with an old bull wisent a hundred feet away in the center of the meadow. The old bull had formidable horns. Its hide was shaggy, with thick, curly, dark-brown hair on its forequarters and scars on its flanks.

The bull's head was lowered and its horns were pointed at the gryffon which stood almost as tall but must have been only half the wisent's weight.

The gryffon's eagle head screamed again and the wisent charged. Wings unfurled, the gryffon rose above the wisent, rotated in flight, and came down with outstretched talons on the wisent's back. Seconds later, Eynon watched as the gryffon's beak opened the wisent's neck. The gryffon's white feathers were suddenly red as the old bull sank to the ground. He turned away, impressed by the gryffon's talent in taking down such a large enemy, but not wanting to draw the predator's attention.

Attack from an unexpected direction, thought Eynon. He filed the memory away for future reference.

Eynon circled the meadow and continued on, moving west and a bit north toward the rising towers of steam, keeping as far away from the feeding gryffon as he could manage. He could smell the tang of spilled blood and hear the dying *chuffs* of the wisent as the gryffon began to feast. A cat's snarl joined the sounds from gryffon and wisent. Eynon turned and saw an opportunistic mountain lion had staked out the wisent's hindquarters while the gryffon's beak and claws were tearing through the wisent's neck.

He increased his pace before the fresh kill drew a pack of wolves who might find him a less-contested meal.

After climbing for more than two hours, Eynon was glad to start heading downhill a quarter mile past the meadow. His path took him near a formation of rock spires interspersed with flat tables of granite. When he looked closer, he saw that the granite had the same pattern of colors as the polished slab next to the main sink back in the castle. He hoped the person who'd lugged the slabs back to be polished had a sturdy cart or magical assistance to move them.

Judging that he was far enough away from the gryffon and mountain lion, he sat on the edge of a broad, flat piece of granite bathed in late-morning sun. What looked like a strange formation of black stones was piled in a circle quite far back on the slab. Eynon knew he couldn't take a long break, but didn't think a few minutes off his feet would pose a problem. He put his staff on the table of rock, placed his pack next to it, and leaned back until he could look straight up into the clouds. A few deep breaths calmed him after the excitement of seeing a gryffon make its kill.

He couldn't stop for long, so he shifted to take off a glove and remove one of the rolls from his pack. He enticed Chee's head out of his coat with a generous morsel. The raconette ate gratefully, then licked crumbs from his paws. Eynon ate the rest of the roll, pleased with how his baking had turned out. The yeast was good here, at least. It gave the rolls a nutty flavor.

After eating the roll, Eynon realized he was thirsty. He squirted water from his goatskin into his mouth and swallowed. It tasted better than he'd expected—he must have been a bit dehydrated. Chee pointed to his own mouth and Eynon understood. He allowed his little friend to hold the skin up while he squeezed, then returned the goatskin to his belt.

It felt wonderful to sit in the sun now that the temperature wasn't cold enough to freeze his earlobes off. It almost made him wish he didn't have to hurry to get to the hot springs before noon. Eynon leaned back again and closed his eyes against the light. He promised himself it would only be for a minute, but it wasn't even that long before Chee insisted on attention with a loud *chee-chee-chee-chee,* followed by a retreat deep into Eynon's coat.

"What is it?" asked Eynon. "I didn't fall asleep."

He felt a warm breeze on his face and opened his eyes slowly. A pair of copper-colored eyes as wide as his palm stared down at him. They had vertical pupils and seemed to shine out from a leathery black face. Eynon froze. Below the eyes was a long snout, and below the snout were rows of sharp teeth the size of eating daggers. The analytical part of Eynon's mind said *wyvern,* while the more primitive part of his brain was torn between *don't move* and *run.* For the moment, *don't move* won.

The nostrils at the end of the wyvern's snout sniffed him. Eynon hoped his wisent-robe didn't make him smell too much like a wisent himself, since he expected the big bovines were frequently on the menu for wyverns. While his body remained still, Eynon's mind raced. He was an apprentice wizard, after all, if a very junior one.

He called on the blue magestone around his neck and summoned a sonic shield to cover his body. None too soon, it snapped into place above him, like the upper half of one of the lenses he'd created to distill clean water.

The wyvern's tongue reached out to taste Eynon, but encountered the magical shield instead. Surprised, the huge beast licked again. It liked the taste of magic. Eynon needed to get the wyvern to back away so he could attempt to escape. He pulled one of the five remaining rolls from his pack and tossed it over his head, farther back on the flat rock.

With its wings still furled, the wyvern turned its sinuous neck and sought out the roll, using its long, forked tongue to pick up the bread and convey it to his mouth. The beast swallowed the roll in a single bite, then moved its head from side to side quizzically, as if trying to decide what to make of the baked dough.

Eynon took advantage of the wyvern's distraction to stand. He quickly closed his pack and donned it, snapping the back half of the sonic shield in place around his body. Before he could reclaim his staff, the wyvern decided the roll wasn't nearly as interesting as the taste of Eynon's magic. It turned back to run its tongue across the front surface of his shield again.

"Magic tastes good to you, does it, big fellow?" asked Eynon softly, as if he was soothing a plow horse.

The wyvern answered with another lick. It didn't seem like he wanted to eat Eynon—just taste his shields. The beast's hide was both leathery and scaly, with its wings more the former and its body more the latter. It was massive, twice the size of the gryffon, with a pair of thick, chicken-like legs and wings that extended six or eight feet above his back when they were furled. The wyvern's wings were membranes across what would have been the fingers of its hands, like bats, though when the creature was on the ground, it looked like it was walking on its elbows. A snake-like tail as long as its body stretched behind.

The constant licking from the wyvern's long tongue was rapidly shifting from intriguing to annoying. It would slow Eynon down just as much to be licked by a wyvern as eaten by one, though the former outcome would be less permanent, or painful, than the latter.

"Are you hungry?" Eynon asked. "I'm not much of a meal, but I know where you could get most of an old bull wisent if the gryffon and mountain lion haven't eaten it all yet."

The wyvern stopped licking for a moment and stared at Eynon, almost as if it understood him. Eynon concentrated and created a bright yellow ball of solid sound at a slightly higher frequency. It was the first time he'd tried making solid sound that was anything except transparent, but the blue magestone made it easy and helped him adjust his spell.

He guided the ball to float in front of the wyvern's nose. The beast's tongue shot out and licked the ball tentatively, then with enthusiasm. As Eynon hoped, the ball tasted better than his shields.

Not knowing quite how he did it, he used wizardry to send the ball flying hundreds of feet into the air. It moved in a huge arc back in the direction of the meadow.

"Fetch," said Eynon with a grin.

The wyvern bounded up, giving chase, and was soon out of sight behind a stand of tall, straight pines.

"I hope that gryffon is wise enough not to put up a fight, big fellow," said Eynon. "And I hope there's enough wisent left for you when you get there."

Eynon made the best time his snowshoes allowed as he tried to hurry away from the sunny spires and flat rocks. From the position of the towers of steam to the west, it wouldn't be long until he reached the hot springs—unless he ran into a pack of wolves or a dragon or something.

He was glad the wyvern hadn't had a toothache.

Chapter 18

"Curiosity is best when mixed with caution."
— Ealdamon's *Epigrams*

Eynon pushed his way through tightly packed pines. He sensed he was getting closer to the hot springs when the rotten eggs smell grew more intense. After a dozen paces, he reached the top of a rise, but suddenly stopped because the trees ended and a bowl of barren white ground stretched before him. There were patches of scrubby grass and stunted trees here and there, but most of the vista was white, dotted with multicolored pools of steaming water and natural cauldrons of bubbling gray mud.

Damon had been right about the snow—there was little of it to be seen and that only on the edges of the odd landscape. When Eynon looked closer, he saw that the white-colored ground was grainy, like it was covered with salt. He knew Melyncárreg in general was strange, but the current locale was particularly so.

Far in the back of the field of hot springs, one particular spring stood out for its spectacular colors. The center of the spring was red and circles of orange, yellow, green, blue and purple formed a rainbow of well-defined rings out to where the spring's edge met the basin's stark white ground. Eynon felt compelled to explore it and resolved to check out the rainbow-colored spring first, if only to determine why it had such a fascinating color pattern.

A steep, snow-covered slope, more suited to a goat than a man or woman, led down to the bad-smelling basin. Someone had set narrow, upright pine logs into the hillside every six feet and lashed long poles between them to help visitors ascend and descend. Eynon silently thanked the people who'd made the railing for their efforts.

He held on and eased his way down, taking in the odd landscape below him as he shuffled along. A bubble as big as his head formed and broke with a lugubrious *plop* in a mud pot close by. Mud pots were the name Eynon remembered Nûd had used for them, at least.

The big servant had been more forthcoming than Damon about finding magestones when he'd helped Eynon strap on his snow-shoes several hours earlier. Eynon replayed their conversation.

* * * * *

"I've been told by the Master that magestones are formed deep in the earth," said Nûd. "That's where their congruencies are created by the *cuddio tân.*"

Eynon nodded as his boots were secured. *That made sense,* he reasoned. There were stories from across the sea about mountains that belched fire and rivers of molten stone, after all. *Why couldn't hot springs toss up magestones?*

"From time to time, magestones find their way to the surface," Nûd continued, "especially where the ground is weak and water and mud seep through."

"I understand," said Eynon.

"Not *all* magestones are found that way," said Nûd. "Some are buried in very old rocks that have been squeezed and folded deep underground. Hot springs and mud pots make them easier to find without mining."

"We have mines for green slate and marble in Wherrel, back in the Coombe," said Eynon. "Mining is backbreaking work. I'd rather pick magestones up off the ground, if I had a choice."

"I hope *your* magestone shoots out of the first hot spring you pass and lands in your hands."

"Where's the adventure in that?" asked Eynon. *If only it could be that easy.*

"Getting back to sharing one of the Master's lessons, slate and marble are shale and limestone that performed well under pressure," said Nûd. "Magestones need a lot more time and pressure to cook."

"Are there magestones *in* the hot springs and mud pots?" asked Eynon.

"Sometimes," Nûd replied, "but if they are, you won't be able to get them. You need to look for ones tossed out onto safe ground by jets of steam or bubbling mud."

"What if I see a magestone in a hot spring? Couldn't I stick my hand in and grab it?"

"There's a reason hot springs are steaming," said Nûd. "If you reached in, your hand and arm would be cooked in seconds."

"Then I definitely won't do that," Eynon said with a smile.

Nûd raised an eyebrow, then wiggled it until Eynon laughed.

"You'd better not," said the big man. "Then I'd have to go back to eating my own cooking."

Eynon tested the snowshoes on the thick powder a few feet beyond the castle's side door. They worked well on the deep snow.

"We can't have that, so I'll be careful," said Eynon. "Thank you for the snowshoes—and the good advice."

"Glad to help," said Nûd.

"One more question," said Eynon.

"Only one?" asked Nûd.

"For now," said Eynon. "Damon didn't want to tell me, but how will I know a magestone when I see it? How can I tell a magestone from an ordinary piece of rock?"

"Damon was right to say little," Nûd answered. "Anyone with the talent for wizardry you've displayed using a training magestone will be able to sense which is which."

"If you say so."

"I do," said Nûd. "And be careful where you step. Use your staff to test the ground before you put your weight down anywhere, though usually if something is growing on it, the footing is solid."

"I'll remember that," said Eynon.

Nûd rubbed the top of Chee's head where it showed at the collar of Eynon's coat underneath the bottom of his long scarf.

"Be sure to keep this little fellow out of trouble. Hot springs and mud pots are not good places for raconettes," said the big man.

"I'll watch out for him," said Eynon. *But who will watch out for me?*

* * * * *

When he reached the bottom of the slope, Eynon answered his own question. *I'll have to watch out for myself.*

Nûd's scenario about a magestone shooting out of a hot spring and into his hands wasn't likely. Eynon was more interested in the polychromatic spring farther back than anything close at hand. It pulled him, somehow. He'd have to figure out how to get from where he was to where he needed to be, without scalding himself or falling into a sinkhole.

Eynon checked on Chee, but the raconette remained burrowed deep inside his coat.

Maybe it smells better in there than out here? he considered.

The rotten-egg smell was particularly bad near the field of mud pots to his right. Eynon saw ground ahead of him supporting grass dusted with gray mud and stubborn shrubs with a few small leaves clinging to their branches. He sat on a nearby rock and took off his snowshoes, which weren't much good without snow. He put them on top of the rock, gripped one end of his staff, and walked forward, testing the ground with every step.

A crystal-clear pool was on his left. It was only gently steaming and had an orange and yellow ring around its edge. Eynon spared a moment to look for stones or clods of earth that might be magestones anywhere around the pool, but he didn't see anything promising. He carefully steered his way between mud and water hazards, making slow progress toward the multicolored spring farther back.

Directly ahead was an empty circular stretch of white ground about as far across as he could throw a rock the size of his fist. The center of the circle gently sloped up to a modest rise, topped by a truncated cone-shaped formation that looked like a melted candle. Thin lines of darker colors, like streaks of rust, radiated out from the cone and converged on the downhill side of the circle, closest to the mud pots.

The footing seemed solid, despite the lack of vegetation, so Eynon allowed his curiosity to win out over his sense of self-preservation. He approached the formation cautiously. Chee stuck his head out of Eynon's coat. Eynon glanced down to see the raconette's eyes scan back and forth and his nose wrinkle.

"I don't like the way it smells here any more than you do, little fellow," said Eynon. "But I do want to check this out. I don't think it's an insect mound. I've never seen one that big!"

Eynon used his staff to tap the ground, feeling for hidden sinkholes. He realized that the surface around the cut-off cone seemed *more* solid than most of the ground in the basin. It reminded Eynon of the coating of ice he'd had to chip off his family's farm wagon when a rare sleet storm descended on the Coombe three winters back. When he struck the ground with his staff, the white surface made a *tink-tink* sound instead of a *thump-thump*.

"So far, so good, Chee," said Eynon, stroking the raconette's head with two fingers.

He was nearly at the cone, about to look down inside it, when he heard the beast hiss. A heartbeat later, he realized it wasn't Chee making the noise—it was the cone. A thread of steam rose from its center and the hissing grew louder. It was joined by a rushing sound that reminded him of the waterfalls near the castle.

Chee broke into a frantic chorus of *chi-chi-chi-chees*, repeated over and over. He pawed Eynon's chest from inside his coat.

"I'm with you, my friend," said Eynon. "Let's get out of here!"

He turned and ran back over ground he'd already tested, his staff rocking back and forth in his left hand with each stride. The waterfall sound grew louder and it felt like something liquid was rushing by not far beneath Eynon's speeding feet. He didn't stop until he was outside the circle of white ground, near the field of mud pots. Then he spun around on the toes of his boots to see what was happening.

With a fierce sound like every mountain lion in Dâron growling simultaneously, a jet of steaming water shot out of the top of the truncated cone until it was at least ten times taller than Eynon.

Accompanying the roaring jet was a hissing that could have come from a batsnake as large as a dragon. Sunlight through the mist generated by the jet made the water droplets in the air sparkle. A few drops, carried by a slight breeze, landed on Eynon's face. One rolled down his cheek and he captured it with his tongue.

It was bitterly alkaline and made the atrocious cider he'd had for yesterday's breakfast taste good by comparison.

The water continued to thunder upward for a few more seconds. When it stopped, Eynon saw a strange creature emerge from a bubbling cauldron in the field of mud pots to his right. It looked something like a lizard, but was built like an armored weasel, with a sinuous body and long tail covered in hundreds of thick, mud-gray plates. It had an extended snout, longer and wider in proportion than a wolf's, and a mouth lined with sharp pointed teeth. Waves of heat radiated from its body and the mud that covered it had baked into a second skin in the few seconds since it had emerged.

Eynon had no idea what sort of creature it was. There weren't any beasts remotely like this monstrosity in the Coombe. Then the creature from the mud pots spotted him and turned to stare in his direction. Its eyes were hypnotizing. They were deep red and twice as large as they should have been for an animal of its size. Eynon was captivated. He couldn't look away as patterns of something dark—he didn't know what—swirled in the glistening red spaces surrounding the vertical black pupils.

The small part of Eynon's brain that wasn't held in place by the beast's gaze gave the creature a name. *Basilisk*. The species was briefly mentioned in the middle of a long chapter toward the end of Robin Goodfellow's *Peregrinations*. Some of the beasts lived on a large island near a fire mountain in the middle of an inland sea. Goodfellow reported that they could turn people to stone. Instead, Eynon realized, they froze their prey in place with their eyes so they'd be easier to capture and eat.

Eynon could feel the blue stone on his chest pulsing a warning, but it didn't help. Like a mouse facing a batsnake, he couldn't move or break eye contact.

The mud-covered beast lumbered toward Eynon on legs that splayed out to the sides, using the same gait as the tiny lizards that skittered about on warm rocks in the Coombe. When it was a dozen yards from Eynon, the basilisk opened its mouth like it was yawning, revealing a bright red palate and purple tongue.

The part of Eynon's mind that wasn't entranced saw that the movement was designed to expand the basilisk's jaw so it would be able to consume Eynon whole, not waste time cutting him into bits with its teeth.

The monster set its feet and wiggled its rear hips like a house cat preparing to pounce on an unwary songbird. The free portion of Eynon's brain thought of Merry and how much he wished he was still with her back in the Blue Spiral Tower.

Ouch! Eynon was in pain. Sharp claws were digging into his chest and neck. It was Chee. The little beast climbed up to his hat, clutching the beaver fur with his front paws and hanging down. The raconette's body covered Eynon's eyes and broke the basilisk's hypnotic gaze. Eynon turned away. Chee quickly flowed his flexible form back inside Eynon's coat.

Eynon's feet propelled him of their own accord. He ran deeper into the basin with the steaming basilisk in literal hot pursuit.

Chapter 19

"Searching is as much about the seeker as what's sought."
— Ealdamon's *Epigrams*

It's not easy to work magic when you're running for your life, thought Eynon.

From the sound of its footfalls, the basilisk was gaining on him, despite Eynon's much longer legs. Eynon focused on speed, not safe footing, though he kept enough sense of self-preservation to mostly put his feet on patches of ground with vegetation.

Ahead was another steaming circular hot spring—this one ringed in blue and green. Eynon lengthened his stride and pulled slightly ahead of the basilisk until he put the spring between himself and the mud-caked monster. There was enough steam rising off the surface of the spring to interfere with the basilisk's hypnotic gaze. Eynon could keep track of the beast's location without having to worry about being mesmerized.

The hungry creature circled to the left. Eynon matched its movements to stay on the opposite side of the hot spring. The beast turned back and circled right. Eynon changed course as well—stalemate.

The basilisk sniffed at the water in the hot spring and growled. Eynon had been afraid the menacing monster would jump into the spring to swim across and attack him, but the mud-dwelling lizard-thing didn't seem inclined to get wet. It stared at Eynon and he looked away, unwilling to risk a chance of being frozen in place by the basilisk's gaze.

In the lull as the young man and the monster considered their next moves, Eynon finally focused enough magic to generate a rudimentary round-shield of solidified sound. If the basilisk tried to attack him now, Eynon could interpose the shield between the basilisk's teeth and his own vulnerable flesh.

The beast didn't attack him, though. Eynon could see its mind wasn't as quick as its four-limbed gait. It was still trying to figure out why chasing the tall human around the hot spring wouldn't work. Eynon had an idea, based on how his sister would discourage their cats when they wanted to help her peel vegetables at the sink back home.

He *pushed* the solidified sound round-shield away from him with the bottom inch or two of the shield just skimming the surface of the spring. A spray of hot water flew up and struck the basilisk's face and shoulders. The beast growled and retreated a few paces back toward the mud pots.

It doesn't like water, Eynon determined. *Maybe it doesn't like losing its protective layer of mud?*

Splashing water with his shield only sent the liquid flying a short distance, so Eynon reformed the simple, one-piece magical barrier into a more complex construct.

It looks like a giant milkweed pod, he realized, *or an unshelled almond as big as a prizewinning blackseed melon.*

He lowered the lens-shaped structure into the hot spring and increased its permeability so it would fill with water. Then he lifted the lens out of the water, brought it close to the basilisk on the far side of the spring, and pressed the top and bottom of the lens together with wizardry, allowing a jet of water to squirt from an opening he'd created at the tip.

The stream of high-pressure heated water struck the basilisk on its nose, evoking a low-pitched grunt of surprise and a series of indignant squeals from the gray mud-covered beast as it abruptly turned and retreated back to its original field of mud pots.

It worked! thought Eynon. *A lot like the water shooting up from the tall mound! Maybe that's what planted the idea in the back of my head?*

No matter what had inspired the concept, Eynon was glad to be safe, at least for now. He had bigger expectations for his life than ending up as a basilisk's lunch. Chee stuck his head up at Eynon's coat collar and gave a satisfied *chi-chee* of approval. He kept his head out to supervise.

Eynon refilled the transparent lens with more spring water and directed it to hover at-the-ready behind his head in case more monsters emerged from mud pots on his way to the multicolored hot spring. *It never hurts to be prepared,* he considered, realizing that would make a good epigram if he lived long enough to write it down.

With a quick hop, Eynon jumped up on a small boulder to take stock of his surroundings. He was pleased to see he was a lot closer to his planned destination than he'd expected. His feet must have carried him in that direction when he'd run from the basilisk.

Climbing down and using his staff to check the ground, Eynon crossed a narrow isthmus between two broad fields of mud pots and finally reached the polychromatic hot spring that had initially captured his interest.

It was every bit as intriguing close up. The hot spring was circular and close to fifty feet across, Eynon estimated. Now that he was next to it, he could see the colors came from something floating on the surface of the water, like the green algae or scum that formed on the edges of farm ponds or horse troughs back in the Coombe. The red, orange, yellow, green, blue and purple rings around this hot spring had colors far more intense than the muted green Eynon was familiar with, however.

Eynon scanned the area, looking for threats, and realized there was a large, pale rock formation at the back of the spring. It was taller than he was, but hard to spot because it was the same uniform shade of white as the rest of the land in the basin. Carefully checking his footing, Eynon tapped his way around the spring's perimeter until he reached the rock. He hoped to climb up it somehow, to gain a better view of the spring's rainbow of colors.

He was pleased to see someone had carved narrow steps into the side of the rock away from the hot spring. Eynon ascended until he reached a flat spot no bigger than a boy's sleeping pallet at the top. He was high enough to have an excellent view of the hot spring and its translucent rings of color. To Eynon's surprise, the center was transparent, not translucent.

The red color in the middle of the spring was not from floating plants. It came from something resting on top of a small white pillar in the spring's exact center—a brightly glowing red gem, easily visible through the clear water. When Eynon saw it something snapped into place in his brain.

That's my magestone!

Now he understood what Damon had meant by, "You'll know it when you see it."

From his elevated vantage point he could see the gem pulse and sparkle, as if it was calling to him from the depths of the spring. The blue magestone under his coat and shirt was vibrating, sharing his excitement. Eynon couldn't tell if it was jealous of the red stone as a competitor or happy that he'd found *his* stone at last.

You're mine, thought Eynon, *but how do I get you?*

He wasn't interested in losing his skin by diving into the steaming, toxic water. Maybe if he knew the secret of controlling animals, he could entice the basilisk into entering the spring to retrieve the stone, but given that monster's antipathy for water and its evident unpleasant disposition, Eynon would have to come up with another solution.

With a hand shading his eyes, Eynon scanned the trees nearby, looking for one tall and slender enough to help him reach for the glowing red magestone. Unfortunately, all the nearby trees—where *nearby* meant a quarter to half a mile away—had trunks too thick to serve in that capacity. Besides, he knew it would be wrong to mar the chromatic symmetry of the rainbow-colored hot spring by stirring its waters with a pole, no matter what its diameter.

Could I summon the stone to my hand? mused Eynon. There were tales of wizards demonstrating great feats of levitation, though most moved their own bodies through the air on magic disks, at least according to an illustration he'd seen in *Peregrinations.* After half a day of training, Eynon was pleased he could make simple shapes from solidified sound. Levitation must be a future lesson.

Wait! he realized. *I know how to cast fireballs, sort of.*

That idea also fell by the wayside. If inserting a pole in the spring would be wrong, disturbing its delicate equilibrium with a fireball would be a travesty. He had to find a better way. Eynon could almost hear the red magestone calling to him. Something inside him ached to hold it in his palm, to feel it against his skin, but he was stymied. There *had* to be a way.

Nûd had said, "I hope *your* magestone shoots out of the first hot spring you pass and lands in your hands." Eynon considered that he might have enough fine control to flash-boil a few ounces of water directly below the red gem, tossing it out of the hot spring where he could catch it with a construct of solidified sound. He focused his mind and called on the same wizardry that boiled water for clean dishes earlier. Unfortunately, despite Eynon's most intense concentration, all he managed to do was cause the water near his magestone to bubble more vigorously.

Why did Damon think I was ready to find my magestone? wondered Eynon. *I need to learn a lot more magic before I can do anything useful.*

He wiped his forehead where he had been sweating underneath his fur hat, not sure whether the extra perspiration was from mental exertion or steam from nearby mud pot fields. Eynon looked down and saw a broad shadow flicker over the rock where he was standing. It moved across the surface of the spring before disappearing. Eynon tilted his head back and spotted a black wyvern—probably the one he'd encountered earlier—circling fifty feet above him.

Where's your yellow ball, big fellow? thought Eynon.

While maintaining the basilisk-discouraging lens filled with water behind his head, Eynon created another tasty ball of solid sound and sent it high into the sky. The wyvern beat its wings and gave chase, like a hound fetching a pheasant. The wyvern was a distraction, for now, but with careful handling, the two-legged dragon-like creature wouldn't be dangerous.

Creating the ball for the wyvern to chase gave Eynon an idea. He could control the motion of his solidified sound constructs, up to a point. What if he pushed a ball into the center of the hot spring and made its bottom semi-permeable, like Nûd pushing the bar of soap into the lens with the dishwater back in the castle? He could push the ball down on top of the red gem and retrieve his magestone. That might be something he could handle with his limited magical abilities.

It's worth a try, thought Eynon.

He formed a transparent ball of solidified sound as wide as his outstretched palm, without worrying about its color or taste. Then he guided the ball down into the center of the hot spring until it was directly above the red gem. An extra push moved the stone from the top of the white pillar to *inside* the ball—Eynon was almost there.

The gem seemed to blink at him encouragingly, though perhaps it was just a trick of the light reflecting underwater.

With a nudge of his magic, the ball expanded to the size of his head. The enlarged ball ascended until it was out of the water and hovering in front of Eynon's station atop the rock. He opened a small hole in its base so the boiling alkali water could drain out. Then, with a *pop* he dispelled the bubble of solidified sound. Eynon caught the magestone as it fell into his hand.

Success! The magestone was warm in his palm, nestling against his skin like it belonged there.

Unfortunately, Eynon wasn't able to relax after his accomplishment. He heard several more threatening pops, plus thick, gooey plops accompanied by deep grunts and growls. Two dozen basilisks had emerged from the mud pot fields on both sides of the multicolored hot spring and were fast approaching Eynon's rocky perch. He gulped and stared at first, but didn't completely succumb to the beasts' combined hypnotic gazes.

After a deep breath to clear his mind, Eynon directed the water-filled lens behind his head toward the lead basilisk and compressed it, sending a jet of liquid into the monster's face. It stopped momentarily, but the other mud-covered beasts continued to approach. Soon, the one he'd squirted shook off the effect of the water and joined them. Four basilisks were now on the makeshift stairs leading up the rock to Eynon's position.

The combined magic of the blue and red magestone gave Eynon confidence, despite the monsters below him. With his staff in one hand, the red gem in his other hand, and the blue stone around his neck, he formed new spheres of solidified sound the size of melons and sent them down to smash into the beasts' noses. That proved counterproductive. It only made them angry.

Three of the basilisks were already at the edge of the flat space on top of the rock.

Eynon created steps of solidified sound and climbed them until he was standing on top of an invisible tower two feet wide and six feet tall. Basilisks roared and snapped below him, sending drops of gray mud up to spatter his coat. Eynon could feel Chee cowering below his sternum. It would only be seconds before more basilisks arrived and climbed over the ones already in place to reach Eynon and snatch him from his magic-generated pedestal. He didn't want to look down, in case a basilisk caught his gaze and froze him in place, but it would be only moments before he became food for the mud monsters.

A shield of solidified sound around his body might protect him from the beasts' teeth and claws temporarily, but he didn't know how long he could keep such a shield in place, and the monsters didn't seem inclined to leave. Eynon wondered if he could shape a sled, like half a barrel, out of solidified sound and ride down over the backs of the attacking basilisks, but realized that would return him to the ground where he'd be even easier prey.

Eynon was considering other, even less attractive options for escape when all his choices were abruptly taken away. Pain and surprise made him scream as the tips of massive claws pierced his skin.

Chapter 20

"The world looks different from the clouds."
— Ealdamon's *Epigrams*

Eynon was torn from his magical pedestal and felt himself rising, his face buffeted by downdrafts from the beating of broad, bat-like wings. Below him, the landscape of hot springs and mud pots was getting smaller. The angry grunts of thwarted basilisks faded as Eynon gained altitude. He could feel Chee quivering inside his heavy wisent-skin coat and was glad that garment was thick enough so that the wyvern's claws only pricked the skin of his shoulders instead of creating deep punctures. Above him, Eynon could see the beast's massive black chest. It was all he could do to hang on to his new magestone in one hand and his staff in the other.

I hope it didn't decide I'm a snack-sized wisent? thought Eynon.

The two-legged dragon-like beast was flying back in the general direction of the Academy. It circled above the clearing where Eynon had seen the gryffon take on the old bull wisent and descended rapidly, coming in for a none-too-gentle landing. The beast dropped Eynon a second before its own taloned feet touched the ground.

Eynon rolled, protecting Chee with his arms, and used his staff to help him stand. His shoulders burned, but Eynon didn't have time to worry about minor injuries—the wyvern was turning to face him, its toothy mouth open wide.

Eynon threw up a shield of solidified sound just as the wyvern's tongue flipped out to lick him. Saliva dribbled down the far side of the shield, making Eynon laugh in an unplanned release of nervous tension. The wyvern's expression resembled a puppy's throw-me-a-ball face. Eynon shifted gears from concern to relief. The wyvern could eat him in a single gulp, but that didn't seem to be its intent.

"Who's a good boy?" said Eynon to the scaly beast, using the same tone of voice he'd take with a friendly dog.

The wyvern's tongue shot out and licked Eynon's shield a second time. Slobber dripped from the corners of its mouth. The monster's pointed external ears flicked up and its striking copper eyes opened wide. Clearly the creature was expecting something.

Without dropping his shield, Eynon formed another bright yellow, high-frequency ball of solidified sound. The wyvern's long, pointed tail thumped excitedly against the ground. Eynon could feel Chee's head poke out from his coat, but didn't have time to spare to check on the raconette.

With a burst of magical energy, Eynon sent the yellow ball a hundred feet into the air. The wyvern launched itself after the ball and captured it in its mouth before it fell more than a dozen feet. Eynon watched as the massive creature, three times the size of the bull wisent, circled and gracefully landed back in its original position. Once in place, the wyvern opened its mouth and allowed the ball to roll out on the ground, where it bumped against Eynon's shield with a soft *click*.

"Do you want to play, boy?" asked Eynon.

He sent the yellow ball up again, this time spinning it on a high arc behind the wyvern. The beast shot skyward, made a quick midair turn, and retrieved the ball a second time, dropping it in front of Eynon with a gentle bow of its head.

"Good boy," said Eynon.

Eynon didn't know if the wyvern was male or female or something else unique to its species. He wasn't interested in examining its hindquarters close enough to check, either, so *good boy* would have to do for now.

The beast's fascination with the ball of solidified sound gave Eynon an idea. He moved the yellow ball off the ground until it floated in front of the wyvern's nose, then slowly guided it to the left. The wyvern's head followed the ball. Eynon lowered his shield—still keeping it at the ready if necessary—and stepped to the beast's right side. He lowered the ball so the wyvern had to crouch to stay level with the ball.

Eynon moved the yellow sphere in small circles to keep the wyvern's attention. He put his new magestone in his pouch for safe-keeping and slid his staff in next to the shard strapped to his pack.

Then he stepped up on the creature's right leg and found a flat spot to sit between the wyvern's wings.

Two protruding bony knobs a hand's breadth in front of the wings gave Eynon something to hang on to. For extra safety, he took off his scarf and used it to anchor himself securely in place.

The wyvern didn't seem to notice Eynon on his back. Its focus was completely on the yellow ball, which it licked every few seconds. Now that he was on top of the beast, Eynon could feel a rumbling below him—whether from the wyvern' hunger or happiness, he couldn't tell. Eynon gently urged the ball up and the wyvern followed. Once aloft, he got his bearings and directed the ball southeast toward the castle.

Eynon eased forward and peered over the front edge of the wyvern' beating wings. He couldn't see the fields of hot springs and mud pots behind him, but did see rising clouds that he thought must be connected to the waterfalls near the Academy. They were on course.

Dozens of other towers of steam rose, marking additional hot springs distributed around Melyncárreg. The colors of the terrain below were the dark green of pine trees and the white of the winter's remaining snow. A few miles ahead, Eynon spotted the Academy's outer walls and towers, their gray stones standing out against the stark background. Far in the distance were the deep blue waters of a lake surrounded by low hills.

It's beautiful, thought Eynon as he gazed at the land rolling by below him. *I wonder if I can spot the Coombe if we go higher?*

Eynon decided not to try for more altitude. Somehow, he knew that his homeland was far away. If Melyncárreg was anywhere near the Coombe he would have heard of its strange wonders from passing travelers or would have read about it in Robin Goodfellow's *Peregrinations.* Besides, flying made him cold, even through his heavy coat. He'd be glad to have some hot soup and a couple of the rolls he had in his pack. It would be time for lunch in an hour, after all.

The wyvern's wings made Eynon's return journey much faster than his outbound trip. They were circling the castle in minutes.

Eynon sent the yellow ball down to rest a few dozen feet from the side door that led down to the castle's kitchen and the wyvern followed it. He left his scarf in place in case he ever needed to ride on wyvern-back again and slid down the beast's flank to stand in the snow. The black beast kept its focus on the yellow sphere, which Eynon moved back and forth on the ground in front of him.

To reward the wyvern for its help, Eynon took one of the four remaining bread rolls out of this pack and surrounded it with a second ball of solidified sound, infusing the roll with some of the flavor of his magic. He guided the second ball next to the first one in front of the wyvern and dispelled its protective sphere. The wyvern sniffed at the magic-enhanced roll where it rested on the white ground, then stuck a claw-tip in it and brought it up to his mouth.

"Go ahead. Eat it, boy," said Eynon.

While the beast investigated the baked dough, Eynon slowly walked over to the kitchen door. He thought he could escape through it if the wyvern decided Eynon meant eat *him,* not the roll. He watched as the wyvern popped the small bit of bread off the end of its claw, savored it on its tongue, and swallowed.

The wyvern's response to the treat made him smile. It was much more intense than the armored creature's reaction to the non-magical roll earlier. The big beast turned over on its back and writhed against the snow-covered ground in apparent ecstasy, emitting a high-pitched hum from its throat that Eynon interpreted as a sign of pleasure. Eynon took a second roll from his pack, seasoned it with a touch of solidified-sound magic, and tossed it to the wyvern, earning a repeat performance.

"I'm glad you like my baking," he said to the wyvern's armored belly.

Behind Eynon, the kitchen door opened with a creak. He turned to see Nûd standing inside the entryway, wearing an expression that looked like he'd been struck in the back of the head with a piece of cord wood.

"What. Is. That?" asked the Master's young servant.

"He followed me home," said Eynon. "Can I keep him?"

Chapter 21

"Be careful about exceeding expectations.
Others may come to expect it."
— Ealdamon's *Epigrams*

Nûd looked up to mark the sun's position, then laughed so hard he had to bend part-way over and put his hands on his knees.

"What's so funny?" asked Eynon.

He kept one eye on the wyvern, who was happily licking the yellow ball of solidified sound that had rolled thirty feet downslope.

After taking a deep breath, Nûd controlled his laughter, but kept a big smile on his face. He straightened up and answered.

"You're back well before noon," said the big man. "I don't think anyone's ever done that before."

"I hitched a ride," said Eynon, glancing at the wyvern and smiling back at Nûd.

"You don't understand," said Nûd. "Usually, candidates come staggering in close to supper time or the following day after lunch."

Eynon nodded. Nûd's face grew more solemn.

"Some don't come back at all."

"I think I know why," said Eynon, remembering the basilisks.

He started to tell Nûd what had happened, but the big man interrupted.

"Wait," said Nûd, holding up his hand. "Not now. You can tell me *and* Damon over lunch in the kitchen."

Eynon remembered he had two rolls left in his pack.

"I'll make some soup," he said.

"A wise plan," said Nûd with a grin. "What about your oversized associate outside?"

"He just ate," joked Eynon, though he wasn't sure how much of the bull wisent had been left after the gryffon had feasted.

He created two more balls of solidified sound—one blue, one green—to add to the yellow sphere, in hopes of keeping his new friend occupied and out of trouble.

After a final check on the wyvern, Eynon followed Nûd down the stairs to the kitchen. He took off his pack, hung up his hat and coat, and leaned his staff in a corner. Then he fed Chee a dried cherry, and set off to gather ingredients from the pantries, while Nûd went to the library to find Damon.

In the cold pantry, which was exposed to the frigid outdoor temperatures, Eynon discovered half a wisent carcass hanging to age. He sliced a modest chunk of meat from it, then collected several different root vegetables—turnips, rutabagas, carrots, and onions— plus a quarter-wheel of soft cheese, dried peas and a handful of spices from other storage locations.

Eynon cubed most of the meat, chopped the vegetables, and put them all in a pot over the fire with the dried peas and the spices. He added enough clean water from the system of magical lenses still running over the main sink to cover all the ingredients. Unfortunately, the soup wouldn't be ready until dinner time, but he had a plan for a tasty lunch.

He sharpened his knife again and used it to cut thin slices from the remaining wisent meat and dice a large onion. A follow-up trip to the pantries helped him locate a bottle of sunflower seed oil and a large bulb of dried garlic. Eynon minced two cloves and put them near the wisent steak and onions. Then he took a large cast iron frying pan from a peg on the wall near the fireplace and suspended it a foot above his prep table on a hollow cylinder of solidified sound.

Here goes, he said to himself.

Drawing on the power of the congruencies inside both the red and blue magestones, he added heat to the bottom of the frying pan, which he'd already covered with a layer of oil. Soon the oil was bubbling and crackling. Fire magic seemed to come even easier, now that he had help from *his* magestone.

"Nûd!" Eynon shouted. "Damon! Lunch time."

He calculated that it would take the pair a few minutes to get to the kitchen—if they'd heard him—so he'd have time to finish cooking their noon meal before they arrived. First, he browned the meat. It was so thin it was ready in seconds. He moved it to one side of the pan and tossed in the onions and garlic. They added their savory smells to the kitchen and must have wafted up the stairs, because Nûd appeared a minute later, with Damon behind him. The older man was beaming.

"Eynon!" he said. "Good lad! You've set a new record."

"For what?" asked Eynon as he moved the meat and onions back and forth in the pan with a long-handled ale-cake turner.

Nûd anticipated what Eynon would need next and brought three pewter plates over to the sizzling pan.

Damon didn't respond—he didn't want to distract Eynon from his culinary efforts.

Eynon portioned out the meat, onions, and garlic. Nûd and Damon took their plates and sat at the broad kitchen table. Reaching down, Eynon took his last two rolls out of his pack and gave them to Nûd and Damon. They used them to sop up the cooking juices.

"Did the Master like my rolls?" Eynon asked Nûd.

The big servant brought his hand to his forehead.

"I'm a fool," he said.

Damon nodded his agreement, but didn't stop chewing.

"I never took the rolls up to him," Nûd continued. "They're still in a cloth bag in the dry pantry. I'll get them."

"Won't the Master be upset if he doesn't get his rolls?" Eynon asked Nûd's departing back.

Damon winked at him and wiped juice from his chin.

"What the Master doesn't know won't hurt him," said the older man.

"Oh," said Eynon.

He'd hoped that the Master would like his rolls, and therefore might want to meet the newest student in the Academy face to face. Now Eynon would have to come up with another strategy to bring himself to the Master's attention.

When Nûd returned, Eynon saw there were only four rolls left in the bag. Nûd looked guilty.

"Damon and I each had one for breakfast," he said. "The Master doesn't usually have a big appetite, so we didn't think he'd mind if we ate his."

Eynon wagged a finger at Nûd in mock disapproval and took two of the rolls, leaving the others one more each. Then he brought his own palm to his forehead.

"Now I'm a fool," said Eynon. "I forgot the cheese."

Eynon cut the quarter-wedge in thirds and passed pieces to Nûd and Damon. Chee saw the cheese and decided to descend from a kitchen rafter where he'd been sleeping to join the humans below. Eynon fed him bits of roll and morsels of cheese. A minute later, the raconette's cheek pouches were bulging and he was sprawled out on the table amid the plates.

"I'm thirsty," said Damon. "Break out that bottle of the good stuff I know you're hiding. We need to celebrate!"

"Since you asked so nicely," said Nûd.

The big man walked back into the warren of pantries and returned with three small glass goblets and a tall, dusty, thick-walled bottle. Eynon read the label. *Applegarth's Finest.* He smiled in anticipation.

Nûd removed a wax seal and extracted the bottle's cork with a loud pop. The scent of apples wafted across the table. The big servant poured the potent apple-flavored liquor into the goblets and handed one to Eynon. A sip later, Eynon was convinced the applejack lived up to its name. Its complex, fiery flavor was amazing. He'd have to compliment Baron Derry next time he saw him.

It was still hard for Eynon to think of Merry's father as a nobleman. Derry seemed so down-to-earth and friendly, not like the tales he'd heard about stuffy nobles who thought they were better than yeoman farmers and artisans.

"Nûd told me you tamed a wyvern," said Damon with a kindly smile.

"Yes, sir," said Eynon. "And I found my magestone."

"Remember to call me Damon, lad. Calling me *sir* makes me feel old."

"But you *are...*" began Nûd.

Damon stopped him with a raised finger.

"You can tell us about the wyvern later. Let's see what you found," Damon continued.

"Yes, sir—I mean, yes, Damon," said Eynon.

He removed his magestone from his pouch and carefully placed it on the table. The stone's red glow washed across the wooden surface. Chee opened one eye and stared at it for a few seconds, then returned to napping. Damon leaned in to examine the magestone more closely.

"It's *red,*" said Nûd.

"Your powers of observation astound me," said Damon dryly.

"Is that bad?" asked Eynon.

"Not at all," said Damon, "but it is unusual. As I'd told you, most wizards from Dâron resonate with blue stones, just as Tamloch's wizards favor green."

"And wizards from the Eagle People use purple or black magestones?"

"You were paying attention, lad," said Damon. "Very good."

The older man shifted position so he could get a better look at the far side of Eynon's magestone.

"A red stone is uncommon?" asked Eynon.

"A red stone is unprecedented," Damon replied.

"Maybe the Master knows about wizards with red stones?" offered Nûd.

Damon looked at the big servant and raised an eyebrow.

"Maybe," said the older man, shaking his head from side to side. "This one is half the size of a hen's egg."

"Is that large for a magestone?" asked Eynon.

"Yes," said Damon. "It certainly is. Most magestones are no bigger than the last joint of your thumb. This one is four times that size, though it will be smaller when you cut and polish it."

"Cut it?" asked Eynon. He was reluctant to do anything that might damage the stone.

"Don't worry," said Damon. "Your magestone will guide you through the process. Cutting and polishing makes it sparkle."

"It sparkles now," said Nûd.

"After cutting and polishing it will sparkle more," said Damon.

"Of course," said Nûd. The big servant tilted his head to acknowledge Damon's evident wisdom. Eynon watched him stick out his tongue at the older man when Damon couldn't see him.

"What do I need to do after cutting and polishing?" asked Eynon.

"You'll need to craft a setting for it," said Damon. "A stone of this caliber will need an extra-fine gold setting."

"A magestone that big will require a *lot* of gold," added Nûd.

"I don't have any money to buy gold for a setting," said Eynon.

He leaned his elbows on the table and stared at the pulsing red gem. He wanted his magestone to have a worthy setting, but had no idea how he'd pay for gold leaf, let alone a lump of gold.

"That doesn't matter," said Damon. "Wizards find their magestones—and they also find the materials for their settings."

What? thought Eynon.

"I knew a wizard who made her setting out of carved wood," said Nûd. "She didn't have any trouble finding what she needed."

Eynon remembered the unending miles of trees outside the castle. He was considering whether he would make his setting from hardwood or pine when Damon spoke up.

"Nothing but gold will do for *this* stone."

"If you say so," said Eynon. "Where's the nearest gold mine?"

"Hundreds of miles from here," offered Nûd, "but don't worry. You won't have to *mine* it."

"You can pan for it in the river," said Damon. "Nûd will show you."

"Thank you for volunteering me," said Nûd.

"I'm sure the Master would approve," said Damon.

"I'll have words with the Master and confirm that later," Nûd replied. "For now, though, I can show you how to get started."

"The sooner you have enough gold, the sooner you can craft your setting," Damon added. "You should get moving while you still have plenty of daylight. It will take you a week or more to accumulate enough dust."

"I thought I needed gold, not dust," said Eynon.

"Mister Inscrutable is talking about *gold* dust, not household dust," said Nûd.

"If you needed household dust, I would have sent you upstairs," said Damon. "Due to someone's lack of attention, the third floor is covered in the stuff."

"I'll clean the third floor when there's good reason to," said Nûd. "With so few students and wizards in residence, I have better things to do with my time than clean vacant rooms."

"As you say," said Damon. "I'm surprised the Master tolerates such a lack of attention."

"I'm surprised you're allowed to teach apprentices, old man."

"Excuse me," Eynon inserted. "Where do I have to go to *pan* for gold, please?"

"Just a few miles upriver from the falls," said Damon.

"Get your coat and snowshoes," said Nûd. "I'll take you to a good spot and show you how it's done."

"Ummm," said Eynon.

"What?" asked Nûd.

"The snowshoes you gave me are back at the hot springs."

"Oh. Well, that can't be helped," said Nûd. "I'm sure I can find another pair around somewhere—unless we're traveling on wyvern-back."

"That could probably be arranged," said Eynon with a smile.

"This I've got to see," said Damon. The corners of his mouth were turning up.

"One thing first, though," said Eynon.

"What?" asked Nûd.

"I want to start some bread for dinner."

"An excellent idea," said Damon. "All in favor?"

He raised his hand and so did Nûd and Eynon.

"The ayes have it," said Damon. "Now get cooking, and be quick about it. The sun sets early in Melyncárreg at this time of year."

"Yes, sir," said Eynon.

"Yes, *Damon,*" the older man corrected. "Call me when you're ready to set out. I want to see your new pet."

* * * * *

Six loaves of bread were proofing in a niche near the fire when Eynon and Nûd were ready to set out. Eynon had strapped his shard-sword on the back of his pack and hung his crossbow on his belt. Nûd had given Eynon two glazed ceramic dishes, like pie pans, and several small drawstring bags of tightly woven cloth. *For the dust,* Nûd had said. Chee was perched on top of Eynon's fur hat, where he could properly supervise the humans' activities.

Nûd shouted up the stairs to the library. "We're leaving, old man. Come down if you want to see Eynon's wyvern."

"On my way," came Damon's voice in reply.

The older man took his coat down from a peg and put it on. He followed Nûd and Eynon up to the castle's side door. Eynon tried to push the door open, but couldn't. Something was blocking it. Nûd added his strength and they were slowly able to push the obstacle out of the way. A dozen feet back from the door, the big black wyvern was sitting on its haunches, playing with the three balls of solidified sound.

Nûd tugged on Eynon's arm. He looked down and saw what had been blocking the door. It was the carcass of a large buck, with odd white markings and strange-looking antlers. From what Eynon could tell, the wyvern must have left it as an offering.

"We haven't had pronghorn in a few months," said Nûd. "They're good eating."

Eynon filed it away that the unusual deer were called pronghorns. Reexamining this one's antlers, he thought the name was apt. And he was quite fond of venison.

"Thank you," said Eynon to the wyvern.

The beast nodded and kicked the yellow ball to Eynon, who picked it up and tossed it back. Chee chattered at the wyvern from the safety of Eynon's hat.

"I didn't know they were intelligent," said Nûd.

"Wyverns, or pronghorns?" asked Eynon.

"Wyverns, of course," answered Nûd.

"Older dragons are wiser than most humans," said Damon, "and wyverns are close cousins to dragons."

"Too bad humans don't always grow wiser as they age," teased Nûd.

"I was born wise," said Damon. "Unlike certain other individuals I might name."

"Of course, *grandpa*," said Nûd, trying to give back as good as he got. "Your venerable self is a font of wisdom and I'm the base brute who makes the beds and takes out the trash."

"I believe I've just been insulted, Eynon," said Damon.

"Yes, sir," said Eynon with a smile. "By ironic exaggeration."

"See," said Damon to Nûd. "Even when he's explaining your insults, he's still polite."

Nûd laughed and turned the palms of his gloved hands up in defeat.

"You win, Damon," he said. "I'll put in a good word for you with the Master the next time I see him."

"See that you do," said Damon with a smile.

"Would you like help with the pronghorn carcass?" asked Eynon. "I could carry it down to the cold storage pantry if you'd like."

"Not unless your muscles have muscles," said Nûd. "It's going to take at least two of us to get it inside. A big buck can weigh a hundred and fifty pounds and that's one of the biggest I've seen. Looks like I'll have to teach you how to pan for gold tomorrow, Eynon. We'll have to dress the buck now and set out at first light."

"Nonsense," said Damon. "Try to keep your wyvern amused, lad, and wait a few minutes."

The older man headed back inside, waving to them as he left. Eynon and Nûd exchanged glances, then moved apart and played three-way catch with the wyvern, using the blue ball this time. Nûd found a spot to stand down the hill.

"That's interesting," said Nûd when he'd had a chance to observe the ground around him.

"What's interesting?" asked Eynon.

"I don't think you need to worry about your wyvern getting enough to eat," Nûd replied.

"Oh?"

"There's blood on the snow down here and a pronghorn's severed head is sitting in a snowbank," said Nûd. "Your beast must have caught two of them."

Eynon circled down to inspect what Nûd had found. He tossed the blue ball up a hundred feet to keep the wyvern busy. Blood didn't bother him—he was raised on a farm, after all—and he was impressed by the neat cut from the wyvern's teeth.

"It makes sense," said Eynon.

"What does?"

"Not wanting to eat the pronghorn's head and horns. They'd probably be painful to swallow."

Nûd took another look at the pronghorn's long, sharp antlers.

"You've got a point," Nûd confirmed. "What are you going to call the beast?"

"I don't know."

"It's *your* pet," said Nûd. "You've got to name it."

As if on cue, the wyvern returned with the blue ball. Eynon tossed the *green* ball high in the air this time. The bat-winged black beast launched himself after the ball like a bolt from a crossbow.

"Cheeeeee!" chirped Chee as he watched the wyvern climb skyward.

"Chee named himself," said Eynon. "Maybe I should wait for the wyvern to tell me his name, instead of giving him one."

"Sounds like a plan," said Nûd. "But don't wait too long, or his name will be *Wyvern.*"

"That's good advice." Eynon rubbed his chin, considering alternatives.

The wyvern returned with the green ball in his mouth, releasing it so it would roll down to Nûd and Eynon. Then he furled his wings and walked—*like a chicken,* Eynon thought—over to a tall, irregular pile of snow. Standing on one leg, the wyvern scratched at the snow pile, revealing a mound of irregularly shaped stones, ranging in size from Eynon's fist to his head. The big beast opened his mouth and shoveled a quarter of the stones from the rocky mound inside.

"He not only walks like a chicken, he eats grit like a chicken," said Nûd.

"I thought chickens ate pebbles to help digest their food," said Eynon. "He's got teeth to cut his meals up into smaller pieces, so I don't see why he needs to eat rocks."

"Look at the blood on the ground," said Nûd. "Do you think he cut the pronghorn into bite-sized pieces?"

"There's not enough red snow for that," said Eynon, observing the scene. "Just enough to go along with cutting the buck's head off. I think he got rid of the head, then swallowed the rest whole."

"Which would explain why he needs to eat rocks," noted Nûd.

"True," said Eynon, "and now I have a name for him."

"Chicken?" asked Nûd.

"No," said Eynon. "Rocky."

"Good choice," said Nûd as he watched the wyvern consume more of the pile of stones.

"Cheee!" agreed Chee.

Rocky swallowed a rounded stone even larger than Eynon's head. It made a visible bulge as it slid down the beast's neck.

"Your name is *Rocky*," said Eynon.

The wyvern's answering belch echoed off the castle's walls.

Chapter 22

"The way it's always been done isn't necessarily best."
— Ealdamon's *Epigrams*

"Would you two please stop annoying the wyvern and help me with this buck?" asked Damon from the door to the kitchen.

Eynon remembered a juggler who'd passed through the Coombe on a midsummer festival day a few years ago and tried moving the three balls in what the itinerant entertainer called a shower pattern. As the spheres circled in front of his eyes, Rocky seemed entranced and playfully reached out with one of his legs to try to capture a ball of solidified sound.

Nûd and Eynon walked back to Damon. A strange-looking disk a yard wide was hovering an inch above the ground, close to Rocky's pronghorn offering. The material the disk was made from reminded Eynon of the shards he'd found near the burning oak back in Applegarth.

What could shatter a disk like that? Eynon wondered. He decided to save that question for later.

"You take the head and I'll take the feet," said Nûd.

"Right," said Eynon, but before he could move, Rocky trotted over to them.

Damon moved his hands in the pattern of a defensive spell, but it was unnecessary. The wyvern gently picked up the pronghorn buck in his mouth and transferred the carcass to Damon's disk. Then Rocky leaned back and pranced from side to side.

"Good boy," said Eynon.

He scratched Rocky's chin with the end of his staff.

"That was unexpected," said Damon.

"Rocky is a fast learner," said Eynon.

"Uh huh," said Damon.

"Do you need help getting the buck down to the kitchen?" asked Nûd.

"No, I can do it," said Damon. "If you hurry, you can still head upriver and teach Eynon how to pan for gold before it gets dark."

"If you say so," said Nûd, who took a long look at the wyvern, then turned to Eynon.

"What?" asked the younger man.

"Are we walking or flying?"

"Flying would be faster," Eynon answered. "Let's see if he'll carry us both."

Eynon approached Rocky's side and used scales on the wyvern's leg to climb onto its back. Rocky looked at Eynon curiously over his shoulder, but made no move to attack. Reluctantly, Nûd climbed on board as well. The two of them wrapped their hands around the ends of Eynon's scarf, which was still anchored to the pair of knobs between Rocky's wings. Chee scampered from Eynon's hat to his refuge inside Eynon's coat, anticipating a windy trip.

Looking back, Rocky nodded his huge head as if to confirm his passengers were securely aboard, then faced forward. Eynon dispelled the three balls he'd created earlier and made a larger ball of solidified sound marked in alternating white and green segments. He gave the new ball a slight spin and set it hovering in front of Rocky's wide muzzle. The wyvern licked it and generated rumbling noises deep in its chest.

"Which way are we headed?" asked Eynon.

"A bit south, then west along the river a few miles," said Nûd. "There's a spot where the current slows and gold dust collects."

"South, then west it is," Eynon replied.

He sent the spinning multicolored sphere in an arcing parabolic course toward the river. Rocky extended his wings and smoothly ascended to follow it. From his new, elevated vantage point, Eynon could see the churning water of the river cutting through the green, forested land like a game trail. To the west, Eynon saw fast-moving rapids, followed by a broad stretch of quieter water.

"Put us down there," shouted Nûd over the wind in their ears. The larger man indicated a flat beach strewn with pebbles on the south side of the quiet segment of the river.

Eynon used the spinning ball to guide Rocky to Nûd's recommended location. The pebbled beach featured four or five large driftwood logs close to the water. A recently-downed tree's roots had caught on the logs. Its crown extended into the river. Nûd used a conveniently angled log to help him descend from Rocky's back. Eynon slid down Rocky's leg and joined Nûd. The wyvern moved back from the riverbank. He circled twice, with his nose chasing his tail, then curled up on a broad stretch of sun-warmed pebbles.

"Now what?" asked Eynon.

"Now I show you how to pan," Nûd replied.

"I can make three different kinds of pie crust in pans," said Eynon. "My sister says they're quite good."

"Is your sister pretty?"

"I'm her brother, but yes," said Eynon. "Several of the boys in the Coombe think so."

"Hmmm," said Nûd. Then he got back to more immediate topic. "Panning for gold is different—and I should have warned you. You're going to get wet."

"The water is barely above freezing," Eynon noted.

"You'll still have to do it," said Nûd.

"Show me. I'll watch you do it first—then I'll get wet."

"If you must," said Nûd. "Stand guard while I do, since Rocky's eyes are closed."

"Right," said Eynon.

He took off his pack and stood at the ready with his small crossbow cocked in his left hand and his staff in his right. Chee moved from his current spot at the neck of Eynon's coat to back on the crown of his fur hat.

Nûd took off his own pack and removed a pair of shallow, circular ceramic pans as wide as the distance from his wrist to his elbow. He stepped out into the river onto a pair of flat rocks, and squatted down so he could scoop up half a pan full of sand and gravel from the riverbed. The rest of the pan was full of water. Nûd stood and turned to show the contents of the pan to Eynon.

"There are flakes of gold in the sand," said the big man. "And sometimes nuggets. Gold is heavy, so it sinks to the bottom. Panning is a way to wash away all but the gold."

"That makes sense," said Eynon. "How did you learn how to do it?"

"My mother taught me," said Nûd. "We'd come here and have picnics when I was young."

"That sounds like fun," said Eynon.

The other man seemed lost in thought for a few moments. Eynon tried to picture the scene replaying in Nûd's mind. It was hard for Eynon to picture Nûd as a small child, since the other man was so big now, but Eynon tried, holding back a smile.

"If people have been panning for gold here for a long time, how can there be any gold left for us to find?"

"The river brings new gold flakes and nuggets downstream all the time," said Nûd. "It washes out of veins of metal in the mountains and collects in places where the current slows and it can sink."

"Oh," said Eynon. "That's a lot better than trying to dig it from a mine."

"You might not agree after a few days of standing in a cold river," said Nûd. The big man took off his gloves and stuffed them in his coat. "Let me show you how to pan properly. You swirl—and tip."

Eynon stepped closer to follow Nûd's movements. The big man tilted the pan from side to side until the water was rotating and beginning to slosh over the edge of the pan. Eynon saw there were ridges around the upper part of the pan that would catch the tiny flakes.

"I get it," said Eynon. "You want the water to carry the lighter sand out of the pan..."

"Leaving the heavier gold dust behind," Nûd continued. "Right. First you get most of the sand and silt out of the pan."

Nûd expertly manipulated the water in his pan until it was mostly gone. Eynon could see larger pieces of gravel and flecks of shiny yellow dust in the bottom.

"Always check for nuggets at this stage," said Nûd, "and remove big pebbles that clutter things up while you're at it."

Holding the pan in he left hand, he picked out small stones with his right, dropping them into the river with a series of tiny *blip* sounds. Chee clapped his front paws and Nûd bowed. Then Nûd squatted again and put more water in his pan.

"You repeat the process to eliminate all the lighter stuff, and what's left will be gold—or lead or platinum, sometimes."

"Fascinating," said Eynon.

"It takes lots of patience," said Nûd, "but when you're done, flakes of gold will be left in the bottom."

"How long does it take to get an ounce of gold dust?"

"An ounce? Days and days," Nûd replied. "You'll probably be out here for a month to get enough for a setting for your magestone."

Eynon considered spending a month out in the cold, standing in frigid water with his hands chilled and his feet wet.

There's got to be a better way, he considered. Eynon reviewed the method he'd used to make sweet-tasting water back in the castle's kitchen. *Maybe he could turn panning for gold into a continuous process?*

Nûd had finished two more rounds of washing away impurities. He showed the contents of his pan to Eynon. A dozen yellow flakes remained in the bottom.

Now Eynon understood why it would take so long to get enough gold to make a proper setting.

"That's an interesting technique," said Eynon, "but I've got an idea that should speed it up."

Nûd stepped back on shore and moved next to Eynon.

"I don't doubt that you do," said Nûd. "How can I help? Your ideas often pan out."

Eynon grinned at Nûd's pun, then gave him a serious reply.

"Please stand guard," said Eynon, handing his crossbow to Nûd.

When Nûd inspected the weapon, he seemed surprised, but didn't say anything.

Eynon leaned his staff against one of the larger driftwood logs and approached the riverbank. Carefully considering distances and angles, he constructed an open, translucent cylinder of solidified sound the diameter of Nûd's pan and twice as long as Eynon's staff. It was shaped like a larger version of the terracotta pipes that brought water to cottages in Haywall. Eynon thought about the ridges in the ceramic disk Nûd had used for panning, and added ridges to the inside of the cylinder to help trap gold dust.

He lowered the pipe into the current and tilted it, so the downstream end was a bit higher than the upstream one. Nûd closely followed Eynon's progress, while simultaneously scanning the area for threats. Eynon created a hemisphere of solidified sound and used it to scoop up gravel from the riverbed, then dump it into the downstream end of the cylinder. Nûd's face lit up.

"I see what you're doing," said the big man. "You think the current will wash away the lighter stones, leaving the gold dust in the ridges."

"Precisely," said Eynon. "It's a lot faster than collecting dust one pan at a time."

"Maybe," said Nûd, "but you'll lose a lot of dust because you're trying to do things faster."

"Not necessarily," said Eynon.

He let the current stream through the cylinder for a quarter hour, then lifted it from the water so he could inspect what had collected in the ridges. It was hard to see colors against the walls of the translucent cylinder, so Eynon adjusted his spell and turned the ridges black. Flecks of gold were now clearly present.

"It's working!" Eynon declared, seconded by an enthusiastic *chee-chi-chi-chee* from his raconette.

"How will you get the gold dust out of the cylinder?" asked Nûd.

"That's easy," Eynon replied.

He put Nûd's panning dish on a rock, rotated the cylinder until it was oriented vertically above it, and removed the ridges. Eynon instructed his red magestone to send a gentle puff of warm air down the cylinder and watched precious yellow dust fall into the panning dish like a shower of pine tree pollen. Eynon's approach had collected ten times as much dust as Nûd had when he'd demonstrated earlier.

"At this rate," said Nûd after he'd examined the bowl, "you'll have enough gold for your setting in a week."

A shadow passed over the dish holding the gold dust. Eynon looked up and saw a large, oddly shaped hawk circling high above.

Wait! That's not a hawk! thought Eynon. That's a gryffon!

The monster wasn't attacking them—but it was descending in a spiral path, trying to determine whether or not Nûd and Eynon would be good eating.

Perhaps it's the same gryffon I saw this morning? Eynon considered. *It might not have had a chance to finish the old bull wisent back in the clearing and was still hungry.*

Nûd brought up Eynon's small crossbow and was prepared to shoot, but Eynon held him back with a hand on his arm.

"I want to try something."

Eynon launched the translucent cylinder toward the gryffon, imparting a rotation to the long tube as it went up to add stability. He tweaked the base of the cylinder, adding a resonance slot to transform it into a giant flute.

As it came close to the gryffon's altitude, the cylinder sounded a deep, mournful note, like the baying of a giant hound. When the cylinder brushed the gryffon on its upward journey, the creature decided that Nûd and Eynon were more trouble than they were worth and flew off toward the north.

Nûd lowered his crossbow and looked at Eynon with more respect.

"That was impressive," said the big man.

"I wasn't sure what would happen," Eynon admitted.

"Neither was the gryffon," said Nûd with a grin.

Chee chittered at them both and Rocky opened one of his massive eyes to confirm his attention wasn't needed. The wyvern returned to napping and soaking up the afternoon sunlight.

Eynon dispelled the cylinder of solidified sound before it could fall into the river and put his hand on his chin. Something about the gryffon's spiraling path in the sky and the rotating cylinder was tugging at his brain. He thought back to how the farmers in the Coombe moved water up to their high fields in the summer, using screws inside a series of hollow logs.

Drawing on the congruencies inside both the red and blue magestones, he constructed a new, even larger and longer translucent cylinder of solidified sound. Inside it, he crafted a long spiral— an Archie screw, the farmers had called it—to lift the water. He added a vertical baffle to the lowest turn of the screw at the bottom and moved the entire thing out into the river with its lower end in gravel and its upper end a few feet above the water. He took a deep breath and directed the cylinder to rotate as he exhaled.

This might work, thought Eynon.

Nûd was staring at Eynon like the younger man had grown three heads.

"You're either a genius or a fool," said the big man.

"We should know one way or the other in half an hour," said Eynon.

It didn't take that long. After fifteen minutes, Eynon lifted the lower end of the cylinder out of the gravel and they could see a sizable collection of gold dust and even a few nuggets gathered against the baffle. When he dumped out what had accumulated, the nuggets made loud *clinks* against the ceramic of the panning dish and gold dust covered the bottom.

"You're a genius, then," said Nûd. "At this rate, you'll have enough gold for your setting before sundown."

"Or maybe sooner," said Eynon, quite pleased his idea had worked.

"What are you planning now?" asked Nûd. "I can tell you've got *something* creative in mind."

"Not creative," said Eynon. "Duplicative."

"Oh," said Nûd.

The big man laughed and slapped his hand against his forehead while Eynon returned the cylinder to the river. Eynon focused his concentration and constructed seven more cylinder-screw combinations, placing four along each bank. When all eight were all properly situated and rotating, he used his blue magestone to magically lock them in place and leaned against a driftwood log, finally able to relax.

Eynon glanced back at Rocky sleeping on the beach and envied the wyvern.

"I could use a nap myself."

"Here," said Nûd, holding out a leather bottle. "Have a drink. You've earned it."

Eynon extended his hand and grabbed the bottle. He squirted a jet of liquid into his mouth, unsure what he was drinking.

"Honey wine!" he exclaimed. "It's delicious."

He sent more of the amber fluid down his throat.

"Be careful," said Nûd. "That's not honey wine. It's winter mead—and that's a lot stronger."

"Winter mead?" asked Eynon.

"You leave honey wine outside during the winter and collect what doesn't freeze," said Nûd.

"Like applejack?"

"Exactly," said Nûd.

The big man pulled a small package wrapped in leaves from his belt pouch and handed it to Eynon.

"This should go well with your drink," he said. "It's candy made from maple tree sap. You'll need to replenish your energy after working so much wizardry."

"Thanks," said Eynon. "I can feel it taking a toll."

He unwrapped the candy from a maple leaf and found that the confection was shaped like a small maple leaf itself.

"How do you..." said Eynon.

"Molds," said Nûd.

Eynon felt like less of a genius for not realizing such an obvious answer. He put the candy in his mouth and smiled at Nûd, feeling his energy return.

"Thank you," said Eynon. "That was exactly what I needed. How do real wizards manage great feats of wizardry, like building castles, without running out of energy?"

"First," said Nûd, "you *are* a real wizard, just quite a junior one."

He gave Eynon a stern look, then smiled to make sure Eynon knew he wasn't upset.

"Second, by and large, wizards don't build castles, at least not using wizardry. They hire architects and workers to construct them, like nobles do."

Eynon nodded as he enjoyed the maple candy melting on his tongue. It was *very* sweet.

"Third," Nûd continued, "most wizards can only do very small magics, like the hedge wizards, or very large magics, like casting fireballs, shooting lightning, or building gateways from this place to that. The Master told me that it's only been in the last decade that more intricate workings, like your cylinders, were even possible. He said it seemed like the congruencies had become more nuanced, able to support more subtle works of wizardry."

Eynon was quite interested now. He leaned forward.

"The Master said that only wizards closely attuned to their congruencies can work this new kind of magic," said Nûd. "I think you've got the knack for it."

"That would be great," said Eynon. "I wasn't thrilled with the first fireball I cast. I blew up a tree."

Nûd laughed.

"You can tell that story to Damon and me over dinner," he said.

Eynon realized that he'd said more than he should. He wasn't ready to tell Nûd and Damon about finding the artifact with the blue magestone at the crossroads. *Dinner was several hours away,* thought Eynon. *Maybe Nûd would forget about his comment by then?*

"I get the sense that you're not interested in being a military wizard?" Nûd continued.

"I'll fight if I have to," said Eynon. "But I'd rather learn how to build things with wizardry, not destroy them."

"I hope you'll have that choice," said Nûd. "There are times when conflict comes to your doorstep and you can't ignore it. As you heard from Doethan, the young king is trying to get the Master to join the war effort."

"And he doesn't want to?"

"So far, he's not convinced it's necessary," said Nûd. "The young king has plenty of wizards."

"But none of them are as powerful as the Master?"

"I don't know about *powerful,*" said Nûd. "Wise, perhaps. The Master was the old king's most capable Crown Wizard and the head of the Conclave."

"Did he retire when the young king took the throne?"

"Long before that," said Nûd. "He came to Melyncárreg to get away from the intrigues at the court."

"Now *that* sounds wise," said Eynon. "Where *is* Melyncárreg?"

"Far to the west of the Coombe and Dâron."

"How far?"

"Far," said Nûd. "Too far to travel without a gateway."

Eynon's face fell, even though he tried to hide it. He wouldn't be able to walk home—or back to Merry.

"How did you end up here, working for the Master?" Eynon asked, realizing he knew next to nothing about Nûd.

"I grew up here," said Nûd. "My mother lived here and my father wasn't in the picture. When my mother left, I stayed."

Nûd's face fell. It seemed to Eynon that he was reliving unhappy memories.

"And the Master offered you a job?" asked Eynon, hoping to distract Nûd.

"Something like that," Nûd replied, his expression more neutral now. "I was a lot younger at the time and fell into the position."

"It must get lonely without anyone your own age to talk to."

"Tell me about it," said Nûd. "No, better yet, tell me more about your sister."

"If you'd like," said Eynon. "She's fifteen, a bit over a year younger than I am, and her skin is covered in freckles."

"With red hair?" asked Nûd.

"Uh huh," said Eynon. "Long red hair. She keeps it braided. Her name is Braith."

"Is she tall? Short? Thin? Buxom?"

Eynon was uncomfortable with Nûd's questions—his sister was his sister. They teased each other constantly, but each would rush to the other's defense when necessary.

"She's well-proportioned and pleasing to the eye," said Eynon. "She also sings like a songbird and can shoot a cherry off a tree at a hundred yards."

"Braith sounds like an accomplished young woman," said Nûd. "A musician *and* an archer."

"I'd be glad to introduce you if you're ever in the Coombe."

"I'm not likely to be in the Coombe unless the Master leaves his tower," said Nûd.

"And joins the other Crown Wizards to serve the young king?"

"Yes," said Nûd. "I don't know which outcome I'm truly hoping for."

With that, Eynon decided enough time had passed to check the cylinders for more gold. He moved them to shore, one by one, and emptied their collections into the panning dish. To his surprise, and Nûd's, they'd collected enough gold dust and nuggets to fill six small cloth bags with the precious metal.

"You must have a pound of gold here," exclaimed Nûd as he hefted the bags. "That's enough for four or five settings, even for a magestone as big as yours.

"Great," said Eynon. "Does that mean we can go back to the castle and I can cook dinner now?"

"It certainly does," said Nûd.

"Chi-chi-chi-CHEE!" said Chee.

The raconette was making it clear *he* was ready for dinner.

"There's only one more thing to accomplish," said Eynon after he'd put his pack back on his shoulder and reclaimed his staff and crossbow.

"What's that?" asked Nûd.

"We have to do something my grandfather said a person should never do."

"Which is?"

"Wake a sleeping wyvern!"

Merry

Fercha's workroom was at the top of the tower, of course. On the climb up the interior spiral staircase, Merry was surprised dust wasn't everywhere. The tower had reputedly been abandoned for years, after all. Then she remembered the animated broom and the moving black circle that substituted for a dust pan and knew why the tower was tidy.

The workroom was half library, half storeroom, with books and scrolls on one side and shelves filled with oddments on the other. In the middle of the circular room were two large worktables topped with dark, polished granite. Beneath the tables were chests of drawers with round brass pulls. A tall, wide, highly-polished mirror in a wooden frame stood against one wall. The room smelled of furniture oil, plaster dust, old leather, lye soap, oak galls, and a hundred other exotic scents Merry couldn't recognize.

A horned owl regarded Merry from a high perch.

"Hoo hoo!" it called to Fercha.

"I know, I know, I'm late," said the Blue Wizard. "Things came up."

"Hoo?" asked the owl.

"Verro, that's who," Fercha replied. "I don't want to talk about it."

The owl sat impassively, then swiveled its head to stare at Merry, who stared back.

"Hoo?" asked the owl again.

"This is Merry," said Fercha. "I found her at the gate pool. She's my new apprentice."

The owl shrugged and let its feathers fall back into place. Merry sensed the night-hunting bird didn't approve of her. She stuck her tongue out at the owl when Fercha wasn't looking and the horned bird blinked twice and shifted position on its perch.

"Be nice, Tuto," said Fercha.

"I don't think your owl likes me."

"Tuto doesn't like very many people," said Fercha. "He's mostly unhappy about me mentioning Verro. He's one of his least favorite individuals."

"Who's Verro?"

"A wizard from Tamloch," Fercha answered. "He's powerful, but not to be trusted."

"If he's from Tamloch, doesn't that go without saying?"

"Don't believe everything you hear, Merry. Not everyone from Tamloch is an ogre."

"You sound like my father," said Merry. "He always looks for the good in everyone."

"Your father is a wise man," said Fercha. "Don't worry about Tuto. He'll warm to you if you read to him, won't you Tuto?"

"Hoo-wheet!" said the owl.

"What kinds of books does he like?" asked Merry.

"All kinds," said Fercha, "though he's partial to bestiaries."

"I'll keep that in mind."

"Good," said Fercha. "You can read to him tonight."

"With pleasure," said Merry.

She hesitated for a moment, remembering something, then spoke tentatively.

"Fercha...?"

The wizard in blue read the worry in Merry's eyes.

"What's on your mind?"

"I need to get a boat loaded with four tuns of cider to Tyford for my father. It's tied up to the dock under the tower. I don't want to break my word."

"Don't let it concern you further," said Fercha. "I'll send Tuto with a message for Madollyn at Flying Frog Farms. Maddy is wiser than she seems. She'll have Llyffan send a crew downriver to get your cider to the city."

"Thank you!" said Merry. "I'll gladly read to you from a beastiary tomorrow night, Tuto."

The owl nodded, as if that was an absolute requirement of Merry's continued existence.

"Don't let the old bird intimidate you," said Fercha. "Madollyn always feeds him well, so he's glad to make the trip."

Merry smiled at Tuto. The owl blinked twice.

"Very good," said Fercha. "Now that your cargo's disposition is settled..."

"Ummm," said Merry.

"Is there something else?"

"Yes," said Merry. "Doethan has Rowsch, Eynon has Chee, and you have Tuto. When will *I* get a familiar?"

Merry watched Fercha hide a smile.

"I don't know," said the short-haired mage. "I've known powerful crown wizards who've never been chosen by a familiar, and simple hedge wizards with two, or even three."

"But what if I never..."

"You're young. You have plenty of time to be chosen."

"I guess so," said Merry. "Being patient is hard."

"You don't need to be patient about everything," said Fercha. "It's time for you to pick out a magestone."

"Pick one out? From where?"

Merry scanned the shelves filled with unusual objects, looking for blue gems.

"I don't see any."

"Don't look with your eyes—reach out with your senses," said Fercha. "If one of the stones in my workroom resonates with you, you'll know. Give it a try."

Merry closed her eyes and visualized the room at the top of the tower. Her mind detected over a dozen glowing points of blue light. The training stones around her neck and at Fercha's throat glittered like tiny stars. Two *very* bright glows elsewhere in the room particularly captured her attention. She told the other woman about the nearer one first.

"I can feel a magestone at the back of the topmost shelf," said Merry. "It's whispering to me."

"You can't have that one," said Fercha. "That's mine. Keep trying."

Merry extended her senses again, seeking the other bright blue glow, and made contact. Instead of whispers, this stone was shouting. When her attention touched it, the magestone seemed to say, *"Mine!"* She felt a tight link to the gem snap into place.

"I've connected with the magestone in the lower drawer, over there," said Merry, pointing with her right hand. "Underneath the far worktable."

"Ah, that *is* a good one," said Fercha. "I look forward to teaching you how to use it."

"And I'm looking forward to learning," said Merry. The corners of her mouth turned up and she bounced on the balls of her feet.

"Get it, then," Fercha instructed. "Now that you've connected, it's best if it stays close to you."

Merry ran the five steps to the chest she'd indicated earlier and pulled out the bottom drawer. She didn't need to *see* the magestone—it called to her and snapped up into Merry's palm the second her hand touched it. She held it in front of her, admiring its inner glow and symmetrical beauty. Fercha moved to stand beside her and examine the gem.

"It's one of the largest I've ever seen," said Fercha. "It must be half the size of a plum, and as blue as a glacier-fed lake."

"What's a glacier?" asked Merry.

"A river of ice a hundred feet tall."

"I'm *glad* I've never seen one. They sound terrifying."

"They are," said Fercha, "but they move slowly. Their ice is a blue so intense it hurts, and the lakes they leave behind when they retreat are cold and deep."

"If you say so," said Merry. She was more focused on her new magestone than Fercha's words.

"Don't worry," said Fercha. "The glaciers are all north of Tamloch now—north of the dragonship raiders in Bifurland, too, for that matter."

Merry had grown up hearing tales of the dragonship raiders from the older men and women in her father's levies. The Northmen from the Kingdom of Bifurland had attacked Dâron a generation ago, before she was born. They had rowed their way up the Moravon as far as Tyford, looting and burning as they came.

The men and women who'd fought with her father told Merry stories about how fierce the invaders were in their conical helmets and round, iron-rimmed shields, painted with dragons and krakens. Merry's mother had once told her that a scar on her father's upper arm marked where one of the dragonship raiders' axes had cut him, but Derry never spoke of his own role in Dâron's defense.

Her magestone pulsed in her palm, filling the room with blue light.

"It's so beautiful," said Merry, staring into the gem.

Fercha closed Merry's hand around her stone.

"Careful. It's all too easy to be enchanted by your stone, instead of being its master," said Fercha. "Put it on the worktable and we'll cut and set our stones together."

Fercha crossed to the shelves and collected the other magestone Merry had identified, along with two small, odd-looking vice-like wooden stands.

"Here," she said when she returned to Merry. "Mount your stone for cutting."

Merry wasn't sure what the older woman meant, but figured it out when Fercha mounted *her* new magestone in a stand. Felted clamps could be adjusted to hold the stones firmly in place. The older woman opened a drawer below the worktable and produced two wooden mallets and a roll of soft cloth with slots holding a dozen fine cutting chisels in graduated sizes.

Fercha handed a hammer and the largest chisel to Merry, keeping the second-largest for herself.

"Now you cut," she said.

"I've never cut a gem before," said Merry. "Don't jewelers train for years to learn how to do it?"

"They do," said Fercha, "but their stones don't guide their hands. Just breathe, hold the chisel loosely, and let the stone instruct you."

Merry took a deep breath, opened her mind to her magestone, and positioned her chisel. Her hand seemed to know the exact pressure needed on the mallet to chip away its outer layers, revealing an even more beautiful faceted gem within. When she finished, she had a round stone with a flat circular center and beveled edges coming down to a point, so that anyone looking into the center of the stone would see dozens of reflected sparkles of blue light.

Fercha had finished cutting her own magestone and leaned over to inspect Merry's.

"Very nice," she said. "Here's mine."

Merry saw that Fercha's new stone looked a lot like the one in the artifact Eynon had found. It was oval, with a smooth upper surface, but like Merry's, it sparkled inside from facets cut into its lower half. Both stones pulsed with strong blue light that reflected off the whitewashed walls of the workroom.

"Do all magestones glow like that?" asked Merry.

"They do," said Fercha. "Though the glow responds to the will and emotional state of the wizard."

"So mine is glowing brighter because I'm excited?"

"That, and because the magestone itself is pleased to be used," said Fercha. "Now we need to make settings for them. Doethan did tell you the secret of wizardry, didn't he?"

"He did," said Merry. "Congruencies."

"Correct," said Fercha. "Did he also tell you about what's happened to wizardry since you were born?"

"What has my birth got to do with wizardry?" asked Merry. She raised one eyebrow, accentuating her question.

"Nothing, that I know of," said Fercha. "You're what? Fifteen?"

Merry nodded. "My wander year starts in a month."

"You know the kinds of magic crown wizards typically perform, right? It's flashy, to amaze farmers and townspeople, or destructive to demoralize attacking armies."

"Y-e-s," said Merry, drawing out the word.

"What's strange is that starting about fifteen years ago, wizards have been able to work increasingly sophisticated magic, far more subtle than we had before," said Fercha. She rubbed her chin. "We don't know *why* things changed, but they have."

"Clearly, it's because *I* was born," said Merry with a smile.

"Don't confuse correlation with causation," said Fercha in mock-admonishment.

"That sounds like one of Ealdamon's epigrams."

Fercha snorted in disgust.

"I'm sorry," said Merry. "I was trying to compliment you."

"You won't do it with that comparison," said Fercha.

She turned to face Merry.

"Did you know that some old-guard wizards insist apprentices find their own magestones in the field?"

Merry tilted her head and regarded her mentor.

"They also require their apprentices to collect the materials for their own settings," Fercha continued. "How would you like to spend a month in a silver mine?"

"I wouldn't," Merry replied.

"Good," said Fercha, "because I've got plenty of precious metals, beeswax for carving, and plaster for molds right here."

"Wonderful," said Merry. She paused for a few heartbeats then posed a question. "Is Doethan an old-guard wizard?"

"No," said Fercha. "He knows the difference between custom and practicality. During the last war with Tamloch he trained thirty apprentices in less than..."

Fercha stopped herself.

"You don't need to hear old stories—at least not right now," she said. "You need a fully functioning, well-set magestone to continue your training, and I certainly need *my* new stone in that condition as well. Storm clouds are gathering and so are the armies of Dâron, Tamloch and Occidens Province, for all I know."

"Occidens Province?" asked Merry. "The Eagle People?"

"Correct," said Fercha. "Dragonships may be sailing south, too, and there are rumors of the barbarians in the northern and southern Clan Lands arming."

"It sounds like the whole of Orluin is preparing for war," said Merry.

"It does indeed," said Fercha. "So, let's get on with crafting settings fit for our marvelous stones."

"Full speed ahead," said Merry.

She thought about shooting the water gap by Rhuthro Keep with Eynon and wondered how he was faring on the other side of the gate. Maybe when she had a fully-functioning magestone, she could figure out a way to contact him?

For that matter, maybe she could talk Fercha into helping her? That would probably be faster.

First things first, she said to herself. She followed Fercha's example, took a block of beeswax, and began to carve.

Chapter 23

"The power of magic is enhanced by the proper setting."
— Ealdamon's *Epigrams*

"Eynon," said Damon, "at the risk of giving you a swelled head, you've amazed me three times today." The older man pushed back from the table and patted his stomach. Chee raised his head from his spot in the middle of the table where his midsection was quite rounded from stuffing himself on carrots, onions and wild rice.

"Three times?" protested Nûd. "I only count twice. Once when Eynon returned on wyvern-back with his new magestone, and once when he collected over a pound of gold in a few hours."

Damon smiled at Eynon. "The third time I was amazed was when I ate dinner tonight," said the older man. "The soup was wonderful. Every meal you cook is better than the one before, lad."

"Thank you, sir," said Eynon. "I'm glad you enjoyed it."

"I certainly did," said Damon.

He noticed Eynon leaning forward on his chair, as if he had something to say.

The older man decided not to string Eynon along any further.

"What is it, lad?" he asked. "You look like you're ready to leap out of your seat."

"I'm just excited," Eynon replied. "I've got my magestone—and I've got the gold you asked for. When do I make a setting fit for my stone?"

"Tomorrow," said Damon. "Meet me in the artifact studio after breakfast and we'll get started."

"Wonderful," said Eynon. "Where's the artifact studio?"

"Don't let the old man tease you," said Nûd. "He won't miss one of your meals. You can count on him showing up with a big appetite in the morning. The two of you can head off together after you eat, while I clean up."

"In that case," said Eynon, "I'd better start mixing up the dough for the honey-raisin rolls I promised you in the morning."

"Don't let us stop you," said Damon.

Nûd smiled and started clearing supper dishes.

* * * * *

"It's not fair," said Damon the following morning as he led Eynon up a flight of stairs and down a long hallway to the artifact studio. The older man was licking his fingers and smiling.

"What's not fair?" asked Eynon.

"Serving us honey-raisin rolls on a day when we have to carve wax and cast a setting."

"My apologies," said Eynon. "I'll never do it again."

"Hah," said Damon. "An apprentice who can give as good as he gets! Don't worry, our fingers won't be a problem."

When they arrived at the artifact studio a few minutes later, Eynon saw why. Nûd had somehow made it there ahead of them. He'd left them two basins of water and a pair of linen towels on top of a waist-high stand just inside the door.

Damon and Eynon each put their hands in a basin to wash off honey from the rolls.

Eynon noticed a bowl of coarse white powder between the basins.

"What's that for?" he asked.

"Cleaning plaster off your hands," said the older man. "It's part soap and part scrubbing sand and comes from the desert west of here. You may need it later."

"Interesting," said Eynon. "Are there maps in the library so I can get a better understanding of where we are?"

"No," said Damon as he dried his hands.

Eynon's face fell and a familiar voice interrupted from the doorway.

"Don't tease him like that," said Nûd. "It's not kind."

Nûd leaned against the door frame, watching Damon.

"Oh, all right," said older man. "I was going to tell him in a minute."

"You mean there *are* maps in the library?" asked Eynon.

"No, they're not in the library," said Damon, pausing theatrically. "They're in the map room."

"There's a map room?"

"I'll show you in a few days. For now, you need to focus on cutting your magestone and creating a setting to hold it."

"A few days!"

"Or sooner, if your efforts today go smoothly," said Damon, glancing at Nûd.

Eynon had an extra incentive to do well, now. He finished drying his hands, hung his towel on a bar on the side of the stand, and took in the room's details.

The artifact studio was large, though not as big as the library. It had tall glass windows divided into panes and faced east to catch the morning sun. Every corner of the room was filled with light.

Chee jumped from Eynon's shoulder to a set of shelves nearby and curled up to nap on a folded fleece that strangely sparkled where the sun caught it.

Without thinking, Eynon took his new magestone out of his belt pouch and rubbed its surface with his thumb.

"Damon?"

"Yes?"

"Why do magestones need settings? Why can't I hold my stone in my hand and make magic?"

Eynon held up his stone and admired its surface.

"You can," said Damon. "For that matter, you already have, from what you told us at dinner last night."

Eynon had managed to dodge questions about casting a fireball with the blue amulet by telling Nûd and Damon about building a tower of solidified sound with his red magestone before Rocky swooped down to rescue him from the basilisks.

"Then why do I need a setting?" asked Eynon.

"Why don't you answer your own question, lad? Tell me why a wizard might want his magestone in a setting."

Eynon thought for a few seconds, then spoke.

"To keep his hands free."

"Bravo!" said Damon. "Most apprentices miss that one—it's too obvious."

"Not to me," said Eynon.

He remembered the challenge of holding his makeshift shard-sword in one hand and his staff in the other. *What about other reasons?* he considered. Eynon thought back to the fireball that went off when he touched a particular spot on the silver metalwork of the blue magestone around his neck.

"I wonder," Eynon said tentatively. "Can settings hold triggers for specific spells wizards need to cast quickly? Or ones they have to cast all the time?"

"Very good," said Damon. "How did you figure that out?"

"It was a lucky guess."

Damon smiled and gently shook his head. Eynon wasn't sure how to interpret the older man's expression.

"Any other reasons?"

"To impress non-wizards?" offered Eynon.

"Hah!" said Damon. "Perhaps you're right, but there are things you don't know about settings. They help strengthen the link between the magestone and the mage and constrain magestones' power in normal circumstances so it's harder to accidentally summon a fireball big enough destroy a castle instead of just knocking down a wall."

"You mean I could release a giant fireball by accident?" asked Eynon. He quickly put his red magestone back in his belt pouch.

"If you're not careful," said Damon. "The Master says there's no telling what might happen if a truly angry wizard held a naked magestone."

"I hope I never find out."

"I do, too," said Damon. "Let's get busy."

Damon walked over to a low table near the windows. On its white marble top were two small pine mallets, a tray filled with tiny chisels, a jar of reddish powder, and a soft-looking cloth a bit larger than Eynon's outstretched hand. The center of the table held an arched wooden mechanism incorporating several felt-covered clamps. A wooden bench decorated with carved and painted knotwork patterns was nearby. The older man moved the bench into place next to the table and indicated to Eynon with a nod.

Eynon nodded back and sat down.

"Take out your magestone and clamp it in place," said Damon.

"Why?" asked Eynon, as he moved the gem from his belt pouch to the device.

Chee jumped from his spot on the shelf to the tabletop and sniffed the magestone, regarding the glowing red gem from all sides as Eynon locked it securely in place.

"He asked you a question," said Nûd.

"Who's the instructor and who is the servant?" asked Damon, wagging a finger at the big man.

Eynon smiled to himself but didn't let it show.

"Your magestone is impressive now," said Damon, "but with artful cutting, it will be magnificent."

"You want me to *cut* my stone?" asked Eynon.

"I want you to listen to your magestone and shape it to maximize its beauty," said Damon. "Let your magestone guide your hand."

"If you say so," said Eynon.

He regarded the mallets and chisels warily, then turned to his stone on the table. Eynon inhaled deeply, filling his lungs and letting his breath out slowly. *I can do this,* he thought. He set his jaw and closed his eyes so he could listen to whatever advice his magestone had to share, then opened them again with a start when Chee rubbed his velvet-soft fur against Eynon's hands. He instinctively rubbed Chee's chin, his concentration broken.

"I don't think that table is a good place for a raconette," said Nûd.

The big man picked up the furry familiar and cradled Chee in the crook of one of his massive arms. Nûd produced a small treat from his pouch and fed it to the raconette to distract him.

Eynon bowed his head briefly in thanks, then barely noticed the raconette's presence in the room. He had connected with his magestone and was listening intently as the stone whispered to him wordlessly. Without conscious thought, Eynon's hands found a mallet and chisel and began to tap.

Thirty minutes later, the cutting was finished. Damon clapped Eynon on the shoulder, bringing him out of his unplanned trance.

"Very nice, lad. Very nice indeed. A little polishing will make it even better."

Eynon looked down at his magestone, somehow seeing it anew. He'd thought its smooth, round surface was amazing before he'd cut it, but now, with facets adding depth and sparkle, its luminous beauty almost overwhelmed him.

"Use the red powder and the smooth cloth to polish it," said Damon.

A few seconds of work made the surface of his magestone glisten. When he gazed into its surface, his vision was almost pulled inside the gem. He leaned back to get another perspective on the glowing red stone, admiring it from a distance.

"Careful, don't tip over," said Damon.

The stool was precariously balanced on two legs until Damon's knee pressed against the middle of Eynon's back and set him upright.

"Are we done for the day?" asked Eynon.

He wasn't sure how he felt about the magestone using his hands to do the cutting. The blue stone around his neck had also advised him, but never taken control. It still felt wonderful to hold *his* stone.

"We're just getting started," said Damon. "It's time to work on your setting."

Eynon stood and followed as the older man led him over to a long, high, well-lit worktable against one of the side walls. Several disks of beeswax as thick as Eynon's little finger rested in the center of its dark stone surface, along with a set of wood and metal tools for wax carving. Two tall stools were placed nearby, and three substantial leather-bound books were within arm's reach at the far end of the table.

"Sit," said Damon, pulling up a stool for himself.

Eynon sat on the other stool and picked up one of the wax disks.

"Your magestone is round," said Damon, "so I thought you might want a round setting, but the design is completely up to you."

"A round setting is fine," said Eynon. "I think I'd like it to be a medallion or amulet, something that suggests protection, not power."

"Interesting," said Damon.

"You don't approve?"

"It's not my place to say one way or another," said the older man. "The setting for a wizard's magestone is a deeply personal choice. It should reflect who you are, not what any other wizard suggests."

"That makes sense," said Eynon. "Please give me a few minutes to think on it."

"Certainly," said Damon.

The older man busied himself by taking small bags, like miniature grain sacks, from a lower cupboard. Fine white dust scattered up into the sunlight when he placed them at the end of the table opposite the books, next to a large pitcher of water.

Too many ideas were streaming through Eynon's head. He needed advice.

"What sorts of designs have other wizards selected?" he asked.

"I wondered if you'd ask me that," said Damon. "Those books record the settings and stones for every wizard in Dâron for the past two hundred years."

"The records go back that long?"

"They go back a good deal longer, but two hundred years is far enough for these purposes. If you choose the same design as a Master Mage from a thousand years ago, I'll let you know."

"I'm not likely to do anything like that," said Eynon.

"Hah," said Damon. "You've surprised me at every step in your training so far. Why would you stop now?"

Eynon recognized a rhetorical question and didn't answer with anything more than a smile.

Damon reached over Eynon and pulled one of the leather-bound books in front of him.

"The volumes on the table show three different broad categories of designs," said Damon. "I call them Animal, Vegetable, and Mineral. This one is Animal—take a look."

Eynon opened the offered volume and grinned when he saw an illustration of a setting made from etched silver. It featured dozens of painted white cloisonné rabbits hopping away from a magnificent round blue magestone along four flat arms etched with knotwork.

A wide ring ornamented with more white cloisonné rabbits carrying books, staffs, swords, cakes and crossbows circled the four arms. The setting had more than a touch of whimsy. It made Eynon laugh, even though he knew a design of this sort wasn't for him.

Other examples in the Animal book had illustrations of pairs of real or magical beasts supporting magestones, including lions, unicorns, and goats. Eynon thought they were unimaginative and didn't want to consider what a wizard with goats on his or her setting was trying to prove. *Might as well use a satyr,* he though. He kept the book open to a page showing a gold setting with light blue wyverns entwined around a deep blue magestone and picked up the volume with Mineral on its spine.

This one wasn't just minerals, though it did have many examples of crystals in different configurations. It also featured geometric shapes etched into metal or soldered onto it. None of the drawings resonated with Eynon, but he kept the book open to a fascinating picture of a rock egg filled with angled white crystals. The illustration called it a *geode,* and some wizard had used a slice from the egg's center to mount a magestone.

Let's see what the Vegetable book has to offer, thought Eynon. *Maybe I'll see the setting for the magestone I found at the crossroads? It has floral motifs worked in silver,* he remembered.

As he paged through the drawings, Eynon felt more at home. He had grown up on a farm, after all, and appreciated the symmetry of many of the designs that featured plants. His hand involuntarily reached into his belt pouch for his new magestone. The gem felt reassuringly warm under his fingers. The magestone around his neck pulsed to remind Eynon of its presence.

While Damon puttered about the studio, Eynon looked at every illustration in the Vegetable book until he located the one he'd found at the crossroads. A small notation below the illustration gave the wizard's name and location.

Fercha. Blue Spiral Tower, Rhuthro Valley.

Eynon had been so close—and now he was far away, though he wouldn't know how far until he had a chance to visit the map room.

At least he knew the name of the wizard who owned the artifact around his neck. He'd return it—as soon as he could get back to the Blue Spiral Tower, and Merry.

Sitting up straight and squaring his shoulders, Eynon went back to selecting a setting design for his red magestone. Instead of going with a variation another wizard's setting, he and his new magestone decided on an original openwork design with lots of flowing curves. Eynon could see it clearly in his mind's eye.

Flowers and vines covered the circular disk, surrounding his red magestone and reinforcing its capabilities with the life and beauty of the natural world. He could feel the blue magestone around his neck add its approval. Without conscious thought, Eynon's hands picked up the wax carving tools and transferred the image he saw in his head to the wax over several hours.

When the carving was complete, Eynon was exhausted. Damon pushed a plate filled with dried meat and cheese toward him and Eynon ate like he hadn't had a meal in days. With a knock on the door frame, Nûd appeared. He entered the artifact studio from the hall and offered Eynon more maple candy.

"Thank you," said Eynon after he'd swallowed the sweet treat and consumed the dried meat and cheese. "Is it always like that?"

"No," said Damon. "You seem to do everything faster than most. The typical apprentice takes a few days to carve their setting."

"You did it in a few hours," said Nûd.

"It felt like a few months," said Eynon. "Do you have any water?"

Nûd brought him a tall mug he filled at a sideboard. Eynon drained it and handed back the mug with a yawn and a sigh.

"Thank you. Can I sleep now?" Eynon asked. His eyelids were bars of lead.

"Not yet," said Damon. "You have to prepare the mold and let it harden, so we can pour this afternoon."

"What time *is* it?" Eynon asked.

"Not quite noon," said Nûd.

"Let's hurry," said Eynon. He could tell his mind was fogged from his earlier effort. "I still have to cook something for lunch."

"You're eating cheese and wisent jerky for lunch today," said Damon. "You can sleep as soon as you prep and pour the plaster."

Eynon yawned. "Will you talk me through it?" he asked.

"Every step," said Damon.

He guided the younger man down to the far end of the table where a flat wooden form two inches tall had joined the sack of white dust and pitcher of water.

"First, mix up the plaster."

Nûd appeared at Damon's elbow with a tall ceramic vessel halfway between a cup and a soup bowl and put it on the worktable. The older man helped Eynon combine the water with the fine white powder in the vessel. The older man handed Eynon a flat wooden stirrer and illustrated the motion needed to mix the ingredients properly. Eynon tried his best, despite his lack of energy, and stirred the mixture until it formed a thick slurry.

"This is like making mud pies when I was small," said Eynon. "Except the mud is white, not brown."

"It is at that," said Damon. "Now pay attention—this is tricky."

"Yes, sir," said Eynon, rolling his head back to crack his neck. It had gotten stiff when he'd been bent over the wax disk, carving the design.

"Fill the mold halfway up with plaster," said Damon. Eynon poured white mud into the square wooden form and waited to be told what to do next.

"Put your carved wax model in the hardening mixture, but don't push it down too far," instructed Damon.

Eynon complied, using his waning attention, and stepped back while Damon added wax sprue cones where the gold would be poured.

"Now pour in the rest of the plaster," said Damon. "Try not to slop any on the table—or yourself."

Eynon leaned close to the mold and topped it off with the plaster slurry, using the exaggerated care he remembered some of the men from the Coombe used when they were trying to plow after too much beer at midday.

"That's it for now," said Damon. "Take him back to his cell and let him rest, Nûd. He's earned it."

"Gladly," said the big man.

He partly supported Eynon as the two of them staggered down the hall to Eynon's room.

Carving settings is hard work, thought Eynon. *I'm glad I'll only have to do it once.*

Nûd was doing more and more of the work, since Eynon's limbs were slow to respond to mental commands. Eynon felt as tired as he had after bringing in the harvest back in the Coombe. When they got to his cell, he fell on his narrow bed with one hand holding his new magestone and the other wrapped around his pillow. Sleep claimed him in seconds.

Two hours later, he woke up feeling refreshed and reinvigorated. The time when he'd carved the setting for his magestone seemed hazy, as if someone else had done the work and he'd looked over their shoulder, so he was still a bit disoriented.

I've got a lot to learn about magestones, thought Eynon.

He shifted to put his feet on the floor and realized Nûd was standing at the door to Eynon's cell, holding a mug and a plate of small delicacies Eynon didn't recognize.

"Have some of this," said Nûd, extending the mug.

Eynon's nose smelled mint. He took the mug with both hands and tasted its contents. It was honey-sweet, but had a bite from vinegar and a wonderful minty aroma. He savored a few more sips, then put the mug down and turned his attention to the plate.

"What are those?"

"Sesame candies," said Nûd. "Sesame seeds, honey, breadcrumbs, and ground sesame paste. Don't worry. I didn't make them."

Eynon reached for the plate eagerly and popped three of the candies into his mouth in six heartbeats. The candies were sticky, sweet, crunchy, and quite delicious. Feeling more himself, Eynon stood up and shifted his weight from one foot to the other until he confirmed he could keep his balance without falling over. He reached out to grasp one of Nûd's hands with his own.

"Thank you," said Eynon.

"My pleasure," said the big man. "Are you feeling better?"

"Much better."

"Good," said Nûd. "Because your mold has hardened and it's time to finish your casting."

Nûd and Eynon hurried back to the artifact studio where they found Damon flipping through the Animal book.

"Ready?" asked Damon.

"I think so," Eynon replied. He squared his shoulders.

"Good," said Damon, pointing to a small cast iron door halfway up one of the walls of the artifact studio. "I've been heating the oven."

Nûd found Eynon thick gloves and a pair of long, iron tongs. Damon opened the oven door. Eynon slid the plaster mold inside with the tongs and Damon closed the door with a clang.

"How long do we wait?" asked Eynon. "Is there a count?"

"Nûd can't help us with counting even if he takes off his shoes and socks," teased Damon. "I'm counting to three hundred in my head and he can't manage higher than twenty."

"I was solving trigonometry problems before my legs were long enough to ride a horse, old man," Nûd replied. "Sixty-seven, one thirty-nine, two eighty-eight..."

"Stop!" Damon protested. "You'll throw me off count."

"Senility is always a problem for aging minds," said Nûd.

He winked at Eynon, who put up his hands, determined to stay out of *this* argument.

"At this rate, you won't have to worry about getting old enough to *be* senile, you disrespectful young behemoth."

"Don't worry," said Nûd to Eynon. "He's got a sphere of solidified sound in the oven designed to explode when the temperature of the mold is hot enough to ensure the wax is melted. It will be ready when we hear a *pop*."

As if on cue, the specified sound came from inside the oven.

"Time to remove the mold," said Damon, opening the oven door.

Eynon took the mold from the oven with the iron tongs and followed Nûd's gaze to a thick-walled soapstone basin on the floor.

"In there?" he asked.

"Correct," said Damon. "Pour the wax there. Hold it in place for a few minutes, to ensure all the wax comes out."

Eynon complied, holding the mold upside down so the wax could drain away. When his muscles began to tremble, he put the plaster mold on the worktable.

"Excellent," said Damon. "You're doing a great job and can take a break for an hour while the gold is melting in the oven."

Why couldn't Damon have started melting the gold while I was napping? thought Eynon.

"Excuse me, sir," said Eynon. "Am I right in thinking it's important for an apprentice to handle every step in the process of making his artifact himself?"

"Absolutely," said Damon. "That's how it's always been done and always will be."

"Yes, sir," said Eynon. "I mean, yes, Damon."

That explained why Damon hadn't started melting gold earlier.

"Don't worry about the occasional *sir*, lad. I know you're distracted," said Damon. "At least you're respectful, unlike some."

He glanced at Nûd in mock anger that turned to laughter when the big man artfully mimed being struck in the heart with a crossbow quarrel.

Eynon decided to take advantage of the others' good moods.

"Would you mind if I tried my own idea for melting the gold, instead of heating it in the oven?" asked Eynon. "I think it might be faster."

Nûd teased Eynon by stepping outside the entrance to the artifact studio and peeking his head around the corner.

Damon ignored Nûd.

"Go ahead, lad," he said. "Let's see what you have in mind."

"I'll need your help, Nûd," said Eynon. "Can you add the gold dust when I give the word?"

"I'd be glad to," said Nûd, stepping back into the room.

"Great. One bag of dust should be enough," said Eynon. "Stand over there."

Nûd collected a bag of gold dust and nuggets from farther down the table and stood in front of the mold.

"Take two steps to the left," said Eynon.

Nûd complied.

Eynon concentrated and used his magic to create a bubble of solidified sound above the mold. He gave the bubble a slight bluish tint so it would be easy to see, then formed an opening at its top.

"Pour in the gold, please."

"I think I see what you're doing," said Nûd as he dumped the contents of a bag into the bubble.

"So do I," added Damon.

Eynon sealed the bubble and added heat, just like he'd done to boil water in the kitchen. This time, he added more and more heat until the dust and nuggets flowed together and puddled at the bottom of the bubble. He slowly extended a thin tube of solidified sound from the bubble down toward the mold and a rivulet of yellow metal followed its course.

Eynon was about to open the tip of the tube and begin filling the mold when he was shaken by an invisible force and thrown roughly to the floor. The bubble and tube shot up to the ceiling and broke open, spraying molten metal on the gray stone blocks above them.

Damon and Nûd also lost their footing when the castle shook, but they reacted quickly, crawling into an open space beneath one end of the worktable. Eynon wasn't far away, but drops of liquid gold were forming on the ceiling and would soon be falling.

"This way!" shouted Nûd. "Come in here with us."

Eynon scrambled closer. One of Nûd's long arms grabbed Eynon's wrist and skidded him across the floor as a dozen drops of hot metal fell. Eynon heard a sizzling sound and realized molten gold was eating through the thick leather of one of his boots. He kicked it off faster than he thought was possible, then tucked his feet under him as he huddled in, crowded together with Nûd and Damon under the table.

No one said anything for a few seconds.

"What was *that?*" asked Eynon after his heart rate slowed to something closer to normal.

"Ground shake," said Nûd calmly. "A pretty big one. You'll get used to them."

Damon also seemed to take the shaking in stride.

"The land around Melyncárreg is unstable," he said. "That's one of the reasons for all the mud pots and geysers."

"Geysers?" asked Eynon.

"Water and steam shooting out of the ground," said Nûd.

"Oh," said Eynon, remembering his recent close encounter with one.

He noticed Chee's frightened and disapproving face peeking out from under the fleece on the high shelf and gave the raconette a reassuring, if not completely convincing smile. Eynon was glad the little beast appeared unharmed.

"Sometimes the energy from the *cuddio tân* is expressed by ground shakes," said Damon. "We have thousands of small ones and two or three large shakes a year."

"Can you tell when they're going to happen?" asked Eynon.

"Not at all," said Nûd.

"Great," said Eynon. "Just great."

He had a sudden wave of longing for his brief time on the river with Merry, when the worst thing he had to worry about was fighting off kidnappers and thieves. Eynon wondered how she was faring on the other side of the gate. Maybe when his magestone had a setting, he could figure out a way to contact her.

Chapter 24

"Even those who learn from their mistakes still repeat them."
— Ealdamon's *Epigrams*

"The Master always wanted a gilded ceiling," said Damon.

"Just not quite like *that*," said Nûd, once the molten gold had solidified in explosive patterns above their heads and in large droplets on the floor.

Damon, Nûd, and Eynon had crawled out of their protected space under the table to survey the damage. Eynon looked closely at the back of the boot he'd removed.

"It's a good thing I took this off quickly," said Eynon. "A few drops went through the leather."

He turned the boot upside down and two small pellets of gold hit the stone floor of the artifact studio with a muted *clink*. Eynon shook his head in disappointment.

"Looks like we'll have to wait to pour my artifact."

"Nonsense," said Damon. "You have to return to slay the dragon that burned you."

"But..." protest Eynon.

"It wasn't your fault," Damon continued. "Your concept was sound—just keep your focus and be ready to handle the unexpected this time."

"Like aftershocks," said Nûd.

"What are aftershocks?" asked Eynon.

"Never mind about them," said Damon. "You've got plenty of gold to try again, and Nûd can clean up the mess from your previous try later."

"Shouldn't Eynon clean it up?" asked Nûd.

"I'd be glad to clean it..."

"Focus, lad," said Damon. "Create another sphere for heating. I'll add the gold dust this time."

"Yes, sir," said Eynon.

Damon smiled at Nûd and the big man shook his head from side to side in resignation.

"I'll add the gold," said Nûd. "You be ready with a shield spell in case anything unforeseen happens, not that something would necessarily be unforeseen in this case."

"Very well," said Damon. "Center your mind, lad, and get busy."

"Right," said Eynon.

He tilted his head back and rotated his shoulders until his neck cracked, then found a solid stance and started again. He created a modest-sized sphere of solidified sound, gave it a light-blue tint, and opened a hole in the top. Nûd poured in gold dust and nuggets from a second bag, then moved five paces away to stand close to the open space under the worktable.

"Don't you have faith in Eynon?" asked Damon.

"I have faith in Eynon," Nûd replied, "but I'm standing over here in case we have another ground shake."

"Hah," said Damon. "Say what you will, but I have full confidence in the lad."

"Thank you, sir," said Eynon. "You might want to stand near Nûd, though. I'm going to heat the gold again and don't want to hurt either of you if something goes wrong."

"An admirable sentiment," said Damon.

He made a slight bow and moved to join Nûd.

"Proceed," said the older man.

Assured they were both out of harm's way, Eynon confirmed that Chee was still safely underneath the fleece, then added heat to the sphere until the gold was molten. He shook his construct gently to ensure the dust and nuggets were completely melted and well-mixed. Then he created another tube to one of the sprue holes at the top of the mold and let the glistening metal flow into it until a slight dome of gold formed at the top and metal showed at the second sprue hole.

Eynon let out a breath he hadn't realized he'd been holding.

"You've done it, lad," said Damon.

Nûd grinned and clapped his hands twice in approval.

Eynon smiled and realized there was still hot metal in the sphere. *Can I take heat away as easily as I added it?* he wondered.

He shrank the sphere until it was less than an inch in diameter and pulled the heat away from it, leaving a small gold ball that fell into his hand with a weighty *smack* when he dispelled the construct of solidified sound.

"What should I do with this?" Eynon asked.

"Keep it," said Damon. "It could prove useful if you're ever short of funds."

"But paint it gray," said Nûd, "so no one murders you in your sleep to get it."

"Good idea," said Eynon.

He put the small gold ball in his pouch and held his hand over the mold. The metal in the sprue holes was solid and not radiating heat.

"Now what?" Eynon asked.

"Guess," said Damon.

The older man handed Eynon a heavy wooden mallet made from a thick section of tree branch.

"Tap, don't smash," Nûd advised.

Eynon took the mallet from Damon and tentatively struck the plaster mold. Nothing happened except for a few flecks of white dust falling to the table.

"Keep tapping," said Nûd.

Shifting the mallet to one side of the mold, then the other, Eynon gave it a series of stronger taps. Fine cracks developed in its outer surface, but the mold stayed intact. Damon watched Eynon closely, waiting to see what he would do.

"I have an idea," said Eynon. "Why can't I try vibrating the mold the same way the ground shake made *us* vibrate?"

"No reason not to give it a try," said the older man.

Nûd moved away from the space beneath the worktable and stood in the doorway to the artifact studio. Damon noted Nûd's new position, but stayed a few feet from Eynon, indicating encouragement by waving his hands in a circular motion.

"Come on, lad," he said. "Get on with it."

Eynon created another sphere of solidified sound, just big enough to hold the rectangular mold. He moved the sphere to float above the worktable and gently pushed the mold inside it, until the construct looked like two slices of bread inside a translucent ball.

Feeling like a puppeteer manipulating a marionette, Eynon put his hands above the ball and wiggled his fingers. The ball began to vibrate at a faster and faster speed, emitting a rising tone that increased until it abruptly stopped when the solid plaster of the mold turned into a cloud of fine white dust.

In the center of the sphere, hidden within the dust cloud, was the setting for Eynon's artifact. He stopped moving his fingers and the construct ceased to move, allowing the tiny white particles to fall to the bottom. The golden design hovering within was now clearly visible. Eynon dispelled the sphere and caught the setting as it fell. Nûd wiped plaster dust off the worktable with a wet rag.

"The setting is beautiful, but dull," said Eynon as he turned the ornate gold disk in his hand.

Nûd gave Damon a pointed look and the older man took a deep breath before speaking.

"I won't say the obvious," said Damon. "Eynon is far from dull. We've had more excitement since he's arrived than we've had since..."

Nûd raised an eyebrow.

"Best not to go there, either," said Damon, nodding his head in unspoken agreement with Nûd. "Water over the waterwheel and all that."

Eynon was oblivious to their byplay. He removed his red magestone from his belt pouch and tested it to confirm it fit the opening in the center of his artifact.

"You need to polish your setting before you mount your stone," said Damon.

Slowly, Eynon realized the older man had spoken.

"How do I do that?"

"With jeweler's rouge and a fine cloth. It will take you hours to make your setting gleam."

"No it won't," said Eynon with a grin.

He generated another small bubble of solidified sound, poured the red jewelers' rouge powder inside, and added the setting.

Then he repeated the vibration process that had liberated the setting from its mold. A few seconds later, every speck of remaining plaster dust had been removed and the surface of the setting was as bright as the sun at midday. He even returned the excess jeweler's rouge to its box.

Damon put his arm around Eynon.

"You have the makings of a fine wizard, lad," he said. "You're not constrained by the traditional ways of doing things."

"You might even say he's broken the mold," said Nûd with a grin.

Damon groaned and Eynon smiled, enjoying the fact that he understood Nûd's joke this time.

Eynon dispelled the sphere and retrieved his polished setting, admiring how it caught the light.

"Do I need to glue my magestone in place?" he asked.

"Try it and see," said Damon.

Taking the setting in his left hand and the red stone in his right, Eynon brought the two close together. When they almost touched, the magestone jumped across the intervening distance and snapped into place, its flat top showing sparkling, faceted depths. Eynon and Damon admired Eynon's artifact while Nûd stepped to the workbench and opened a drawer.

"You may find this useful," said Nûd, holding a length of chain made from thick gold links. "It used to belong to the Master."

Damon seemed surprised, but didn't let it show on his face for long. He helped Eynon connect the chain to a pair of loops on the top of Eynon's setting.

"Try it on, lad," he said. "Let's see how it suits you."

Eynon put the chain around his neck. The artifact rested on his collarbone, over his quilted jacket. He hoped the Blue Wizard's artifact wasn't visible as a bulge beneath the fabric.

"It will take me a while to get used to his red stone," said Nûd. "I'm only used to seeing blue ones—and green."

"You've seen a wizard from Tamloch up close?" asked Eynon.

"Very close," Nûd replied. "It's a long story for another time. You look good with a red magestone. It suits you."

"Does it make me an odd duck among wizards in Dâron?"

"It does," said Damon. "But there's nothing wrong with that. I had a student once whose stone was more aquamarine than blue, but we lost her."

"Lost her?"

"In the last war," said Nûd. "There's a high attrition rate for wizards."

"Oh," said Eynon. He hadn't thought much about the down side of being a wizard. "Why is that?"

"Kings and generals use wizards before engaging their armies," said Damon. *"Wizards take territory—soldiers hold it,* is the old saying. Since offensive spells are usually stronger than defensive ones, battles tend to go through a lot of wizards."

"Is that why Dâron needs a big school like this one to train wizards?" asked Eynon.

"There are never enough wizards in time of war," said Nûd.

"And always too many in peacetime," added Damon.

"That sounds a lot like bringing in crops from year to year," said Eynon.

"It's much the same, but with longer cycles," said the older man. "We have to get you enough training so you will be one of the survivors. I have high hopes for you, lad."

Nûd glanced sideways at Damon and muttered under his breath.

"What was that?" asked Damon.

"Nothing," said Nûd. "Do you want to continue Eynon's training now or have him start dinner?"

"That's an excellent question," Damon replied. "What do you think, Eynon? Do we opt for dinner or more instruction?"

"Why not both? I can get a pot of meat and vegetables started in a few minutes, then come right back to learn more about wizardry."

"Get about it, then, lad," said Damon.

Eynon left with a light step, his red magestone pulsing in its new setting on his chest. His hearing must have improved, because he heard Damon's next words to Nûd and grinned.

"We'll let him stew on things a bit, then start him on offensive magic," said Damon.

Eynon didn't hear Nûd's reply, just his groan.

Merry

"Why did you decide on electrum, rather than gold or silver?" asked Fercha.

The older wizard held Merry's artifact in her hand, turning it from side to side to examine its details. It was diamond-shaped with rounded corners, convex like a war shield, and changed its appearance as the light caught it. The artifact's surface was etched with intricately flowing geometric designs and a fine chain attached to points just above its outer vertices.

"I couldn't decide," said Merry. "I like both gold *and* silver. Doethan has his magestone in a gold headband, and you favor silver for your pendant, so it may be a way to acknowledge you both."

Merry took her artifact back from Fercha and put it around her neck. The circular blue magestone in the center of the artifact pulsed once it was in place.

"Alloys are often stronger than pure metals," said Fercha. "Bronze is harder than copper or tin, and steel holds a sharper edge than iron. Perhaps electrum—mixing gold and silver—will serve you well."

"I hope it will," said Merry. "Don't the gold and silver we use have other metals, like copper and platinum in them?"

"They do," said Fercha. "When we're not pressed for time I'll show you how to determine how much of each metal is present using a tub of water. How did you know about the other metals?"

"There's a bench on the street of the jewelers in Tyford where I like to read," said Merry. "It's easy to overlook a girl with a book."

Fercha smiled at the younger woman.

"I think I'm going to enjoy having you as an apprentice. Come with me to the top of the tower. We both need to learn how to use our new artifacts."

"Yours is beautiful, by the way," said Merry when they paused at the door to the roof. "It's a lot like the one Eynon showed me, but different."

"No two artifacts are alike," said Fercha, "just as no two magestones are alike. The artifact is the expression of the bond between the magestone and the mage."

"What happens to magestones when their wizards die?" asked Merry. "Is there a storeroom or museum where they're kept?"

"Magestones die when their wizards die," said Fercha. "The light goes out of them and the settings of their artifacts melt back to puddles of metal. Some of the gold and silver in my stock belonged to wizards who are gone."

"That's so sad," said Merry. "Artifacts are works of art. They should be preserved."

"There are artists in Brendinas who will want to paint a picture of your artifact," said Fercha. "The pictures are kept in books so new wizards can see what their predecessors have created."

The older woman ran her fingers through her short hair, as if her mind was elsewhere.

"What are you thinking?" asked Merry.

"I'm thinking I'll need a picture of *my* new artifact as well. I was remembering when my first artifact was painted. My father arranged for the finest artist at the court to do it. He was a handsome fellow— a visitor to the court from Tamloch. We found out later he was a spy."

"There were artists from Tamloch in Brendinas?"

"That was after both kingdoms had briefly united against the Eagle People," said Fercha. "Ask your father about it when you get a chance. There was even an exchange of wizards between the courts."

Fercha seemed lost in thought again, her hand on the door latch, but not opening it.

"Are we going up to the roof?" asked Merry after a few seconds.

"What?" asked Fercha. "Oh, yes, of course."

They ascended.

Chapter 25

"True strength is in control, not power."
— Ealdamon's *Epigrams*

The booming flash from Eynon's first attempt at casting an offensive spell from the castle's battlements was like standing in the middle of a thunderstorm, except for the lack of rain and the bright afternoon sun. His lightning bolt had been so powerful, it had carved half a circle out of a broad expanse of bare rock close to the castle.

"Perhaps not quite so much power next time," suggested Damon.

The older man had been standing next to Eynon, but was now a few steps away. The remaining hair on his head was standing out straight from his scalp due to the residual magical charge radiating from Eynon. Damon's head looked like one of the brushes Eynon used to clean bottles in his kitchen back in Haywall.

"Sorry," said Eynon.

He wondered what his own hair looked like and reached up to check. He could feel the pulse of Chee's rapid breathing inside his jacket. The raconette had sensibly retreated from his usual perch on Eynon's shoulder after the blast.

"What's going on up there?" called Nûd from the courtyard behind and below them.

"It's none of your concern," said Damon.

"You're frightening the chickens," said Nûd. "They're so upset they won't lay for a week."

"We have chickens?" asked Eynon.

He put his head to his forehead. *Of course, we have chickens. Nûd can't pick up a dozen eggs at the weekly market. There don't seem to be any other people around for hundreds of miles.*

Nûd took pity on Eynon and didn't reply.

"I'll calm them down after my lesson," Eynon offered.

"If you try," Nûd shouted up, "don't bring Chee."

"Right," Eynon replied.

Raconettes were notorious egg-stealers. Chee shifted inside Eynon's jacket and stuck his head out of its front collar.

"Back to your lesson," said Damon.

Chee retreated and curled up on top of Eynon's ribs.

"Focus this time," said the older man. "Even lightning can be a subtle weapon."

"How?" asked Eynon. "Subtle lightning doesn't make much sense to me."

"The Master can spark a horsefly off the king's neck without giving him a shock," said Damon. "That's control."

"Why use lightning when a tiny sphere of solidified sound would do the job more effectively, with less risk?"

"I don't think you're properly understanding the teacher-student relationship," said Damon with a smile. "Try it again, but with more control and less power."

"Because you say so?"

"Exactly. Find the spark inside your magestone and release it a little at a time."

Eynon couldn't hold back a grin as he moved to the edge of the battlements and set his feet. *Maybe power is like salt? A little is good, but a lot ruins the dish.*

He tried summoning lightning again and succeeded, releasing a short blast from his index finger that carved a bit more arc in the circle he'd created in the bare rock earlier.

"Good," said Damon. "Again."

Carefully aiming his blasts, Eynon carved the remainder of the figure in the bare expanse of rock near the cliffs. The bolts left a rounded two-foot wide channel in the stone that curved into a circle, fifty feet in diameter. By the time Eynon finished the last few degrees of arc, his control had improved substantially. He sent a tiny bolt of lightning at a pebble balancing on the edge of the circle, causing it to fall into the shallow channel below.

"Well done, lad," said Damon. "We'll have you sparking horseflies off Nûd's neck in no time."

"I think I'd still prefer using tiny spheres of sound," Eynon replied.

It suddenly became cooler when a shadow passed between them and the sun. Eynon looked up to see if his work with lightning had attracted a storm, but it wasn't a cloud above him, it was Rocky. Eynon waved to the wyvern. Rocky tipped a wing and expertly descended to land a dozen feet farther down the crenellated wall. The scaly black beast looked at Eynon expectantly.

"We still need to work on fireballs before dinner," said Damon. "Tell your *pet* to run along and come back later."

"I don't know if he's my pet or I'm his," said Eynon, "and I'm not sure I can *tell* him anything."

"Then distract him," said Damon. "We have more spells to cover."

"Yes, sir," said Eynon. "I just thought of something that should keep Rocky busy for a while."

Damon crossed his arms and watched as Eynon created a red ball of solidified sound. He brought it close enough to Rocky that the wyvern could lick it and the beast was obviously pleased by its taste. With a wave of one of his hands, Eynon directed the sphere down to the circle he'd carved in the bare rock by the cliffs. Rocky leapt from the battlements and dove for the ball, which Eynon dropped into the circular channel.

The wyvern landed in the center of the circle and batted the ball with a wing-tip. It rolled halfway around the circle's circumference until it was behind Rocky. He turned to follow it and tapped the ball with a wing-tip again. It skittered around the entire circle this time.

Rocky looked up at Eynon and bobbed the dragon-like head on his long neck several times. Eynon bowed back, bobbing his head like the wyvern had.

"I'm glad you like it," Eynon shouted.

The wyvern made a pleased *chuffing* sound and returned to playing with its giant new toy.

Damon shook his head and turned away, but Eynon saw his smile.

"Fireballs?" asked Eynon.

"Yes, fireballs," said Damon. "I was going to have you practice on that stretch of bare rock you'd blasted with lightning, but now that's inadvisable."

"Because Rocky might flame back?"

"Because I don't want you to hurt your pet," said Damon, "even by accident."

The older man shouted down to Nûd, who was still in the courtyard below, pretending to sweep the cobblestones while listening to the magic lessons.

"Fetch me my disk and one of the training disks, and be quick about it."

"Yes, Your Superiorness," said the big man. "I hear and obey."

"More alacrity and less sarcasm, please," said Damon.

"Since you said *please*," said Nûd as he went back into the castle to fetch the requested items.

Eynon enjoyed the way the Nûd and Damon fought. It reminded him of the way his uncles teased him when he paid them visits. They joked about how he was a better cook than a farmer, but ate the small cakes he brought them with obvious relish, despite their mock-disparaging comments.

Nûd soon returned with a pair of thin, flat, translucent disks a yard wide. He tossed both up to Damon, who handed one to Eynon. The disk glowed softly with some sort of inner light. It looked just like the floating platform Damon had used to transport the pronghorn down to the kitchen earlier.

"What's this?" asked Eynon. He was pretty sure he knew the answer.

"It's a flying disk," shouted Nûd from the courtyard. "Damon doesn't want to risk having you set the forest on fire, so he's taking you to the lake."

"That seems sensible," said Eynon.

Damon made a *harrumph* sound that Eynon interpreted as grudging agreement. He was already hovering ten feet above the battlements, looking down on Eynon.

"It *is* a sensible precaution, lad," he said. "Step on your disk and let's be off."

"How do I make it fly?" asked Eynon.

He put his disk in the center of the walkway along the top of the wall, then stood on it and thought about flying. Nothing happened.

"That's not the way to do it," said Damon. "Use your magestone and setting. You can't lift your disk by just thinking about it."

"But..." said Eynon.

"Try again, and use your magestone this time."

"Yes, sir."

Eynon didn't have to reach out to his magestone—he just had to feel their connection. When he tried to lift himself with the flying disk using the power of his magestone moderated by its setting, he rose smoothly from the battlements and joined Damon floating above.

Chee stuck his head out of the top of Eynon's jacket and decided to climb back to his usual perch on Eynon's shoulder.

It makes sense that raconettes wouldn't be bothered by heights, thought Eynon. *They spend a lot of time in trees, after all.*

"The lake is to the south," said Damon, waving his arm in the indicated direction. "Follow me."

"Stir the stew, please," Eynon shouted to Nûd.

He heard the big man's voice saying, "As you wish," as his flying disk sped after Damon's.

The lake turned out to be more of an inland sea than a lake, at least by Eynon's standards. It was far larger than the wide spot in the river near the earl's castle on the Rhuthro beyond the gap. He couldn't see its southern shore, even though he was floating a hundred feet above its northern end. Eynon thought for a moment and wondered why the water wasn't covered with ice. Threads of steam were visible wafting up in the late afternoon sunlight.

"Is the lake..." began Eynon.

"...warmed by the *cuddio tân?*" responded Damon. "It is. The heat varies from place to place. There's one spot near the shore where you can enjoy a pleasant hot bath and another that will boil the meat off your bones."

"I'll stick to the hot bath," said Eynon, "and will save the boiled meat for our stew pot."

"A wise choice," said Damon. "Now it's time to teach you how to cast fireballs. Throw them at the center of the lake where the steam is thickest. You can't hurt anything there."

"Not even fish?" asked Eynon with a smile.

"Any fish straying near the center will be precooked," said Damon, the corners of his mouth turning up. "Let your magestone know what you want. Allow your setting to moderate the extremes of your will and let fly."

Eynon felt his magestone and his mind fit into a comfortable matrix. He rubbed his hands together until his palms were warm, then he cupped his hands, envisioned a fireball forming between them, and cast it like a falling star at the surface of the lake.

The water boiled and hissed. An even larger plume of steam rose up where the fireball struck, but Eynon's flaming missile hadn't done anything to hurt the lake's waters.

"Very good," said Damon. "You're showing restraint. That was a medium-sized fireball. See how small you can make one."

Eynon nodded and clenched his teeth, then relaxed his jaw. He didn't want to make a habit out of tensing up to work wizardry. He imagined a gentle rain of fiery spheres, each no larger than a dewdrop. With a wave of his hand they materialized, falling to the lake's warm waters with a *sssssttt* sound that reminded him of water drowning a campfire. Eynon turned his head to face Damon, hoping for feedback.

"I'm impressed," said the older man. "Most apprentices can't make fireballs smaller than apricots."

"You asked me to make them as small as I could."

"I did," said Damon. "I hesitate to ask how *large* you can make one."

"I'm worried about that, too," said Eynon. "I don't want to vaporize the entire lake by accident."

"I don't think even your magic can do that, lad," said Damon. "Though you can take comfort in knowing any release of energy powerful enough to blast away half the lake would undoubtedly kill us both in the process."

"That's not very comforting," said Eynon.

"Then exercise restraint," said the older man. "Make a somewhat larger fireball, but not a *large* fireball."

"I'll try," said Eynon.

"Try hard," said Damon.

He shifted his flying disk until he was behind Eynon, not beside him.

Eynon looked over his shoulder and saw Damon nod. He turned back and reached out to his magestone, feeling its power shaped by the flowers and flowing vines of its cast-gold setting. Eynon called for power to build, then cut it off before it grew too strong by closing his hand into a fist. He pulled his arm back and brought it forward, opening his hand and sending a ball of orange fire the size of a pumpkin toward the surface of the lake.

Before the fireball could hit, Damon was beside him throwing a bubble of solidified sound around them both. Their protective bubble was thrown backward on a wave of superheated steam. Damon's hand on Eynon's arm kept them both upright and on their flying disks as the bubble tossed and bobbed like an acorn in floodwaters. After half a minute of continued erratic motion, the bubble stabilized.

Eynon stared down at the lake, improbably expecting to see a hole in the water leading all the way to the bottom. Instead, there *was* a hole in the water, but it marked the center of a whirlpool fifty feet across, spinning in a hypnotic pattern that captured Eynon's gaze and held it tight until Chee began to chitter excitedly in Eynon's ear.

"Sorry," said Eynon. "I may have made that one a bit *too* big."

"A bit," affirmed Damon. "I think that red magestone of yours has a special affinity for fire. I've never seen a fireball that size packed with so much energy. You'll need to be very careful casting fireball spells in the future. You could do more damage to your own side than the enemy."

"I hope I never have to use wizardry in battle," said Eynon.

"You may not have a choice in the matter, lad," said Damon, overlapping his flying disk so he could put his arm around Eynon's shoulders. "We can leave that problem for the future. For now, I think we'd best call it a day."

"Good idea," said Eynon. He was shaking as he realized the full extent of the destruction caused by his spell.

"Come along," said Damon. "A bowl of stew will set you right."

"Chi-chi-chi-*chee!*" said Chee from Eynon's shoulder.

"And an Applegarth apple for you, little one!"

Eynon followed Damon back to the castle with the whirlpool still churning in the lake behind them.

Merry

"Well done," said Fercha. "You have good control of all the major offensive spells—fireballs, lightning, sound blasts, tight light, and cold."

"Thank you," said Merry. "I've stored them with triggers in my magestone's setting so I can retrieve them quickly."

"Very good," said the wizard in blue. "I've watched you practicing and was quite impressed with the way you made a boulder shatter by applying intense heat to one side and intense cold to the other."

"I remembered what happened when my mother took a ceramic crock directly from hot ashes and put it in a basin of water to cool," said Merry. "She only did that once."

"Another good lesson," said Fercha. "Learn from your mistakes and don't make them a second time."

"Which is only useful when your first mistake doesn't kill you," said Merry with a grin.

"Not making mistakes that kill you is the beginning of wisdom," Fercha replied with an answering smile. "It's probably best to avoid mistakes that make you wish you were dead as well."

"You sound like you're speaking from experience," said Merry. "I can see that practicing wizardry can be dangerous, especially when other wizards are trying to kill you."

"I *am* speaking from experience," said Fercha. "Painful experience. But my biggest mistakes weren't with wizardry."

"Not with wizardry?" echoed Merry.

"No," said Fercha. "With wizards."

Merry was ready to ask more questions, but Fercha changed the subject.

"I heard from Doethan last night," she said. "He said he has important news from Brendinas and is heading this way. He said he will stop at the tower this evening."

"Doethan's coming here?" asked Merry.

"That's what I said. I think he'll be very pleased to see your progress."

"I think I'll be very pleased to see *him*," Merry exclaimed. "What sort of important news? Do you think it's about the war?"

"I'd be surprised if it wasn't," Fercha replied. "I told him about dueling Verro after I caught him snooping around west of here."

"What do you think Verro was looking for?"

"I don't know, and that bothers me," said Fercha. "It sounds like it bothers Doethan, too."

"Doethan's not a hedge wizard, is he?"

"You already know the answer to that, don't you?"

"Yes," said Merry. "I supposed I always have. He lives like a hedge wizard, but doesn't *feel* like a hedge wizard. From time to time, my father would say things about Doethan that made me sure he was more than he pretends to be."

"And that's one of the reasons you apprenticed yourself to him?" asked Fercha.

"Yes," said Merry. "My da also said I should talk to Doethan if I was curious about wizardry."

Fercha laughed.

"I'll wager he didn't say that in your mother's hearing."

"No," said Merry. "We were on a trip to Tyford together. My da introduced me to Doethan when we stopped at his tower."

"Your father and Doethan were both important advisers to the old king," said Fercha. "It's not my place to tell their stories, but you may want to ask Doethan about his time in the old king's service. When you get back to Applegarth, you can ask your father the same question, though I don't guarantee you'll hear the same stories from both of them."

"My father was an adviser to the old king?"

"He was on the royal council. So was Doethan."

"Neither of them ever said anything about it."

"Think," said Fercha. "Why would Derry settle in the far west of the kingdom? Why would Doethan play the part of a humble hedge wizard not far from Derry's baronial lands?"

"Why does my da never travel closer to Brendinas than Tyford?" mused Merry.

"Good," said Fercha. "You're considering possibilities."

"I feel like I've been kicked in the head by a plow horse."

"I felt the same way when I was a girl and realized my parents must have..."

"I understand," said Merry as Fercha's voice trailed off. "It's strange when you realize your parents must have had sex."

"No, it's not that," said Fercha, "but no matter. It's just ancient history."

"Since you bring it up," said Merry, "do you have any history books in the tower? Ones that cover the relevant years?"

"I do," said Fercha. "I rescued one of them from the flames, but that's another story you don't need to hear. There's no accounting for the foolishness of princes."

"There's no shortage of foolishness," said Merry, thinking of Gruffyd. "Do you think that's why we're at war?"

"I would, if I hadn't spotted Verro scouting the lands west of the Rhuthro valley," said Fercha. "I pushed him back to the river..."

"And dueled and lost your magestone?" asked Merry.

"Correct," said Fercha. "Though I'm not proud of it. Verro was looking for something, but I don't know what."

"I have a friend who knows the lands to the west quite well," said Merry.

"Your lover from the Coombe? The one who found my artifact?"

"Uh huh," said Merry.

"He won't do us much good, unfortunately. If he's where I think he is after taking the gate in the base of the tower, he might as well be across the sea."

"I know how to get in touch with him," said Merry.

Fercha looked at Merry and raised an eyebrow.

"Doethan has an enchanted ring and gave Eynon a matching one," said Merry quickly. "He can talk to Eynon whenever he wants."

"I know the spell he must have used," said Fercha after brief pause. "It's a limited gate that's only good for sight and sound. It's tricky to get the rings' bands to expand, but not too hard once you've done it a few times."

"Could you make a ring like that now, or show me how to enchant one?"

"I could," said Fercha, "but it wouldn't do much good. Rings like that have to be tuned to each other and we don't know anything about the ring Doethan gave Eynon. It's easier to wait until he gets here tonight. Then I can read the tuning on Doethan's ring and make you a copy of it, or teach you how to make one."

Merry grasped Fercha's hands, then did a small, excited dance.

"Could you?" she said. "That would be *wonderful!*"

"I'm glad you're so easily delighted," said Fercha. "This young man must be quite special."

"He's sweet and smart and charming and clueless and very brave and the best cook and..."

"Yes, yes," said Fercha. "I'm sure he's an amazing individual. That's all well and good—but now you need to focus on learning defensive magic so you can stay alive long enough to see him again."

Chapter 26

"Testing reveals the tester as much as the tested."
— Ealdamon's *Epigrams*

"Did Rocky catch a deer?" asked Eynon from the battlements.

"I called a big one to the castle," said Damon, leaning on his staff at Eynon's right. "What your scaly pet chose to do with it is his business."

"I'm sorry I was late and didn't see it," said Eynon. "I had to put tonight's rolls by the fire to proof."

Damon nodded, as if any cooking-related excuse would be accepted without objection. Off to the west, Eynon heard faint grinding sounds, like a giant mortar and pestle in operation.

"There he is," said Eynon, pointing in that direction. "Under those trees. That sound must be from all the rocks he swallowed."

"That wyvern of yours has a healthy appetite," Nûd added from the other side of Eynon. "I'm glad he's eating over there, so I don't lose *my* appetite."

From what Eynon could see at this distance, the big deer's head had already been removed from its body. Eynon noticed that Nûd was holding a loaded crossbow and aiming it out toward the woods where the grinding sounds were coming from. He had a quiver full of bolts slung over his shoulder and at the ready. Eynon hoped the weapon wasn't intended as protection against Rocky.

"He's a good wyvern," said Eynon.

"So long as he keeps his distance," said Nûd. He winked at Eynon and pointed his crossbow down. Eynon wasn't sure if he was being teased, but figured the odds were good. He shifted his attention back to Damon.

"How do you call animals?" Eynon asked the older man.

"That's advanced wizardry," said Damon.

"He put out a salt lick," said Nûd.

"Quiet, you," said Damon, dismissing Nûd's comment with a wave before putting his free hand on Eynon's shoulder.

"You're going to learn advanced forms of shield work today, lad," Damon continued.

"Like the bubble of solidified sound you created to protect us from my fireball at the lake yesterday?"

"Yes," said Damon. "A bubble is one kind of shield. You'll practice creating those, and other types of shields as well."

"What other types?" asked Eynon.

"We'll get there in a minute," said Damon. He looked Eynon up and down, as if trying to determine the extent of his previous education from his physical appearance. "I know you've studied Euclid and have a basic familiarity with plane geometry, but have you read Apollonius of Perga's *Treatise on Cones and Spheres?*"

"I'm sorry, sir, I haven't," said Eynon. "My teacher back in the Coombe never mentioned him."

"Apollonius isn't useful for military engineers, but his writings are quite valuable for wizards."

Damon used the head of his staff to sketch out a three-dimensional cone and sphere in the air in front of Eynon. The figures were drawn in glowing dark blue lines. Eynon stepped back to the inner edge of the path along the top of the battlement to get a better look.

"The sphere is like the bubble you created yesterday," observed Eynon.

"Correct," said Damon. "Now follow along."

The older man formed a third figure—a shimmering rectangle the size of a page of parchment in a book. Instead of being outlined, the rectangle was filled with a luminous shade of sky blue.

Slowly, Damon moved the rectangle through the sphere.

"What do you see?" asked Damon.

"New shapes," said Eynon. "Some are familiar, some not."

"Yes, but consider defensive magic. What do you *see?*"

"I see many ways to make a shield," said Eynon. "A dished circle or oval would protect against an attacker if you kept it turned toward them."

Damon raised one eyebrow and nodded his approval.

"Enough theory," said Nûd. "When are you going to let him generate a complex shield for himself?"

"Soon," said Damon, frowning. "At this stage, it's important for the lad to understand the theoretical basis of defensive wizardry, not just the practice."

Eynon kept quiet about his experience using the blue oval magestone to defend himself from Rocky's initial 'attacks.' What Nûd and Damon didn't know wouldn't hurt them. They already knew he could make sophisticated constructs of solidified sound for boiling water, melting gold, and escaping basilisks. Damon shifted the flat rectangle from the sphere to the cone.

"What do you see now?" asked the older man.

"Flat circles and ellipses," said Eynon. "And arches with rounded tops."

"Parabolas," said Damon.

"How are they useful?" asked Eynon. "Why wouldn't I always want to use a sphere to protect me from all directions?"

"Because you can't fight back effectively through a sphere," Nûd answered.

"At last, you've said something helpful," said Damon.

Eynon covered his mouth so the pair couldn't see him smile at their bickering.

"Do you understand, lad?" asked Damon. "You have many shapes available for shields and they all have their strengths and weaknesses."

"I can see that," said Eynon. "What would you like me to do?"

"Use your flying disk to float up and out from the castle wall," said Damon. "Experiment with different shield shapes until you're comfortable with several of them, and remember, speed is even more important than shape."

"Speed?" asked Eynon.

"You'll see," said Damon. "Getting your shield in place quickly can be the difference between life and death."

Eynon nodded, but he wasn't sure he understood what Damon was trying to tell him. Maybe he'd learn how to generate shields faster with practice. He stood on his flying disk, rose a dozen feet in the air, and moved out away from the battlements. Chee was excited to be flying again and chittered like a field of locusts in his ear.

"Farther out," said Damon.

Eynon complied.

"Farther."

He was a hundred yards from the castle when Damon instructed him to stop and hover.

"Create a spherical shield," said the older man.

Eynon did, taking a fraction more than a second.

"Drop it, and do it again—faster this time."

"Yes sir," said Eynon.

He managed to get his shield up in a heartbeat this time.

"Drop it," said Damon.

Eynon did, then barely had time to register Nûd raising his crossbow and firing. His spherical shield snapped up in an eye blink and the quarrel bounced off it and fluttered down to the stones below.

"What was *that* for?" asked Eynon.

Nûd loaded another bolt and released it, aiming for Rocky at the tree line to the west, not Eynon. Only a quick bit of flying interposed Eynon's shield bubble between the bolt and the wyvern.

"Hey," said Eynon. "Stop!"

Damon didn't respond verbally. Instead he shot a fireball from the tip of his staff, followed by yet another quarrel from Nûd. The fireball splashed across Eynon's sphere, blinding him temporarily. When the flames cleared, Damon and Nûd were only a dozen feet away, floating on Damon's flying disk. Nûd kept shooting and Damon shifted to crackling discharges of lightning that played around Eynon's sphere, confusing him.

They're trying to kill me! thought Eynon.

He readied a fireball of his own and flicked his spherical shield down just long enough to launch it at Damon. The fireball incinerated Nûd's most recent crossbow bolt before striking the circular dished shield that instantaneously popped into place to protect his two attackers.

"Enough!" shouted Eynon.

His body twitched as some of the lightning Damon shot back penetrated his thickening shield sphere. Eynon's shield wavered.

Damon released a brief blast of ice-cold air and soon Eynon found himself shivering as well as twitching. Chee had ice in his fur, matching Eynon's hair.

"I surrender!" he cried, raising his hands over his head. Chee mirrored Eynon and raised his forepaws.

Damon and Nûd stopped their assault and floated close to Eynon and his familiar. A gentle heat spell thawed Eynon's hair and Chee's fur.

"I don't know if I'm happy or sad to see that you're not a prodigy at everything," said Damon.

Eynon shook his head.

"Why did you *do* that?" he asked.

"Your enemies won't take pity on you," said Nûd. "You have to be ready for anything."

"I should have learned that lesson when the ground shook yesterday," said Eynon.

"You should have indeed," said Damon. "Pull yourself together and we'll do this again. Try to fight back this time."

"Now I know why you teach offensive magic before defensive magic," said Eynon as he rubbed Chee's fur to warm the raconette.

An enigmatic smile crossed Damon's face. Eynon was afraid it meant the older man would enjoy teaching him how to defend himself in a literal trial by fire. Nûd looked embarrassed and shrugged his shoulders, which Eynon interpreted to mean the tall servant was just doing what Damon told him to do.

"Does the Master know about the way you teach defensive magic?" asked Eynon.

Nûd laughed and Damon couldn't keep the corners of his mouth from turning up.

"He's the one who insists on training apprentices this way," said Nûd. "The Master says it selects for survivors early in the process."

"Do you at least heal the students who can't get their shields up fast enough?

"When there's anything left to heal," said Damon. The old man had returned to his enigmatic smile, so Eynon couldn't tell if he was teasing or serious. He hoped for the former.

Eynon squared his shoulders and brushed drops of water from his hair—the remains of melted ice from Damon's blast of frigid air.

"I'm ready to try again if you are," he said.

Chee burrowed into the depths of Eynon's jacket, which was fine by him. The little beast would be marginally safer there, Eynon hoped. He moved his flying disk fifty feet away, closer to the trees where Rocky was still digesting, if the continued noisy grinding sounds were any indication.

Eynon opened his arms as if to say *take your best shot.*

Nûd pointed his crossbow at Eynon and pulled the trigger. The bolt leapt toward Eynon as fast as a striking batsnake, but Eynon was faster. His mind and magestone worked together to construct a lens-shaped shield, with a thick concave side close to Eynon and a thinner convex side facing Nûd and Damon. The crossbow bolt didn't bounce off—it was trapped by the outer shield.

Damon's energy attacks came next. It was lightning first this time, then a larger fireball than before, followed by a series of finger-thin beams of tight light that would have bisected Eynon's torso if his new lens-shaped combination shield had let the beams all the way through. More attacks followed. Damon was playing rough.

Eynon remembered what he'd learned from the gryffon attacking the wisent about attacking from an unexpected direction. He'd planned ahead and had a trick up his sleeve—more than one, actually.

The outer part of his lens-shaped shield allowed energy in to hit the sturdy wall of the inner shield. The more wizardry Damon directed at Eynon, the more energy filled the space between the inner and outer shields. Scattered crossbow bolts were held in the outer arc of the lens, which was starting to bow outward from the pressure of the powerful forces captured behind it.

Nûd was reloading and Damon was preparing a bolt of lightning when Eynon dropped the outer part of his lens-shaped shield, releasing the combined energies of over a dozen of Damon's spells simultaneously. The powerful blast struck Damon's shield like a giant's fist and forced the shield and both men three paces back to the far edge of their flying disk.

Damon started to teeter but Nûd pulled the older man back before he could fall. Lightning crackled around them from the older man's prematurely triggered spell.

Shaking himself like a dog coming out of a river, Damon grinned at Eynon and readied a large fireball.

"Go ahead, old man," shouted Eynon, goading Damon on. "If this is a game, I want to win. If it's not, I want to live."

Nûd turned and saw Eynon's second surprise, but didn't warn Damon. Before the older man could release his spell, Rocky flew up behind him and knocked him off his flying disk with the tip of one of his wings. The prepared fireball spell went off, sending a huge, flaming missile high in the air. It exploded above them like a lit candle landing in a box of fireworks.

Damon's staff went spinning down in one direction while Damon himself fell more like a rock than a leaf in another.

Eynon gently caught Damon in a hemisphere of solidified sound before he hit the ground. He lifted Damon up to the castle's closest battlement and flew to join the older wizard, towing Nûd along behind him. He expected Damon to yell at him when he stepped onto the walkway atop the castle wall, and he wasn't wrong—though he was surprised by what the older man said.

"That was *amazing!*" Damon exclaimed.

The older man put his arms around Eynon and hugged him harder than his mother had before he'd left for his wander year.

"How did you come up with that two-ply lens shield, lad?"

Damon was laughing so hard he put his fists to his stomach. It took Eynon a moment to realize Damon was laughing at himself, not Eynon.

"You fooled me completely," said the older man between more rumbling laughs. "How did you get the wyvern to do what you wanted?"

Nûd turned his back on Eynon and Damon. His shoulders were shaking, so Eynon expected he was laughing, too.

"Let me answer your last question first," said Eynon. "Once the two-ply shield began to fill with energy, making it harder for you to see me, I sent a tasty ball of solidified sound to Rocky and flew it around behind you. Rocky chased it, and you know the rest."

Damon slowly gained a measure of self-control after taking several deep breaths.

"And the two-ply lens shield?"

Eynon didn't want to tell Damon how he'd created squirt bottles from solidified sound to discourage basilisks, so he figured out an alternative explanation.

"I thought about my goatskin," he said. "It fills with water, then I can release it all at once."

The older man looked dubious but didn't press Eynon for more.

Nûd took advantage of the break in the conversation to ask a question of his own.

"Why did you have your wyvern knock Damon from his flying disk instead of grabbing him in his mouth?"

"I didn't trust Rocky not to eat Damon under the circumstances," said Eynon.

Nûd and Eynon laughed loud enough for Chee to pop his head out of the neck of Eynon's jacket and chitter along with them.

"Hah hah," said Damon with a pause between each word. His smile said he wasn't too upset, but he did keep looking up from time to time to scan the sky for circling wyverns.

"What's my next lesson, sir?" asked Eynon. "We still have a few hours before I have to make lunch and then the entire afternoon is available. I want to learn how to store spells in my artifact."

"That won't take long," said Damon. "It's a simple matter to attach preconfigured spells. You just..."

The older man stopped in mid-sentence. Eynon leaned forward, eager to hear the rest.

"No," said Damon, shaking his head as if correcting himself. "Best not."

"He's afraid if he teaches you triggers now, you'll want to learn one more thing, then another, and another after that," said Nûd.

Eynon grinned and proved Nûd's point with a litany of things to learn.

"Like gate spells and communications spells and healing spells and the names of all the wizards in the Conclave and..."

Damon raised his hand and Eynon stopped talking.

"Congratulations, lad. You've done so well you can have the rest of the day off. Find a book to read in the library and relax, if you'd like, except for making lunch and dinner, of course."

"Of course," repeated Nûd in a way guaranteed to annoy Damon.

"The library? That would be wonderful!" said Eynon. "Can we eat lunch early so I'll have more time to read."

"Certainly," said Damon. "Now that I think about it, I'd like an early lunch myself. I have projects of my own to attend to. I've been putting them off to instruct a certain precocious new apprentice wizard."

"I'm sorry to take you away from your work," said Eynon.

"Don't be sorry," said Damon. "Teaching *is* my work. The Master put me in charge of apprentice training for a reason—*teaching teaches the teacher* and all that. Still, I'd appreciate a free afternoon. I need to get back to writing my next book."

"You write books?" asked Eynon. "What kind?"

"Oh, this and that," said Damon.

"He writes for his own amusement," said Nûd. "And he's easily amused."

Damon made a disapproving noise in his throat that sounded exactly like the one Eynon's great-uncle made whenever someone expressed an opinion contrary to his own.

Nûd ignored the wordless criticism.

"I could use a free afternoon myself," he said. "The Master has lots of work for me and I have to retrieve someone's dropped staff."

"Thank you," said Eynon. "Thank you, both."

Damon and Nûd gave small bows and walked toward the stairs in the nearest guard tower. Nûd carried his full-sized crossbow, the few remaining quarrels, and Damon's flying disk.

Eynon's spirits were soaring, so he stood on his flying disk and directed it to swoop around the castle courtyard in exuberant curves before landing by the inner door to the kitchen.

Half a day in the library! he thought. *Where do I start?*

Chapter 27

"Books are dangerous things—you can fall into them."
— Ealdamon's *Epigrams*

"Thanks for cleaning up!" said Eynon.

He'd rushed through his lunch and was at the kitchen door, ready to head for the library.

"Go," said Nûd. "I'll take care of things here and check on the dinner rolls."

"You're the best," said Eynon.

Chee was on Eynon's shoulder, nibbling a double-handful of dried cherries.

"No food in the library," Damon admonished.

The raconette pushed all the remaining cherries into his cheek pouches and gave the older man an overstuffed smile.

"Bye," said Eynon.

His footsteps echoed on the stairs.

* * * * *

It took him a moment to catch his breath after climbing the stairs and running down the corridor, which was odd. *Something about Melyncárreg was affecting his endurance.* Then he was at the library.

Eynon stood in the doorway, regarding the books on the shelves. He didn't know how they were organized—if they were—and had no idea where to start. There were so many books—hundreds and hundreds of them.

He wanted a recent history of Dâron, if he could find one. Failing that, he'd be glad to read a copy of *The Venerable History of Dâron from the First Ships,* so he could discuss it with Merry when he made his way back to her again.

Chee decided to jump over to a reading table to take a nap and chew on dried cherries, while Eynon determined his best course was to review the bookcases from left to right.

To his surprise, Eynon couldn't even read the titles of the books on the left-hand shelves. They were written in strange characters Eynon didn't recognize, until he spotted triangles and circles with slashes through them. *Delta, theta* and *phi* were old friends from his geometry lessons. Those books must be written in Athican.

He deduced that the shelves on the left must be for works in other languages and shifted to the next set of bookcases to the right.

The Animal, Vegetable, and Mineral books with pictures of wizards' artifacts were on these shelves, so Eynon assumed all the other nearby books would be about wizardry. He'd return to them if he had time, but now he was looking for history books. There were holes in his understanding of the ancient and recent history of Dâron he wanted to fill as soon as possible.

There it is, thought Eynon when he shifted to the next set of shelves. *The Venerable History* had a dark blue cover and a gold crown on its spine. Eynon was drawn to it like iron to a lodestone. He opened the cover and read the title page to confirm that the book truly was what he expected.

Eynon memorized the spot on the shelf occupied by *The Venerable History* and put it on one of the reading tables. *There must be other history books in the same section,* he reasoned. After opening five more volumes, he found what he wanted.

The Annals of Dârioth XXIV, Volume II, read its title. Dârioth XXIV was the old king. He'd assumed the throne at eighteen after his father fell in battle with Tamloch and had reigned for seventy years. Dârio, as the young king was called, was the old king's great-grandson. Not much older than Eynon, he'd only worn the crown for a year and a month.

I'll bet he hates to hear people say, "That's not how the old king would have done it," thought Eynon.

He opened the leather-bound copy of the *Annals* and began to skim its pages. Chee stirred and moved from one end of the reading table to sit in the middle of Eynon's book like a cat, confident he was the center of Eynon's universe. Eynon rubbed the raconette's head and shifted him to the top of *The Venerable History.*

He hoped the little beast would be satisfied to rest on an unopened book and returned to the *Annals*. From what Eynon could tell, it started recounting events from forty years ago.

Battles with the western Clan Lands. Battles with the northern Clan Lands. Bifurland dragonship raids up the river to Brendinas. Border clashes with the Eagle People. Skirmishes with Tamloch. More skirmishes with Tamloch. New golden statue of Princess Seren to replace one taken by raiders.

Ah! Found it! thought Eynon. Dâron and Tamloch combine to defeat the Eagle People twenty-five years ago.

In the forty-fifth year of the reign of King Dârioth XXIV, may his sword arm be strong and his wisdom ever increase, the Master Mage was summoned from the far west to freeze the waters of the Abbenoth River so the combined armies of Dâron and Tamloch could cross and lay siege to the Eagle People's capital at Nova Eboracum.

Eynon rubbed his chin. *I wonder if it's the same Master Mage as today,* he thought. *And why was he summoned from the far west? Was he here in Melyncárreg then? Why was the Master Mage living so far from Brendinas?*

He read on.

When their supplies grew short, the infantry squares and cavalry of the Eagle People came forth from their walls to give battle. The king's son, Crown Prince Dârioth, fell in combat fighting side by side with Túath, the heir to Tamloch's throne, but their sons avenged them. Young Prince Dâri of Dâron and Prince Túathal of Tamloch slew the commander of the city and his guards, claiming eagle standards from four legions.

Eynon had heard that story from grandfathers and grandmothers in the Coombe who'd served in the levies. They didn't often speak of the battle at the walls of Nova Eboracum, but it seemed like every one of them had been within a hundred yards of the royal princes when they fell.

A book like this should give me the truth of the matter, thought Eynon. It's not the faded memories of old warriors who probably heard the story third-hand around a campfire. He kept reading.

All would have been lost without the actions of two brave, quick-thinking men. Salderwen, a yeoman soldier in the king's guard, blocked a cowardly thrust from an enemy short sword aimed at young Prince Dâri's back. Llandoethan, a newly made crown wizard, cast a shield spell that saved both princes and their armsmen from a great fireball thrown from the walls of Nova Eboracum.

Eynon had hoped for clarity, but ended up more confused than before. Sal*derwen* and Llan*doethan?* Were Derry and Doethan heroes in the war with the Eagle People? If so, why did they end up settling in the far west of the kingdom along the Rhuthro valley, instead of closer to the court in Brendinas? He skipped over a long section detailing the terms of the Eagle People's surrender and the new borders for their territory until he found something relevant.

From what he read, he learned that the old king was grateful to Salderwen and Llandoethan, raising Salderwen to a baron and giving him a generous estate on fertile lands north of Brendinas.

Llandoethan was also rewarded. His magical talents were strong and he was named Senior Crown Wizard—the Master Mage for the kingdom in all but title, since the Master had disappeared again, shortly after creating the ice bridge across the Abbenoth.

The historian writing this volume of the *Annals* was clearly dancing around a sensitive area when discussing the Master Mage. Perhaps that story was in the previous volume. Eynon glanced at the shelf and confirmed the earlier book was there. He'd read that one next, since he also wanted to know more about Princess Seren and what she'd done to merit a gold statue—or two gold statues, if it was true that dragonship raiders took the first.

Eynon knew the romantic daydream version of the story—it had been one of his little sister's favorites when she was small. Princess Seren was the first child born to King Dârioth and Queen Carys, close to seventy years ago. Her younger brother, named Dârioth, like his father, came along a few years later. The princess had striking auburn hair and was a favorite of the court, as beautiful as her wits were quick. She sat by her father's side in court and council from the time she was six, learning how to be a good ruler when her turn came to take the throne.

Years passed, and Princess Seren grew from a precocious child to an impressive young woman. Suitors from noble families across the kingdom vied for her favor, but she put them off, saying she wanted to focus on her work as her father's assistant for a time before considering marriage. She was scheduled to speak to a gathering of stewards and military engineers on the importance of building solid roads and sturdy bridges when she disappeared while walking down a hallway from one room in the palace to the next.

Everyone in the kingdom from blacksmith to baron tried to find the missing princess. The king and queen offered a huge reward to anyone who could help them find her, but it did no good. She had vanished from the land between the mountains and the sea and was never seen again in Dâron.

Eynon's sister Braith had a Princess Seren doll when she was younger. The doll's hair came from a fox tail and was made for her by one of the women a few cottages down from theirs in Haywall. When Eynon was older, he learned that the tail of every fox caught robbing a hen house in the Coombe was used for a similar purpose.

He looked back at the copy of the *Annals of Dârioth XXIV, Volume I,* behind him on the shelf and decided he had time to follow his quest to learn more of Princess Seren's story. Chee didn't stir from his nap when Eynon got up and returned with another thick book.

It was no surprise that the disappearing princess merited her own chapter in *Volume I.* Eynon skimmed the pages and gathered that the romantic tale told to children was largely correct. What it omitted, however, was any discussion of the Master Mage's role in the search for Seren. The book in his hands covered that in detail.

The Master Mage blamed himself for not being able to find the princess. He was convinced she had been abducted by wizardry using a congruency gate. For days, he cast detection spell after detection spell, hoping for details about who might have taken her and where she might be. None were successful.

After a fortnight of failures, he requested an audience with the king and queen and tried to resign his position. The royal couple wouldn't hear of it, but the Master Mage insisted. The king was wise, however, and suggested a compromise, which the *Annals* recorded.

"The kingdom rests on a four-legged stool," said the king. "The crown and its nobles, the wizards, the traders and artisans, and those who till the land."

"That is known to all," said the Master Mage.

The king nodded.

"Each leg must be of equal length for the stool to balance," he continued, "but losing the princess makes the crown's leg shorter. I can already feel the stool begin to tip."

"Only for a short time, Your Majesty," said the Master Mage. "The prince will grow and fill the void."

"That is so," said the king, "but now the stool is swaying. If the wizards' leg grows shorter—if you leave our service forever—I fear the stool will fall."

The Master Mage stood silent. The king looked at him with kind eyes, while the queen's gaze was down. She still wept for her lost daughter.

"Leave the court for a time," said the king. "Take as many days or months or years as you need to find Princess Seren, or find peace."

The Master Mage bowed, acknowledging the wisdom in the king's words. He gave the king a ring that could be used to summon him if the kingdom was ever in grave danger and left the palace.

According to the chronicler who wrote *Volume I,* the Master Mage was not seen again, though Eynon knew he reappeared more than twenty years later when he froze the Abbenoth River at Nova Eboracum.

Carefully lifting the leather cover, Eynon closed the book, then closed his eyes. It was a sad story. Two of the brightest gems in the kingdom had been lost within weeks of each other, forty-five years ago.

Maybe that's why the Master keeps to himself in his tower, he thought. *If he's even the same person.*

He was hoping for answers from history, but all he had were more questions. Eynon heard a tapping on the frame of the door to the library. It was Nûd.

"Time to put the rolls in the oven and get dinner started," he said.

Eynon sat up with a start and wondered how the afternoon had passed so quickly. He smiled to himself, knowing the answer, then put the history books back on the shelf, collected a half-asleep Chee and joined Nûd in the hall.

"I've got a lot of questions for you about the Master," he said.

"I'm sure you do," said Nûd.

His smile, as best Eynon could read it, was enigmatic.

Merry

Merry was practicing her shield work at the top of the tower in the moonlight. The setting sun had turned the western horizon red and gold hours ago. As she practiced, she faced east, watching for Doethan. Merry was gaining confidence in her new magestone and setting, pleased with its power and responsiveness. She snapped spheres and hemispheres and flat walls of solidified sound into place in fractions of a second and dispelled them every bit as quickly.

After Fercha had tagged her on the back with a stinging ball of sound that afternoon while she was using a hemisphere instead of a sphere for protection, Merry and her magestone had devised a very thin sphere of solidified sound that acted as a detector for anything approaching from behind. It was very sensitive and would automatically switch to a full, thick spherical shield in case of an attack from the rear, yet not interfere with working offensive magic when thin. The only problem was its sensitivity. It would snap into place if approached by a midge, not just a missile.

At least I'll avoid mosquito bites, thought Merry. *And better too sensitive than not sensitive enough. I'll have to tell Fercha about it and see what she thinks.*

"Merry," came strong Fercha's voice up the stairs. "Come down. Doethan's here."

"How did..." Merry said out loud, then she stopped herself. *Of course. He didn't fly all the way from Brendinas. He came through a gate.*

She started to speed down the stairs, or tried to. It was hard to run on a spiral staircase. Even at a more measured pace, it didn't take long to get to Fercha's workroom.

Doethan was standing next to Fercha by one of the worktables. He still wore his sky-blue cloak, but his plain white linen tunic had been replaced by a finer white garment edged in gold embroidery. His long gray hair was pulled back and the large blue gem in his circlet pulsed with light. His ironwood staff leaned against the table so both his hands were free to hug Merry. The two held each other for a moment, then Doethan stepped back.

"You've rejected me as a teacher to take up with *this* one instead," teased Doethan with a grin. He put his hand on Fercha's shoulder and they all smiled.

"Your loss, my gain," said Fercha.

"No, *my* gain," said Merry. "Now I've got you both to teach me."

All three laughed.

"I've learned so much, Doethan," said Merry. "Fercha helped me find my true magestone and craft a setting and taught me offensive and defensive magic and..."

"Fercha is an excellent mentor, I'm sure," said Doethan, breaking in. "And I owe her an apology for sending you and Eynon here without her approval in advance. But I'm here with a purpose, and it's best if we get to it."

His expression turned serious.

"We need to know what Verro was looking for in the Coombe. Spies in Tamloch say they're preparing an attack on Dâron territory, and I'm concerned the Coombe may be their target. Verro never does anything without a good reason."

"I'll second that," said Fercha. "That's why I stopped him when I saw him over the Coombe initially. I wanted to talk, but he attacked me."

"I'm sorry," said Doethan.

"Don't worry about it," said Fercha. "I lost my original magestone in that fight, but now I've got another."

"It will take you weeks to get back to..." began Doethan.

"That's my problem, not yours. The wizard makes the artifact..."

"The artifact does not make the wizard," completed Merry and Doethan.

"Fine," said Doethan when Fercha glared at him. "You can take care of yourself—and help me scout the Coombe in the morning."

"Certainly," said Fercha.

"Don't you want advice on the Coombe from Eynon?" asked Merry. "He knows everything about it."

"A nice young man," said Doethan. "Good choice."

"Thank you," said Merry. "If I ever see him again."

"You will, I'm sure," said Doethan.

"She can see him now if you use that ring you gave him," said Fercha. "Whatever made you decide to give him one?"

"Now that I think about it, I'm not sure. But I'm glad I did. I must have seen something special in the lad."

Doethan rubbed the center of his forehead under his circlet, then noticed Merry and Fercha were staring at him.

"What?" he said. "It itches."

"The ring, Doethan," said Fercha.

"Oh, yes," he replied, removing the simple gold band from his little finger and handing it to Merry. "He's your lover. *You* call him."

Merry raised her eyebrows but took the offered ring and held it in front of her in both hands.

"*Gwaloeaden!*" she commanded.

Three bell tones chimed. The ring expanded and a hazy scene began to sharpen inside its enlarged circumference.

"Eynon? It's me."

Chapter 28

"What is commonplace may not be common."
— Ealdamon's *Epigrams*

Nûd had been unresponsive, even evasive, when Eynon had asked him about the Master and Princess Seren.

"That's the Master's business, not mine—or yours," he'd said. "What the Master decides to say to you or anyone is up to him."

"But the Master is the same person who tried to find the princess when she disappeared?"

"He's old enough to be," said Nûd, "but he doesn't confide the details of his personal life to me."

Eynon understood that was the end of their conversation. He wouldn't get more out of Nûd.

When he saw Damon at dinner, he considered asking the older man what he knew about the Master's history. Damon's dour mood at the table—a contrast to his smiles and laughter when Eynon had gotten the better of him this morning—made Eynon think better of it. He now had access to the Academy's huge library—he could live without answers to all his questions with so many new things to learn.

Both men had cleaned their plates, so Eynon assumed they were satisfied with their dinners. Damon went upstairs after he'd finished eating without thanking Eynon for his meal. Uncharacteristically, Nûd shortly followed the older man instead of helping to clean up.

"What's buttered their bread with goose droppings?" said Eynon to himself. That reminded him he'd best get busy if he wanted to have more time in the library before bed. It was still early evening in Melyncárreg, and Eynon thought he could light one of the lamps in the library to read by.

It didn't take him long to get the pots and dishes washed and set out to dry. Then he had to prepare tomorrow's bread. Mixing dough always relaxed Eynon. He enjoyed the smell of the yeast and the feel of combining the ingredients with his hands.

Eynon put the covered bowl of dough on a shelf next to the banked fire and had just finished washing his hands when he heard three bells chime softly. The middle finger of his left hand buzzed like a wasp trapped under a goblet. It was Doethan's ring.

He held the ring's enlarged circle in front of him, saw a blurred image, and heard an oh-so-familiar voice say, "Eynon? It's me."

"Merry?" said Eynon. "It's you?"

"Of course it's me," said Merry. "Pay attention. We don't have much time and we need your help."

Now that the scene through the ring had sharpened, Eynon could see Merry's smiling face. He smiled back, ready to jump through the ring, if that had been possible. He remembered how Doethan's first message had been short and difficult to understand, so he focused on what Merry was saying. Chee leaned in from his usual perch on Eynon's shoulder so he could see Merry, too.

"Right," he said. "You're safe? I'm *so* glad to see you! What can I do?"

"Yes. Me, too. Tell us what Tamloch might want from the Coombe," said Merry in a quick burst.

"What?" said Eynon. "Dâron hardly wants anything from the Coombe besides taxes and levies. What could Tamloch want?"

"This is a waste of time," said a woman's voice he didn't recognize.

"Shush," said Merry. "Think, Eynon. Is there anything of value to Tamloch in the Coombe?"

"Tell him I found Verro snooping toward the northwest," said the unknown woman's voice.

"Particularly in the northwest," said Merry.

"I heard—and unless they want green soapstone griddles or green slate roof tiles, I can't think of anything."

"That could be it," said a familiar man's voice.

"Is that Doethan?" asked Eynon.

"Yes," said Merry and Doethan simultaneously.

"Where would we find the soapstone and slate?" Doethan asked.

"At the quarries in Wherrel," said Eynon.

"Ask him how to find Wherrel," said the woman's voice. Eynon could see a woman with short red hair behind Merry.

"How do we..." began Merry.

"It's in the northwest corner of the Coombe. Look for a village where all the houses are topped by green slate. The quarries are a quarter mile west of there, through a gap in the mountains."

"Thank you," said Merry. "You're wonderful."

"So are you!"

The connection was beginning to lose coherence and fade.

"What's happening?" asked Eynon.

"Later," said the other woman.

"Chi-chi-chi-chee!" said Chee from Eynon's shoulder.

"Take care of him, Chee," said Merry.

The raconette's head bobbed. Then the connection suddenly severed and the ring contracted, surprising Eynon and causing him to drop it on the table. It landed in a dusting of flour left over from bread making, but Eynon barely noticed.

I need to get back to Merry, and the Coombe!

Eynon picked up the ring, rubbed it on his tunic, and stuck it on his finger. He crossed to the stairs and took them two at a time. The library could wait. He had to find Damon and Nûd, tell them about connecting with Merry, and learn how to get home.

Nûd

"Shouldn't we tell him?" asked Nûd. "We're not going to leave him here, are we?"

"That's exactly what we're going to do," said Damon.

The two men stood close together in a small study room near the library, speaking softly.

"Why?" asked Nûd. "He's good-hearted, and a powerful wizard."

"We're not bringing him because he reminds me of someone."

"Who?" asked Nûd.

"Me, when I was his age," said Damon. "I had plenty of raw power and enough imagination to come up with creative ways to use it."

"I'll bet you did," said Nûd. "If he's so much like you, why not bring him along?"

"Remember what happened when I started teaching the... ?"

"Oh," said Nûd, cutting him off.

"Right," said Damon. "If we're going to sort things out between Dâron and Tamloch, we don't want to have a magic-using puppy with big feet bumbling around."

"Eynon's not a bumbler," said Nûd. "If anything, he's more responsible than he should be at his age."

"Yes, but his wizardry is so strong *and* subtle that he could easily turn small problems into big ones with a miscalculation."

"Like that fireball at the lake?"

"Exactly like that," said Damon. "And the red magestone he found is a real wild card. No one at court will know what to make of it."

"I'd forgotten about that," said Nûd. "He seems so ordinary most of the time, it's easy to forget how odd he is."

"Maybe you can forget," said Damon, "but I can't. With his red stone, the young king might think Eynon's a spy from the Eagle People, despite his youth."

"But their wizards only use purple or black stones."

"We're talking about Dârio," said Damon. "It would be just like him to think any magestone that isn't blue or green is from the Eagle People."

"Don't the Bifurlanders use amber stones?"

"They do, but if anyone tried to explain that to Dârio they'd just confuse him," said Damon.

"True," said Nûd. "From what I've heard, that's not hard to do."

"He's not the only one Eynon would confuse," said Damon. "The Conclave of Wizards will be turned upside down if they test him—and they'll want to."

"You know more about that sort of thing than I do," said Nûd. "Maybe it *is* best to leave him here."

"It is," said Damon with authority. "We'll leave early tomorrow morning—well before dawn—when he's asleep."

"If we must," said Nûd. "I guess he'll be fine here on his own. He'll have that wyvern of his to keep him company."

"Woof," said Damon. "The beast acts like a big dog around him!"

"And gave you quite a surprise this morning," Nûd added with a smile in his voice.

The older and younger man both chuckled.

"One thing's for sure, he'll eat better on his own than we did before he got here."

"You're right about that," said Nûd. "I'll miss his stews and his honey-raisin rolls."

"So will I," said Damon. "I knew there was more to Eynon than meets the eye from the moment I first met him."

"I like him," said Nûd. "I hope we're doing the right thing by leaving him here."

There was a pause, then Nûd spoke again.

"Which gate do we take? Brendinas? Tyford? Hers?"

"You know the answer to that," said Damon. "It's farthest west."

"I do, but I wanted to hear you say it. She's not going to be happy if she's there when we arrive."

"We'll have to hope she's not home, then."

"Why did you decide we're going back?" asked Nûd. "It's been a long time."

"It's not because the young king asked," said Damon.

"So...?"

"One of my sources in Riyas tells me that several senior court wizards—particularly Verro—are interested in the Coombe," said Damon.

"You *would* have sources in Tamloch's capital," said Nûd.

"I value intelligence," said Damon.

"Of course," said Nûd. "If Verro's interested in the Coombe, we are too. That goes without saying. I'm so glad you finally got around to telling me."

"Don't be that way," said Damon. "I only found out after dinner."

"Isn't the Coombe where Eynon hails from?"

"It is," said Damon. "That's another reason to keep him out of it."

"Or bring him along."

"He's not coming," said Damon. "Listen to your elders."

"I hear and obey, Your Ancientness."

"Maybe I should leave you here with Eynon."

"Or maybe not," said Nûd. "I'll pack what we need for the trip."

"Good," said Damon. "We'll meet in the couryard outside her tower two hours before sunrise."

"I'll make sure you're up," said Nûd, "and you won't be getting a hot breakfast before we leave."

"Or a good-tasting one," said Damon.

There was a pause, then Nûd spoke.

"Maybe I can have some home cooking when we get there?"

"Let's hope not," said Damon. "I might be the one to be cooked and served."

"Perhaps," said Nûd. "I'll start packing."

Chapter 29

"When you know the right thing to do, do it."
— Ealdamon's *Epigrams*

Eynon moved silently from the position where he'd been standing two steps outside the small room. He was glad Chee had read his mood and kept quiet on his shoulder.

Merry had been right about the listening spell she'd taught him. It had all sorts of uses.

He'd gone looking for Nûd and Damon to tell them about his contact with Merry and Doethan and the other wizard. When he passed the library, he'd seen a light coming from a room down a side hall, along a route he'd never walked before. As he'd approached he'd heard voices—Nûd and Damon's voices—and decided to be a fly on the wall instead of interrupting them.

Now he hurried away and ducked into the library before the others could see him. He lit an oil lamp on one of the tables with his magestone, pulled *The Annals of Dârioth XXIV, Volume II* from its place on the shelf, and pretended to read. Too late, he realized he could have cast a light spell.

Nûd and Damon's overheard conversation raised dozens of questions in Eynon's mind. Thoughts swirled in his brain like the lake water hit by his fireball. Despite his questions, one thing was clear. He would follow the two of them through their chosen gate tomorrow, wherever it led.

Chapter 30

"Doors and gates are often locked for a reason."
— Ealdamon's *Epigrams*

Eynon heard footsteps and looked up to see Nûd standing in the doorway.

"Don't stay up *too* late burning oil," said the taller man with a smile. "You'll have plenty of time for reading in daylight."

After you and Damon leave me here, thought Eynon.

"I'll be heading for bed soon. There are only a few more pages in this chapter."

Eynon was worried his voice might be giving away his new-found knowledge, but Nûd didn't seem to notice anything was different about him.

"Sleep in tomorrow," Nûd offered. "I can get the fire started and put the bread in the oven."

"Thanks," said Eynon. "That would be great. After fireballs and lightning spells yesterday and shield spells this morning, I could probably sleep until noon."

Eynon yawned, not sure he wasn't overdoing things, but it felt right. Nûd covered his mouth to disguise a yawn of his own and they both laughed. Eynon realized his was nervous laughter.

"Go to bed," said Nûd.

The tall man wagged his index finger, like a mother giving the same command to a stubborn child.

"Yes, master," said Eynon.

"I'm not the Master," Nûd replied. "Just a humble servant *to* the Master."

"When will I ever meet this mythical individual?"

"When he's ready to be met, and not before," said Nûd.

Nûd stepped close to the table where Eynon had his book open and read over his shoulder.

"*The Annals,* eh? Good choice," said Nûd. "They're guaranteed to put me to sleep. All that talk about kings and princes."

"And princesses," Eynon added.

"Them, too," said Nûd.

The larger man put his hand on Eynon's shoulder and gave it a supportive squeeze before turning and leaving the room.

Eynon was about to leave himself when he heard more footsteps. Had Nûd returned? No, this time it was Damon at the door.

"How are you feeling?" asked the older man. "Spellcasting can take a lot out of you."

Were they both checking up on him? Eynon wondered.

"You're right," said Eynon. "I'm tired from casting spells, and I also seem to be short of breath from time to time. I never felt that way back home."

"You're quite high in the mountains, lad," said Damon. "The air is thinner, that's all."

"There are mountains all around the Coombe."

"Yes, but these are three times as tall as the tallest peaks back in Dâron," said Damon. "It makes a difference."

"It was worse when I first arrived."

"Your body adjusts to the mountain air," said Damon. "In a few more weeks you won't notice it at all."

Eynon looked thoughtful.

"Where *are* we, sir, if we're not in Dâron?" he asked. "You said you'd show me the map room someday."

"I did and I will," said Damon. "Put your book back on the shelf and douse the lamp. You're a wizard now—use a light spell."

"Yes, Damon."

Eynon complied with the older man's instructions. A glowing ball floated above and behind his head.

"Good," said Damon. "I'll show you the map room so you can see the location of the Academy—then we can both go to bed."

"I hope I'll be able to sleep after seeing all the maps," said Eynon.

"There are several maps in the map room," said Damon as he led Eynon out of the library and down a long perpendicular corridor. "Most of them are safely stored in drawers—but there is one *big* map that should impress you."

Damon and Eynon entered the map room and Eynon was suitably impressed. One entire wall, sixteen feet long by eight tall, was a map far larger than any Eynon had seen before. The older man triggered a large glow globe in the ceiling with a gesture. He led Eynon to the right side of the map where Eynon saw sections marked in five different colors.

The upper-most part was yellow and the section below it was green. The lower part of the map was painted the Kingdom of Dâron's familiar sky blue, while mountainous regions signified by small triangles and rounded humps in the in the lower left and right center were different shades of brown. Lakes and major rivers were marked in deep blue. A bright red-colored section, shaped like a knife, stabbed between the green and sky blue.

Eynon stood staring, as if it would all make sense if he only looked at it long enough.

"Do you understand what you're seeing?" asked Damon.

Eynon replied, reluctantly. "No. It's beautiful, though. Can you explain it to me?"

"Of course," said the older man. "The yellow lands are Bifurland, where the dragonship raiders come from. The green lands are..."

"Tamloch?" asked Eynon.

"Indeed," said Damon. "And the sky blue lands must be..."

"Dâron," said Eynon with a smile. The map was beginning to make sense to him. "That must mean the red strip in the center, on either side of that big river running straight up and down..."

"The Abbenoth."

"...is the province of the Eagle People."

"Correct," said Damon. "What about the brown regions?"

"They're both in the mountains—"

"Yes. So... ?"

"Are they the Clan Lands?"

"Correct again," said Damon. "Both Dâron and Tamloch have Clan Lands and clan barbarians to torment them."

"Clan Lands warriors raided the Coombe the year after I was born," said Eynon. "My mother says they took one of her cousins away with them."

"My condolences," said Damon.

"Our baron and his levies got her back, though."

"That's a surprise. It's not often clan raiders give up their captives."

"They stole casks of mead as well," said Eynon. "My mother said the baron and his men found the raiders a day's travel west of the Coombe, hung over from a night spent drinking the casks dry."

"It's easier to reclaim captives from dead men than live ones," said Damon.

"My mother didn't say anything about that—but I was only eight when she told me."

"Your mother sounds like a wise woman."

Damon pointed at the sky blue part of the map.

"Can you find the Coombe, lad?"

Eynon found Brendinas. It was marked with a star and sat on the west bank of another river that ran up and down. Tiny letters along its length said it was the Brenavon, the Royal River. He scanned to the left and identified Tyford, on the banks of a larger river—the Moravon, he remembered. From what Merry had told him, he located the Rhuthro where it came in north of the city, then traced the route of that river back until he spotted a pattern of triangles that he thought might be the Coombe.

"Here, sir?"

"Very good," said Damon. "I think you've got it figured out. Now let me show you Melyncárreg."

Eynon followed Damon several paces to the left, past vast sections of the map that seemed empty except for five inland seas near the top. Damon stood in front of a part of the map that was filled with thousands of sharply pointed triangles. Another star was drawn there, not as big as the one marking Brendinas. It was a fraction of an inch above a small lake.

"This is the Academy," said Damon.

Eynon looked across the room to the Coombe on the far right.

"How far is it from here to home?" he asked.

"If you started walking and made a steady twenty miles a day, it would take almost four months to get there."

"What if I flew on wyvern-back?"

"That depends on how fast your beast can fly," said Damon. "Do you know anything about that?"

"No," said Eynon.

He realized that he'd *have* to follow Nûd and Damon through a gate if he wanted to see Merry before midsummer. Eynon also thought he knew why Damon was showing him the map tonight. He wanted to make sure Eynon didn't leave Melyncárreg and set out for the Coombe on his own. Seeing the vast distances between Melyncárreg and anywhere in the Kingdom of Dâron was daunting.

"Does this satisfy your curiosity about where you are?" asked Damon.

"Yes, sort of," said Eynon. "But why is the Academy so far away?"

"The Master Mage wanted to be far away from the intrigues of Dâron and Tamloch," said Damon. "The story is he flew to the west until he found the greatest concentration of magic and magestones on the continent, then built his tower."

"The broad, solid-looking one inside the castle walls?"

"Yes," said Damon. "That came first."

"What about the Blue Spiral Tower?"

"The Master doesn't speak of that these days. For many years, he led a solitary existence, then he took his first students and built the Academy and the rest of the castle."

"I guess with gates it doesn't matter if a school for wizards is a thousand miles away," said Eynon.

"More like two thousand," said Damon. "Gates do make travel easier, but they work in both directions."

Eynon nodded.

"And thankfully, they can be locked."

* * * * *

Eynon put pillows under the blankets on his cot in case Nûd came to check on him during the night. He quietly collected all the things he wanted to bring with him—his pack and goatskin bottle, his staff, the small crossbow, and the shard-sword. Eynon put on his quilted jacket and tucked Chee inside it.

He cast the listening spell again so he could hear Damon or Nûd approaching and slipped down the stairs to the kitchen to retrieve the borrowed flying disk he'd left leaning against the wall near the fireplace. Chee stuck his head up, then yawned and retreated.

It was awkward, but he noticed foot straps that he'd missed earlier glued to the disk's surface. Eynon used them to attach the disk to the back of his pack like a soldier carrying a shield. There was no sign or sound of anyone else moving about.

Nûd and Damon had said they'd meet at *her* tower, which could only be the Blue Spiral Tower inside the castle walls. The tower had one visible entrance—broad double-doors made from oak like the ones leading to the circular room in the *other* Blue Spiral Tower. The doors were flanked by tall arrow-slit windows.

Eynon found a sheltered spot behind a pile of dressed stones in the courtyard that gave him a good view of the entrance. The stones looked like a giant stack of children's blocks and Eynon deduced they were probably a teaching aid for more advanced forms of wizardry.

He crouched behind the pile and waited, counting his breaths to stay awake. Eynon had reached fifteen hundred when he heard an odd noise coming from *outside* the castle's walls. It was loud and sounded like a knife scraping around an oiled whetstone. It wasn't until Eynon heard the clicks of massive claws on granite that he identified it. Rocky was playing with the circular channel and sphere of solidified sound Eynon had made for him.

He must be pushing the ball around, thought Eynon. *I didn't know wyverns were nocturnal.*

Then he considered what he knew about his new pet's habits. He'd first met Rocky in daylight.

Maybe he can't sleep?

The noise the ball made as it went around the carved stone path grew softer, almost soothing. Eynon took deeper breaths and pinched himself on the cheeks so he didn't fall asleep. Another hour passed and the noise outside the walls ceased. Eynon could picture Rocky sleeping with his head tucked on top of his tail in the center of the circle.

Footsteps echoed in the courtyard. Nûd and Damon were side
by side with packs on their backs. Nûd was holding Damon's flying
disk and had a full-sized crossbow strapped to the top of his pack.
Damon had his staff in his right hand. It made a *tap-tap* staccato
sound out of synch with the beat of their footsteps.

The two men halted in front of the Blue Spiral Tower's doors.
Eynon watched as Damon stepped close to them and did something Eynon couldn't see because the older man's body masked his
actions. Then Damon stepped back and touched his staff to the
line between the heavy oak portals. A muted blue glow appeared
at the collar of Damon's coat and the doors swung open, revealing
a tall, wide corridor lit by glow balls that reminded Eynon of what
he'd seen at the Blue Spiral Tower along the Rhuthro.

Eynon waited until Nûd and Damon entered before he moved.
He ran from his hiding place, trying to keep his own footsteps
quiet, but proved too slow. The heavy doors closed before he
reached them.

Blast, thought Eynon.

He tried what had worked for Damon and had worked for him
at the other tower. Extended his right arm, he gently tapped the
end of his staff against the center of the doors. A flash of red light
reflected back from the polished wood, but the doors didn't open.

Eynon remembered Damon's words from earlier in the evening.
Perhaps Damon had locked the doors, not just the gate? Could the
older man have been unlocking them when he stepped close to the
doors? Eynon examined them closely. The left-hand one *did* have
a keyhole.

Eynon was sure he could use subtle sensing and manipulating
magic to craft a key from solidified sound, but that would take
time. There didn't seem to be any better alternative. He leaned
down to inspect the keyhole and felt Chee crawl out of the neck of
his jacket and shift to sit on the back of his head.

"Not now, Chee," Eynon whispered. "You're distracting me."

Eynon felt the raconette launch himself toward the doors, then
saw him scamper to one of the arrow-slit windows. He didn't want

to call out to Chee in case Nûd or Damon would hear him, so he left his little friend to his own devices. He extended his senses into the keyhole, feeling out the shape of the tumblers within and sculpting a key that would fit them in his mind.

He'd almost figured it out when Chee landed on his head again. Eynon raised one hand and gently tried to push the raconette away. The construct in his mind disappeared like a dream on waking. *Now it will take me more time to work it out again,* he thought, growing angry.

The clank of metal on stone distracted Eynon and short circuited his anger. A large black key was on the cobbles in front of him. Eynon picked it up, put it in the lock, and turned it, hearing a satisfying click.

"Well done, my friend," Eynon whispered as he removed the key and tucked it in his belt.

"Chi-chee," replied the raconette softly.

The small masked beast earnestly put a finger to its lips and almost caused Eynon to laugh. He repeated Chee's gesture, then raised his staff and tapped it against the doors. This time, after a flash of red light, the doors opened.

Chee tugged his earlobe and Eynon nodded in reply. They made a good team.

Nûd and Damon were not in the corridor ahead of them. Eynon saw a hook to one side of the opening and hung the key in the place where Chee must have found it. He strained to hear any sign of the others. Thanks to the listening spell, he heard their voices far ahead and to the side.

Running on tiptoe, holding his staff out so it didn't touch the floor, Eynon hurried down the hall, checking side passages on the left and right for any sign of Damon and Nûd. Now he could pick up a conversation between the two men from somewhere ahead.

"What will we do if she's home?" asked Nûd.

"Ask for forgiveness and claim it's for the good of the kingdom," said Damon.

"Do you think that will work?"

"Maybe," said the older man.

Eynon could tell he was much closer now. He no longer needed the listening spell to hear them.

"Are you sure you have all the settings right for the gate?"

"Don't teach your grandmother how to spin," said Damon.

"Or my grandfather how to plow—I get it," said Nûd. "He won't be able to follow us."

Eynon ran even faster. He *had* to get through that gate with them.

He heard footsteps and the tap of a staff on the stone floor as he turned into the last room on the right, only to see Nûd's pack and crossbow disappearing into the surface of a tall, wide mirror bolted to the wall of a room tiled in white and blue.

Eynon doubled his speed, aimed himself at the mirror, and jumped toward it, following the pair, then smacked against the mirror's smooth surface with a force hard enough to stun him.

Knocked back several feet by the rebound from the collision, he fell on his tail bone and toppled over, thanks to the weight of his pack. For a few moments, he stayed on the floor, rocking on top of the flying disk and feeling like a turtle left upside down on a fence post.

Chee jumped on his chest and regarded Eynon sympathetically.

He must have hopped off before I hit the mirror, thought Eynon as he got to his feet.

Blast and double-blast! How would they get back to Merry and the Coombe now?

Chapter 31

"When you're lost, return to where you started."
— Ealdamon's *Epigrams*

Eynon tapped the mirror with his staff, willing the gate to reopen. His magestone flashed, but nothing happened except for the mirror revealing a reflection of Eynon's frustrated face. He tried slashing at the mirror with his shard-sword, but his blows bounced off like his body had. The gate was closed and locked.

He slowly walked back to the entrance to the tower and out into the courtyard. Despite feeling down, he did what he thought was the responsible thing and touched his staff to one of the doors. They swung back, resealing the way into the tower and making a deep *thunk* sound like closing an oversized book after reading the last chapter.

Eynon paced across the cobblestones, trying to figure out what to do next. The sky was dark, with no hint of coming dawn, but the moon was half full and cast enough light for Eynon to see by. He took comfort in knowing that the same moon was above Merry and Doethan and his parents back in Dâron.

The knife-scraping sound came from outside the castle again. Rocky was back to rolling his ball.

Didn't the blasted wyvern ever sleep?

Eynon stepped onto his flying disk and floated up to the top of the castle's wall where he could see Rocky at play. The wyvern hadn't seen him, yet. He was focused on the ball of solidified sound rolling in the channel. Eynon smiled and created a second ball on the far side of the circle.

Rocky looked up and saw Eynon outlined on the crenellated wall. The wyvern thumped his tail. Beyond Rocky, in the distance toward the south, Eynon saw something that wasn't snow glinting in the moonlight—the four blue-striped alabaster pillars that marked where he'd appeared when he'd come through the gate he'd found with Merry. There *was* another way back!

The wyvern launched himself into the air and in a few swift wing-beats was hovering above Eynon. He landed gently on the walkway atop the wall, filling it from side to side.

"Ready for a trip?" asked Eynon.

Rocky nodded his head and allowed Eynon to climb from one of the crenellation stones to the wyvern's back. As if reading Eynon's mind, Rocky dove from the wall, extended his wings, and followed a shallow glide path toward the four blue-striped pillars. Seconds later, Rocky, Eynon and Chee were inside the square the pillars defined. Eynon held up his staff, waved it in the air, and thought about being elsewhere.

Instead of disappearing, Eynon felt stupid. Nothing happened except for the snow being packed down by Rocky's weight. Chee looked at Eynon from his new spot on Rocky's neck. It seemed like the raconette was urging him to do something, but he didn't know what.

The little beast put his hands together and opened them out. Eynon shook his head. He didn't get it. Chee repeated the gesture then jumped back to Eynon's shoulder and scampered down his arm to his wrist. Eynon wondered what was wrong with the raconette until Chee leaned forward and touched the gold ring he'd been given by Doethan.

"I'm an idiot," said Eynon.

Chee turned around and nodded, as if in agreement. He hopped back to Rocky's neck.

Eynon took off the ring and held it in both hands. He took a calming breath and said, *"Gwal-o-e-a-den,"* clearly enunciating each syllable.

Invisible bells chimed. The ring expanded. Soon he saw Merry's face sharpen inside the golden circle. Her hair was streaming back in the wind and Eynon could see the mountains east of the Coombe below and behind her.

"Eynon," said Merry, "I'm glad to hear from you, but it's not a good time. Fercha and Doethan and I are flying to Wherrel. I'm still getting used to my flying disk and it's hard to fly, hold the ring, and talk to you at the same time."

"Do you know how to open the gate back to the Blue Spiral Tower?" asked Eynon.

Another voice came through the ring's circle—the other woman from their connection last night.

"Merry doesn't, but I do," came the voice, distorted by the wind.

The images behind Merry stopped streaming by. *They must be hovering,* thought Eynon. The woman with short red hair replaced Merry in the ring's circle. Merry and Doethan floated behind her.

This must be Fercha, the wizard who lost her artifact, Eynon realized. *The Blue Spiral Tower belongs to her.*

"Listen carefully," said Fercha. "There are three simple steps."

Eynon nodded. Now that he knew who she was, he could return her artifact. Eynon focused on her instructions.

"First..."

Chapter 32

"Finding your quarry also means they have found you."
— Ealdamon's *Epigrams*

Rocky exploded from the surface of the well, beating his wings in tight, sharp movements and sending whirlwinds of air spinning off the cylindrical walls of the well shaft. Chee was inside Eynon's jacket and Eynon gripped the scarf tied to the knobs of bone at the wyvern's shoulders hard enough for his hands to turn white. They were at the top in seconds, in the circular room with the high-domed ceiling.

"That way," shouted Eynon, pointing toward the oak doors leading out to the docks. Eynon aimed his staff toward the doors. They slammed open as blue and red light flashed around the chamber. Out of the corner of his eye, Eynon saw the animated broom and dustpan that kept the place clean scurry out of the way of the speeding wyvern.

Eynon directed Rocky out of the tower using his knees and a light touch from his staff to indicate changes in direction. The outer false-rock doors to the river also opened in a hurry as Eynon and his mount approached. Soon, wyvern, man, and raconette were headed west as fast as Rocky's wings could carry them. The barest hint of dawn was showing behind them on the eastern horizon, casting shimmering shadow patterns on the flowing waters of the Rhuthro.

Then they were over mountains—the northeastern boundary of the Coombe. The moon cast enough light for Eynon to scan the horizon. He hoped to see Damon and Nûd, but couldn't spot them. He was sure they couldn't be very far ahead, but two men on a translucent flying disk would be nearly invisible. Rocky was moving faster by far than a flying disk, even one not carrying two people, so Eynon was confident he'd beat them to Wherrel. He also had the advantage of knowing the lands of the Coombe like he knew the lines of his palms. He turned Rocky slightly southwest and looked for landmarks.

Below, he saw a string of bobbing lanterns approaching a long rectangular building with a thatched roof. Haywall's dairy workers were walking to their communal cow barn for the pre-dawn milking. Eynon had often helped with that chore and knew their routine well.

If that's Haywall, Wherrel is close at hand to the northwest.

He directed Rocky lower in that direction, gaining speed from the slight dive.

No lanterns would be lit in Wherrel. Stones don't *moo* when their udders are full and the folk in the quarry town got their milk and cream and cheese from Haywall. Still, someone would be awake in the town—perhaps the baker, or one of the people maintaining equipment for the morning shift digging slate and soapstone.

Rocky glided lower and the few lit lamps in windows allowed Eynon to confirm it was Wherrel. The village's green slate roofs and stone houses made it looked carved out of rock, not constructed from thatch and timber.

He'd been to Wherrel many times and knew the quarry was close—just west of town, through a natural gap in the mountains. From the air, it looked darker than its surroundings, a deep bowl cut into the earth over many generations.

Rocky spiraled down to land in the broad, flat surface at the bottom of the quarry. Eynon sensed something special about the rocks around the quarry, as if they were pulsing with power. He'd started to analyze the patterns when he heard a familiar voice call his name.

"Eynon!"

"Merry!" shouted Eynon.

He dismounted Rocky and created a tasty ball of solidified sound for the wyvern as a way of saying thanks and to help keep the beast occupied. Eynon moved haltingly toward where Merry's voice seemed to come from, then heard Doethan's voice shout *"Llachar!"*

The bottom of the bowl went from dark to bright in an instant, forcing Eynon to close his eyes. Once his vision recovered, he saw Doethan's glow ball floating high above them. Merry, Doethan, and a tall, short-haired woman who must be Fercha, were standing thirty feet away. Eynon crossed the distance in seconds.

"Let us know when you'll be done hugging Merry," said Fercha. She had a smile in her voice, but an underlying seriousness as well.

"That will depend on when *she* lets *me* go," said Eynon, giving Merry and extra-hard squeeze then releasing her. The two lovers held hands and turned to face the other wizards.

"Welcome back, lad," said Doethan. "It's not the best time to return, with rumors of war and invasion buzzing around like angry wolfhornets, but it's clear Merry is glad to see you."

"I am," said Merry. "Very glad. You won't believe it, Eynon. Fercha's taught me so much magic and..."

"I believe you have something that belongs to me," Fercha said to Eynon.

Merry gave Fercha a contrite smile and kissed Eynon on the cheek. His face flushed, but he kept his manners.

"Certainly, good wizard," said Eynon. "It's on a chain around my neck and under my shirt to keep it safe. I'll be glad to give it back."

"I knew it!" said Doethan.

Eynon glanced at the old wizard, then back at Fercha.

"I've wanted to return it since the day I found it, but didn't know who it belonged to."

"It belongs to *me,*" said Fercha.

"Of course," said Eynon.

Now that he had a magestone of his own, he understood just how tight the bond was between mage and magestone. He reached for Fercha's artifact, then remembered something else important.

"I need to tell you—" said Eynon, "—there are others on the way."

"Who's coming?" asked Doethan.

"We are," said Nûd, stepping into the light near Doethan with Damon close behind him.

Fercha stared at Nûd with an amalgam of expressions. Eynon saw love, concern, anger, fear and frustration in her face, partially concealed by an overwhelming sense of surprise. Nûd looked back, with tenderness and a sense of loss in his eyes.

"How are you enjoying your retirement?" Damon asked Doethan. "Do you like pretending to be a hedge wizard in the hinterlands?"

"I'm no more retired than you are, Ealdamon," said Doethan. "You can't resist keeping your hand in, even at a distance. I was asked to serve the young king, and I stepped forward."

"Ealdamon?" asked Merry.

"Ealdamon?" Eynon repeated.

"Old Damon," said Nûd. "The Master Mage of Dâron. Famed author of Ealdamon's *Epigrams*."

Fercha seemed to recover from her shock and composed her face.

"Nûd," she said in a neutral tone.

"Mother," said Nûd.

Their reunion was interrupted by an angry trumpeting as Rocky launched his massive body into the sky, now red-tinged by the rising sun. Eynon followed Rocky's path and saw more than a dozen flying disks pouring over the hundred-foot rim of the quarry.

Two or three people crowded onto each disk—a green-cloaked wizard and one or two Tamloch soldiers.

"Verro!" shouted Fercha. Without another word, she mounted her flying disk and ascended to meet the attackers.

Merry reached for her flying disk, ready to use her magic to defend the realm. Eynon held her arm.

"Wait," he said. "I know why they're here."

Merry's eyes asked Eynon, *"Why?"*

"This quarry is full of green magestones—hundreds of them."

"That's not good," said Ealdamon, almost to himself. "Not good at all."

The old wizard looked at Nûd for a half a second, then turned to Doethan.

"Take Nûd and get word to Brendinas," said Ealdamon. "Fercha and I will hold them off until you return with half the Conclave."

Nûd pointedly looked at Eynon, then at Ealdamon. He tilted his head a few degrees and Ealdamon nodded.

"I stand corrected. Fercha and Eynon and I—" began the old wizard.

"—and Merry!" shouted Merry.

"—will do our best to defend the quarry. Now hurry!"

Nûd took off his pack and untied his crossbow. He hung his quiver over his shoulder, nocked a bolt, and shot one of the descending green wizards in the ribs. The injured wizard's flying disk tipped and both the wizard and the soldier behind him fell fifty feet toward the quarry's floor.

Doethan shrugged. The blue magestone on his forehead flashed. He wasn't going anywhere—not that help would be able to get here soon enough to do much good anyway.

Ealdamon, Doethan, Merry and Eynon stepped on their flying disks, set their shields, and rose to join Fercha in the fight.

To be continued in the second book
of the Congruent Mage series:

The Congruent Wizard

Coming in 2018

MAPS

The Coombe and
the Rhuthro Valley

Liamston

County of
Rhuthro Valley

Rhuthro
Keep

Farnam's Cabin

Blue Spiral Tower

Quarry

Wherrel

Flying Frog
Farms

Campsite

The Coombe

Mastlands

Dorthan's Tower

Bordermarches

Gruffyd's

Barony of
Middle Rhuthro

Brynhill

Applegarth

Haywall

Caercadel

Barony of
Upper Rhuthro

Barony of
Cadelluin

A larger color version of this map is available at:

CongruentMage.com/maps.html

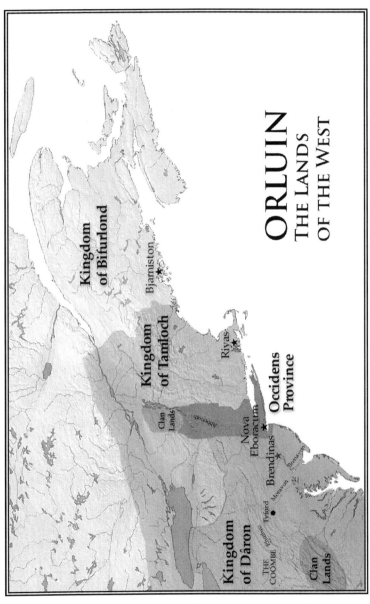

ORLUIN
THE LANDS
OF THE WEST

Kingdom
of Bifurlond

Bjarniston ★

Kingdom
of Tamloch

Rivas ★

Occidens
Province

Clan
Lands

Abovon

Nova
Eboracum
Brendinas ★

Brendinas ●

Tyford ●

Mexton

Kingdom
of Dâron

THE
COOMBE

Clan
Lands

A larger color version of this map is available at:

CongruentMage.com/maps.html

74398341R00189

Made in the USA
Columbia, SC
02 August 2017